YASUNARI NAGATOSHI

All right! The editing staff gave me a copy
of *Puzzle & Dragons Z*!! Let's get right to it!!
Oh right...I don't have a 3DS...Well anyway,
I hope you enjoy *Zo Zo Zombie*, Volume 3!!

ZOMBiE BOY'S METAMORPHOSiS COLLECTiON

BALLOON ZOMBIE BOY

AAGHH.
AAGHH.

He wanders all over the world, drifting wherever the wind takes him and saying "Aaghh" as he goes. He occasionally gets pecked at by birds, collides with planes, or even pops. This zombie has been confirmed to exist in six colors: red, blue, yellow, green, pink, and orange. However, there have also been reports of a golden one. In Japan, he is most often spotted flying in the early spring and so is sometimes referred to as the Spring Delivery Man, or the one who delivers spring to Japan.

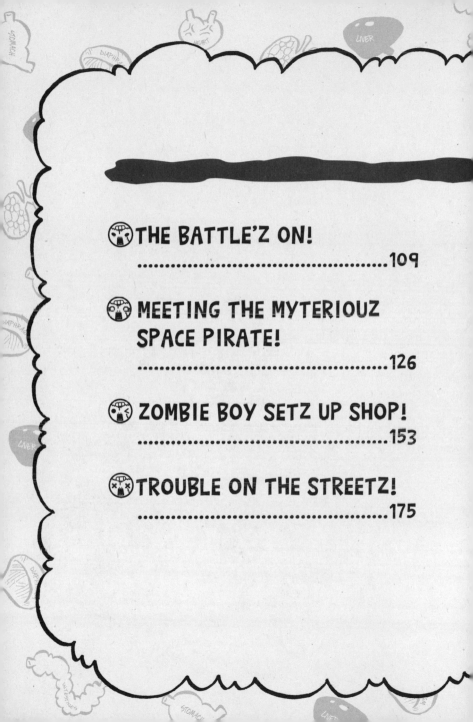

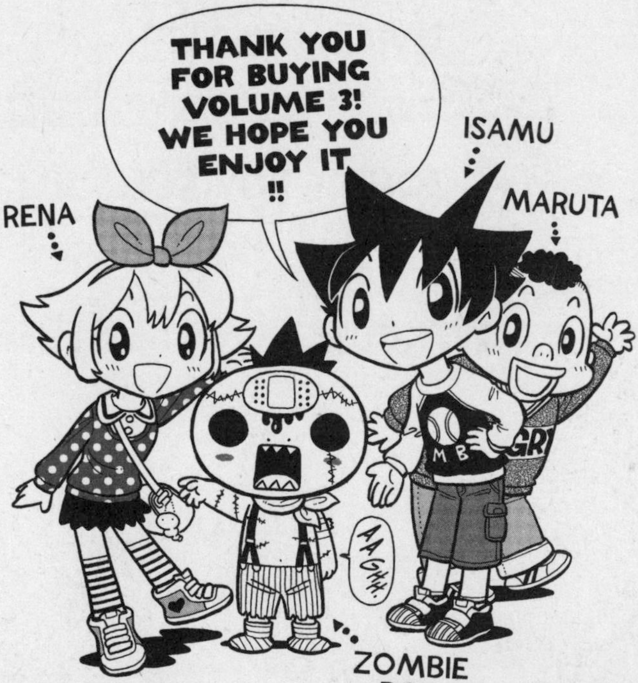
THANK YOU FOR BUYING VOLUME 3! WE HOPE YOU ENJOY IT !!
ISAMU
MARUTA
RENA
AAGHH.
ZOMBIE BOY

VOL.

YASUNARI NAGATOSHI

TABLE OF CONTENTS

MANGA

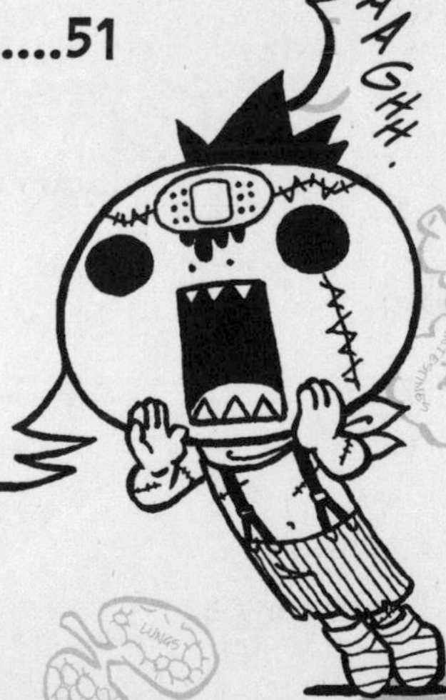

AAGHH.

SWEET, DELICIOUS DEZZERTS!

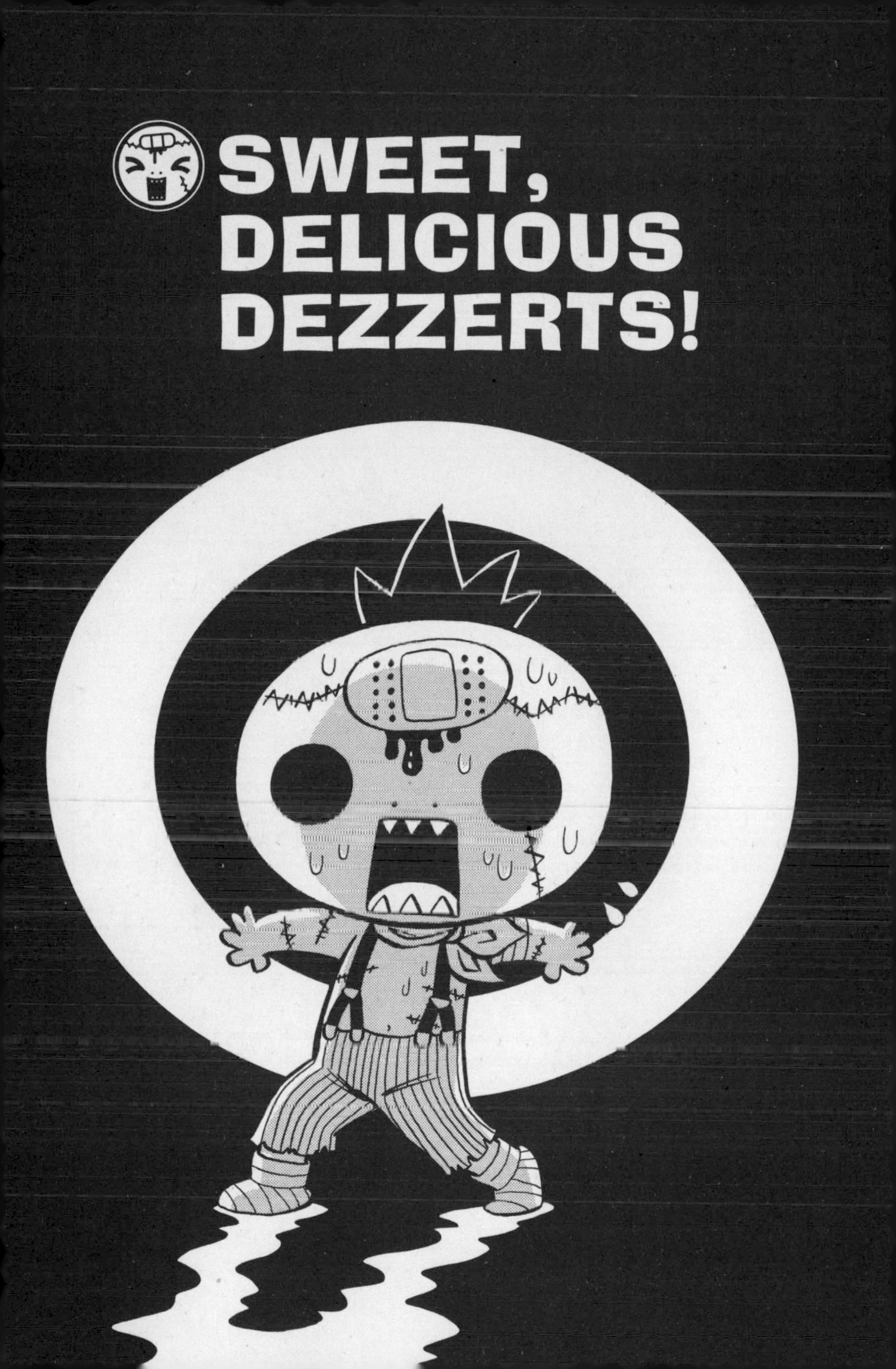

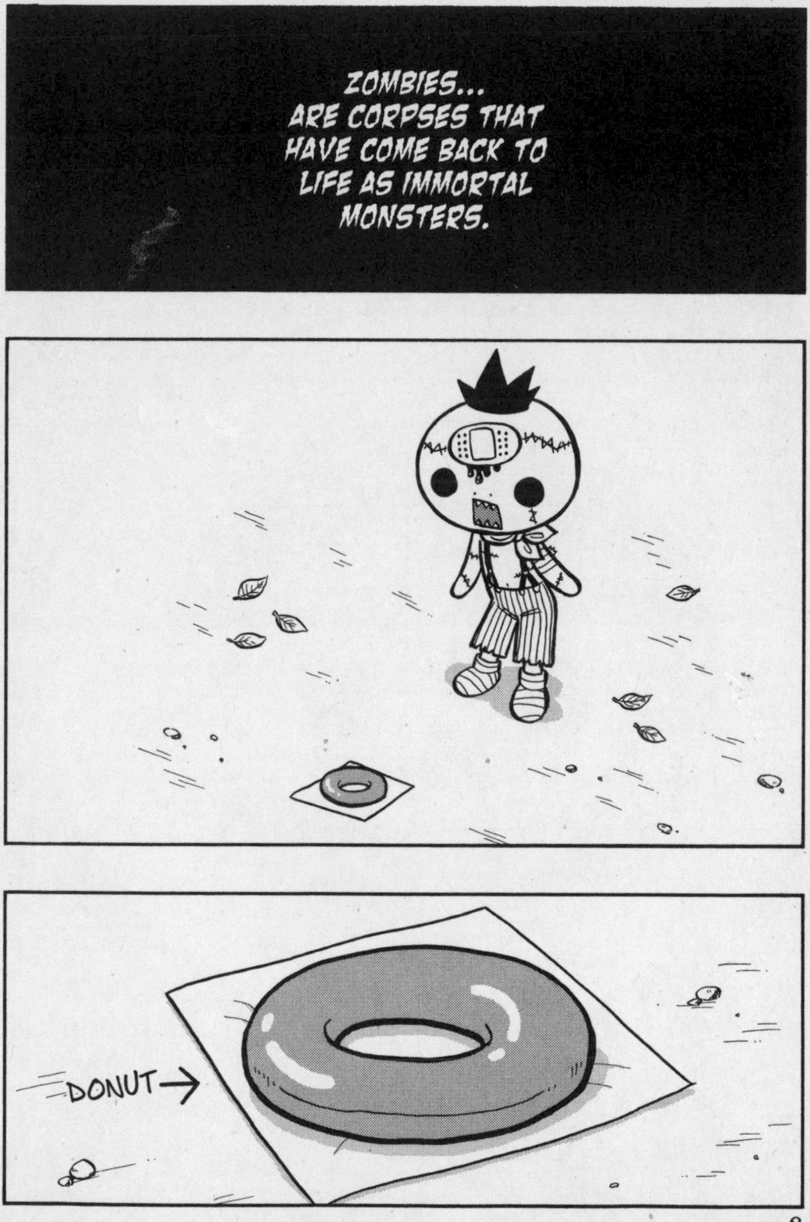
ZOMBIES... ARE CORPSES THAT HAVE COME BACK TO LIFE AS IMMORTAL MONSTERS.
DONUT

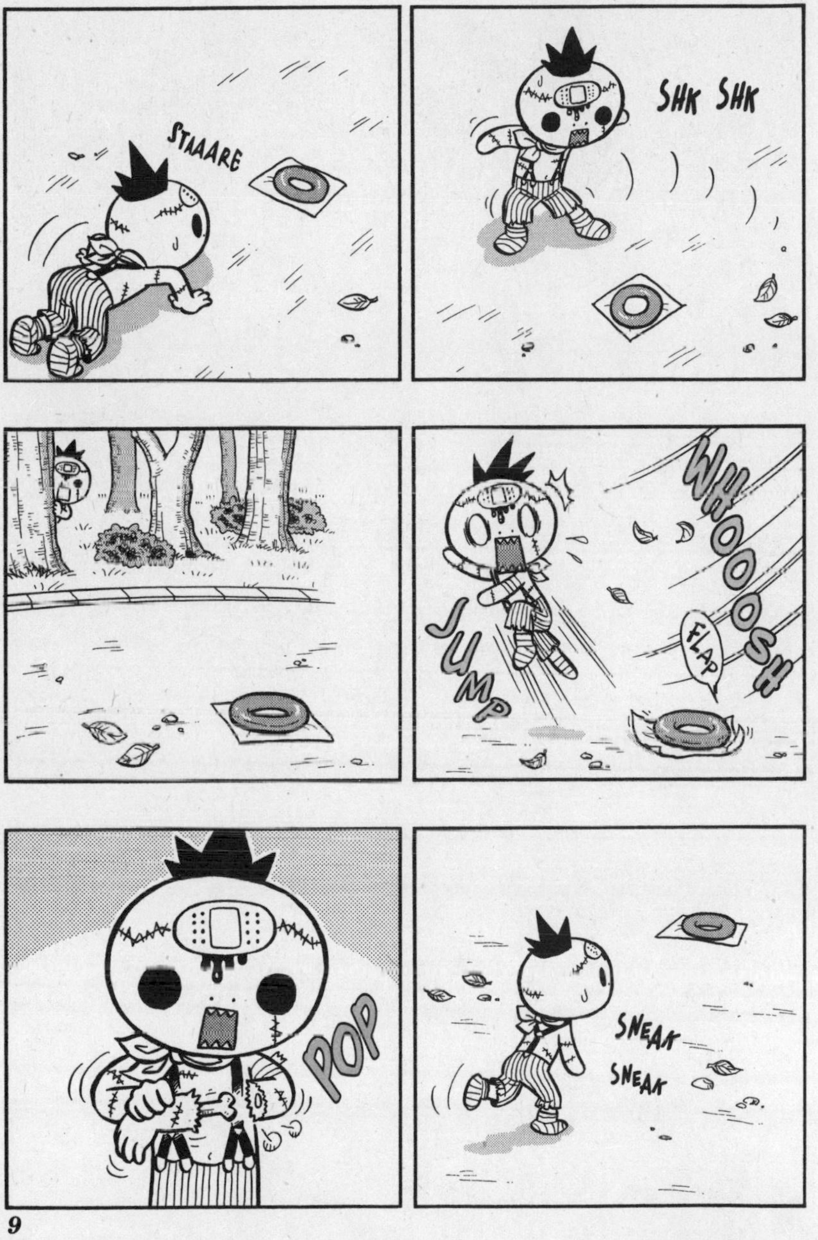
SHK SHK
STAAARE
WHOOOSH
FLAP
JUMP
SNEAK
SNEAK
POP

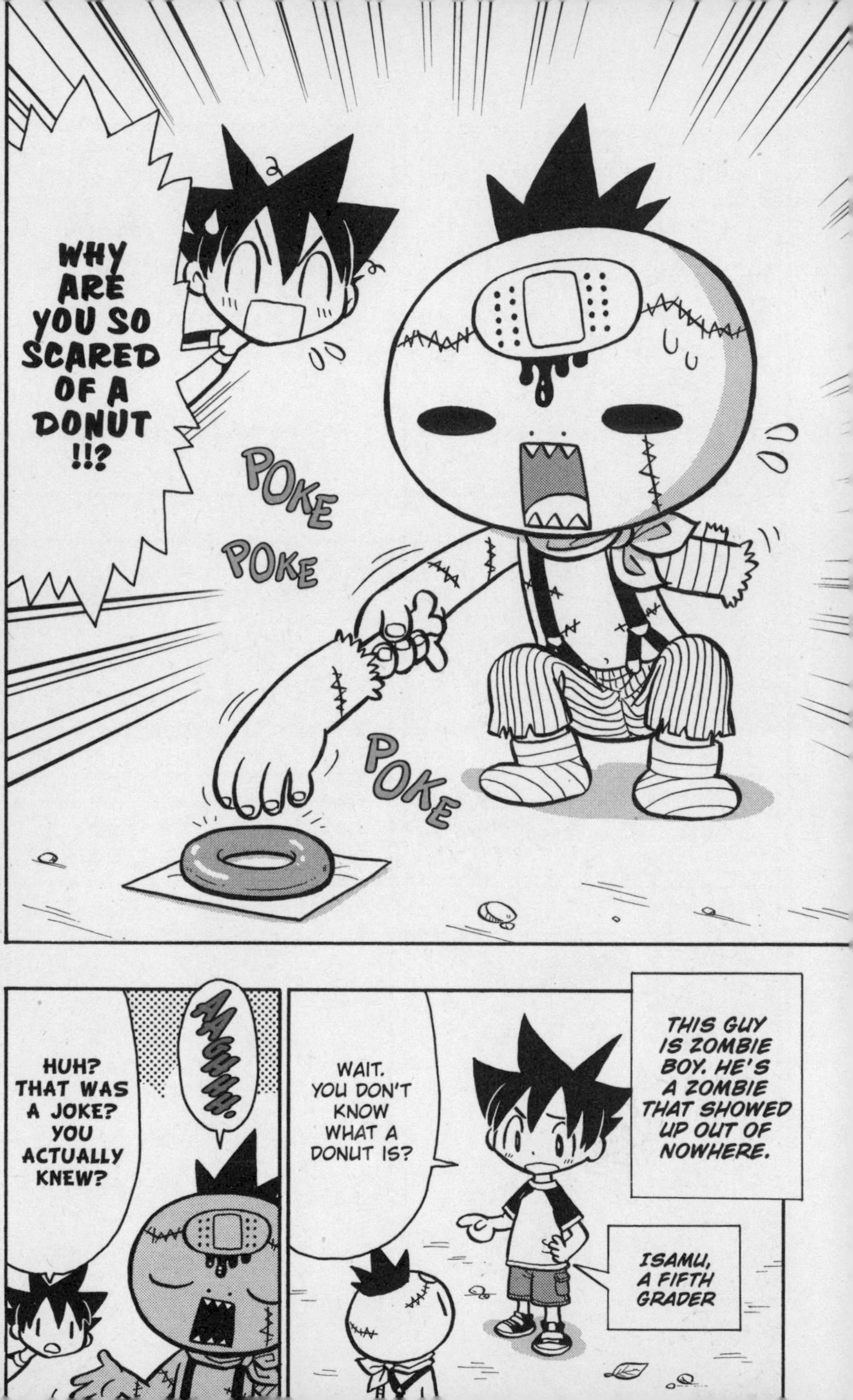
WHY ARE YOU SO SCARED OF A DONUT!!?
POKE
POKE
POKE
THIS GUY IS ZOMBIE BOY. HE'S A ZOMBIE THAT SHOWED UP OUT OF NOWHERE.
ISAMU, A FIFTH GRADER
WAIT. YOU DON'T KNOW WHAT A DONUT IS?
AAGHHH.
HUH? THAT WAS A JOKE? YOU ACTUALLY KNEW?

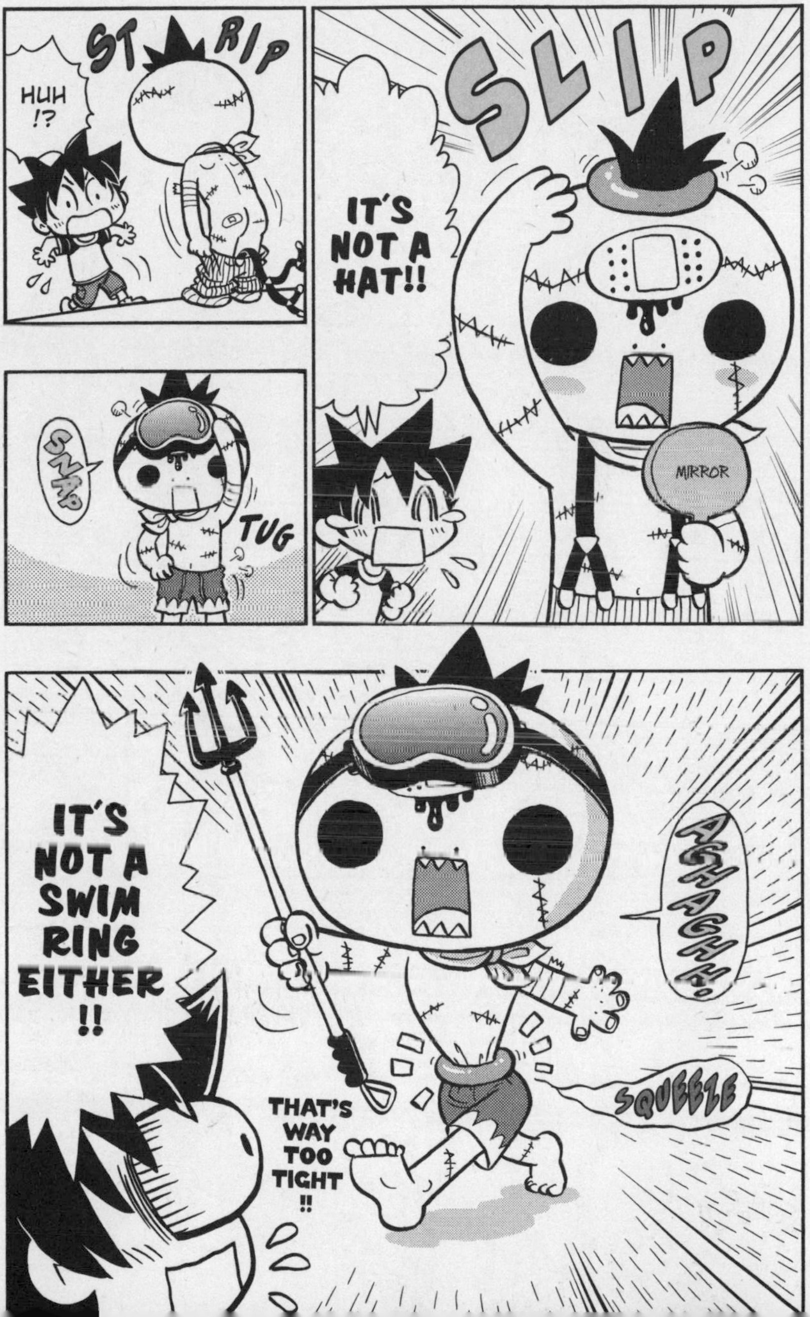
SLIP
IT'S NOT A HAT!!
MIRROR
HUH !?
STRIP
SNAP
TUG
AGHAGH!
SQUEEZE
IT'S NOT A SWIM RING EITHER !!
THAT'S WAY TOO TIGHT !!

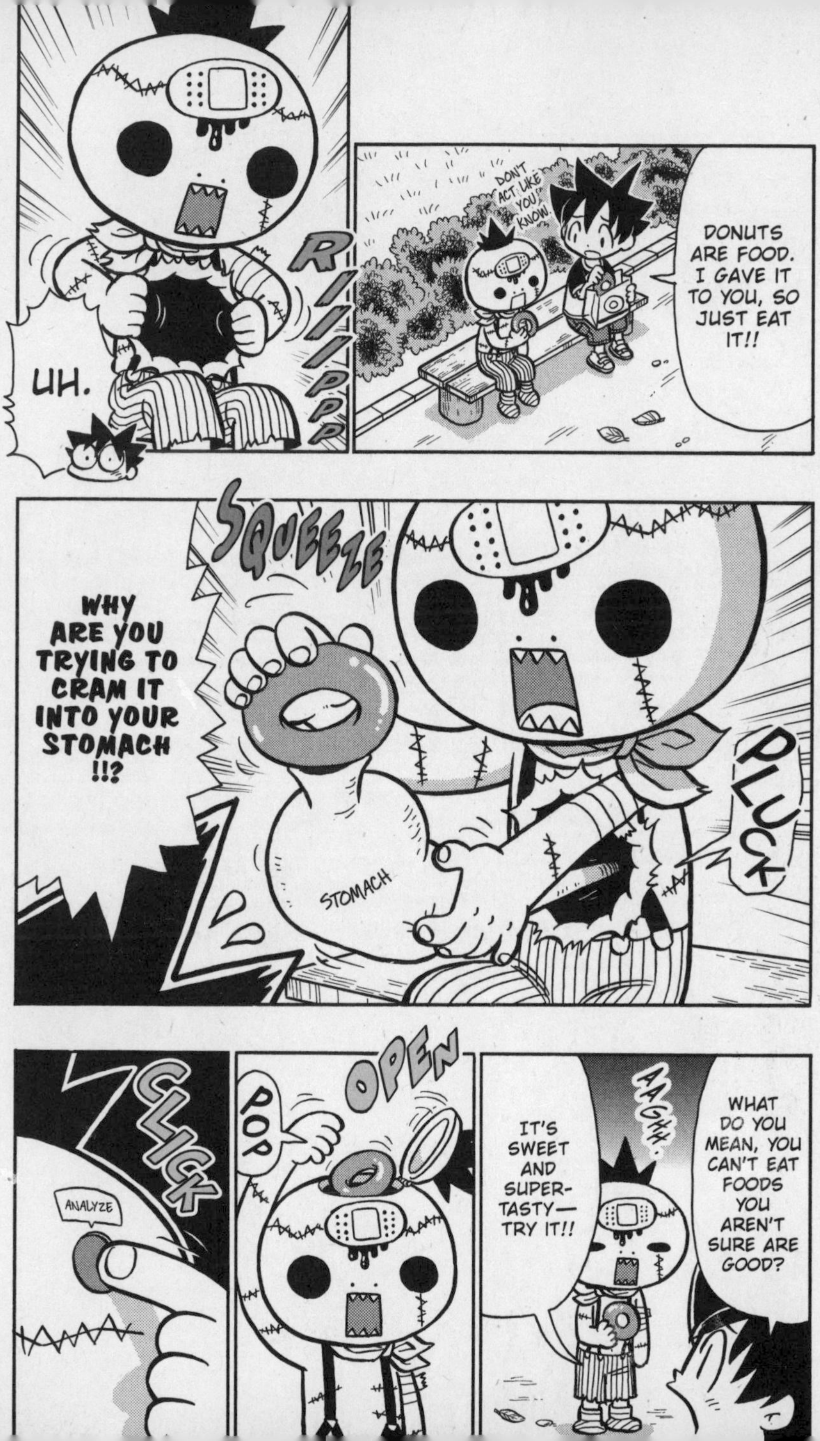
DONUTS ARE FOOD. I GAVE IT TO YOU, SO JUST EAT IT!!
DON'T ACT LIKE YOU KNOW.
RIIIPPP
UH.
SQUEEZE
PLUCK
WHY ARE YOU TRYING TO CRAM IT INTO YOUR STOMACH!!?
STOMACH
WHAT DO YOU MEAN, YOU CAN'T EAT FOODS YOU AREN'T SURE ARE GOOD?
AAGHH.
IT'S SWEET AND SUPER-TASTY—TRY IT!!
OPEN
POP
CLICK
ANALYZE

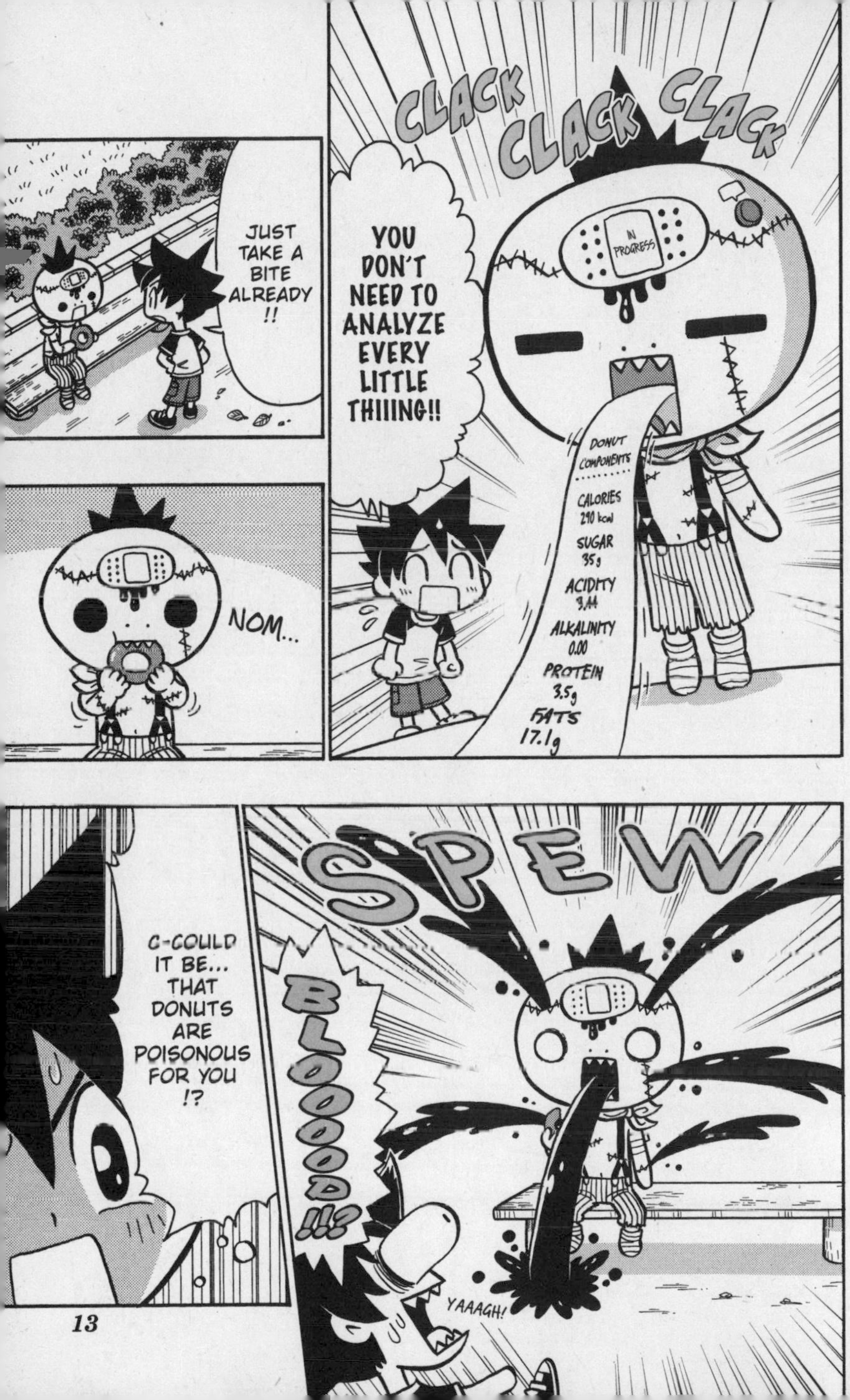
CLACK CLACK CLACK
YOU DON'T NEED TO ANALYZE EVERY LITTLE THIIING!!
IN PROGRESS
DONUT COMPONENTS
CALORIES 290 kcal
SUGAR 35g
ACIDITY 3.44
ALKALINITY 0.00
PROTEIN 3.5g
FATS 17.1g
JUST TAKE A BITE ALREADY !!
NOM...
SPEW
BLOOOOOD!!?
YAAAGH!
C-COULD IT BE... THAT DONUTS ARE POISONOUS FOR YOU !?

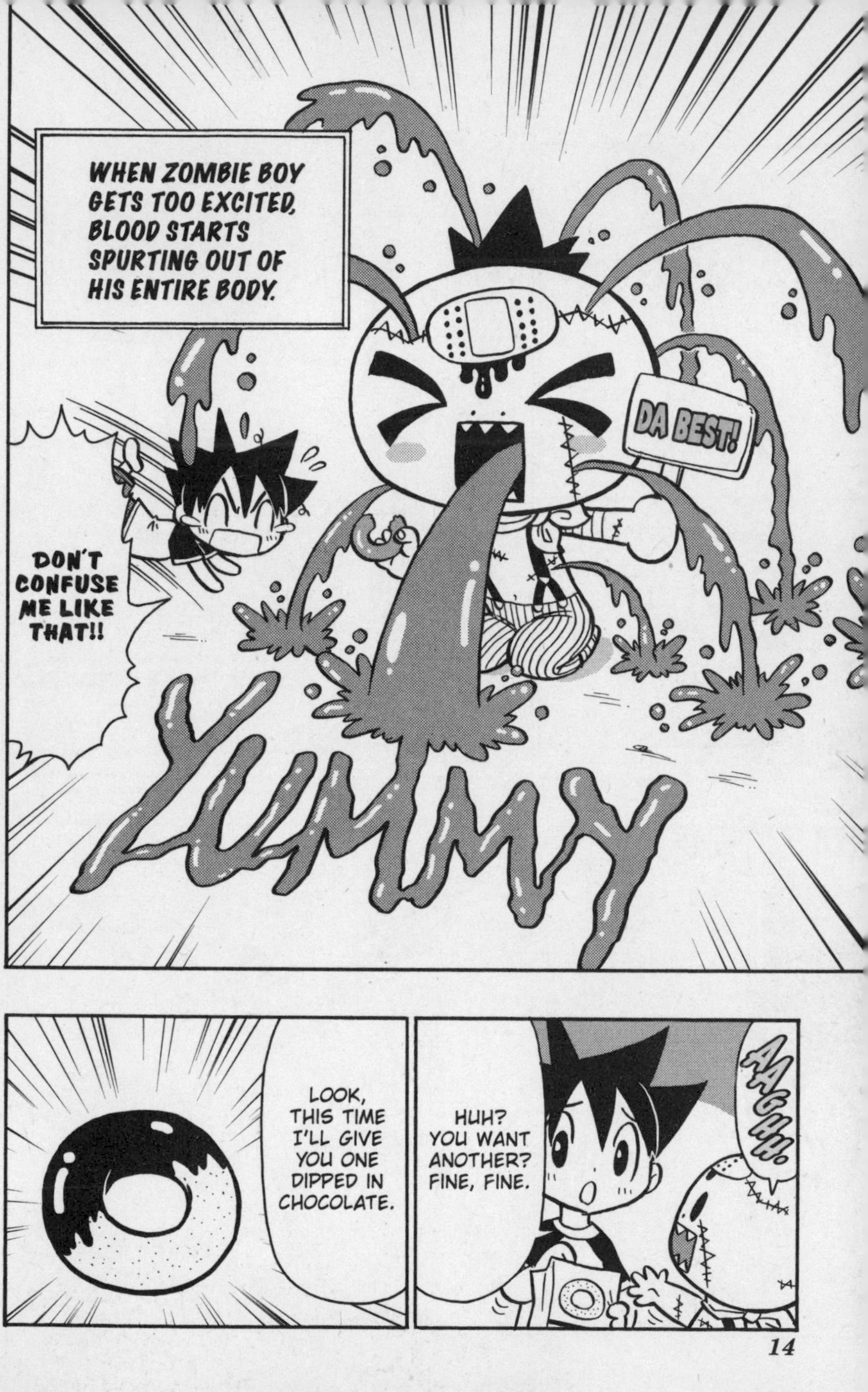
WHEN ZOMBIE BOY GETS TOO EXCITED, BLOOD STARTS SPURTING OUT OF HIS ENTIRE BODY.
DA BEST!
DON'T CONFUSE ME LIKE THAT!!
YUMMY
AAGHH.
HUH? YOU WANT ANOTHER? FINE, FINE.
LOOK, THIS TIME I'LL GIVE YOU ONE DIPPED IN CHOCOLATE.

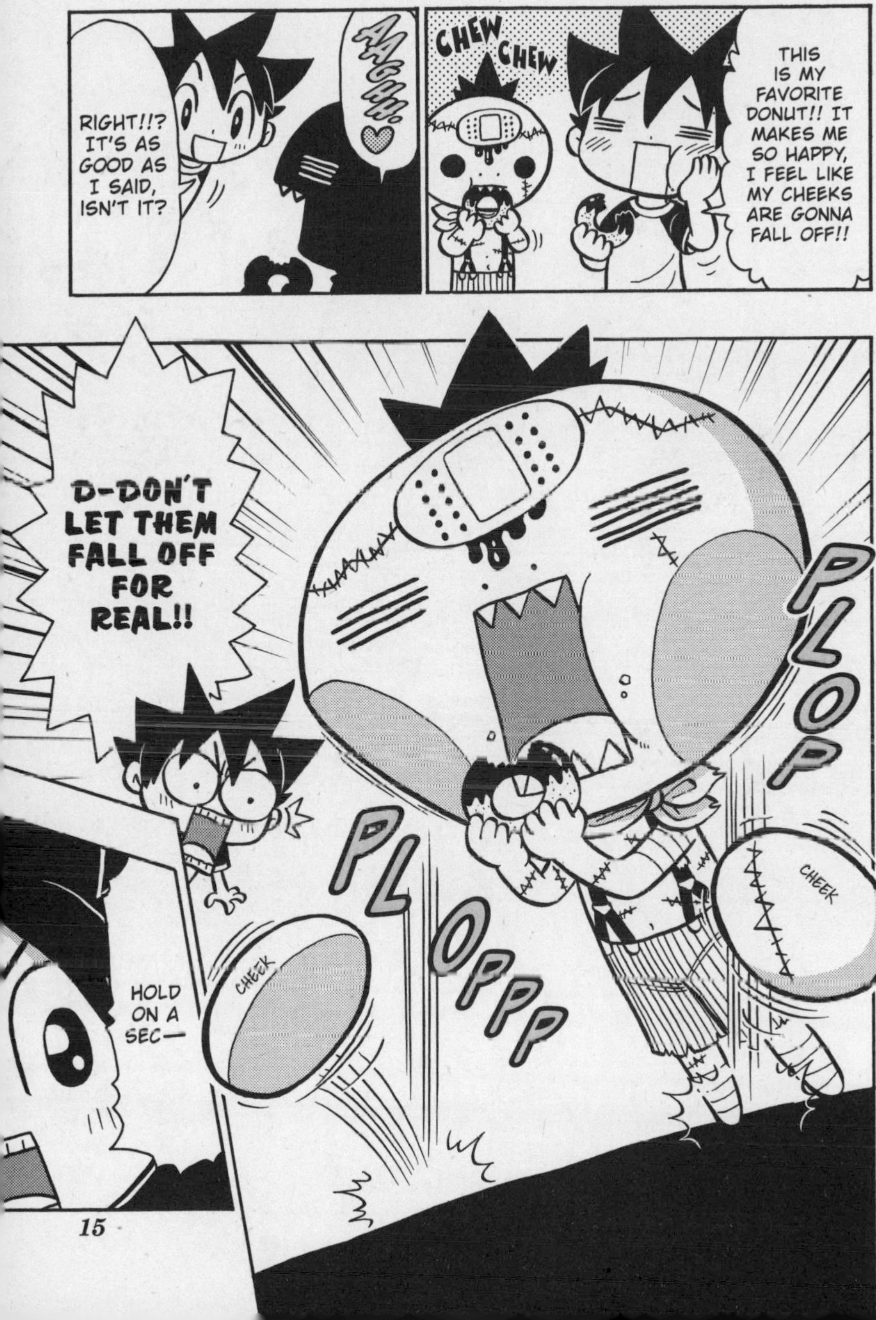
THIS IS MY FAVORITE DONUT!! IT MAKES ME SO HAPPY, I FEEL LIKE MY CHEEKS ARE GONNA FALL OFF!!
CHEW CHEW
AAGHH!
RIGHT!!? IT'S AS GOOD AS I SAID, ISN'T IT?
PLOP
D-DON'T LET THEM FALL OFF FOR REAL!!
PLOPPP
CHEEK
CHEEK
HOLD ON A SEC—

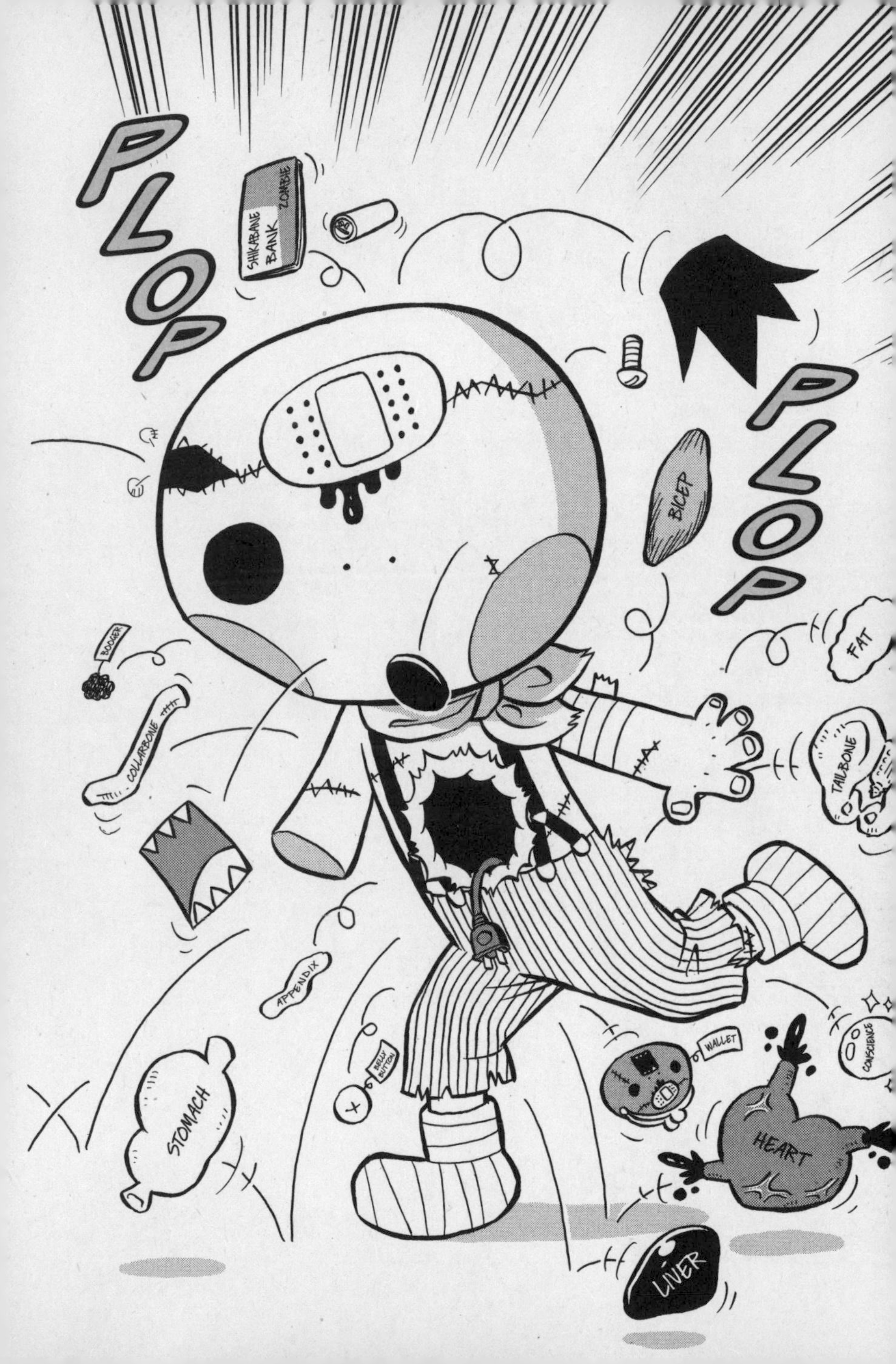
PLOP
PLOP
SHIKABANE BANK ZOMBIE
BICEP
FAT
TAILBONE
BOOGER
COLLARBONE
APPENDIX
BELLY BUTTON
WALLET
CONSCIENCE
STOMACH
HEART
LIVER

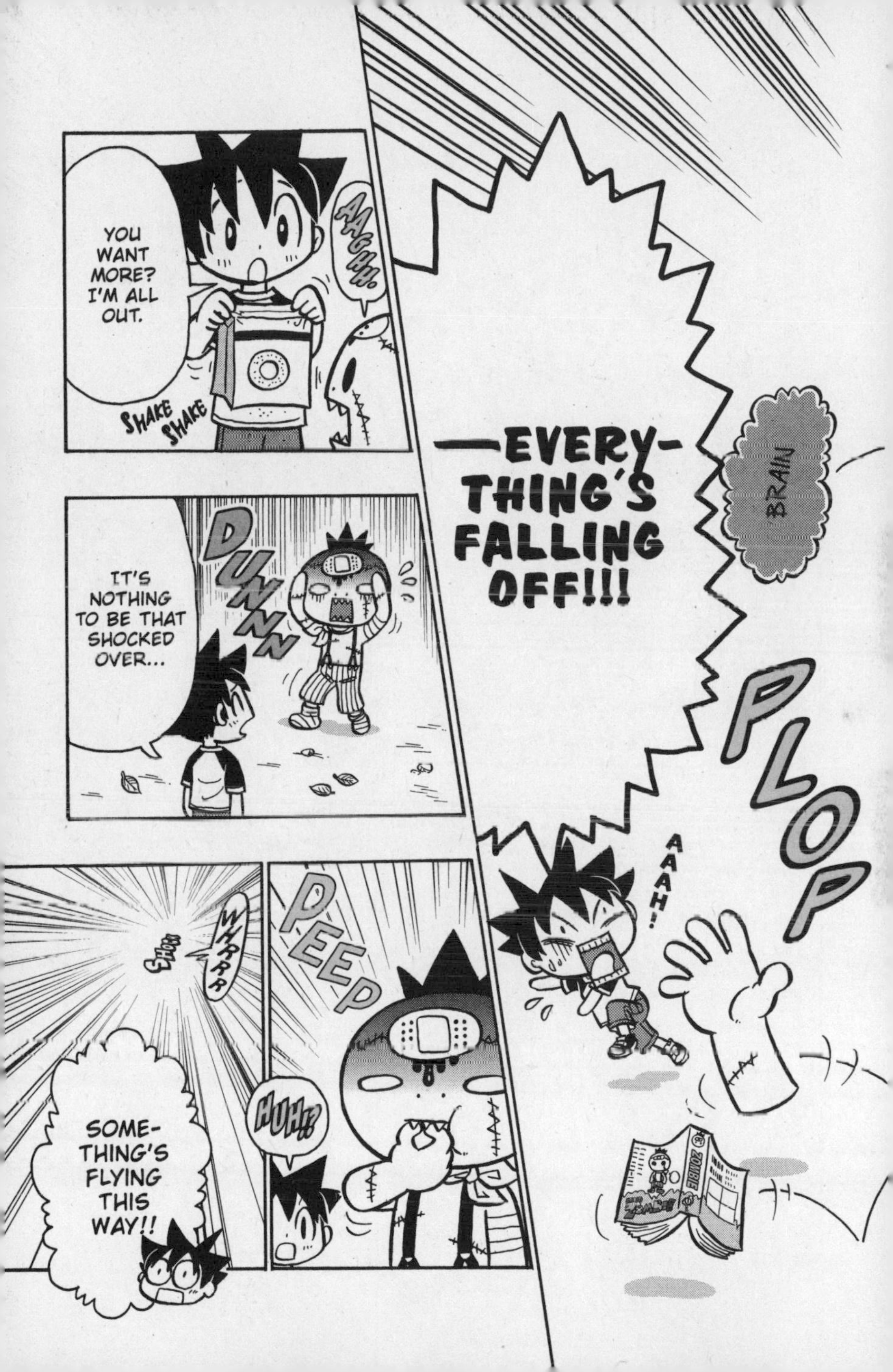
—EVERY-THING'S FALLING OFF!!!
BRAIN
PLOP
AAAH!
YOU WANT MORE? I'M ALL OUT.
AAGHH.
SHAKE SHAKE
IT'S NOTHING TO BE THAT SHOCKED OVER...
DUNNN
PEEP
HUH!?
WHRRRR
SHOOM
SOME-THING'S FLYING THIS WAY!!

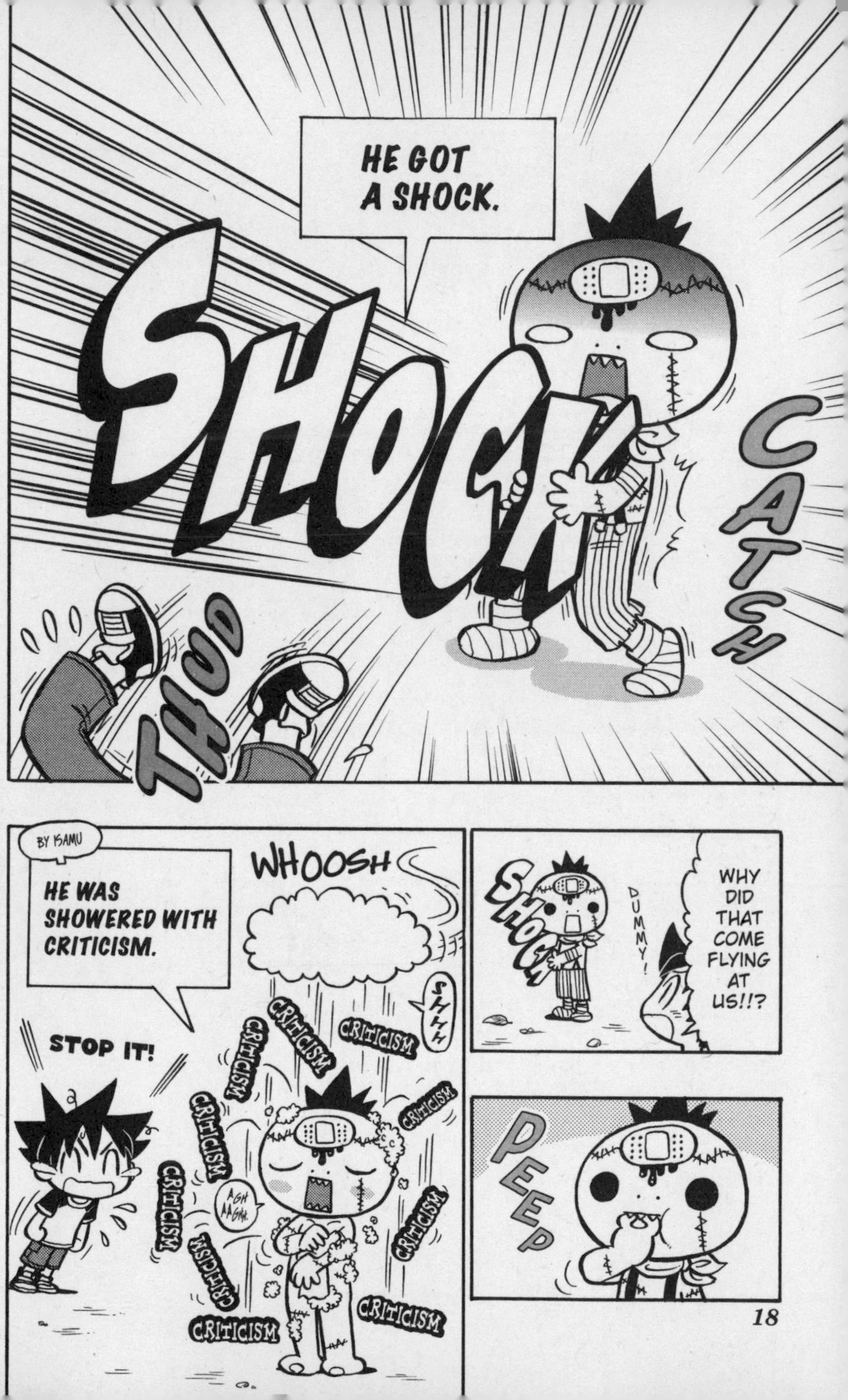
HE GOT A SHOCK.
SHOCK
CATCH
THUD
WHY DID THAT COME FLYING AT US!!?
DUMMY!
SHOCK
PEEP
BY ISAMU
HE WAS SHOWERED WITH CRITICISM.
WHOOSH
SHHH
CRITICISM
CRITICISM
CRITICISM
CRITICISM
CRITICISM
CRITICISM
CRITICISM
CRITICISM
CRITICISM
CRITICISM
CRITICISM
AGH AAGHH.
STOP IT!

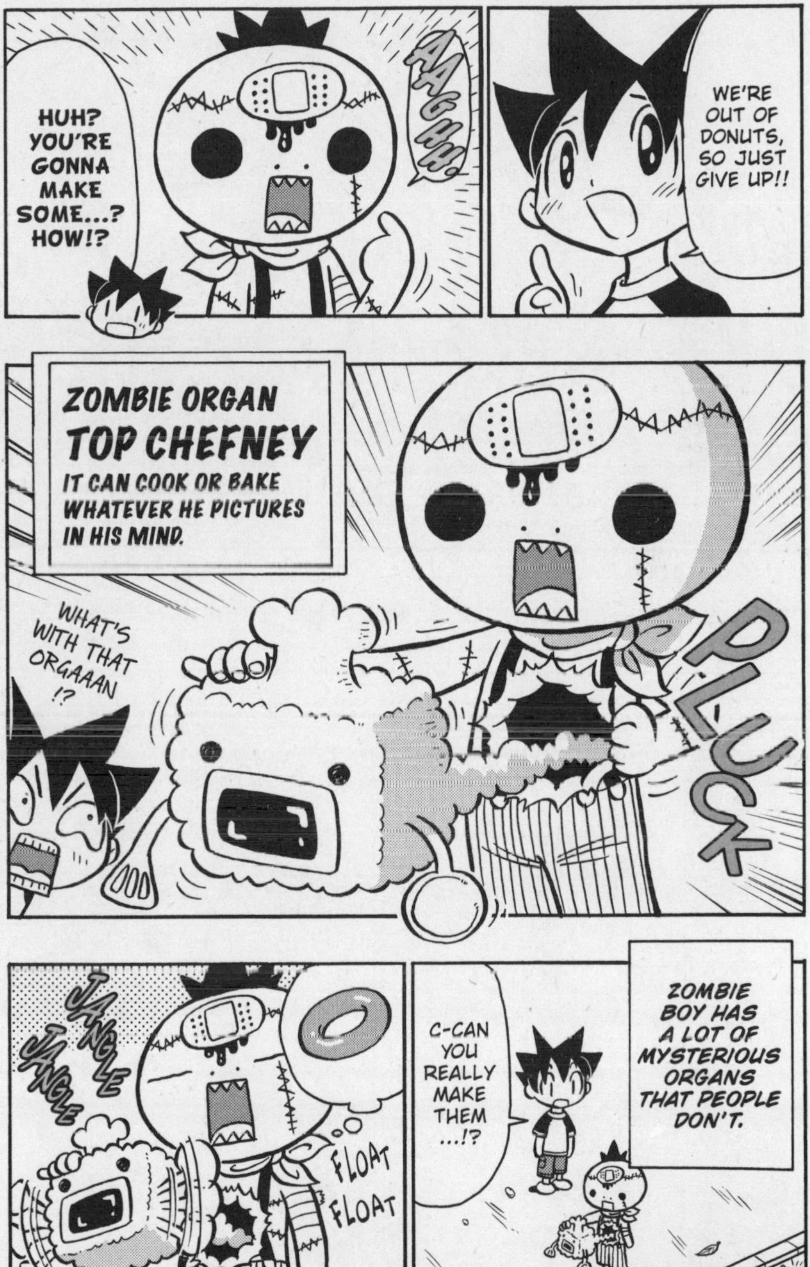
WE'RE OUT OF DONUTS, SO JUST GIVE UP!!
AAGHH!
HUH? YOU'RE GONNA MAKE SOME...? HOW!?
ZOMBIE ORGAN
TOP CHEFNEY
IT CAN COOK OR BAKE WHATEVER HE PICTURES IN HIS MIND.
PLUCK
WHAT'S WITH THAT ORGAAAN !?
ZOMBIE BOY HAS A LOT OF MYSTERIOUS ORGANS THAT PEOPLE DON'T.
C-CAN YOU REALLY MAKE THEM ...!?
JANGLE
JANGLE
FLOAT
FLOAT

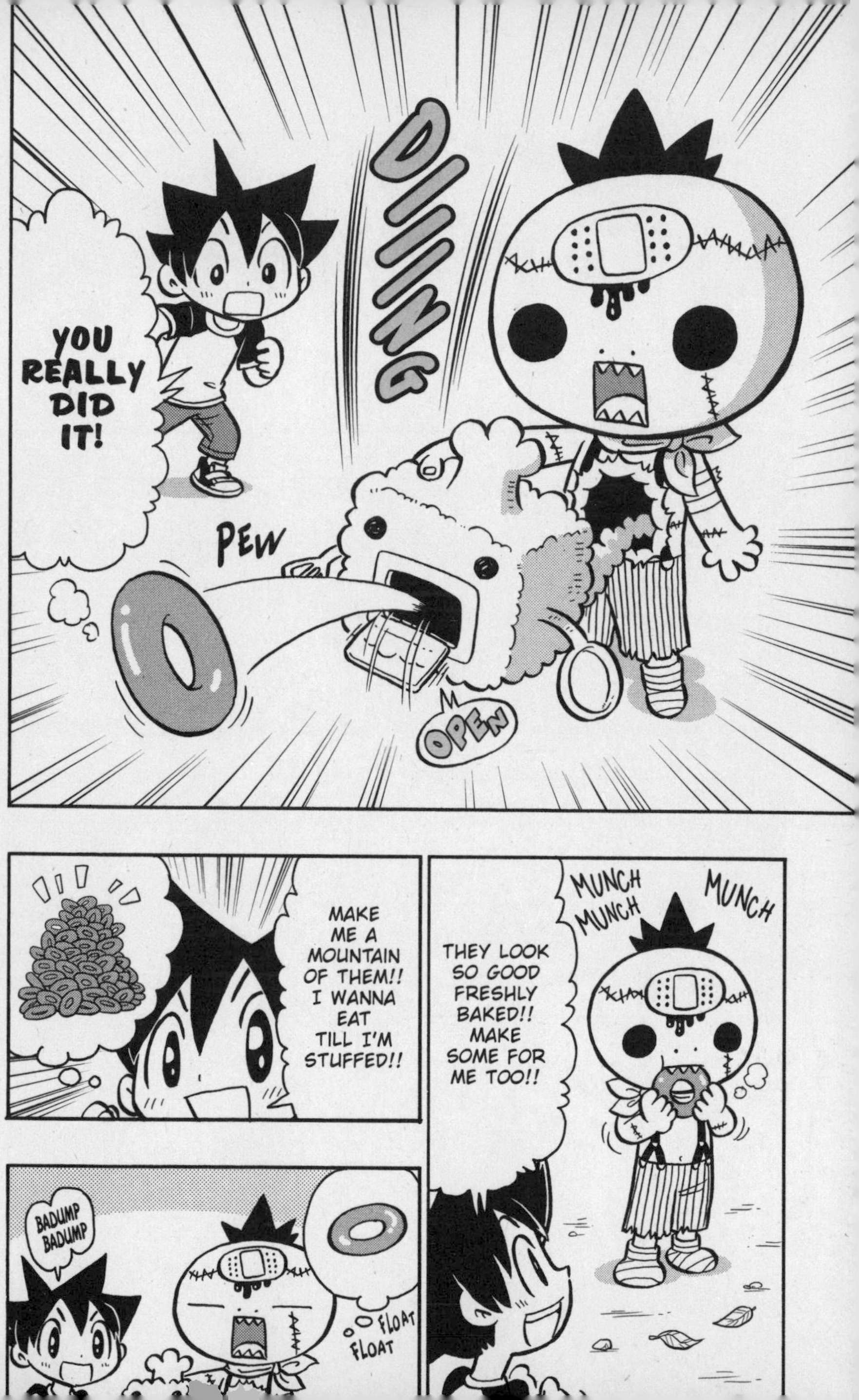
DIIIING
YOU REALLY DID IT!
PEW
OPEN
MUNCH MUNCH
MUNCH
THEY LOOK SO GOOD FRESHLY BAKED!! MAKE SOME FOR ME TOO!!
MAKE ME A MOUNTAIN OF THEM!! I WANNA EAT TILL I'M STUFFED!!
BADUMP BADUMP
FLOAT FLOAT

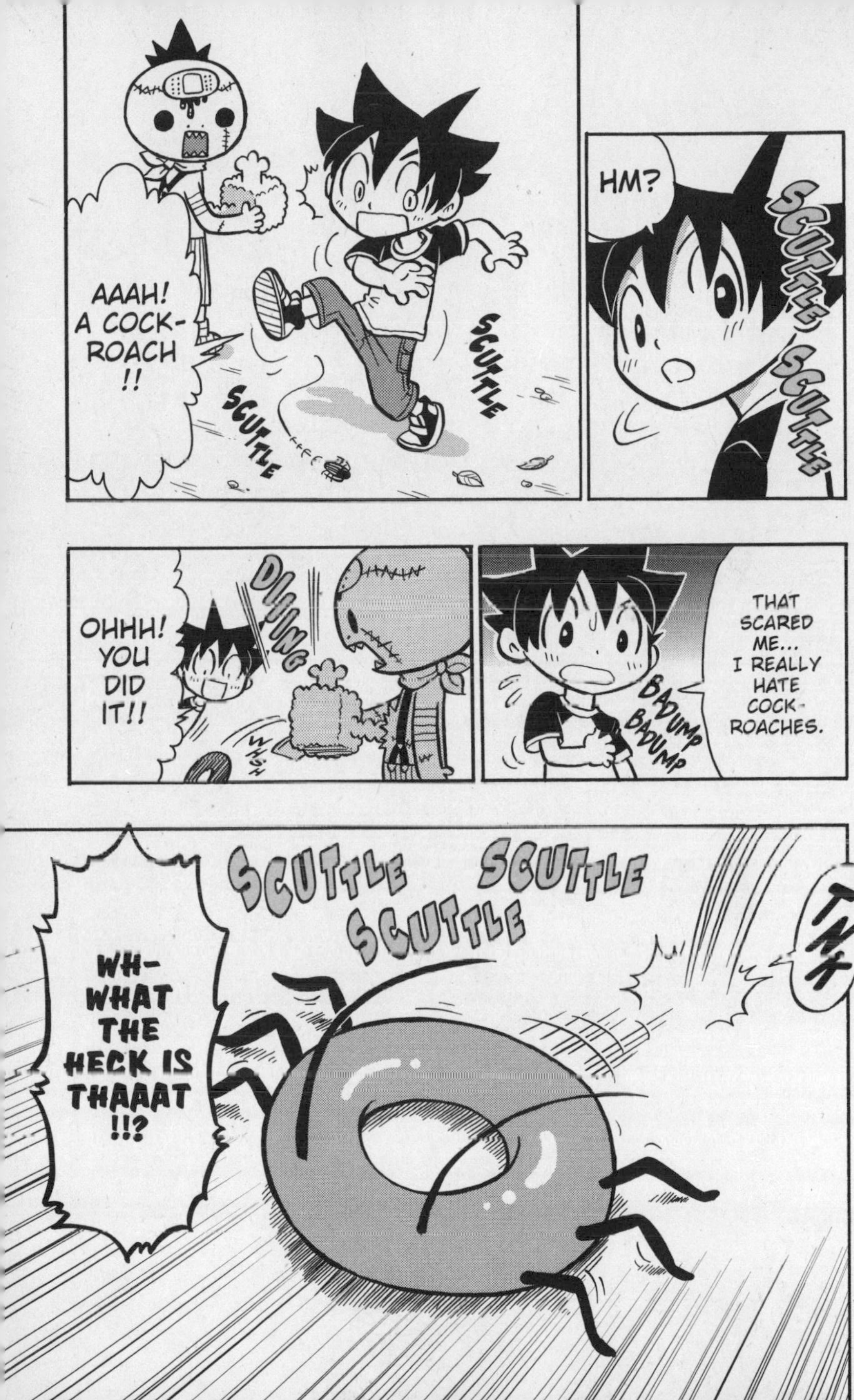
HM?
SCUTTLE
SCUTTLE
SCUTTLE
AAAH! A COCK-ROACH!!
SCUTTLE
SCUTTLE
THAT SCARED ME... I REALLY HATE COCK-ROACHES.
BADUMP BADUMP
OHHH! YOU DID IT!!
DWING
WHSH
TNK
SCUTTLE SCUTTLE
SCUTTLE
WH-WHAT THE HECK IS THAAAT!!?

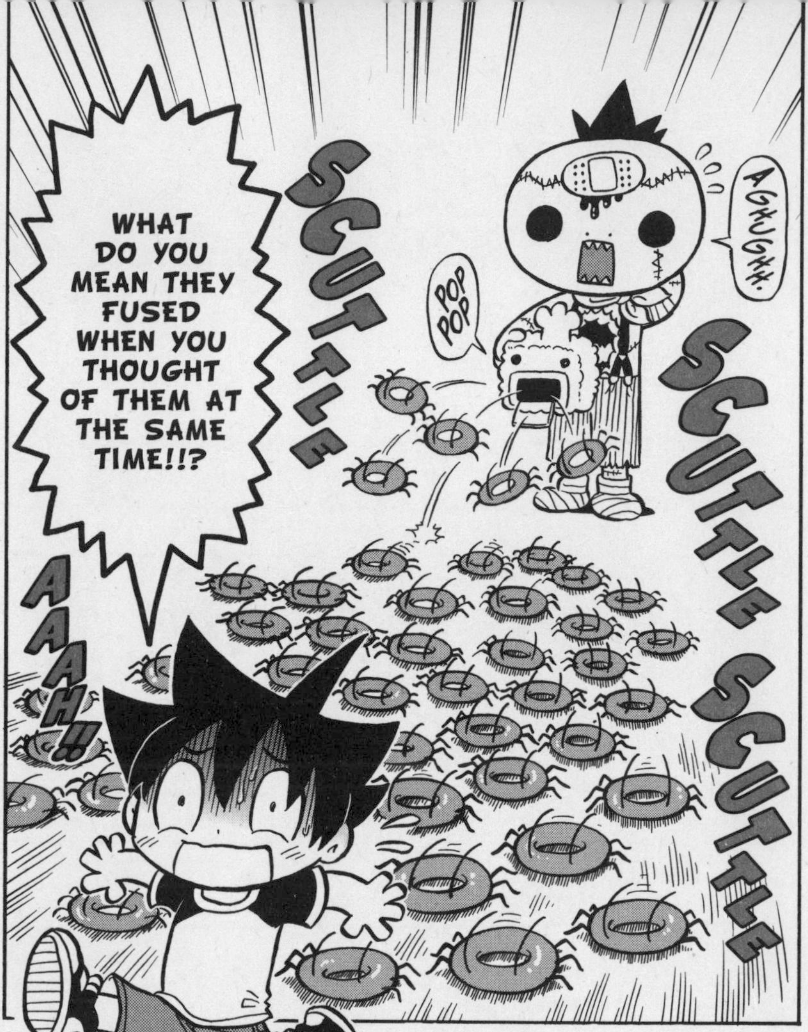
AGXUGXX.
SCUTTLE SCUTTLE SCUTTLE
POP POP
SCUTTLE
WHAT DO YOU MEAN THEY FUSED WHEN YOU THOUGHT OF THEM AT THE SAME TIME!!?
AAAAH!!

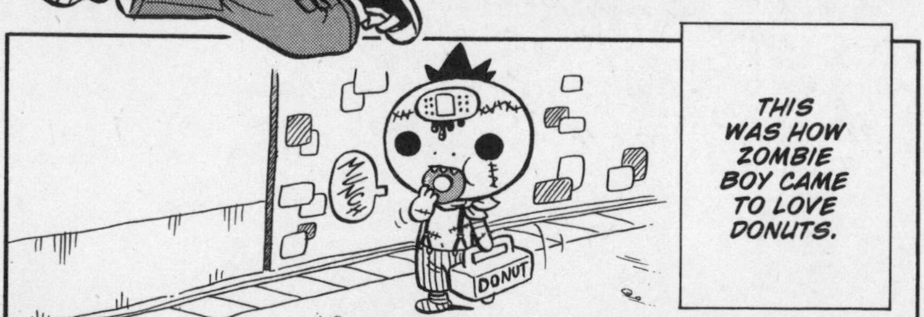
THIS WAS HOW ZOMBIE BOY CAME TO LOVE DONUTS.
MUNCH
DONUT

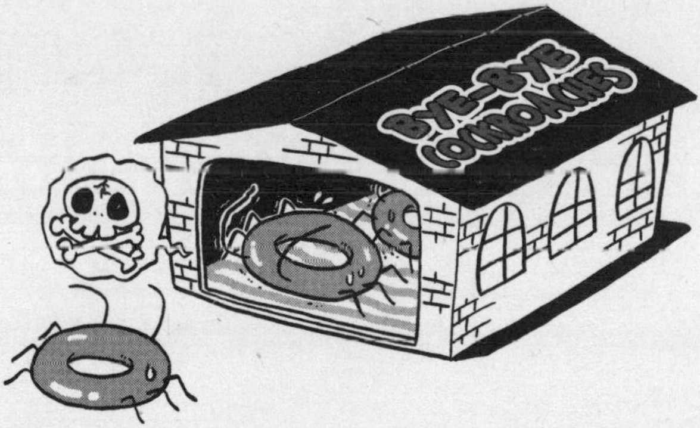
BYE-BYE
COCKROACHES

A STRANGE CREATURE IZ FOLLOWING YOU!

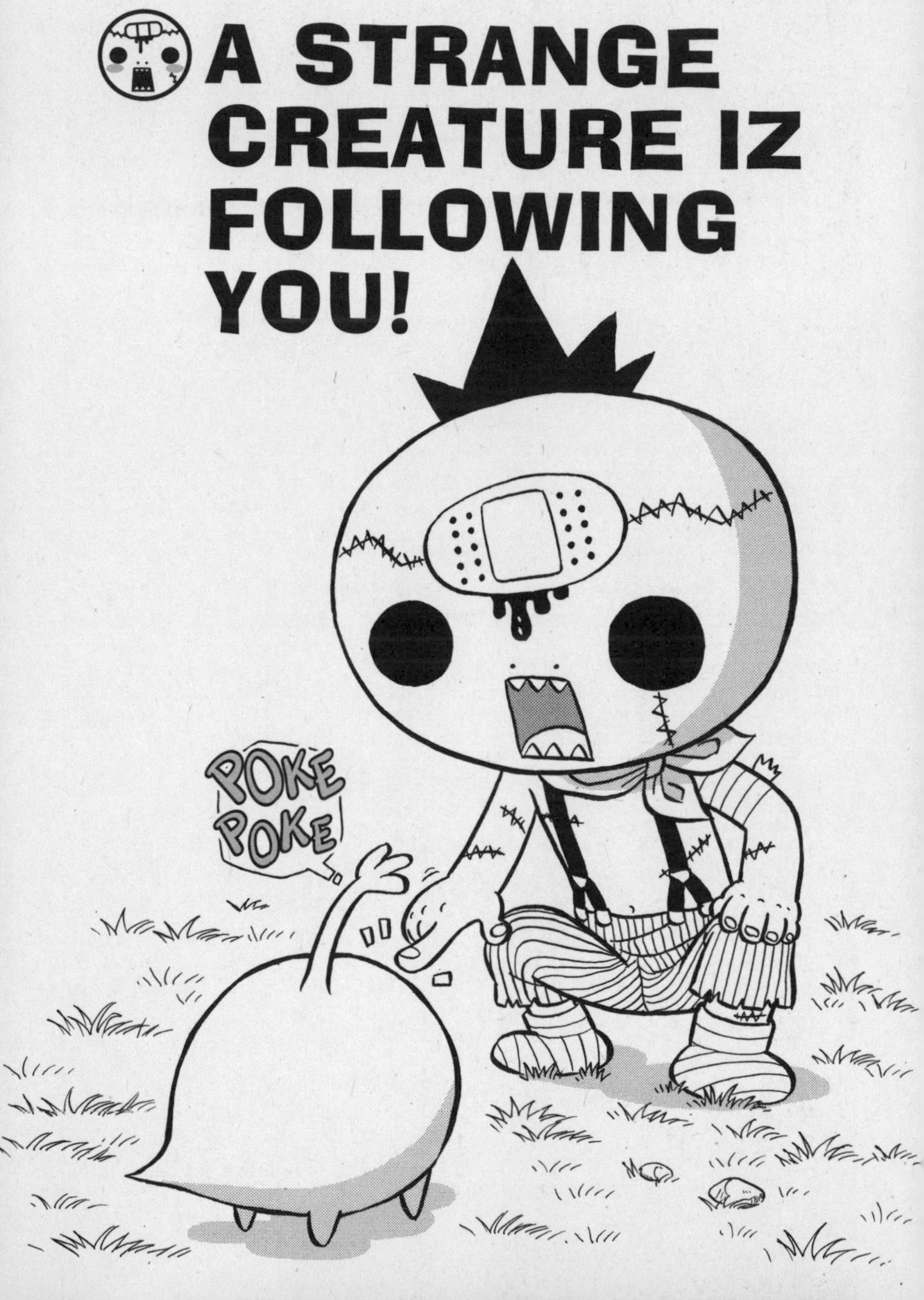
POKE
POKE

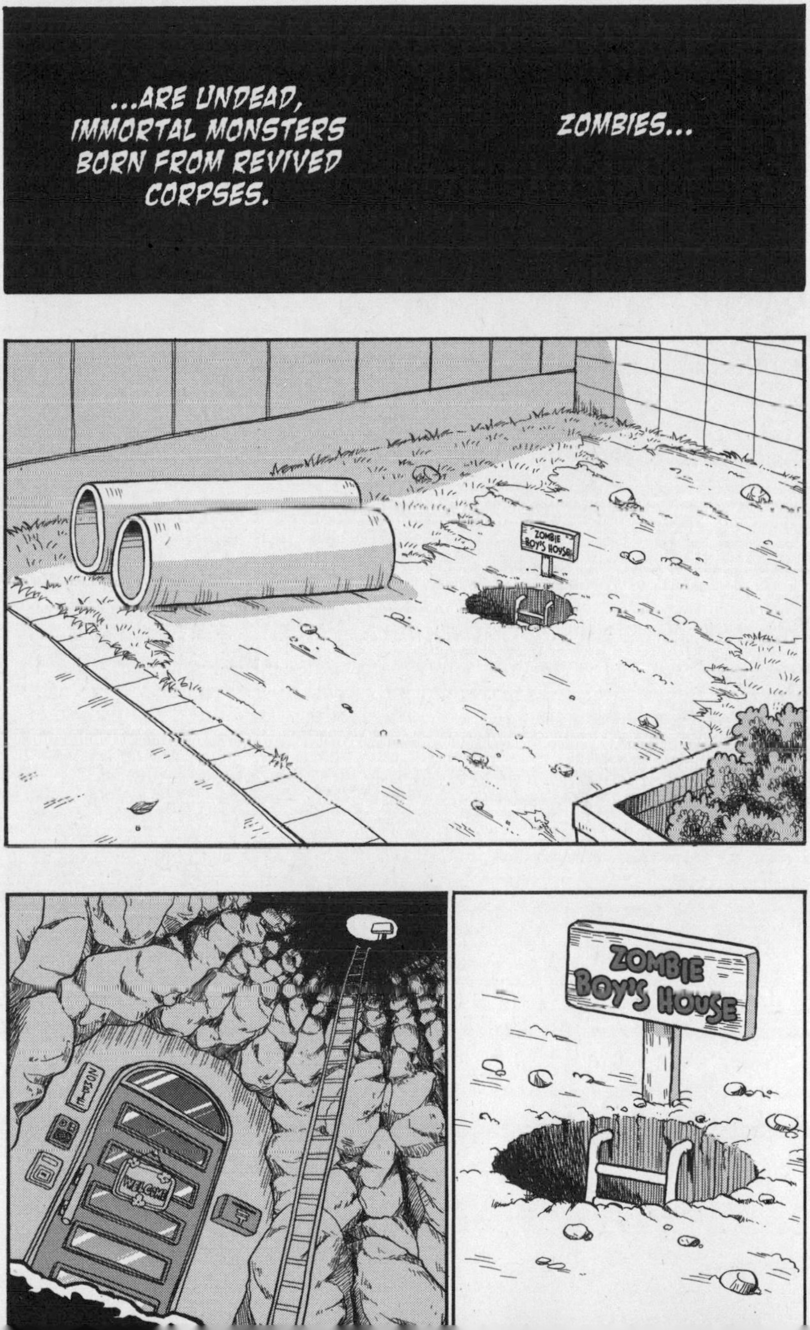
ZOMBIES...
...ARE UNDEAD, IMMORTAL MONSTERS BORN FROM REVIVED CORPSES.
ZOMBIE BOY'S HOUSE
ZOMBIE BOY'S HOUSE

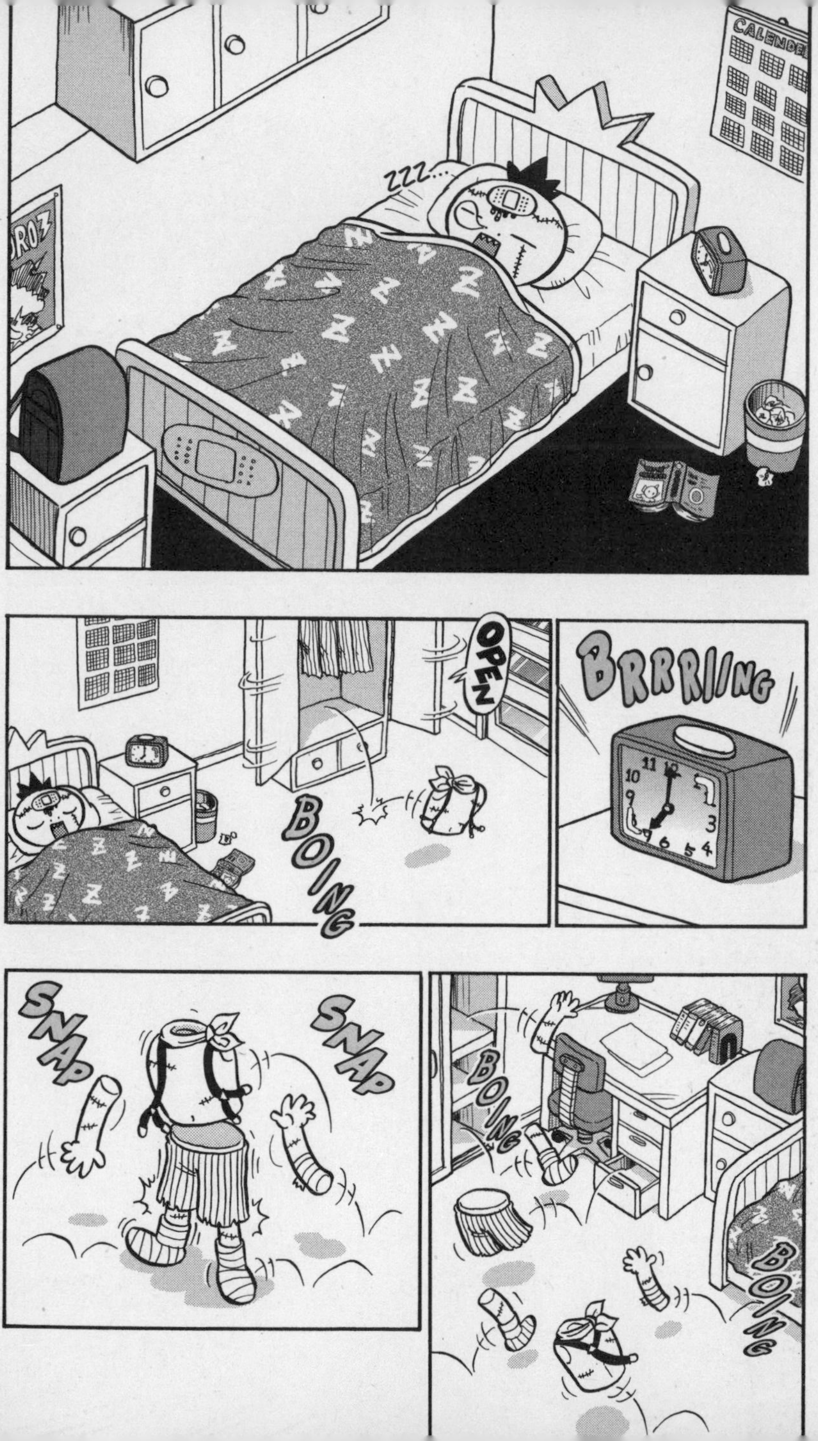

ZZZ...
BRRRIING
OPEN
BOING
BOING
BOING
SNAP
SNAP

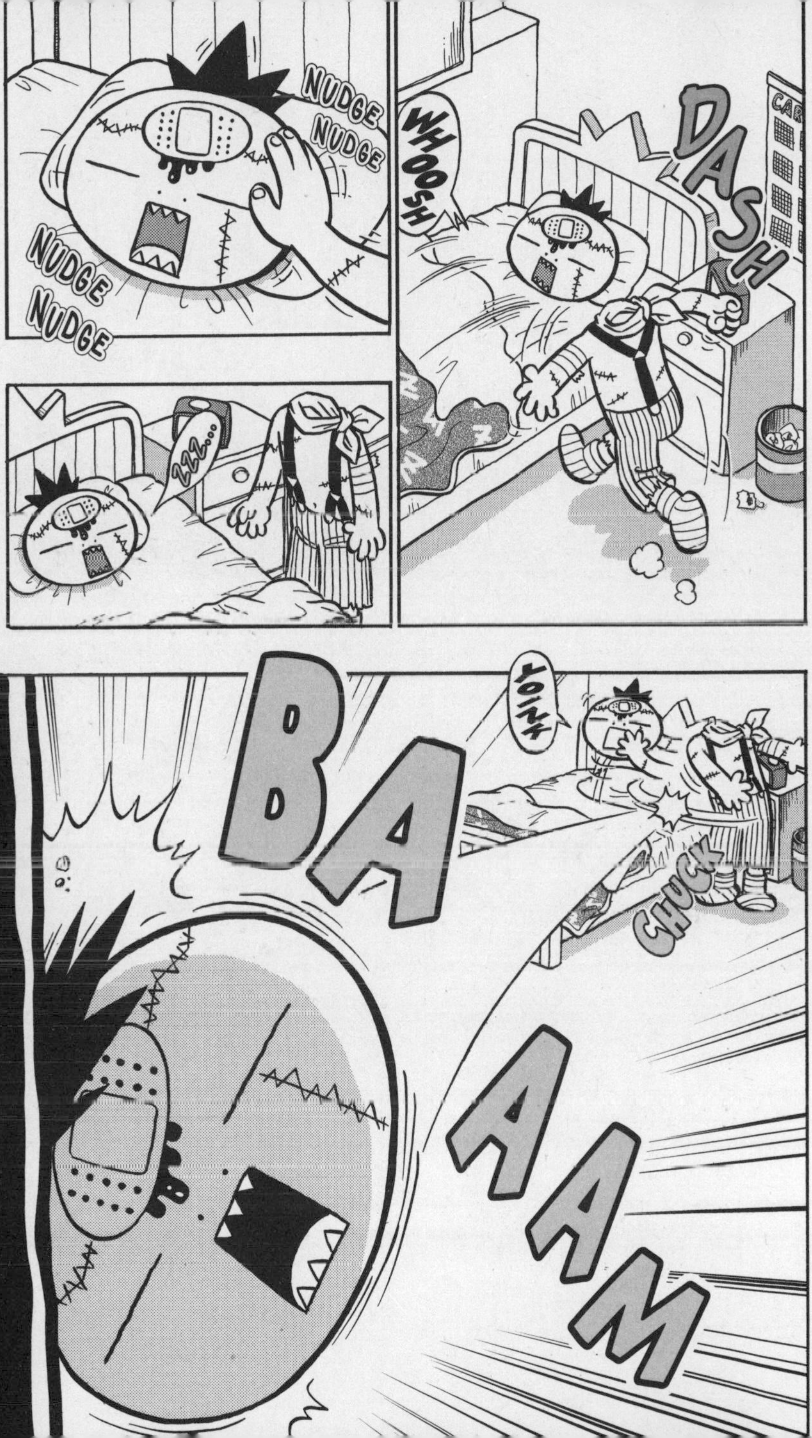
WHOOSH
DASH
NUDGE NUDGE
NUDGE NUDGE
zzz...
YOINK
CHUCK
BAAAM

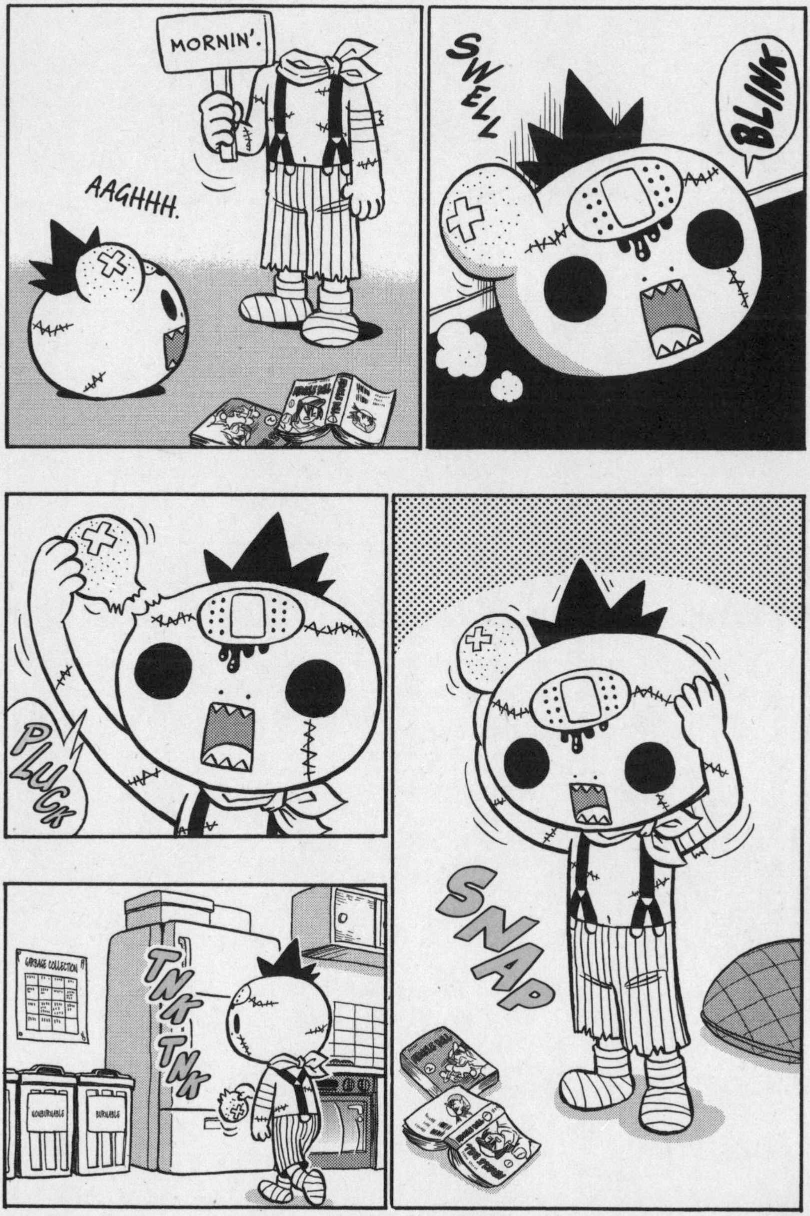
SWELL
BLINK
MORNIN'.
AAGHHH.
SNAP
PLUCK
TNK TNK
GARBAGE COLLECTION
NONBURNABLE
BURNABLE

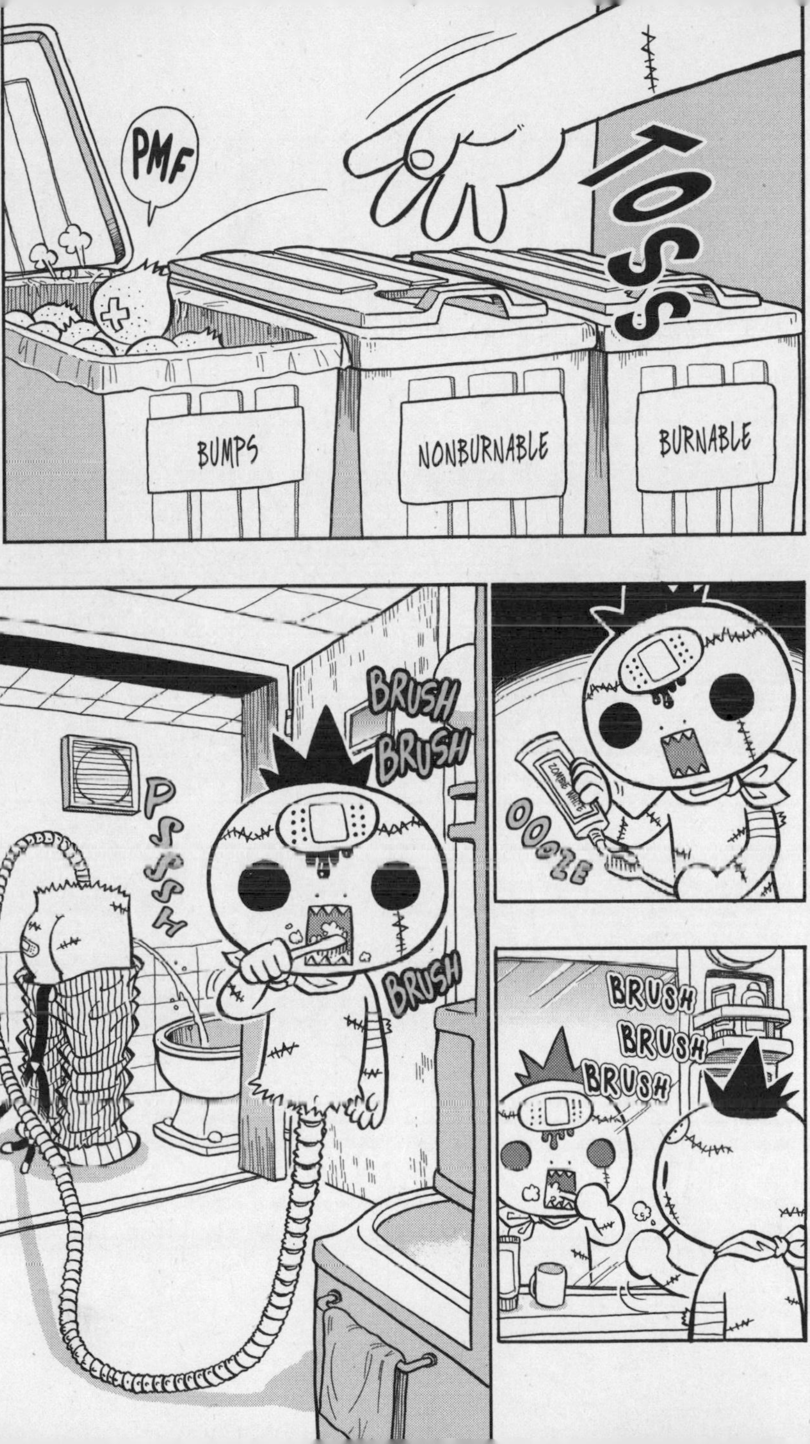
TOSS
PMF
BURNABLE
NONBURNABLE
BUMPS
ZOMBIE WHITE
OOOZE
BRUSH
BRUSH
BRUSH
BRUSH
BRUSH
BRUSH
PSSSH

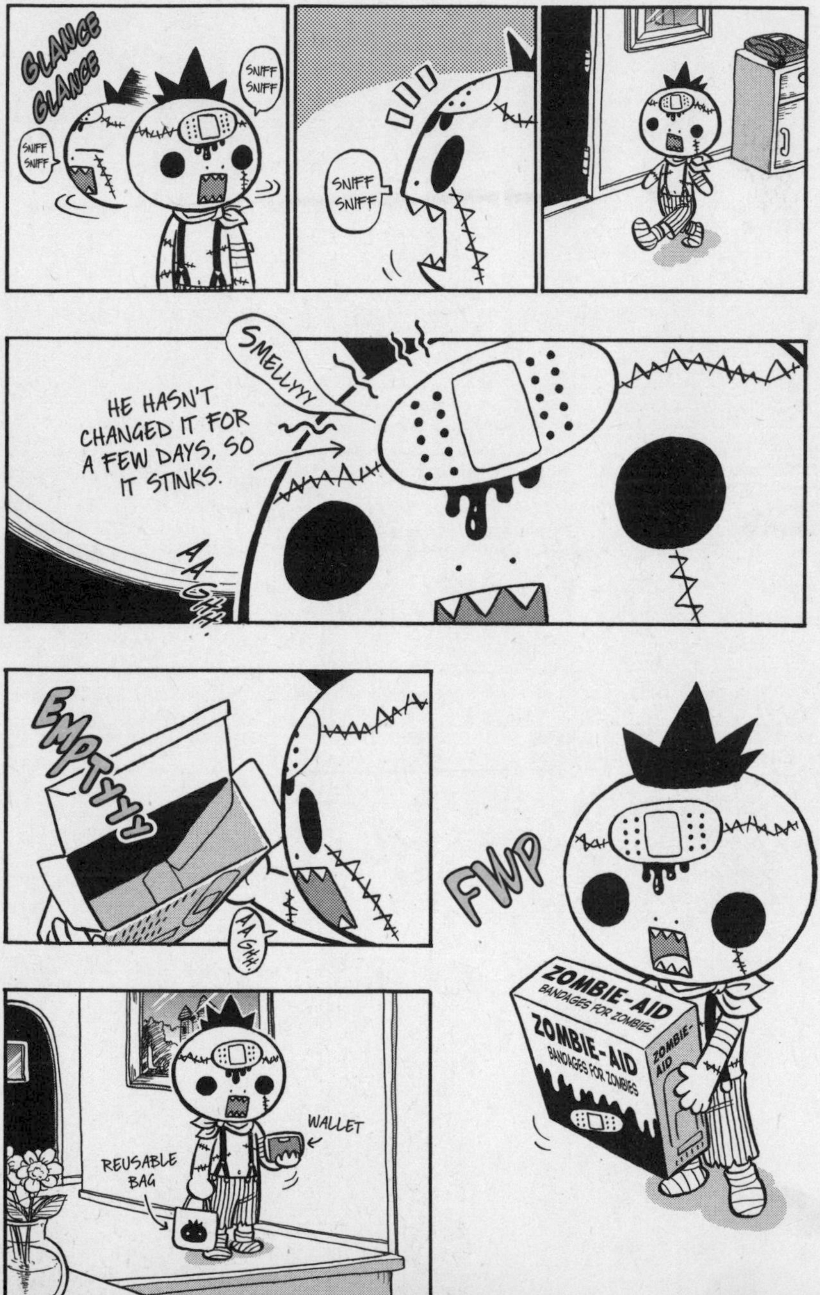
SNIFF SNIFF
SNIFF SNIFF
GLANCE GLANCE
SNIFF SNIFF
SMELLYYY
HE HASN'T CHANGED IT FOR A FEW DAYS, SO IT STINKS.
AAGHH.
FWP
ZOMBIE-AID
BANDAGES FOR ZOMBIES
ZOMBIE-AID
BANDAGES FOR ZOMBIES
ZOMBIE-AID
EMPTYYY
AAGHH.
WALLET
REUSABLE BAG

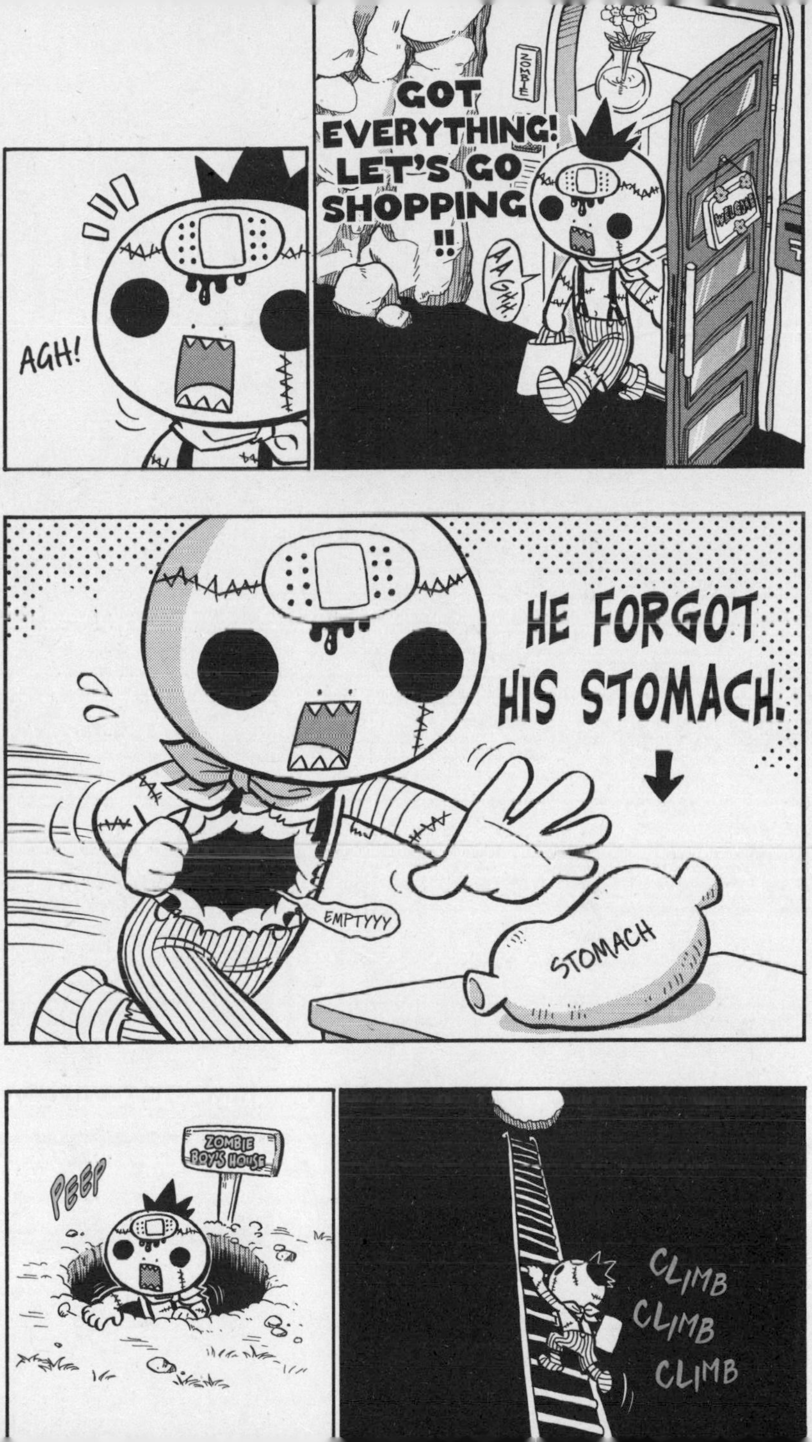
ZOMBIE
GOT EVERYTHING! LET'S GO SHOPPING!!
WELCOME
AAGHH
AGH!
HE FORGOT HIS STOMACH.
EMPTYYY
STOMACH
CLIMB
CLIMB
CLIMB
ZOMBIE BOY'S HOUSE
PEEP

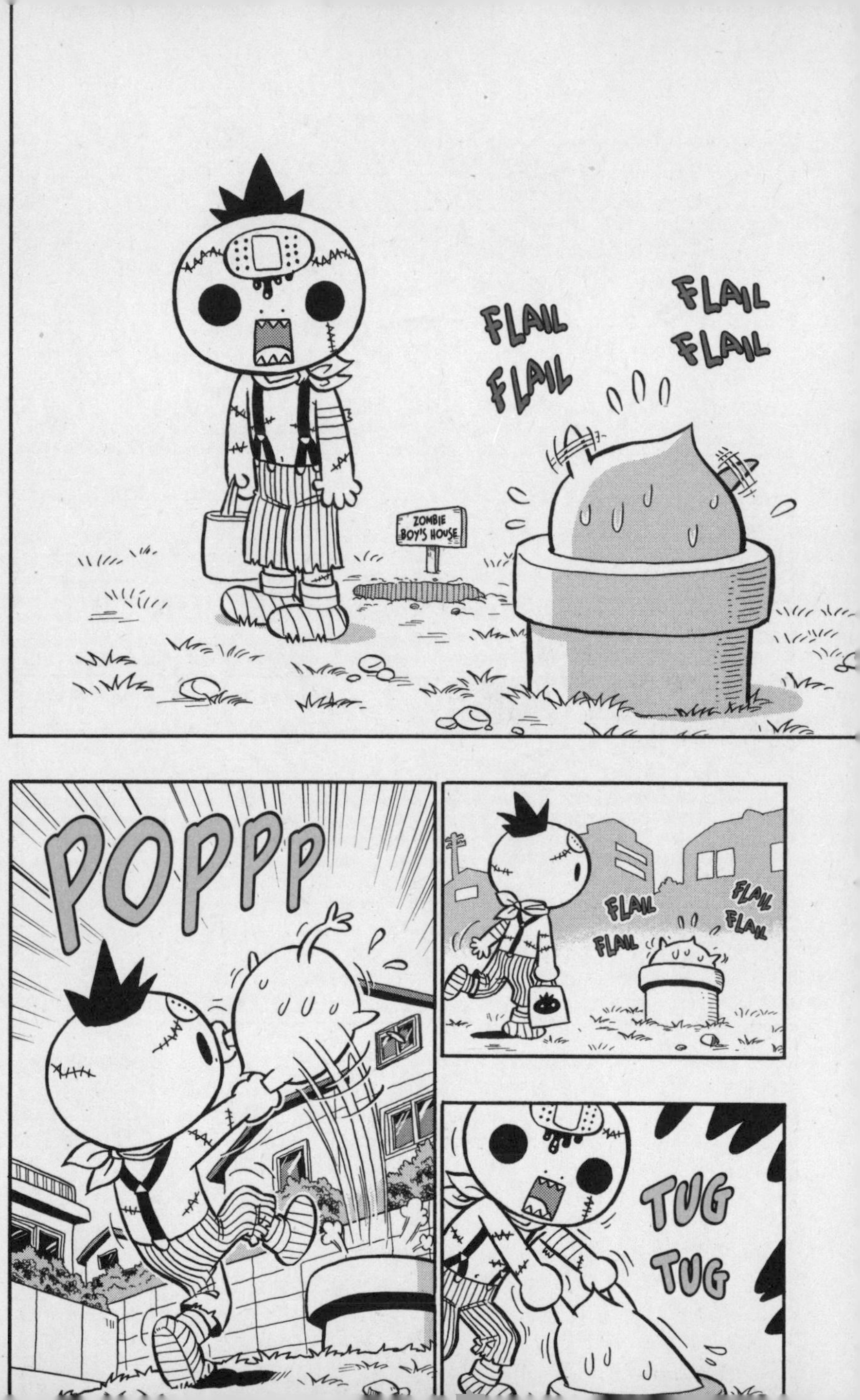
FLAIL
FLAIL
FLAIL
FLAIL
ZOMBIE BOY'S HOUSE
FLAIL
FLAIL
FLAIL
FLAIL
TUG
TUG
POPPP

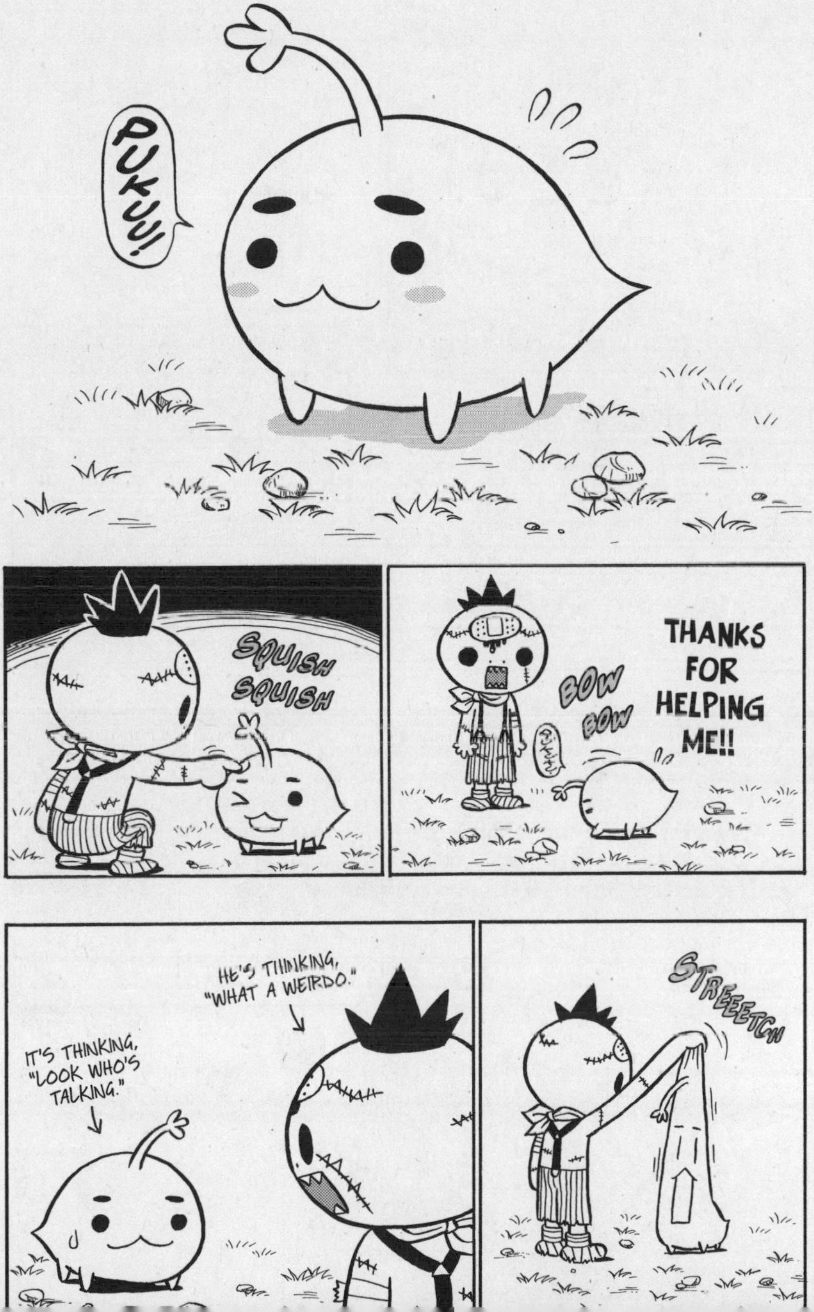
PUKUU!
THANKS FOR HELPING ME!!
BOW BOW
SQUISH SQUISH
STREEETCH
HE'S THINKING, "WHAT A WEIRDO."
IT'S THINKING, "LOOK WHO'S TALKING."

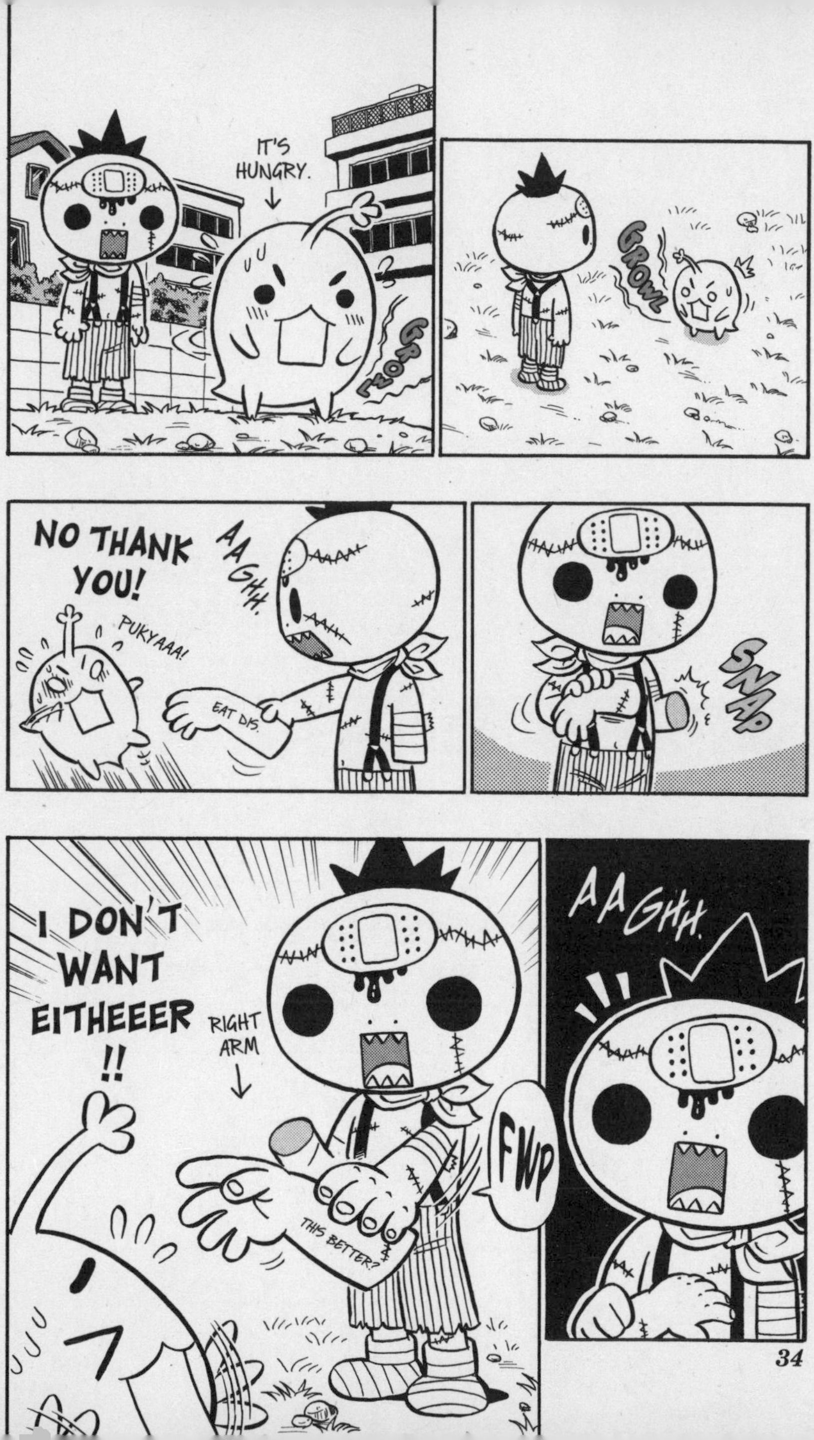
GROWL
IT'S HUNGRY.
GROWL
SNAP
AAGHH.
NO THANK YOU!
PUKYAAA!
EAT DIS.
AAGHH.
I DON'T WANT EITHEEER!!
RIGHT ARM
FWP
THIS BETTER?

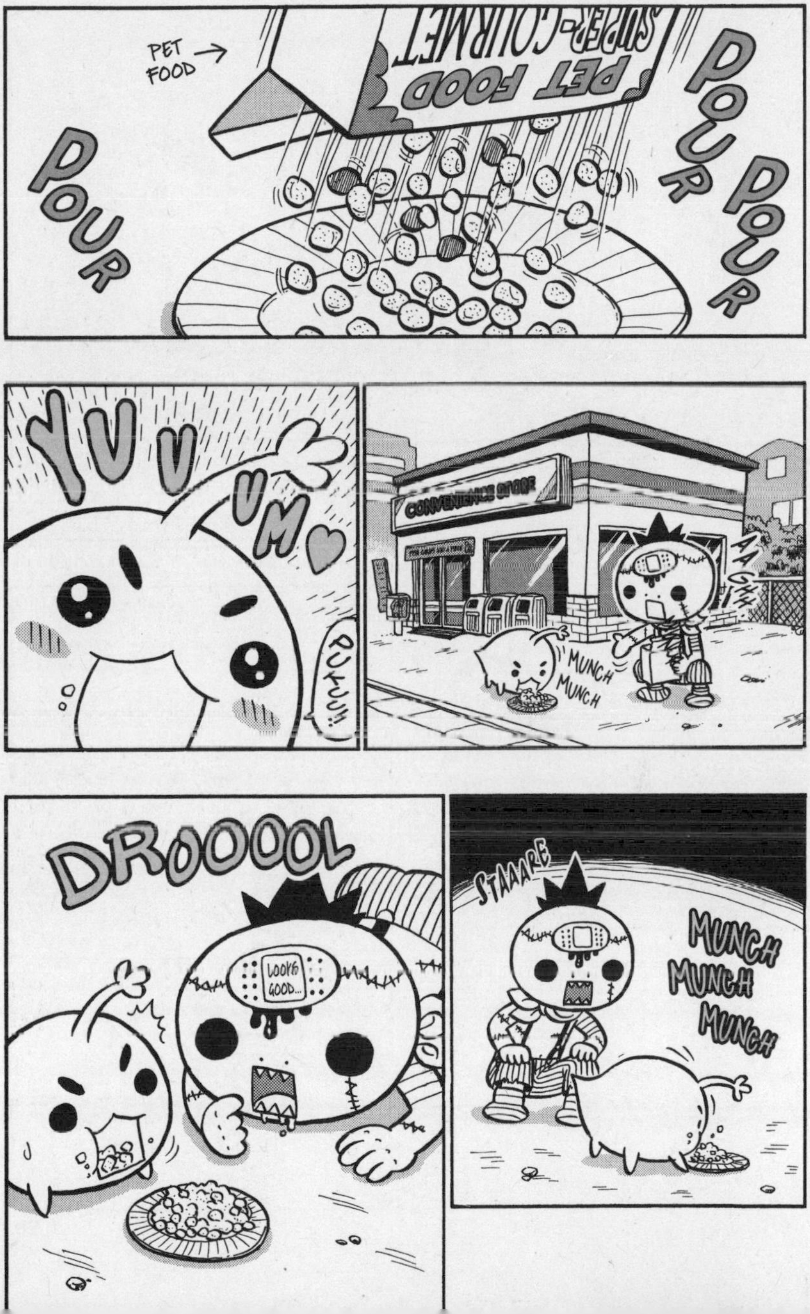

PET FOOD →
SUPER-GOURMET PET FOOD
POUR
POUR
POUR
CONVENIENCE STORE
AAGHH!
MUNCH MUNCH
YUUUUM
PUKUU!!
STAAARE
MUNCH MUNCH MUNCH
DROOOOL
LOOKS GOOD...

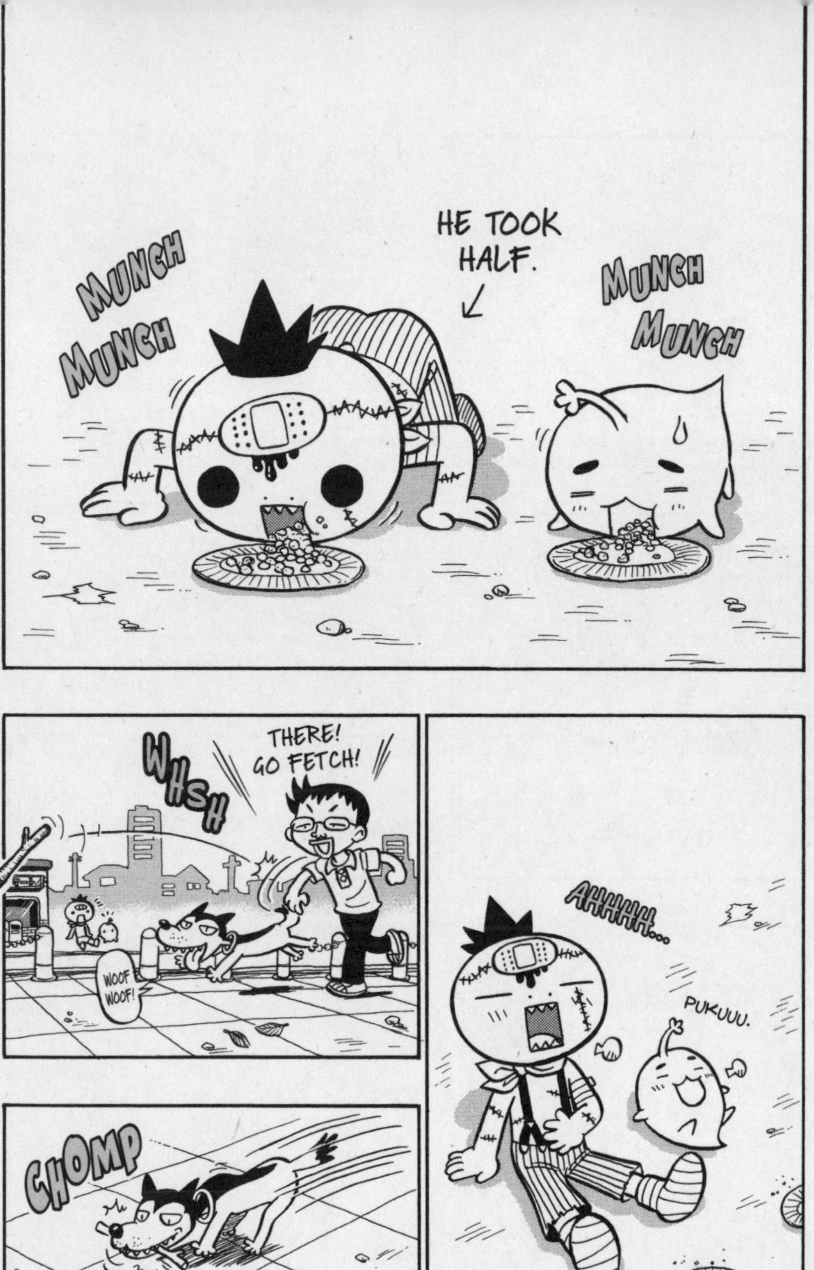
MUNCH MUNCH
HE TOOK HALF.
MUNCH MUNCH
AHHHHH...
PUKUUU.
THERE! GO FETCH!
WHSH
WOOF WOOF!
CHOMP

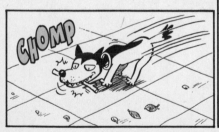

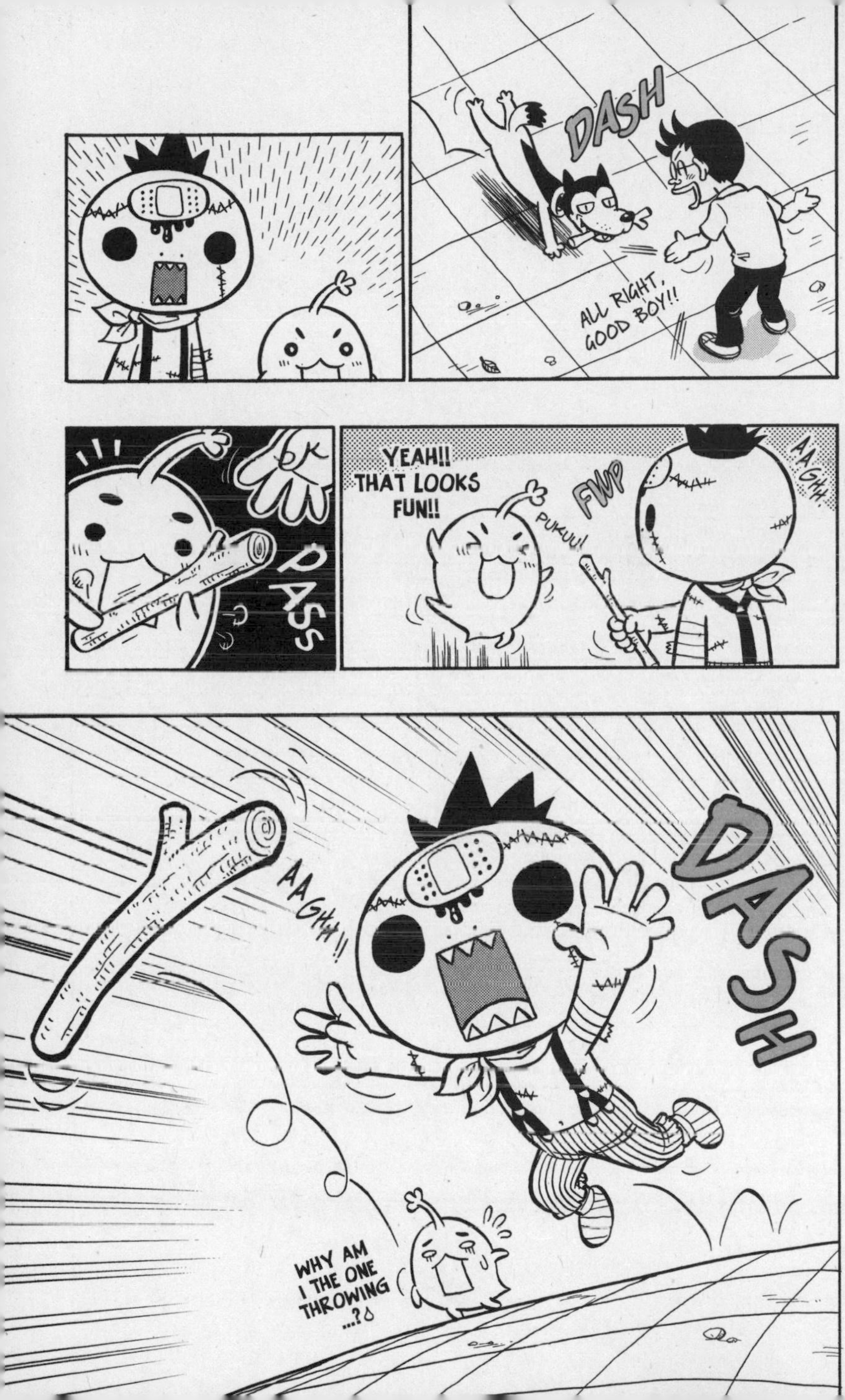
DASH
ALL RIGHT, GOOD BOY!!
AAGHH
FWP
YEAH!! THAT LOOKS FUN!!
PUKUU!
PASS
DASH
AAGHH!!
WHY AM I THE ONE THROWING ...?

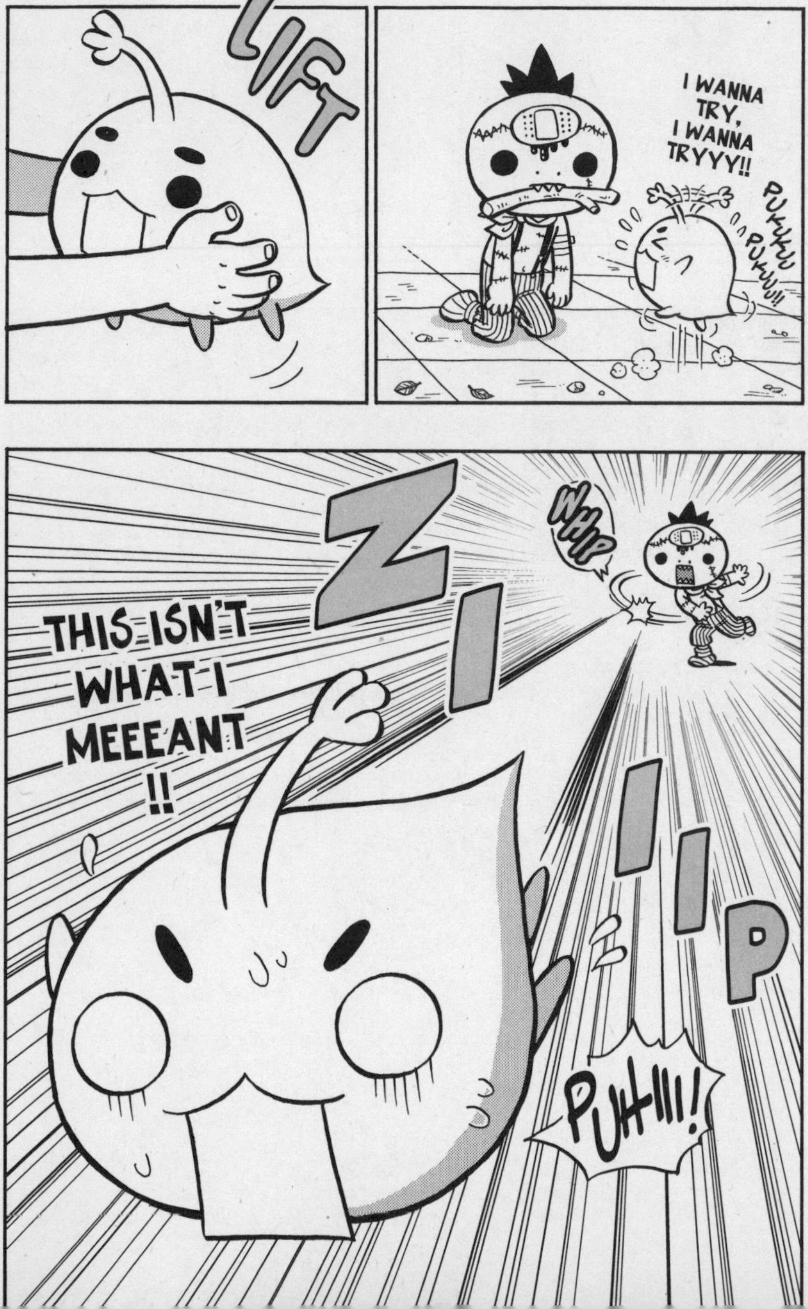
I WANNA TRY, I WANNA TRYYY!!
PUKUU
PUKUUU!!
LIFT
WHIP
ZIIIP
THIS ISN'T WHAT I MEEEANT !!
PUHIIII!

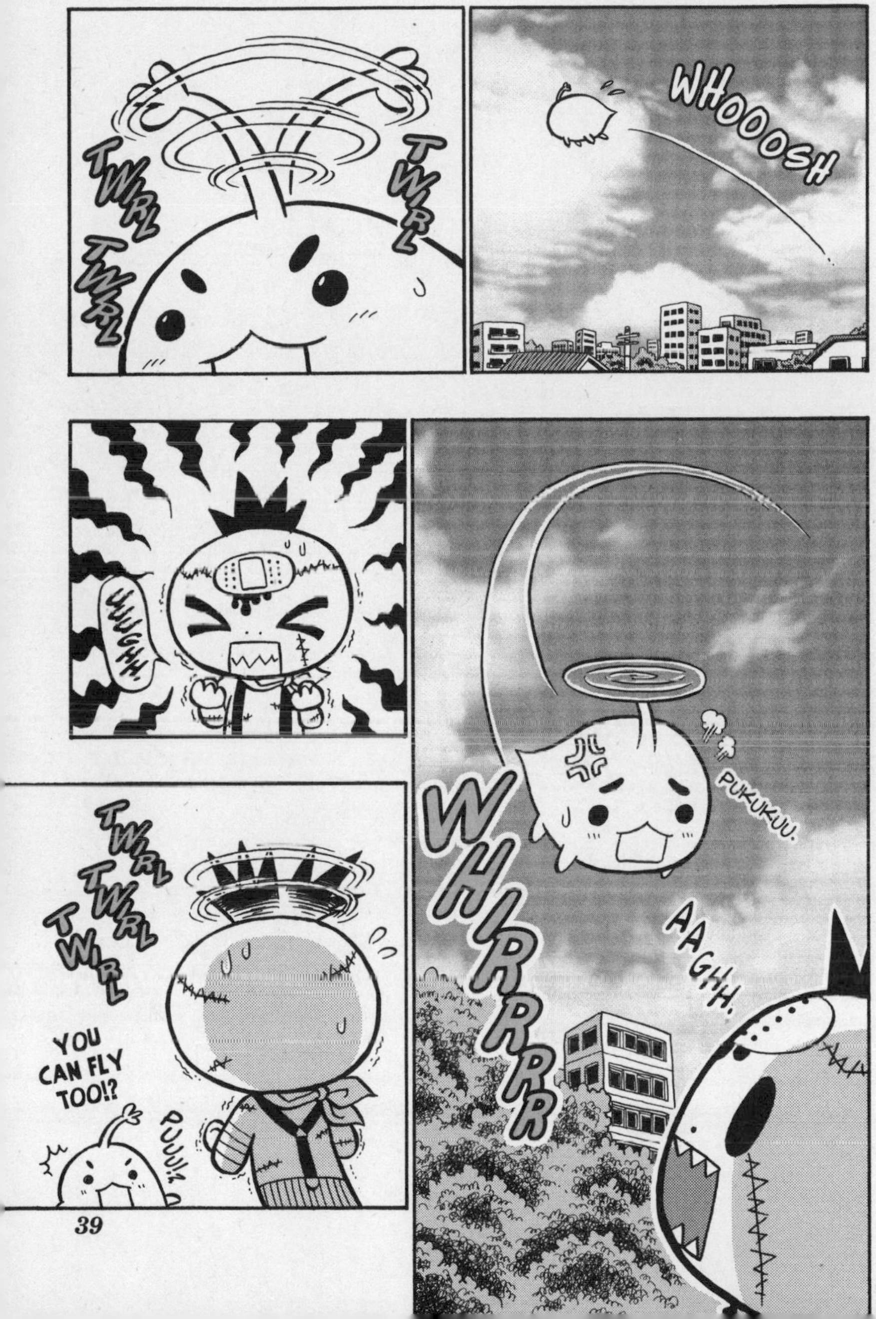
WHOOOOSH
TWIRL
TWIRL
TWIRL
WHIRRRR
PUKUKUU.
AAGHH.
UUUGHH.
TWIRL
TWIRL
TWIRL
PUUU!?
YOU CAN FLY TOO!?

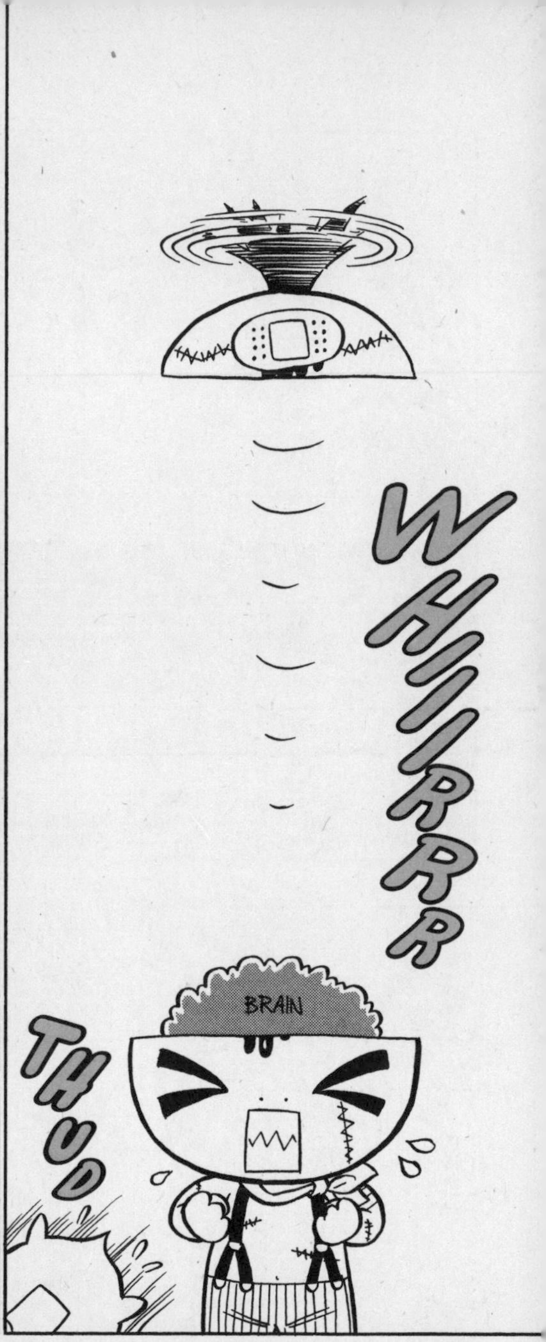
WHIIIRRR
BRAIN
THUD

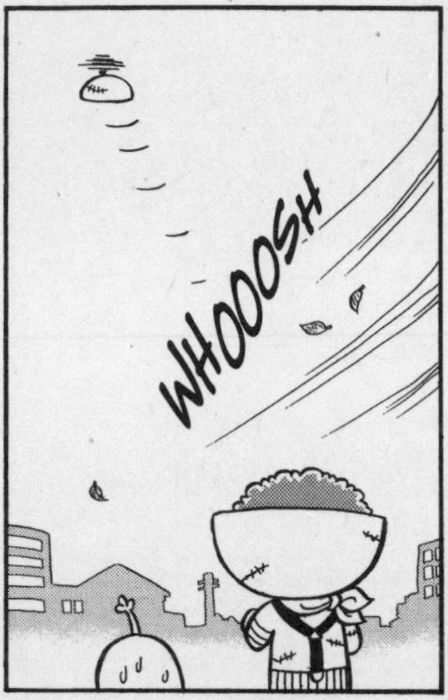
WHOOOSH

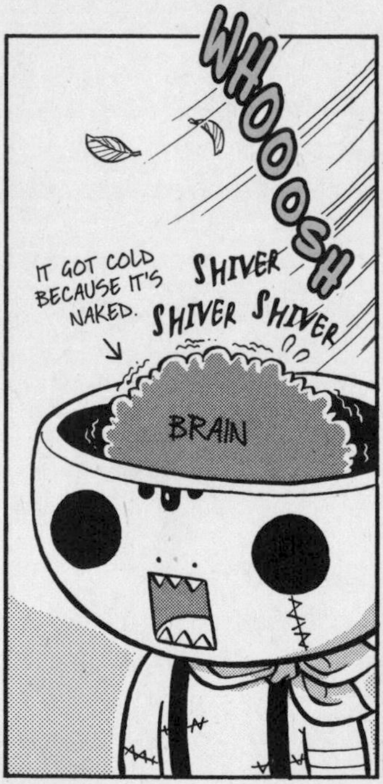
WHOOOOSH
SHIVER
SHIVER SHIVER
IT GOT COLD BECAUSE IT'S NAKED.
BRAIN

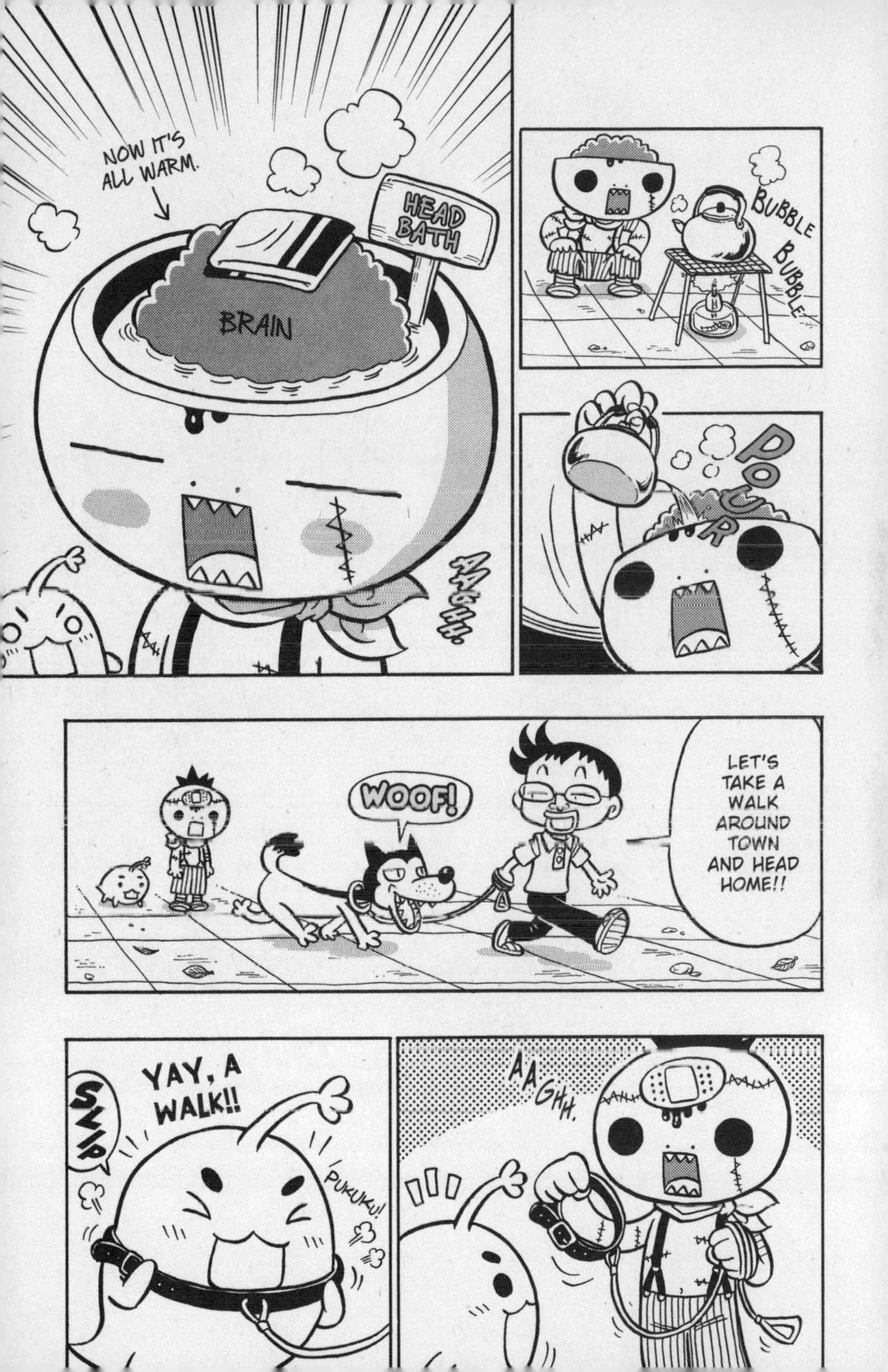
BUBBLE
BUBBLE
BUBBLE
POUR
NOW IT'S ALL WARM.
HEAD BATH
BRAIN
AAGHH.
LET'S TAKE A WALK AROUND TOWN AND HEAD HOME!!
WOOF!
AAGHH.
YAY, A WALK!!
SWIP
PUKUKU!

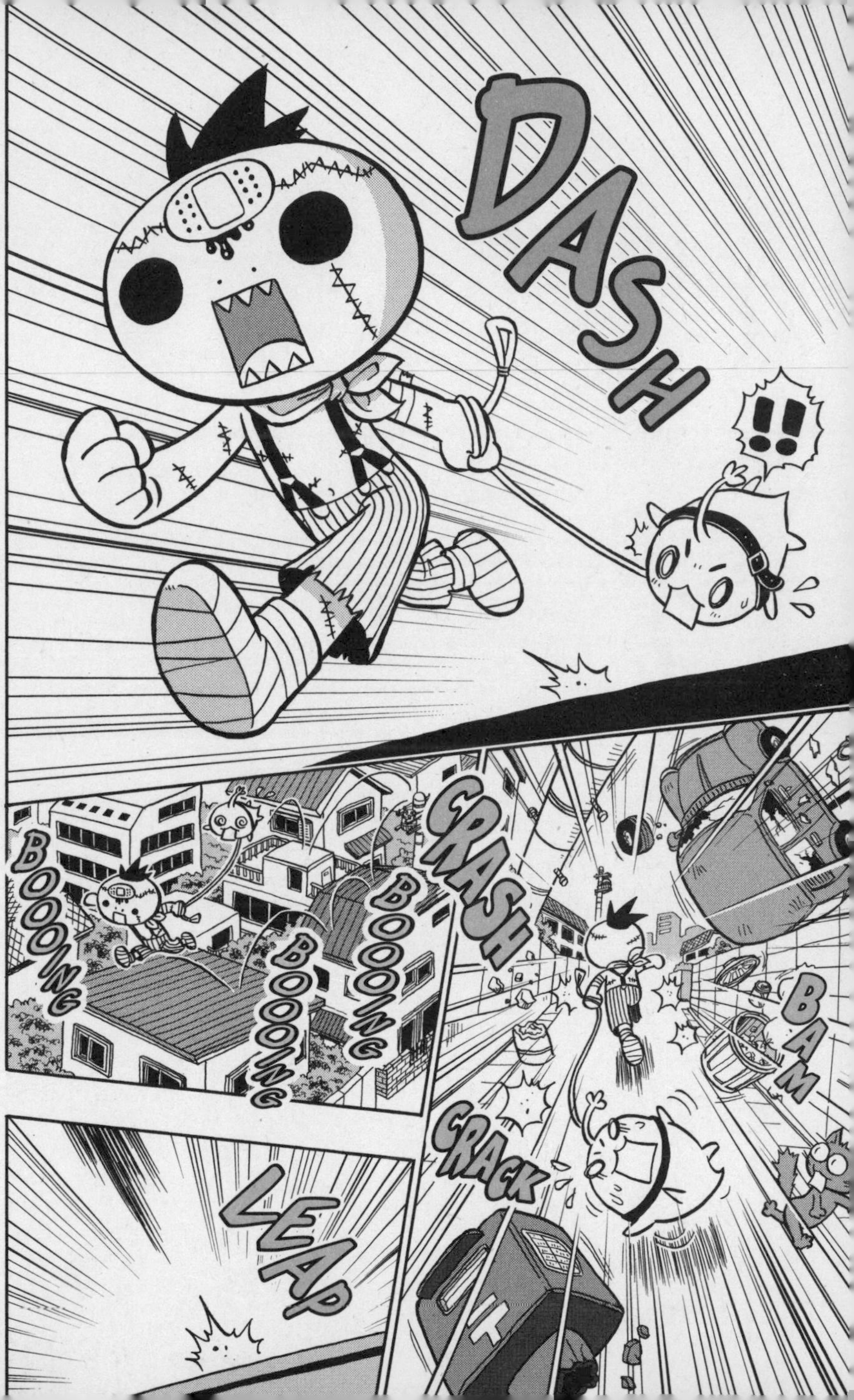
DASH
!!
CRASH
BAM
BOOOING
BOOOING
BOOOING
BOOOING
CRACK
LEAP

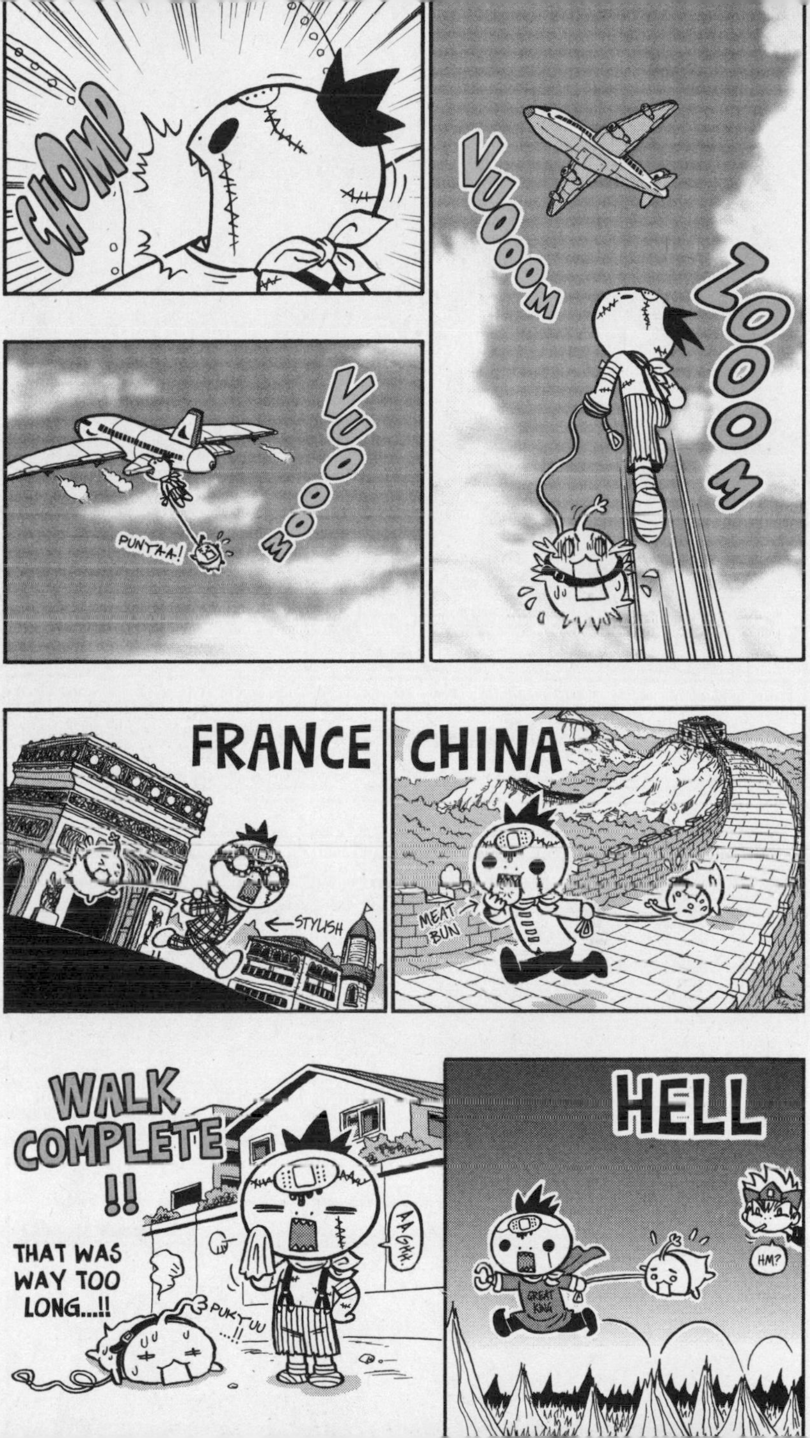

VUOOOM
ZOOOM
CHOMP
VUOOOM
PUNYAA!
CHINA
MEAT BUN
FRANCE
STYLISH
HELL
HM?
GREAT KING
WALK COMPLETE !!
AAGHH.
THAT WAS WAY TOO LONG...!!
PUKYUU ...!!

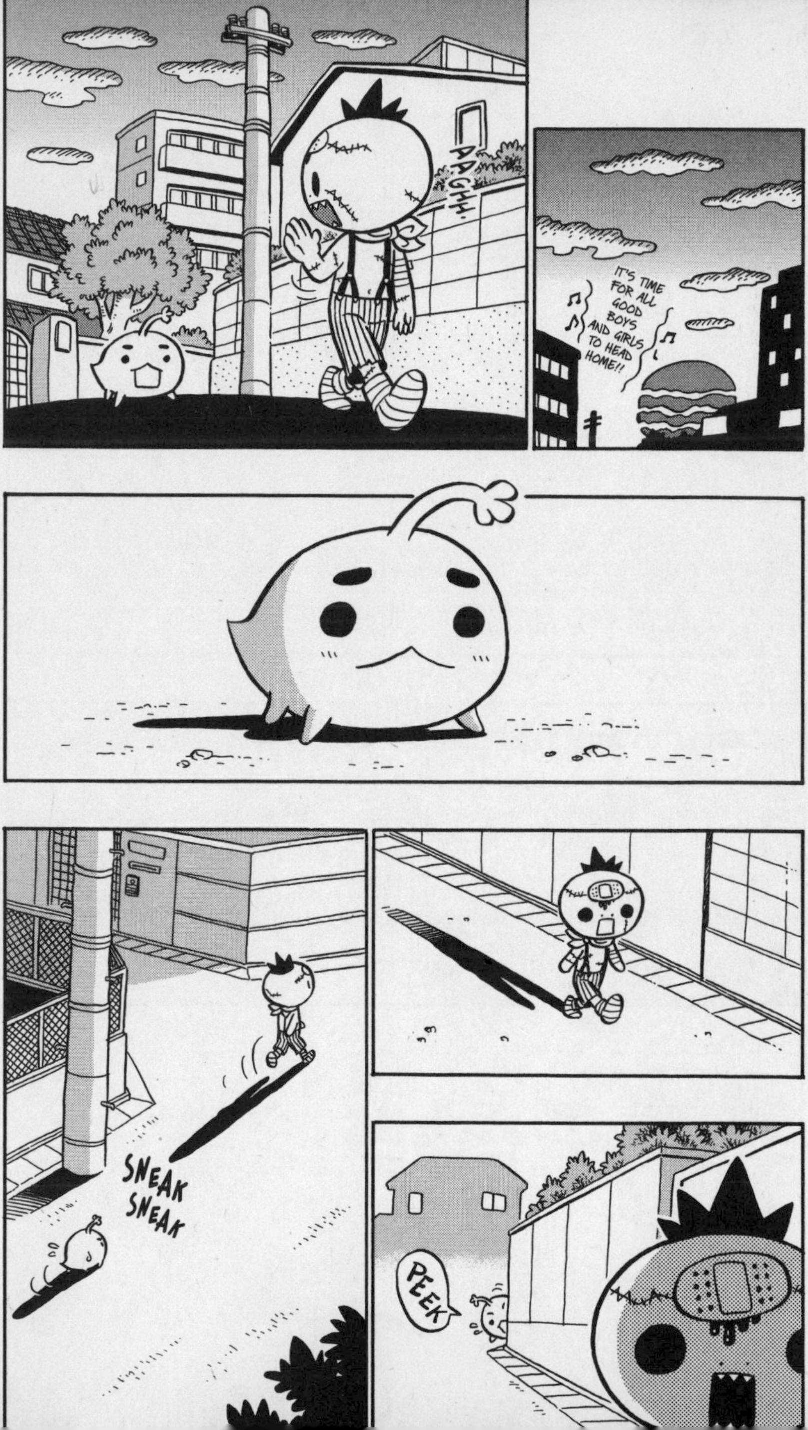
IT'S TIME FOR ALL GOOD BOYS AND GIRLS TO HEAD HOME!!
AAGHH.
PEEK
SNEAK SNEAK

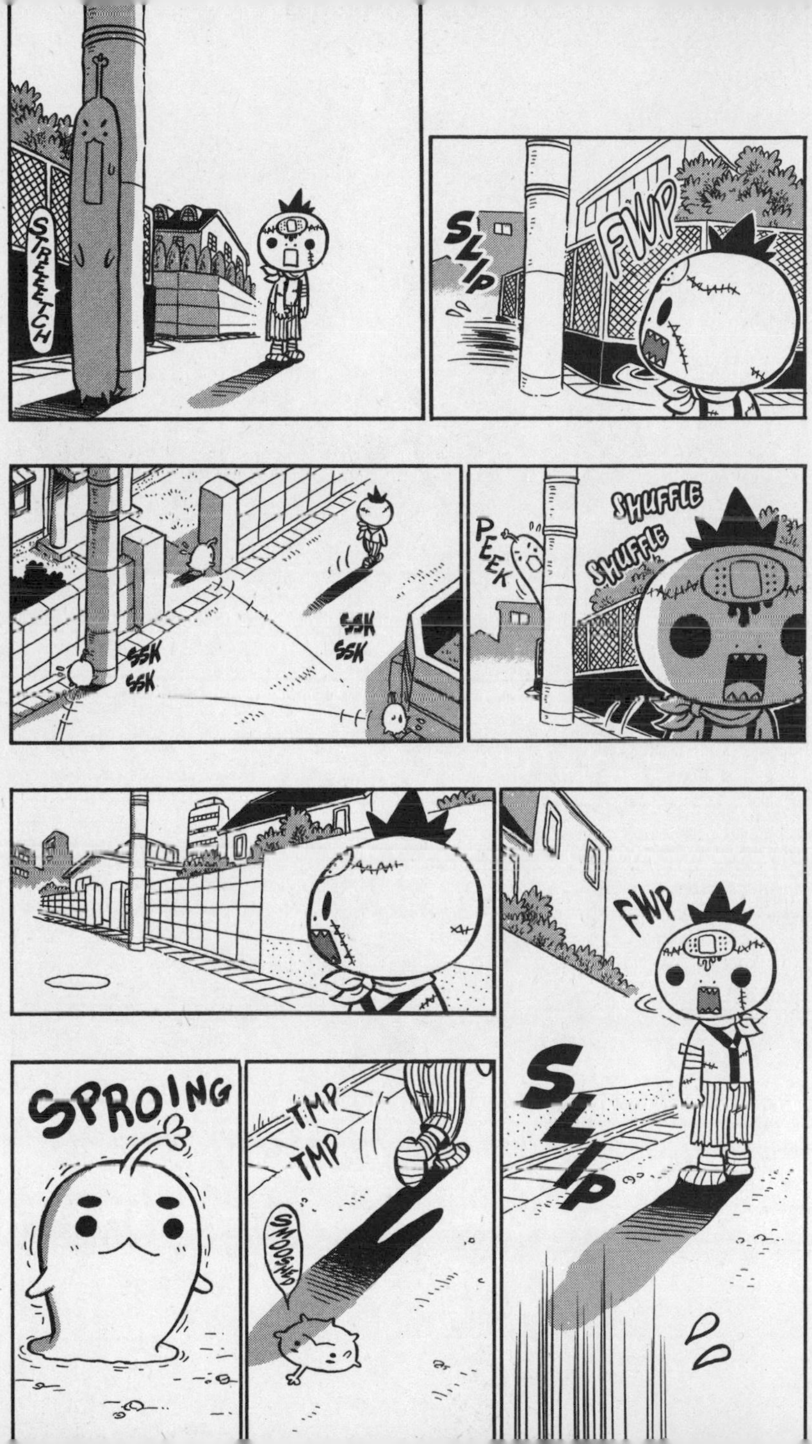
SLIP
FWP
STREEETCH
PEEK
SHUFFLE
SHUFFLE
SSK
SSK
SSK
SSK
FWP
SLIP
TMP
TMP
SMOOSHED
SPROING

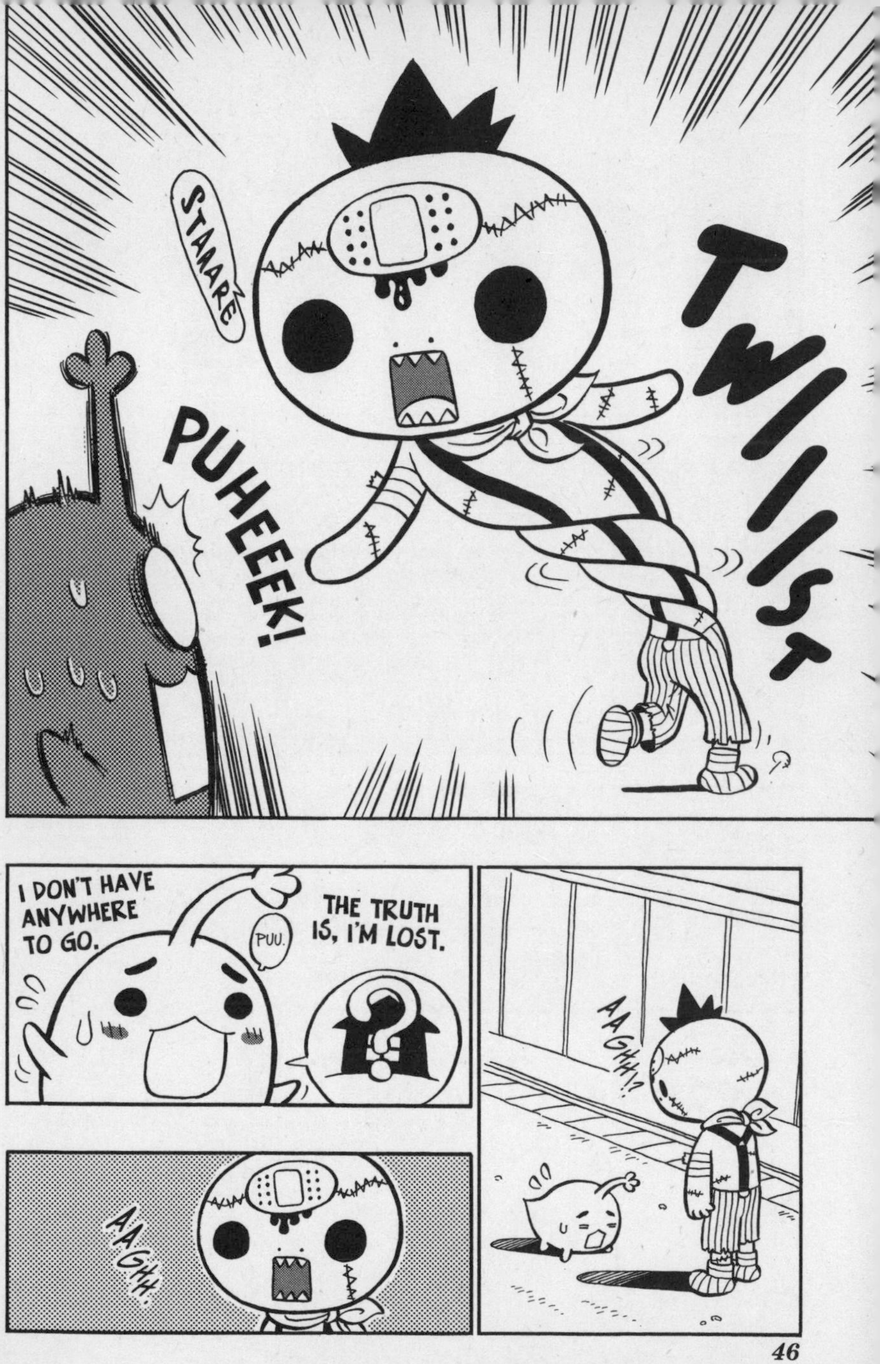
TWIIIST
STAAARE
PUHEEEK!
AAGHH!?
THE TRUTH IS, I'M LOST.
PUU.
I DON'T HAVE ANYWHERE TO GO.
AAGHH.

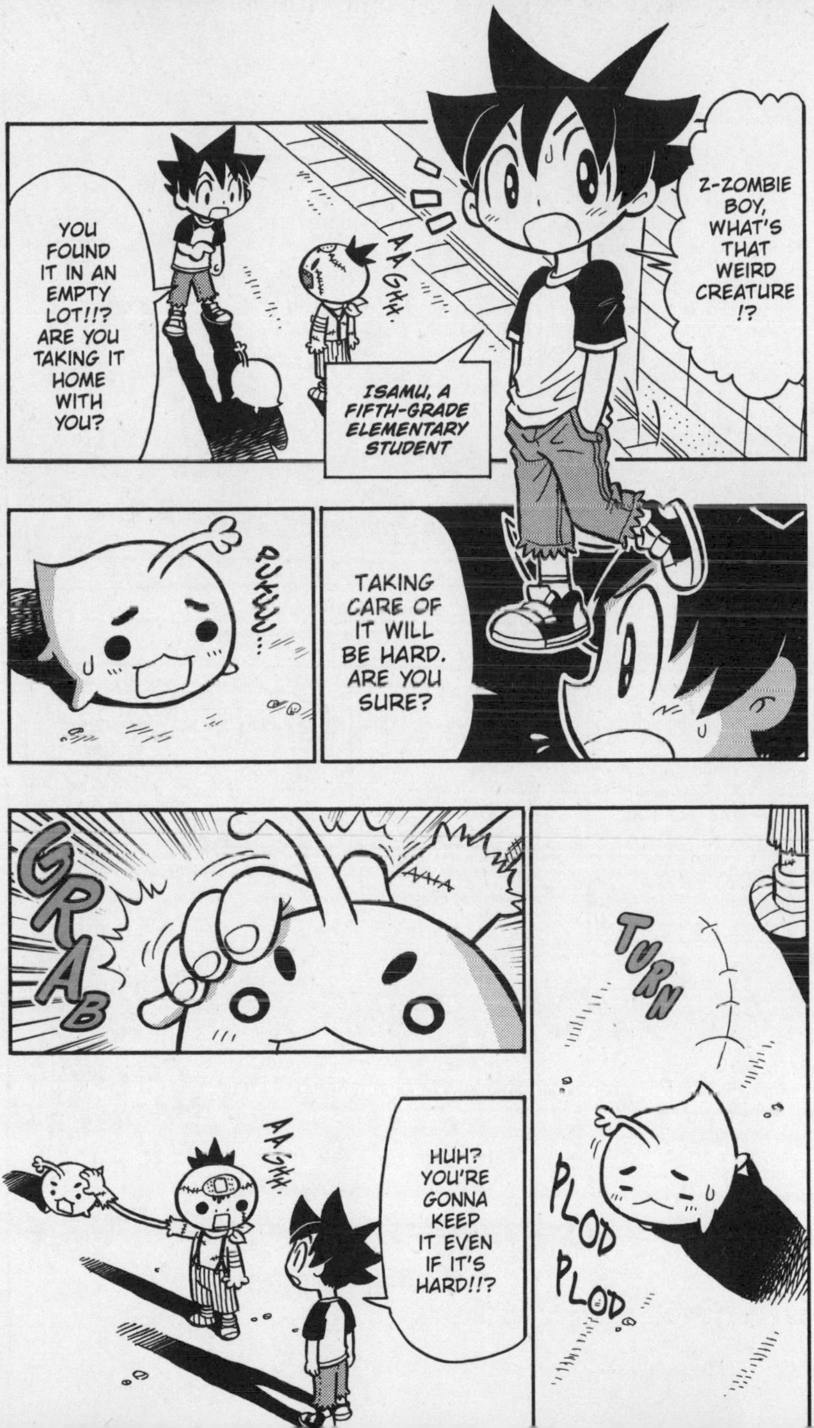
Z-ZOMBIE BOY, WHAT'S THAT WEIRD CREATURE!?
ISAMU, A FIFTH-GRADE ELEMENTARY STUDENT
AAGHH
YOU FOUND IT IN AN EMPTY LOT!!? ARE YOU TAKING IT HOME WITH YOU?
TAKING CARE OF IT WILL BE HARD. ARE YOU SURE?
PUKUU...
TURN
PLOD PLOD
GRAB
AAGHH
HUH? YOU'RE GONNA KEEP IT EVEN IF IT'S HARD!!?

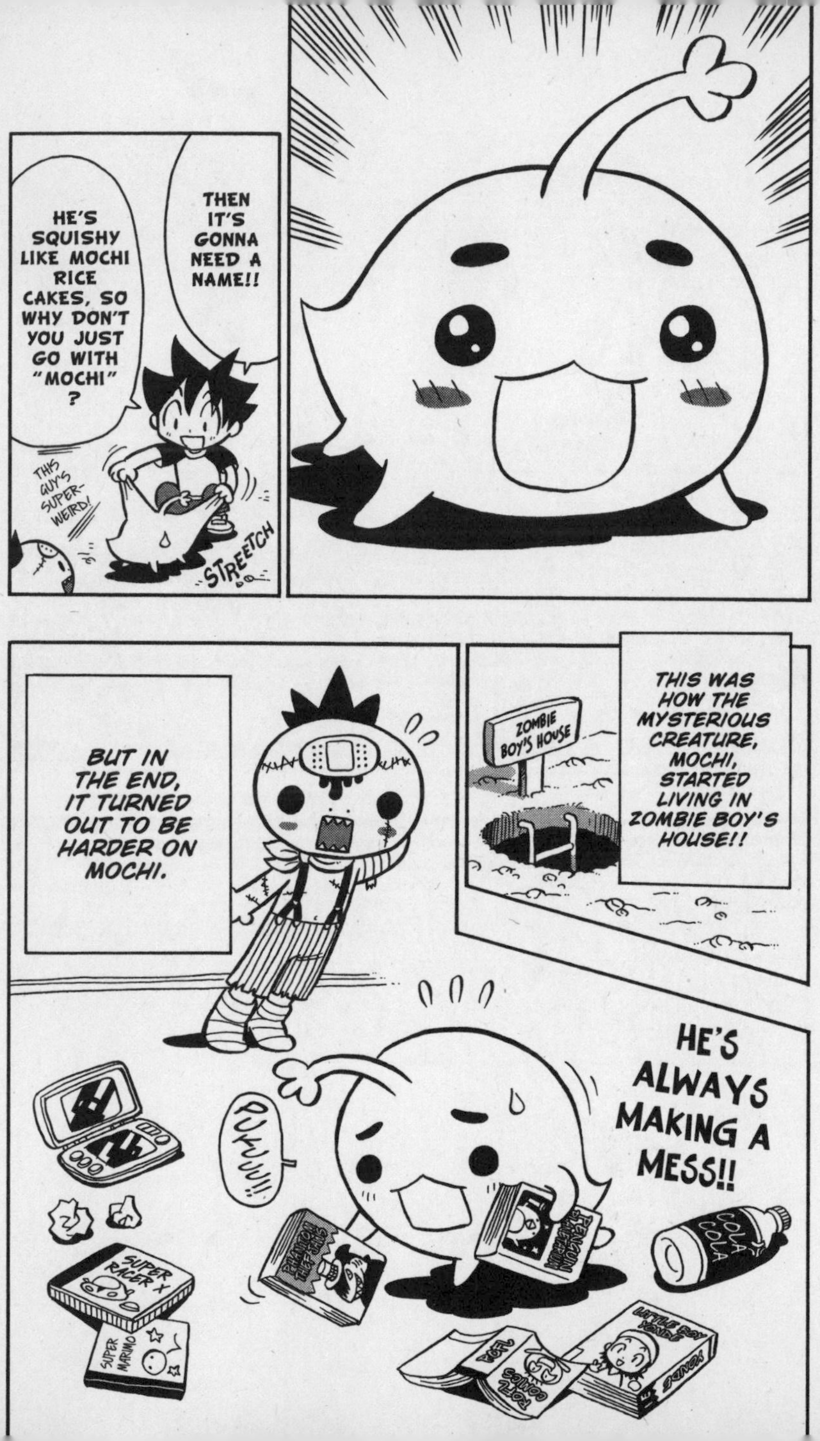
THEN IT'S GONNA NEED A NAME!!
HE'S SQUISHY LIKE MOCHI RICE CAKES, SO WHY DON'T YOU JUST GO WITH "MOCHI"?
THIS GUY'S SUPER-WEIRD!
STREETCH
THIS WAS HOW THE MYSTERIOUS CREATURE, MOCHI, STARTED LIVING IN ZOMBIE BOY'S HOUSE!!
ZOMBIE BOY'S HOUSE
BUT IN THE END, IT TURNED OUT TO BE HARDER ON MOCHI.
HE'S ALWAYS MAKING A MESS!!
COLA COLA
SUPER RACER X
SUPER MARIMO

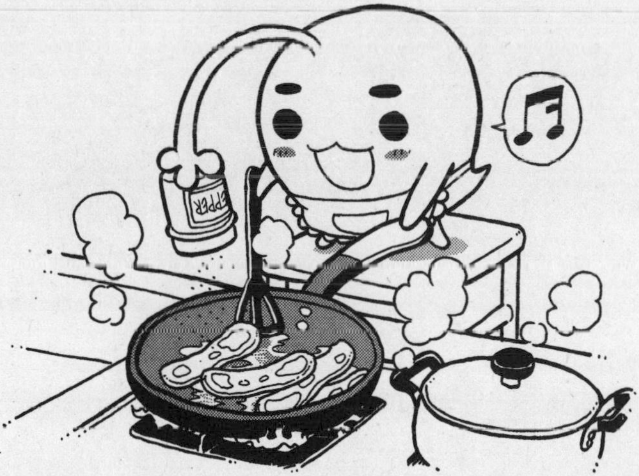
PEPPER

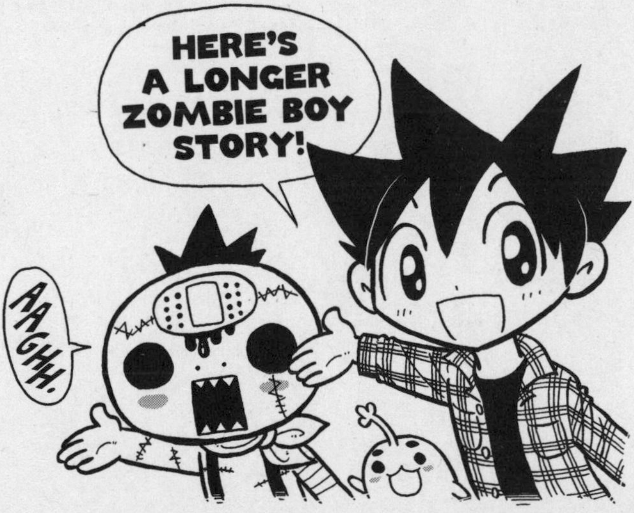
HERE'S A LONGER ZOMBIE BOY STORY!
AAGHH.

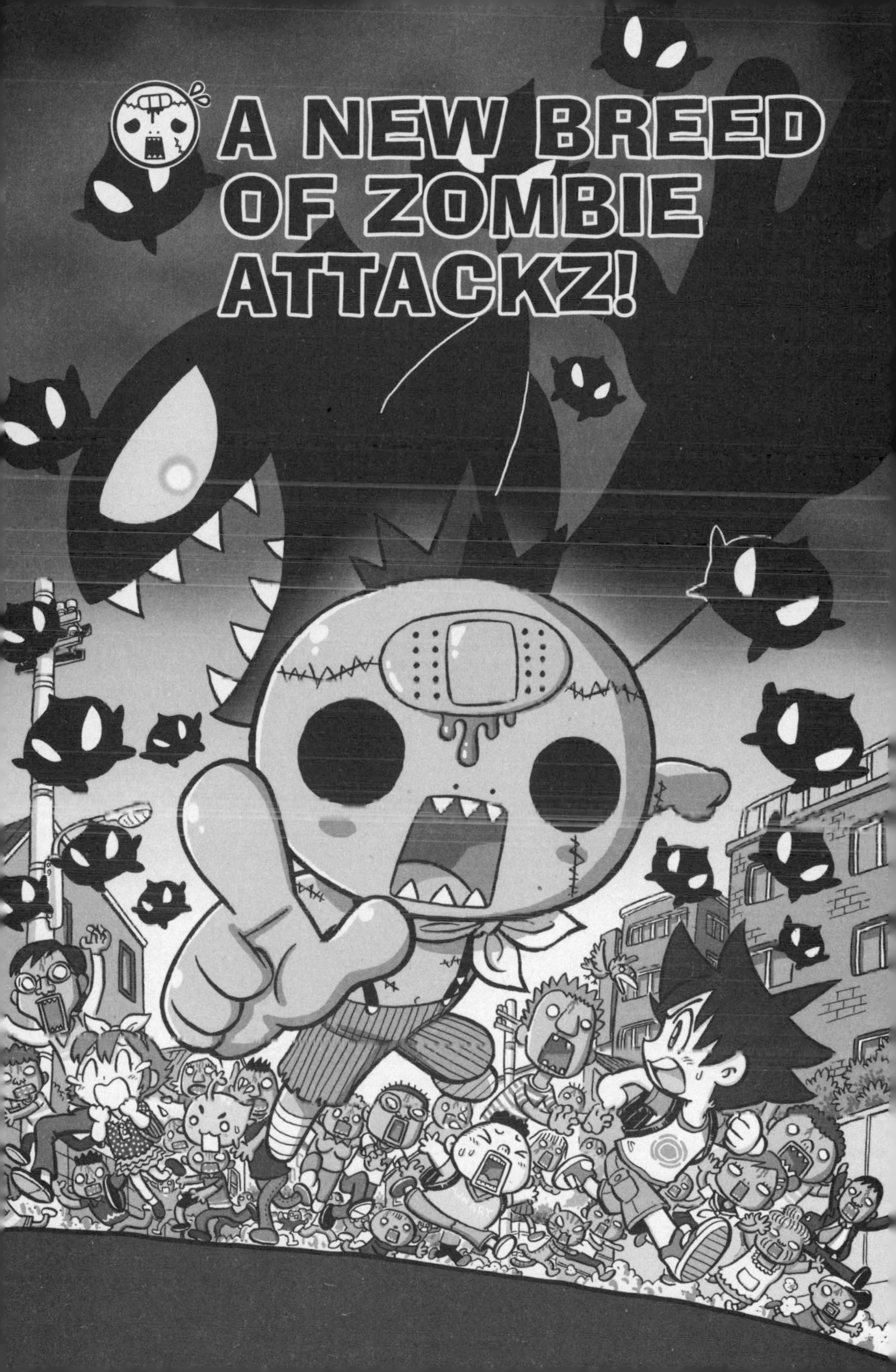
A NEW BREED OF ZOMBIE ATTACKZ!

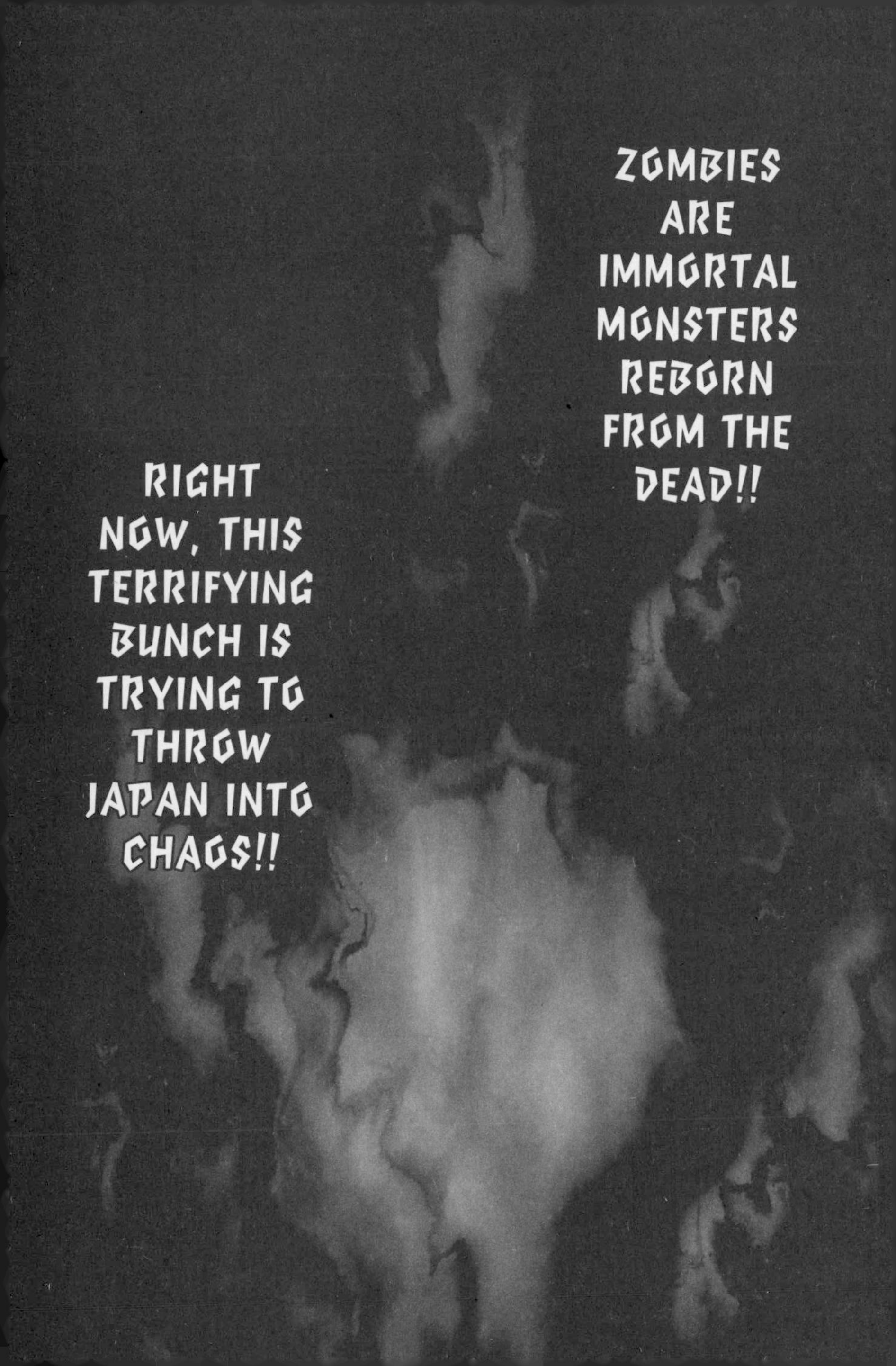
ZOMBIES ARE IMMORTAL MONSTERS REBORN FROM THE DEAD!!
RIGHT NOW, THIS TERRIFYING BUNCH IS TRYING TO THROW JAPAN INTO CHAOS!!

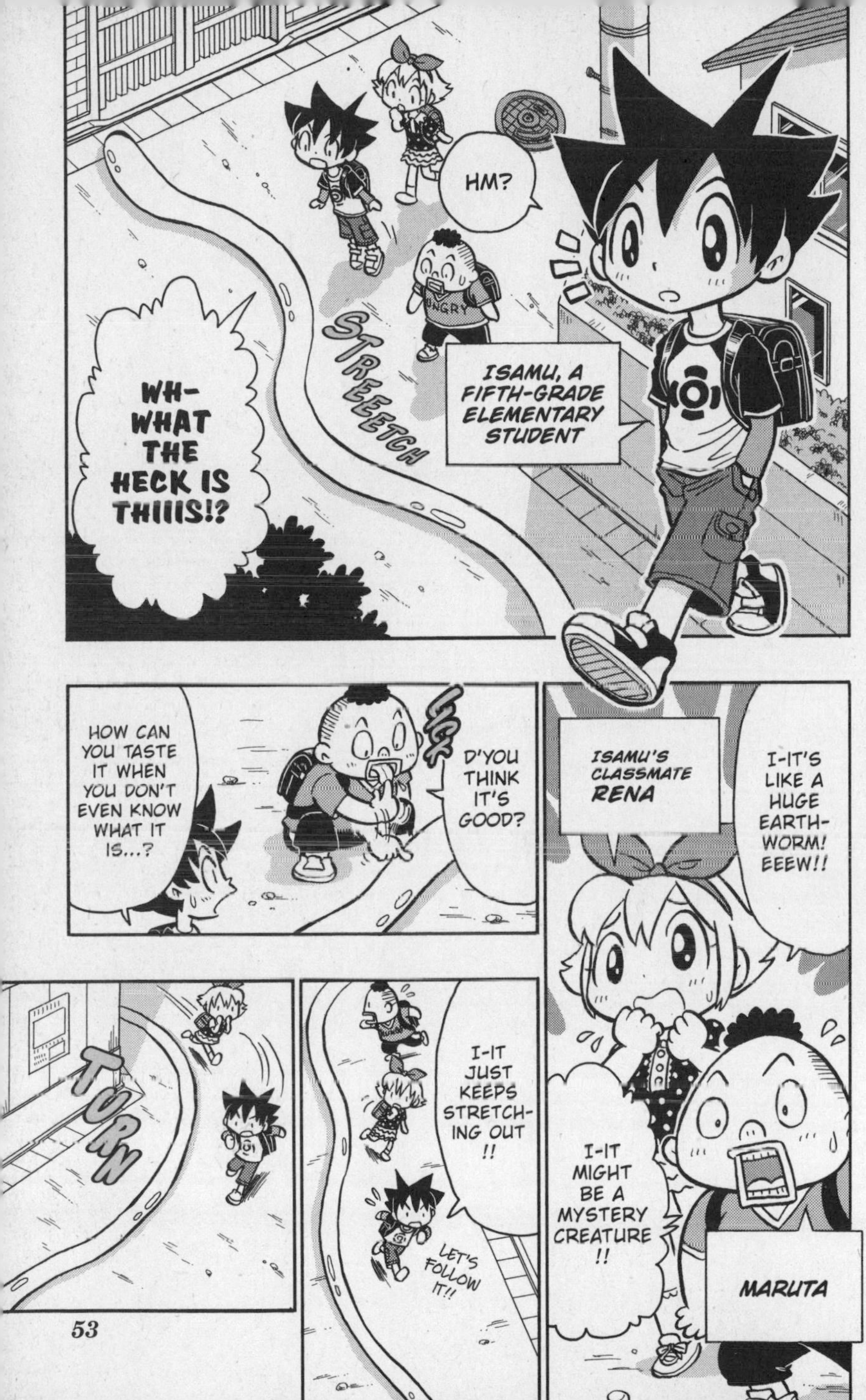
HM?
ISAMU, A FIFTH-GRADE ELEMENTARY STUDENT
STREEETCH
WH-WHAT THE HECK IS THIIIS!?
ISAMU'S CLASSMATE RENA
I-IT'S LIKE A HUGE EARTH-WORM! EEEW!!
I-IT MIGHT BE A MYSTERY CREATURE !!
MARUTA
LICK
D'YOU THINK IT'S GOOD?
HOW CAN YOU TASTE IT WHEN YOU DON'T EVEN KNOW WHAT IT IS...?
I-IT JUST KEEPS STRETCH-ING OUT !!
LET'S FOLLOW IT!!
TURN

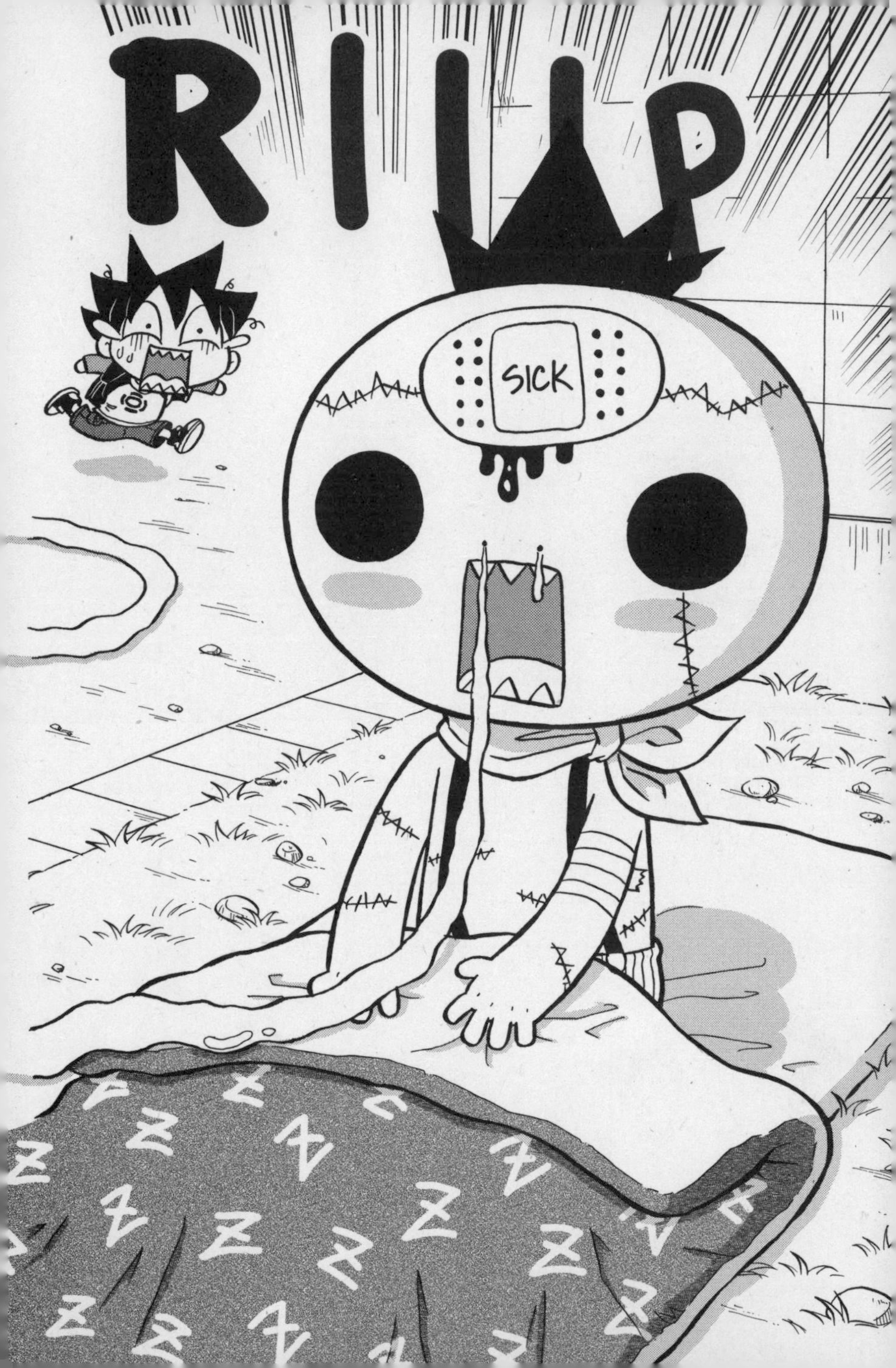
RIIIP
SICK

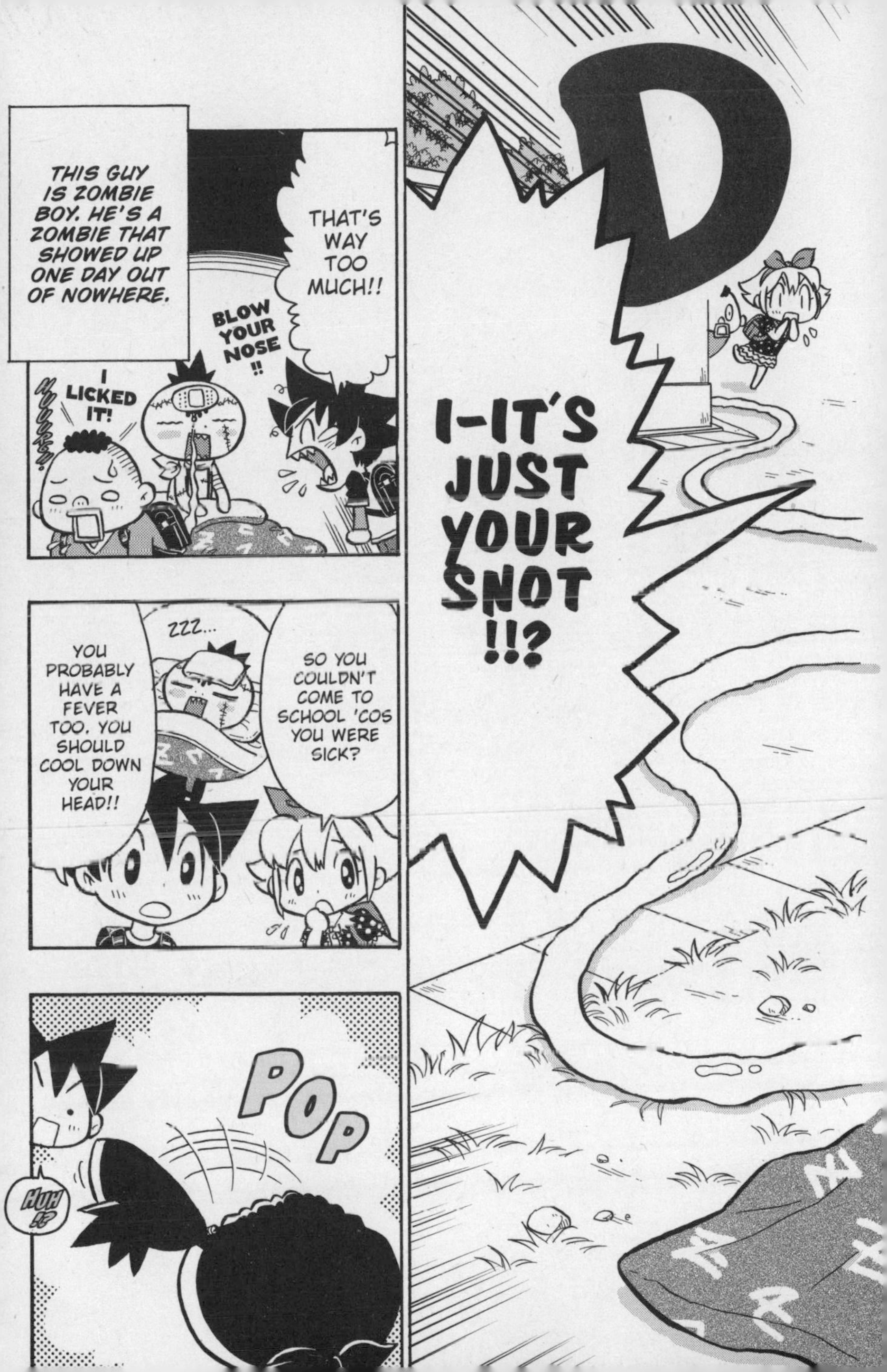
D
I-IT'S JUST YOUR SNOT!!?
THAT'S WAY TOO MUCH!!
BLOW YOUR NOSE!!
THIS GUY IS ZOMBIE BOY. HE'S A ZOMBIE THAT SHOWED UP ONE DAY OUT OF NOWHERE.
I LICKED IT!
SO YOU COULDN'T COME TO SCHOOL 'COS YOU WERE SICK?
ZZZ...
YOU PROBABLY HAVE A FEVER TOO. YOU SHOULD COOL DOWN YOUR HEAD!!
POP
HUH!?

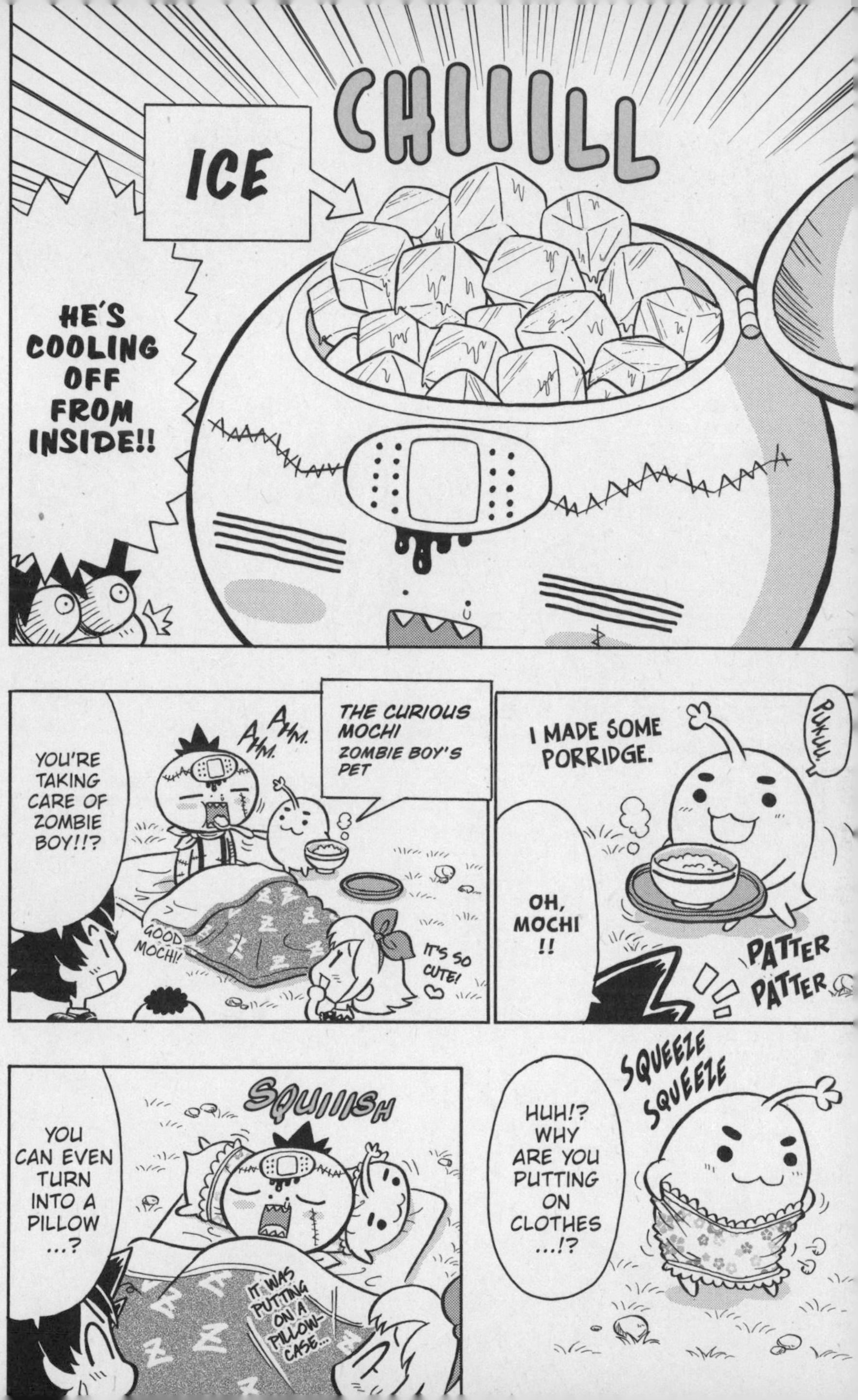
CHIIILL
ICE
HE'S COOLING OFF FROM INSIDE!!
PUKUU.
I MADE SOME PORRIDGE.
OH, MOCHI !!
PATTER PATTER
THE CURIOUS MOCHI
ZOMBIE BOY'S PET
AHM. AHM.
YOU'RE TAKING CARE OF ZOMBIE BOY!!?
GOOD MOCHI!
IT'S SO CUTE!
SQUEEZE SQUEEZE
HUH!? WHY ARE YOU PUTTING ON CLOTHES ...!?
SQUIIISH
YOU CAN EVEN TURN INTO A PILLOW ...?
IT WAS PUTTING ON A PILLOW-CASE...

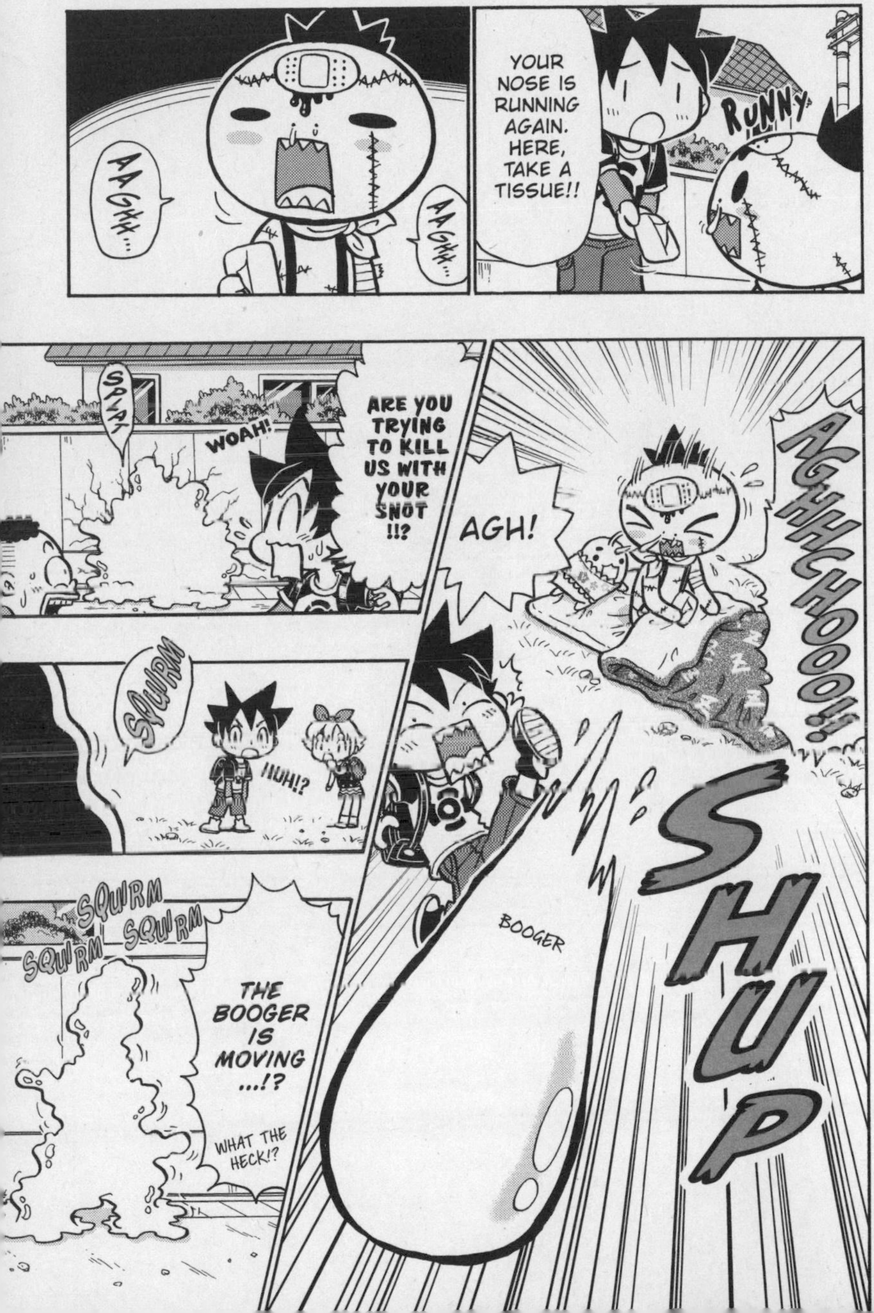
YOUR NOSE IS RUNNING AGAIN. HERE, TAKE A TISSUE!!
RUNNY
AAGHH...
AAGHH...
AGHHHCHOOOO!!
AGH!
SHUP
BOOGER
ARE YOU TRYING TO KILL US WITH YOUR SNOT!!?
WOAH!
SPLAT
SQUIRM
HUH!?
THE BOOGER IS MOVING...!?
WHAT THE HECK!?
SQUIRM
SQUIRM
SQUIRM

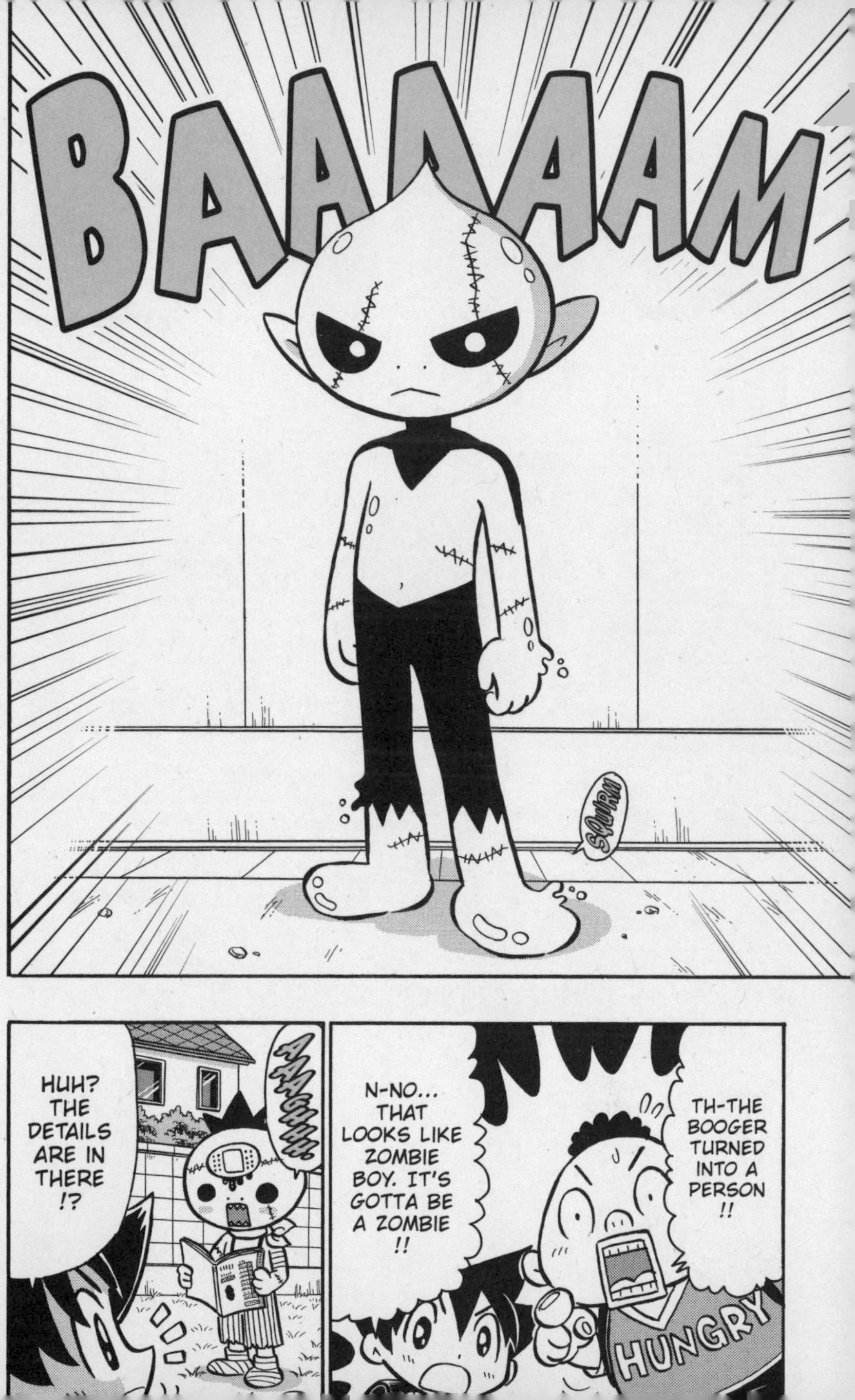
BAAAAAM
SQUIRM
TH-THE BOOGER TURNED INTO A PERSON!!
N-NO... THAT LOOKS LIKE ZOMBIE BOY. IT'S GOTTA BE A ZOMBIE!!
HUNGRY
AAAAGHHH!
HUH? THE DETAILS ARE IN THERE!?

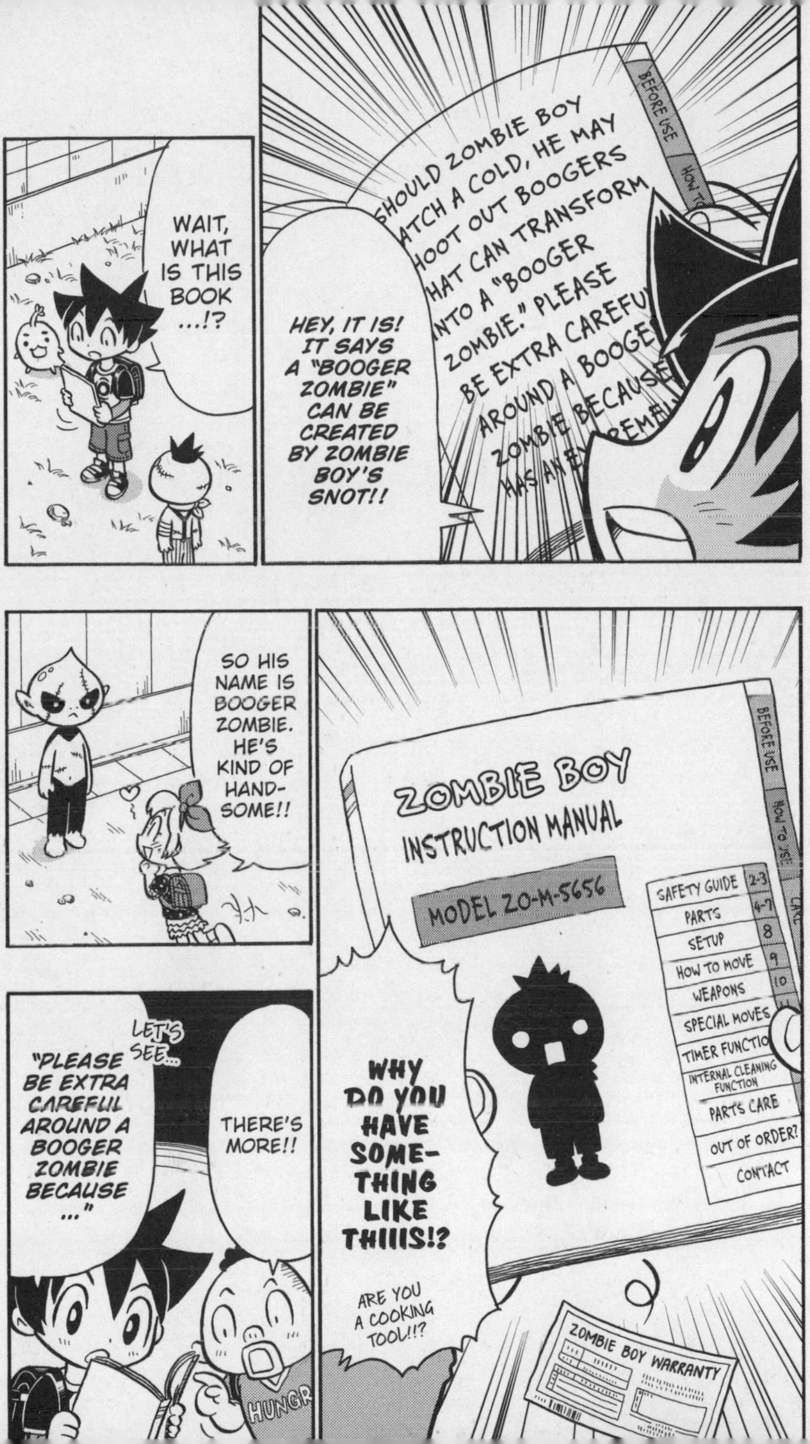
BEFORE USE
HOW TO
SHOULD ZOMBIE BOY ATCH A COLD, HE MAY HOOT OUT BOOGERS HAT CAN TRANSFORM NTO A "BOOGER ZOMBIE." PLEASE BE EXTRA CAREFU AROUND A BOOGE ZOMBIE BECAUSE HAS AN EX
HEY, IT IS! IT SAYS A "BOOGER ZOMBIE" CAN BE CREATED BY ZOMBIE BOY'S SNOT!!
WAIT, WHAT IS THIS BOOK ...!?
BEFORE USE
HOW TO USE
ZOMBIE BOY
INSTRUCTION MANUAL
MODEL ZO-M-5656
SAFETY GUIDE 2-3
PARTS 4-7
SETUP 8
HOW TO MOVE 9
WEAPONS 10
SPECIAL MOVES
TIMER FUNCTIO
INTERNAL CLEANING FUNCTION
PARTS CARE
OUT OF ORDER?
CONTACT
WHY DO YOU HAVE SOME-THING LIKE THIIIS!?
ARE YOU A COOKING TOOL!?
ZOMBIE BOY WARRANTY
SO HIS NAME IS BOOGER ZOMBIE. HE'S KIND OF HAND-SOME!!
LET'S SEE...
THERE'S MORE!!
"PLEASE BE EXTRA CAREFUL AROUND A BOOGER ZOMBIE BECAUSE ..."
HUNGR

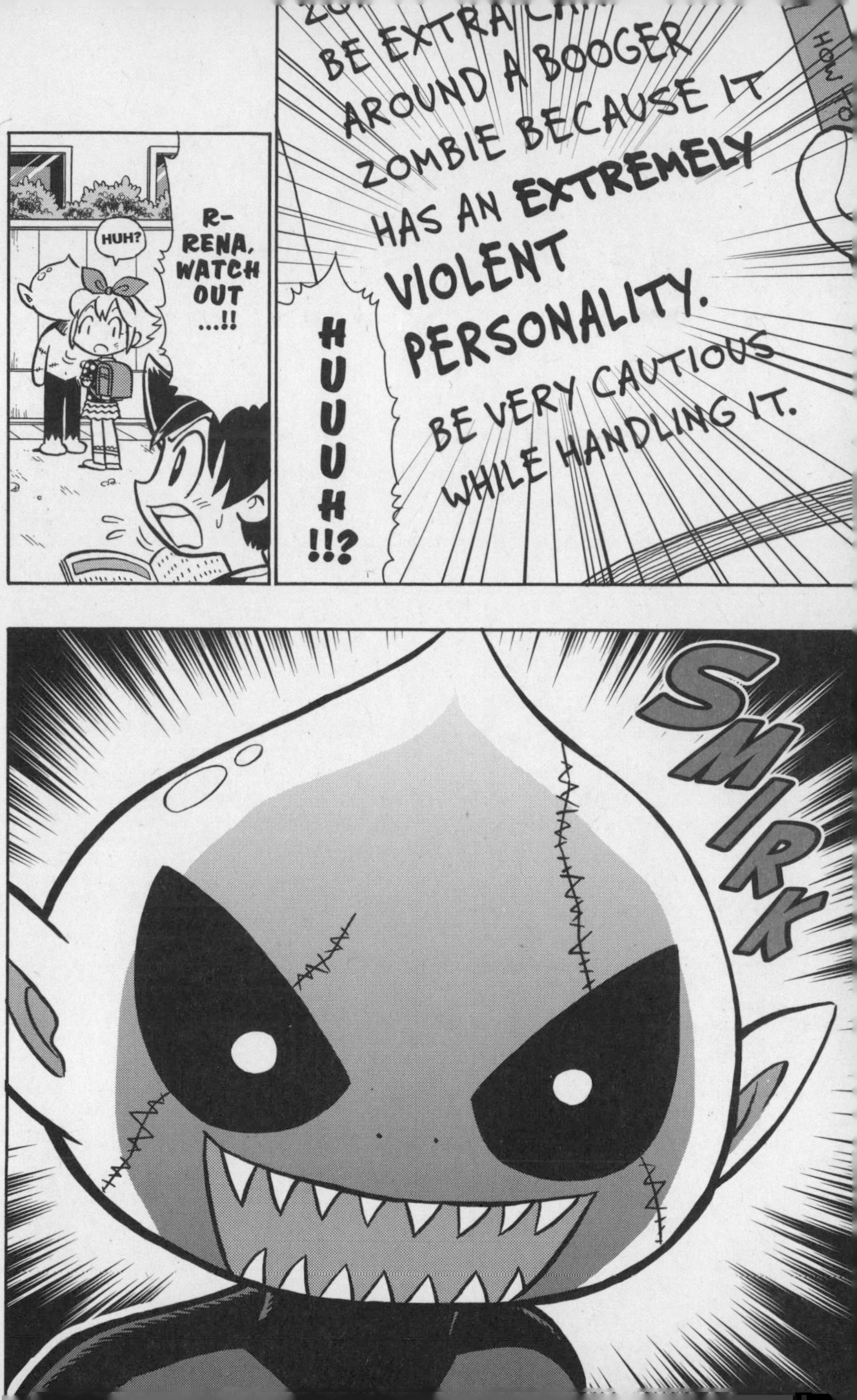
BE EXTRA CA
AROUND A BOOGER ZOMBIE BECAUSE IT HAS AN EXTREMELY VIOLENT PERSONALITY.
BE VERY CAUTIOUS WHILE HANDLING IT.
HUUUUH!!?
HUH?
R-RENA, WATCH OUT ...!!
SMIRK

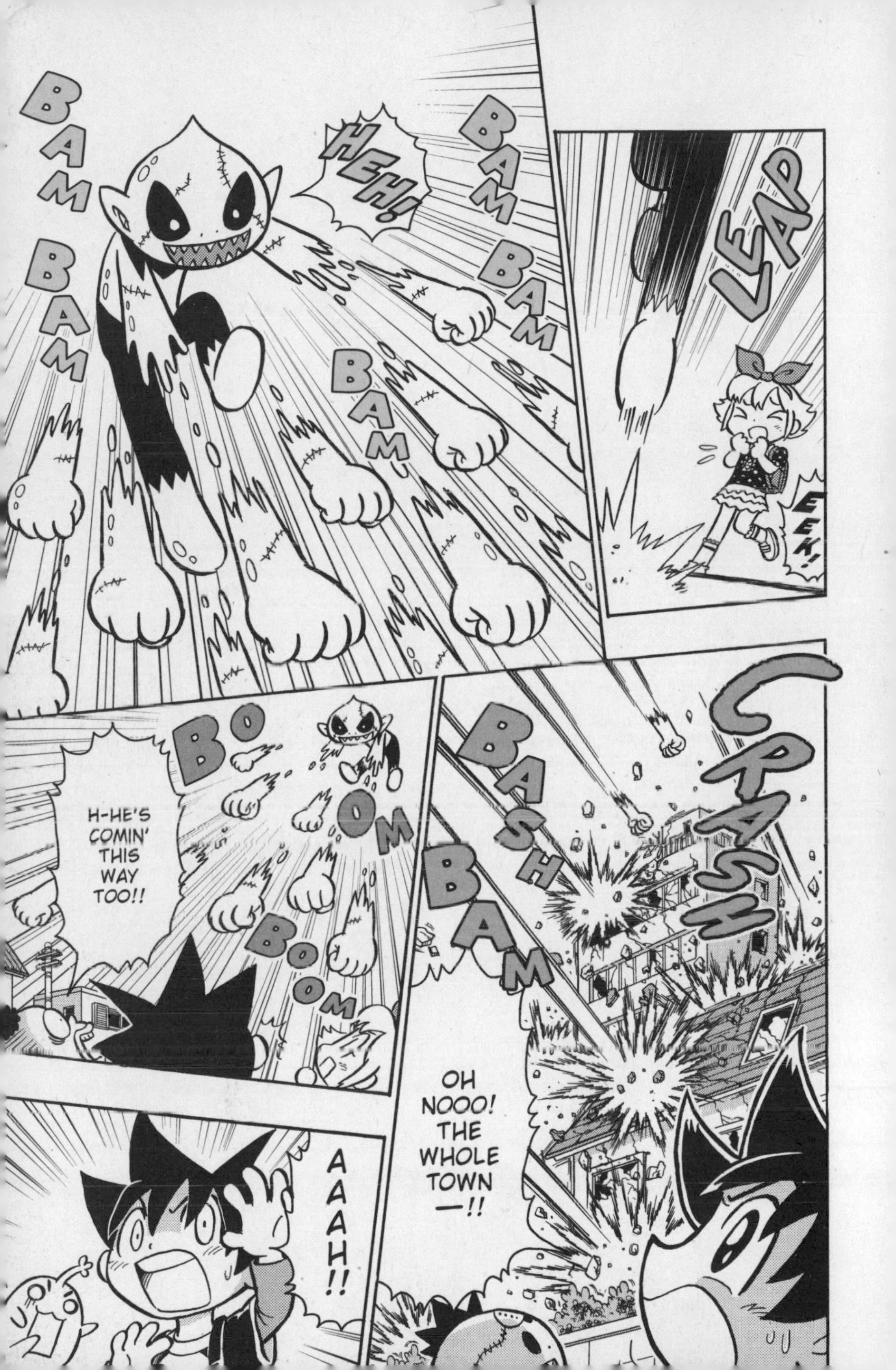
LEAP
EEK!
HEH!
BAM BAM
BAM
BAM BAM BAM
CRASH
BASH
BAM
BOOM
BOOM
H-HE'S COMIN' THIS WAY TOO!!
OH NOOO! THE WHOLE TOWN—!!
AAAAH!!

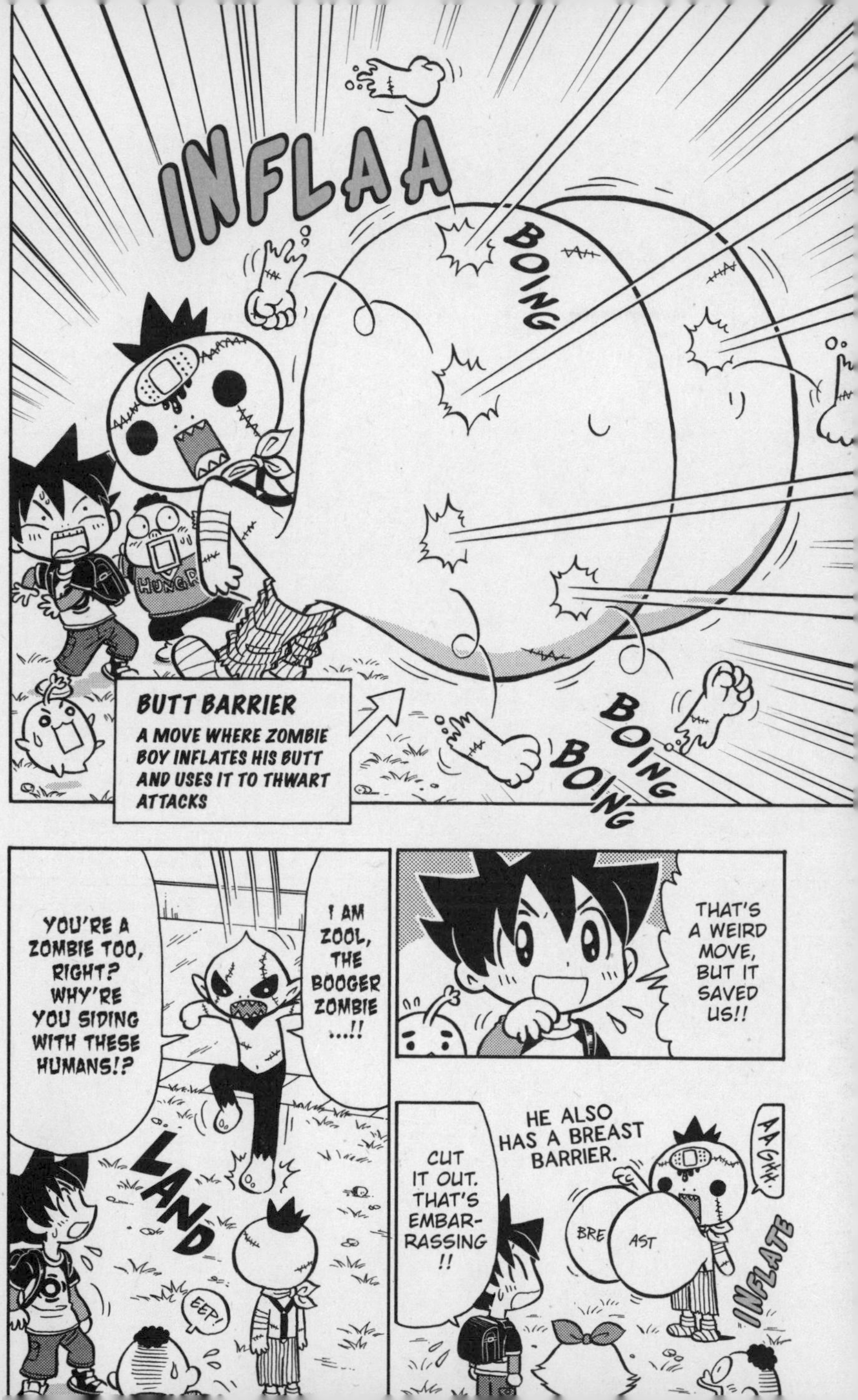
INFLAA
BOING
BUTT BARRIER
A MOVE WHERE ZOMBIE BOY INFLATES HIS BUTT AND USES IT TO THWART ATTACKS
BOING BOING
BOING
THAT'S A WEIRD MOVE, BUT IT SAVED US!!
AAGHH.
HE ALSO HAS A BREAST BARRIER.
CUT IT OUT. THAT'S EMBAR-RASSING!!
BRE AST
INFLATE
I AM ZOOL, THE BOOGER ZOMBIE ...!!
YOU'RE A ZOMBIE TOO, RIGHT? WHY'RE YOU SIDING WITH THESE HUMANS!?
LAND
EEP!

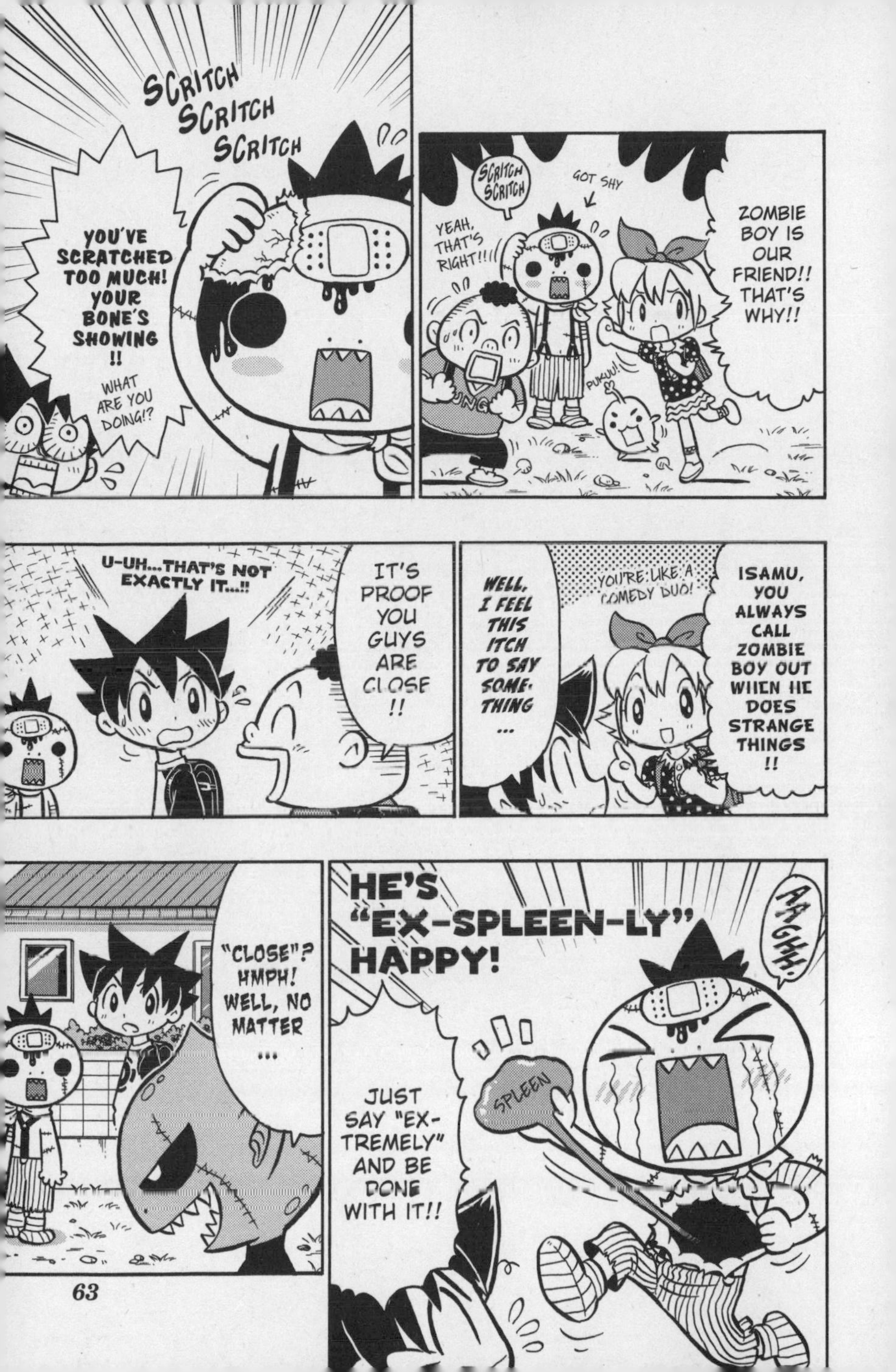
ZOMBIE BOY IS OUR FRIEND!! THAT'S WHY!!
GOT SHY
SCRITCH SCRITCH
YEAH, THAT'S RIGHT!!!
PUKUU!
SCRITCH SCRITCH SCRITCH
YOU'VE SCRATCHED TOO MUCH! YOUR BONE'S SHOWING!!
WHAT ARE YOU DOING!?
ISAMU, YOU ALWAYS CALL ZOMBIE BOY OUT WHEN HE DOES STRANGE THINGS!!
YOU'RE LIKE A COMEDY DUO!
WELL, I FEEL THIS ITCH TO SAY SOME-THING...
IT'S PROOF YOU GUYS ARE CLOSE!!
U-UH...THAT'S NOT EXACTLY IT...!!
HE'S "EX-SPLEEN-LY" HAPPY!
AAGHH!
SPLEEN
JUST SAY "EX-TREMELY" AND BE DONE WITH IT!!
"CLOSE"? HMPH! WELL, NO MATTER...

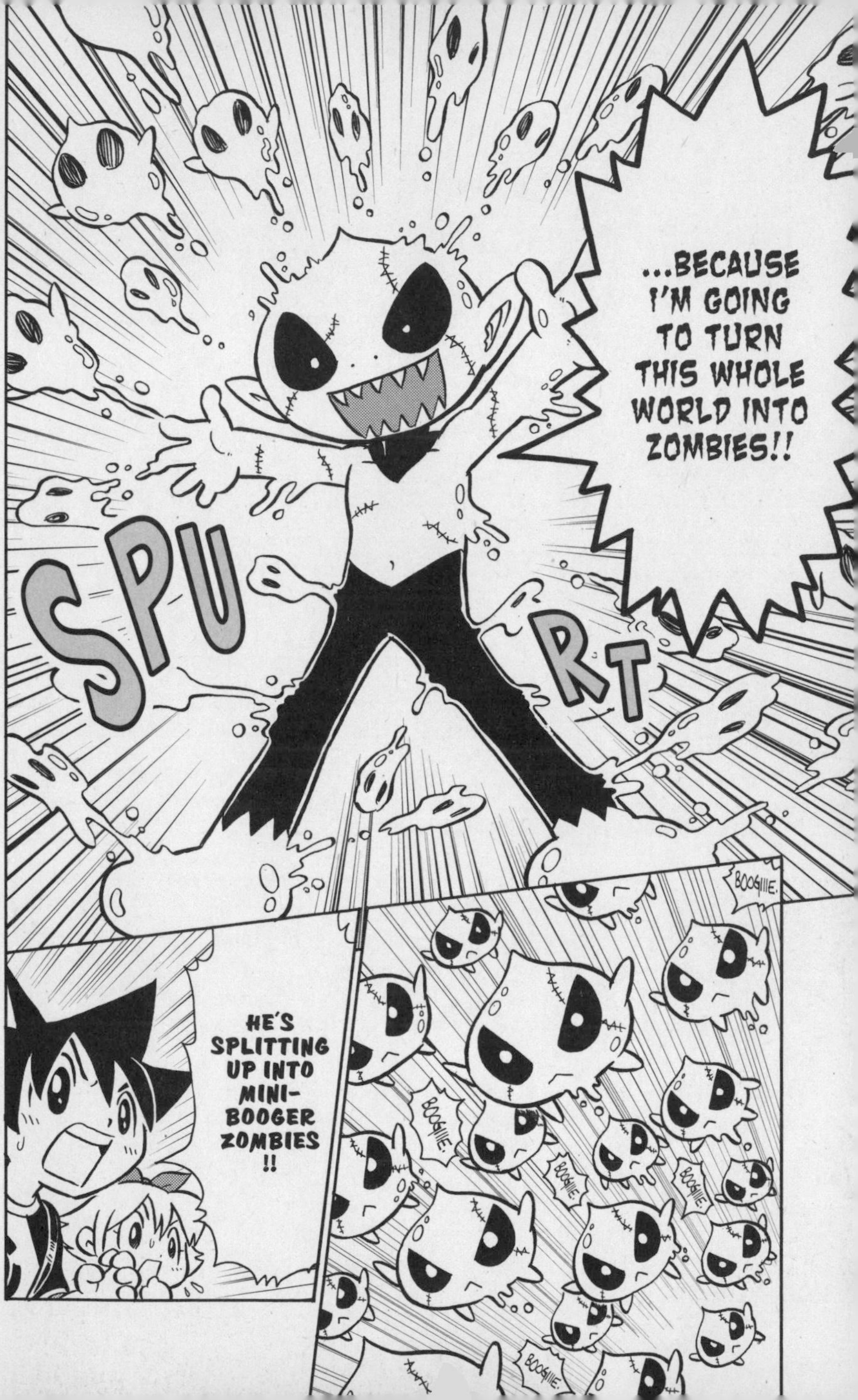
...BECAUSE I'M GOING TO TURN THIS WHOLE WORLD INTO ZOMBIES!!
SPURT
BOOGIIIE.
BOOGIIIE.
BOOGIIIE.
BOOGIIIE.
BOOGIIIE.
BOOGIIIE.
HE'S SPLITTING UP INTO MINI-BOOGER ZOMBIES!!

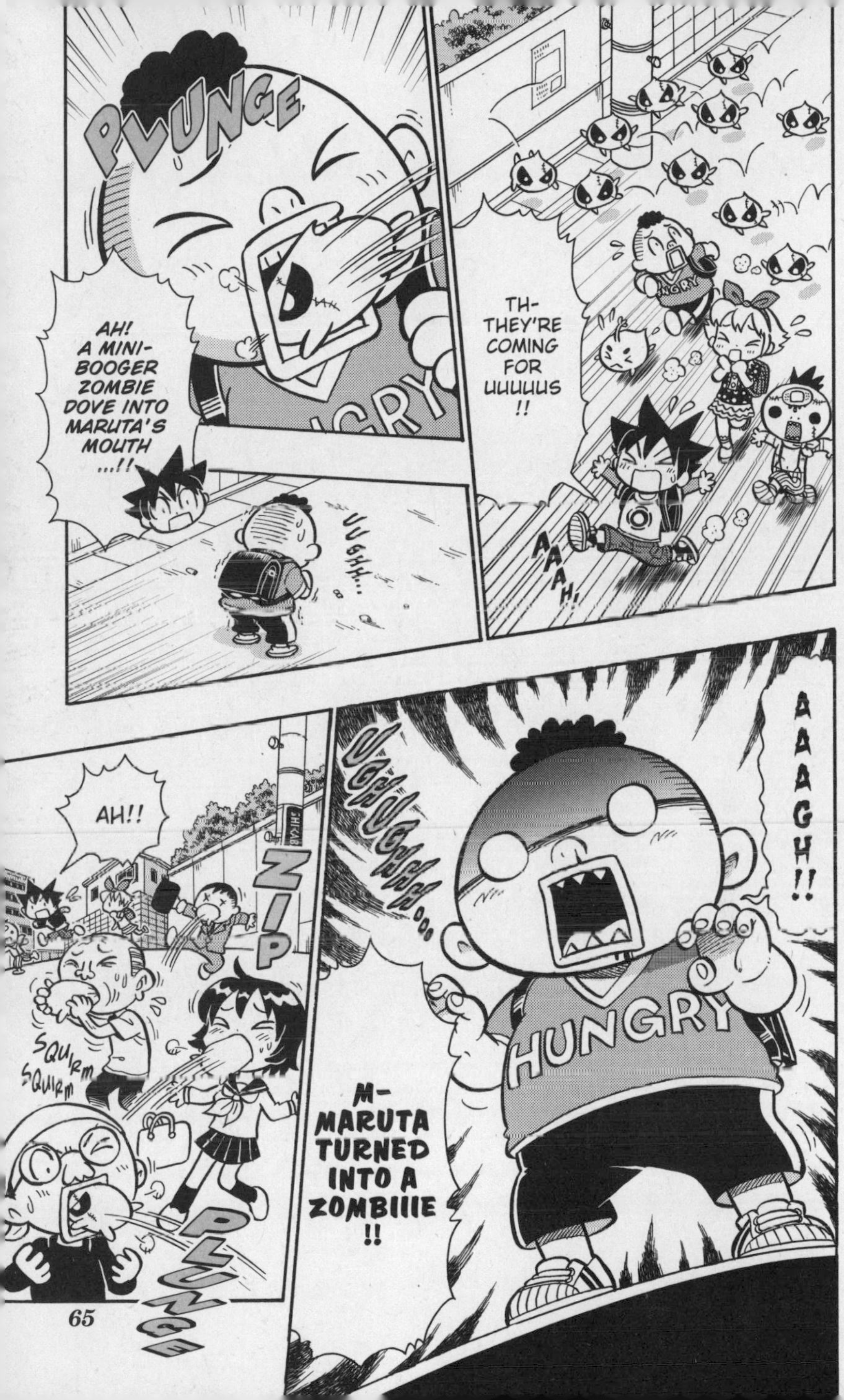
TH-THEY'RE COMING FOR UUUUUS!!
AAAH!
PLUNGE
AH! A MINI-BOOGER ZOMBIE DOVE INTO MARUTA'S MOUTH...!!
UUGHH...
AAAGH!!
UGHHH...
M-MARUTA TURNED INTO A ZOMBIIIE!!
AH!!
ZIP
SQUIRM SQUIRM
PLUNGE

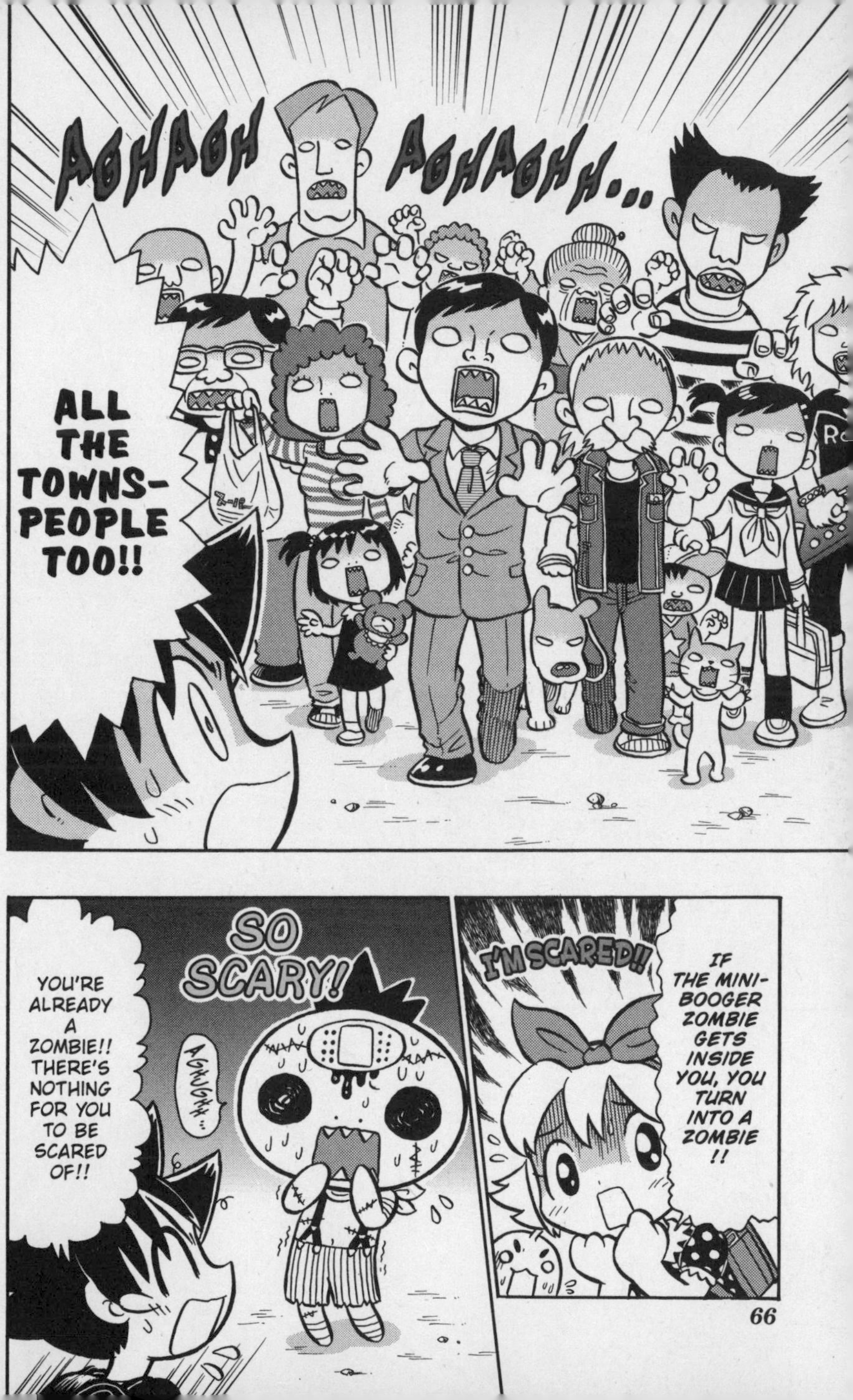
AGHAGH AGHAGHH...
ALL THE TOWNSPEOPLE TOO!!
I'M SCARED!!
IF THE MINI-BOOGER ZOMBIE GETS INSIDE YOU, YOU TURN INTO A ZOMBIE!!
SO SCARY!
AGHUGHH...
YOU'RE ALREADY A ZOMBIE!! THERE'S NOTHING FOR YOU TO BE SCARED OF!!

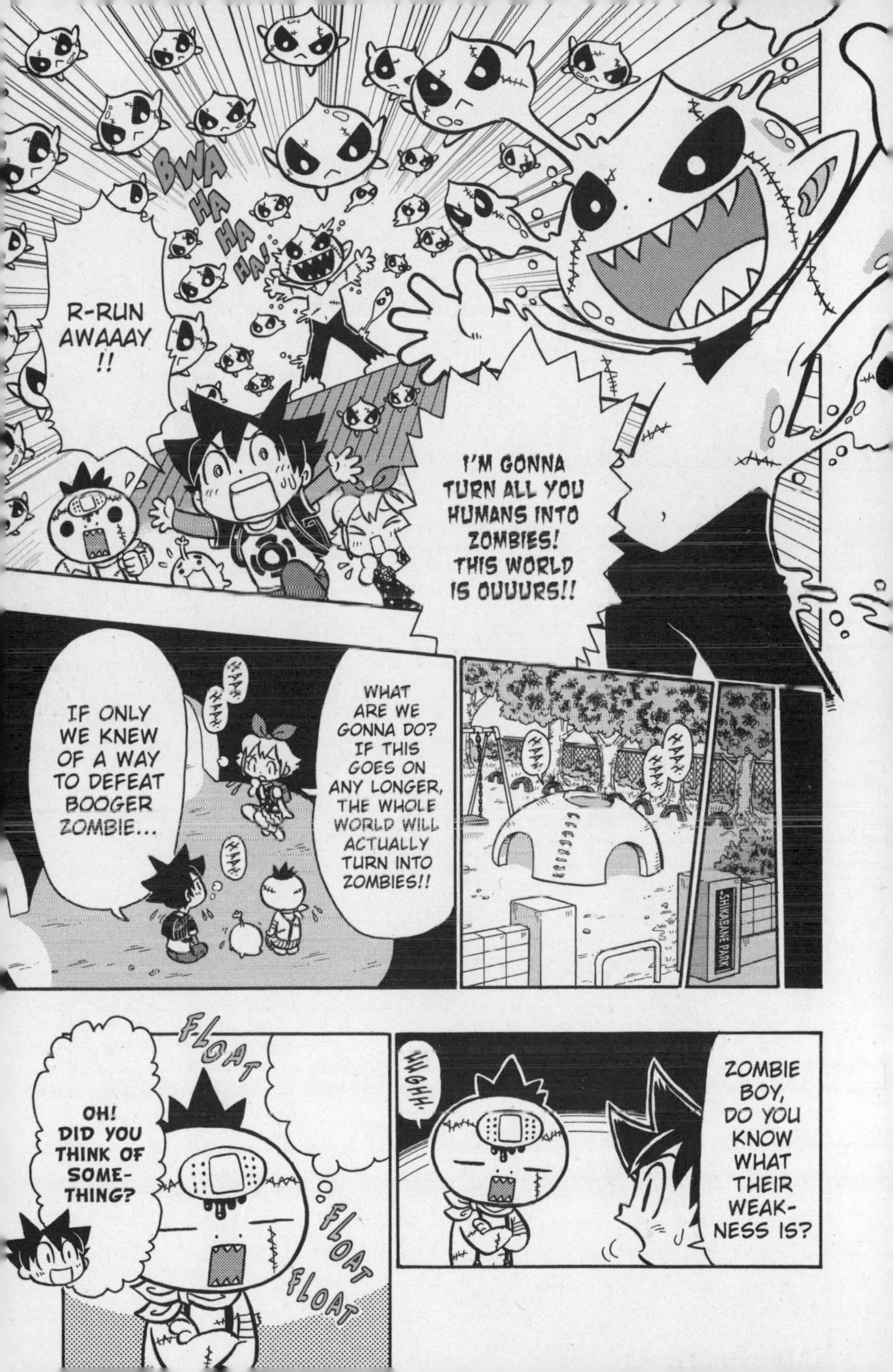
BWA HA HA HA!
I'M GONNA TURN ALL YOU HUMANS INTO ZOMBIES! THIS WORLD IS OUUURS!!
R-RUN AWAAAY!!
SHIKABANE PARK
WHAT ARE WE GONNA DO? IF THIS GOES ON ANY LONGER, THE WHOLE WORLD WILL ACTUALLY TURN INTO ZOMBIES!!
IF ONLY WE KNEW OF A WAY TO DEFEAT BOOGER ZOMBIE...
ZOMBIE BOY, DO YOU KNOW WHAT THEIR WEAKNESS IS?
MMGHH.
FLOAT
OH! DID YOU THINK OF SOME-THING?
FLOAT
FLOAT
FLOAT

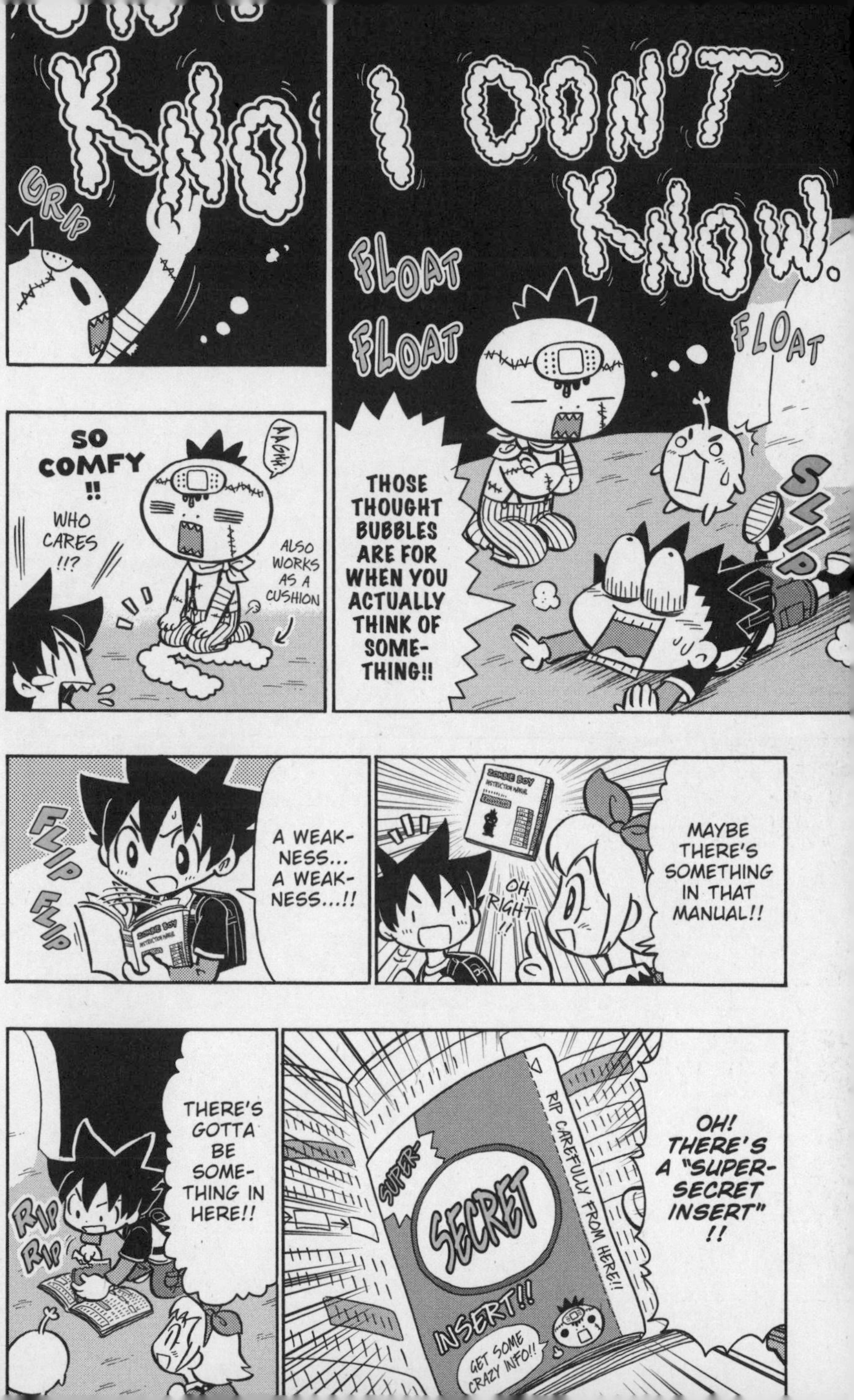
I DON'T KNOW.
FLOAT
FLOAT
FLOAT
KNO
GRIP
SLIP
THOSE THOUGHT BUBBLES ARE FOR WHEN YOU ACTUALLY THINK OF SOME-THING!!
AAGHH
SO COMFY!!
WHO CARES!!?
ALSO WORKS AS A CUSHION
MAYBE THERE'S SOMETHING IN THAT MANUAL!!
OH RIGHT!!
ZOMBIE BOY
INSTRUCTION MANUAL
A WEAK-NESS... A WEAK-NESS...!!
FLIP
FLIP
ZOMBIE BOY
OH! THERE'S A "SUPER-SECRET INSERT"!!
RIP CAREFULLY FROM HERE!!
SUPER-SECRET INSERT!!
GET SOME CRAZY INFO!!
THERE'S GOTTA BE SOME-THING IN HERE!!
RIP
RIP

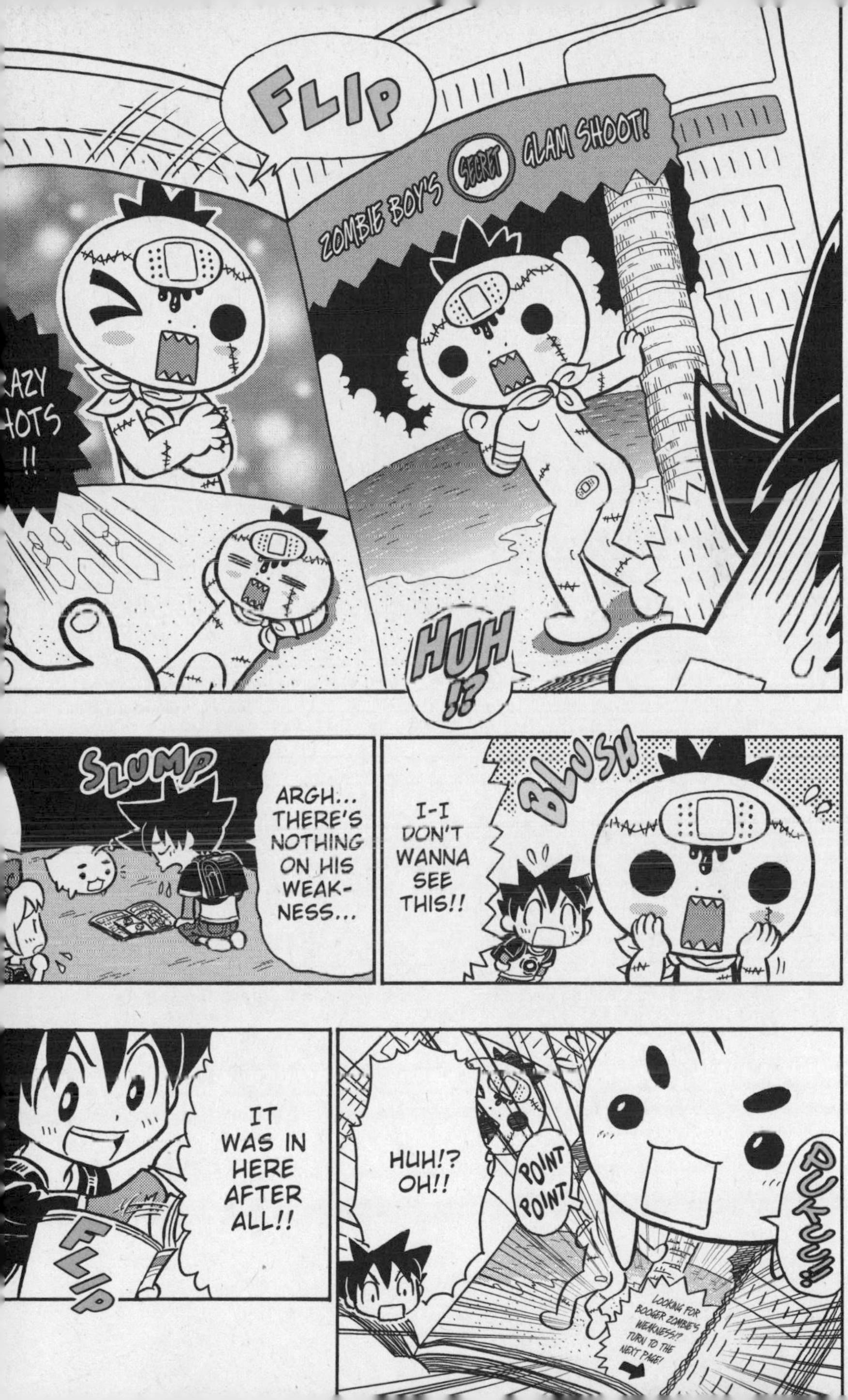
ZOMBIE BOY'S SECRET GLAM SHOOT!
FLIP
HUH !?
AZY HOTS !!
BLUSH
I-I DON'T WANNA SEE THIS!!
ARGH... THERE'S NOTHING ON HIS WEAKNESS...
SLUMP
PUKUN!!
POINT POINT
HUH!? OH!!
LOOKING FOR BOOGER ZOMBIE'S WEAKNESS!? TURN TO THE NEXT PAGE!
IT WAS IN HERE AFTER ALL!!
FLIP

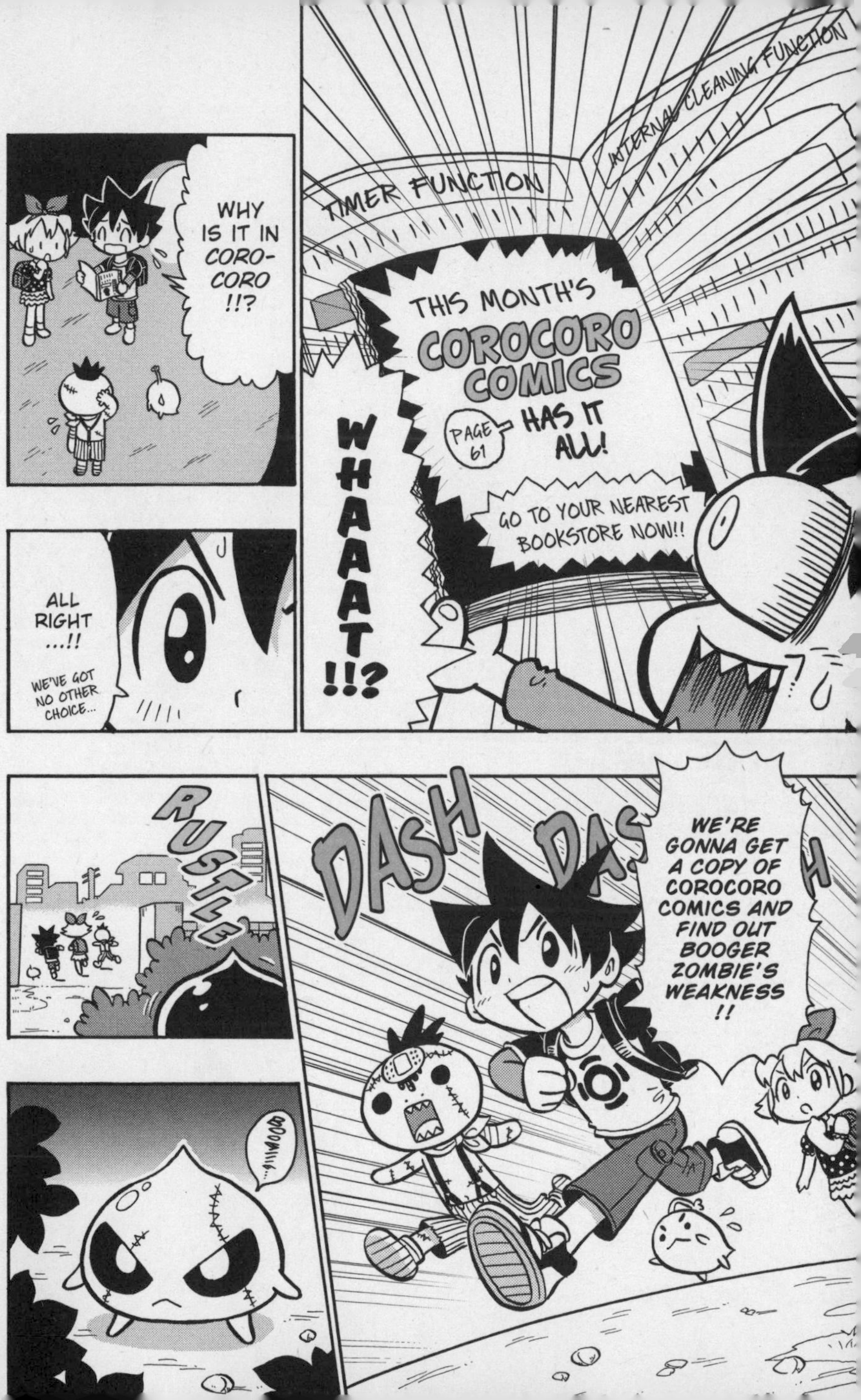

TIMER FUNCTION
INTERNAL CLEANING FUNCTION
THIS MONTH'S COROCORO COMICS HAS IT ALL!
PAGE 61
GO TO YOUR NEAREST BOOKSTORE NOW!!
WHAAAAT!!?
WHY IS IT IN COROCORO!!?
ALL RIGHT...!!
WE'VE GOT NO OTHER CHOICE...
DASH DASH DASH
WE'RE GONNA GET A COPY OF COROCORO COMICS AND FIND OUT BOOGER ZOMBIE'S WEAKNESS!!
RUSTLE
BOOM!!!...

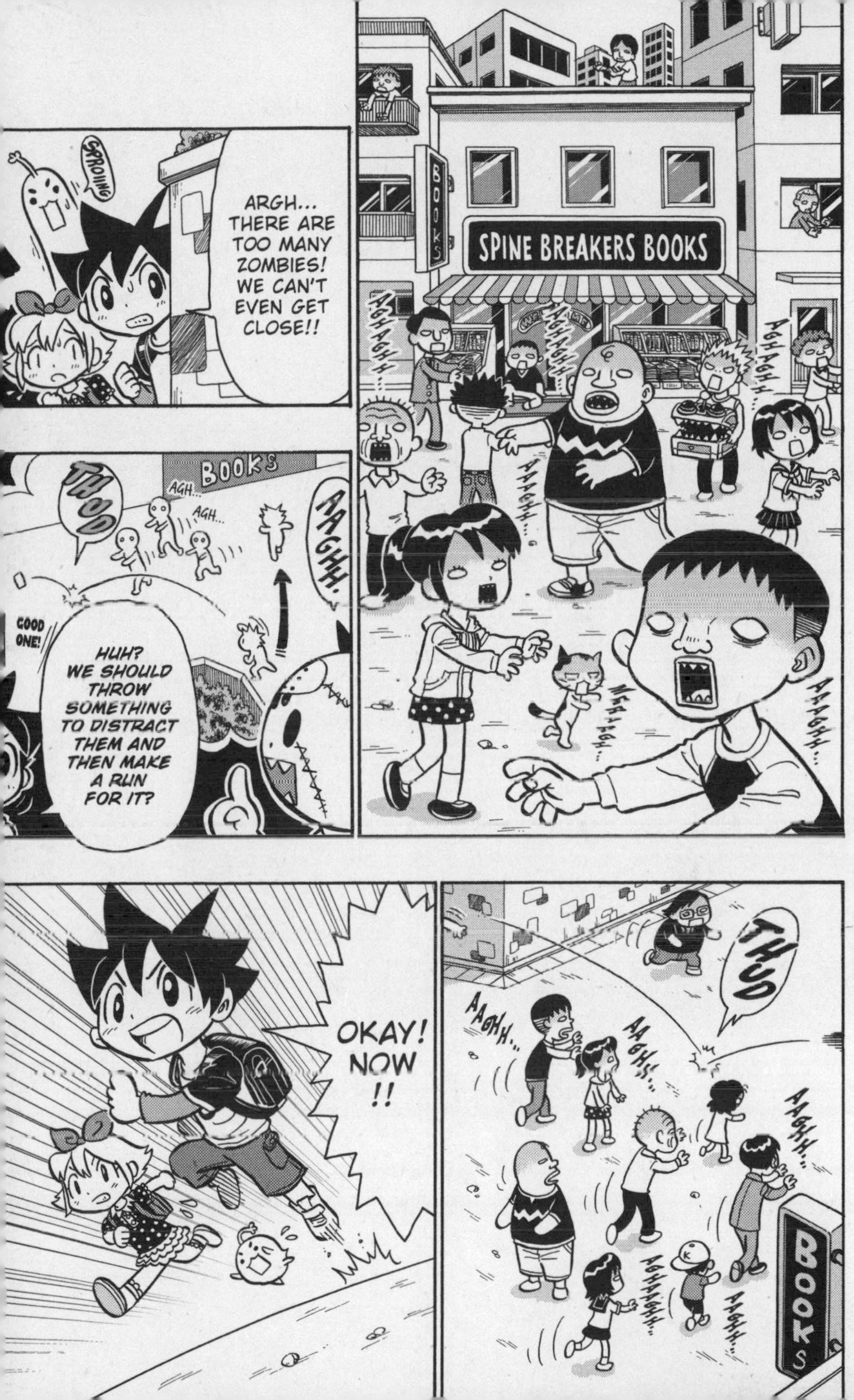
SPINE BREAKERS BOOKS
BOOKS
AGHAGHH...
AAGHH...
AAAGHH...
SPROING
ARGH... THERE ARE TOO MANY ZOMBIES! WE CAN'T EVEN GET CLOSE!!
AAGHH.
BOOKS
THUD
AGH...
AGH...
GOOD ONE!
HUH? WE SHOULD THROW SOMETHING TO DISTRACT THEM AND THEN MAKE A RUN FOR IT?
THUD
AAGHH...
AAGHH...
AAGHH...
BOOKS
OKAY! NOW !!

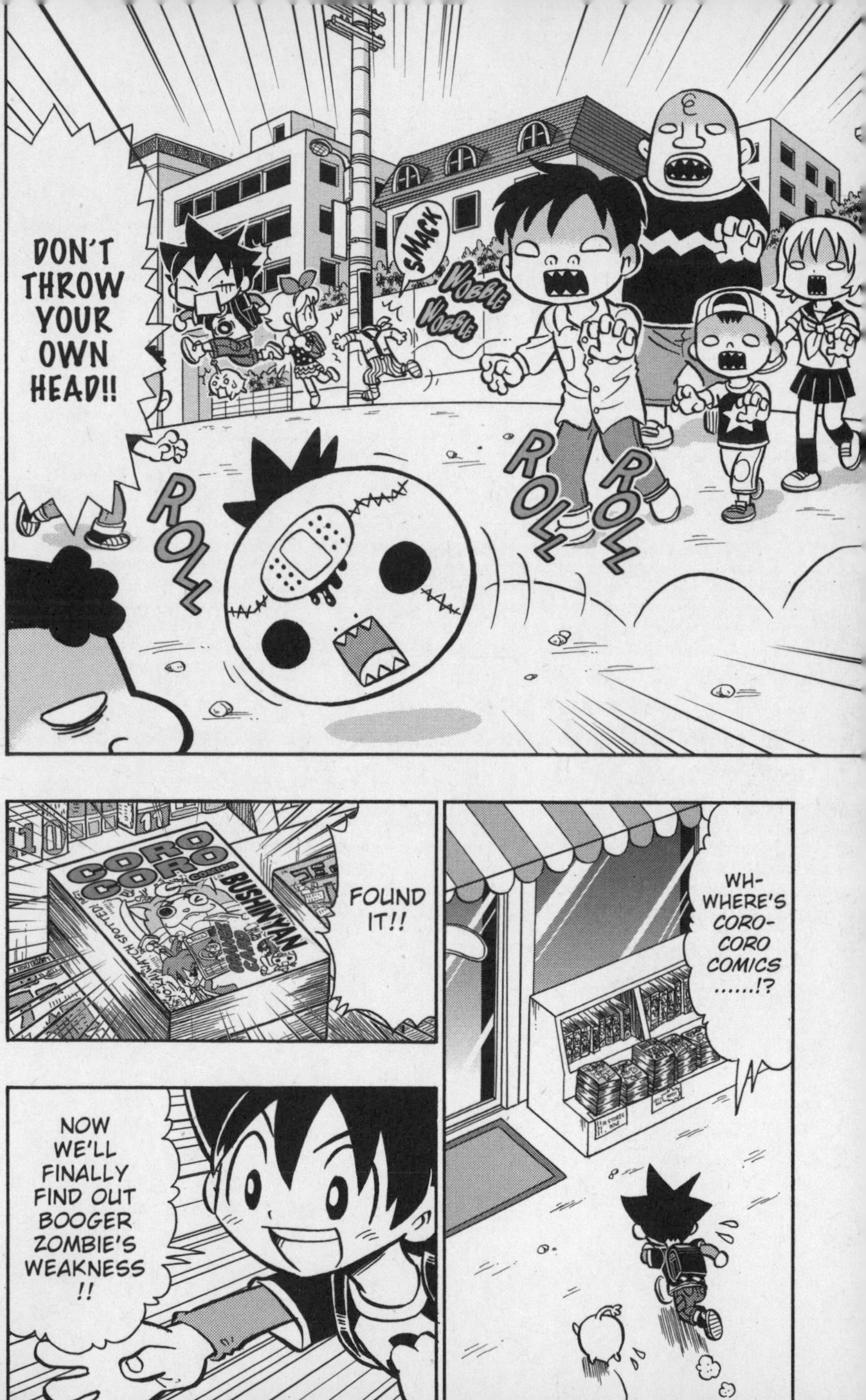
WOBBLE WOBBLE
SMACK
DON'T THROW YOUR OWN HEAD!!
ROLL ROLL
ROLL
WH-WHERE'S CORO-CORO COMICS ......!?
CORO CORO COMICS
BUSHINYAN
FOUND IT!!
NOW WE'LL FINALLY FIND OUT BOOGER ZOMBIE'S WEAKNESS !!

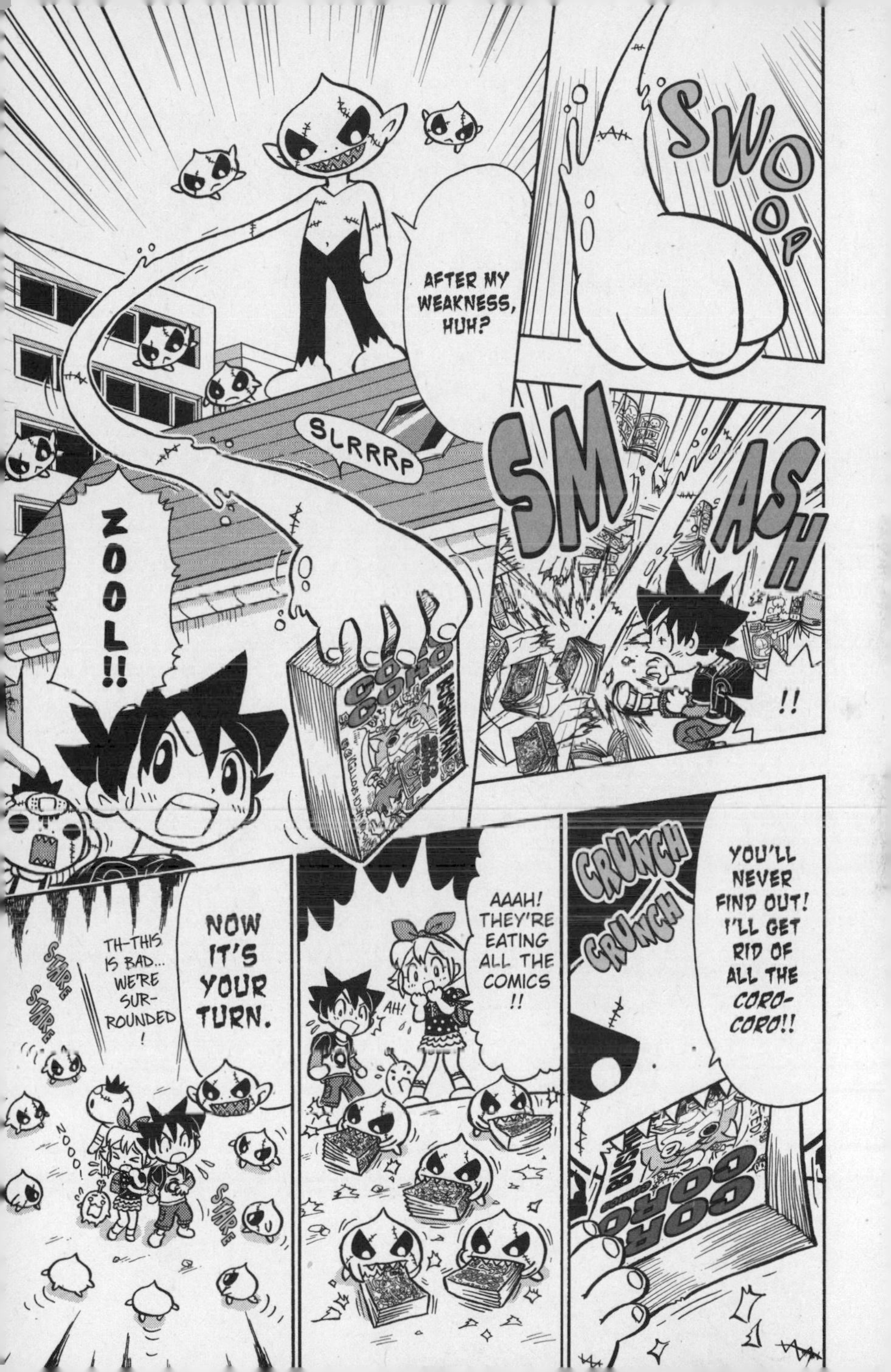
SWOOP
SMASH
!!
AFTER MY WEAKNESS, HUH?
SLRRRP
ZOOL!!
YOU'LL NEVER FIND OUT! I'LL GET RID OF ALL THE *CORO-CORO*!!
CRUNCH
CRUNCH
AAAH! THEY'RE EATING ALL THE COMICS!!
AH!
NOW IT'S YOUR TURN.
TH-THIS IS BAD... WE'RE SUR-ROUNDED!
STARE
STARE
ZOOO!
STARE

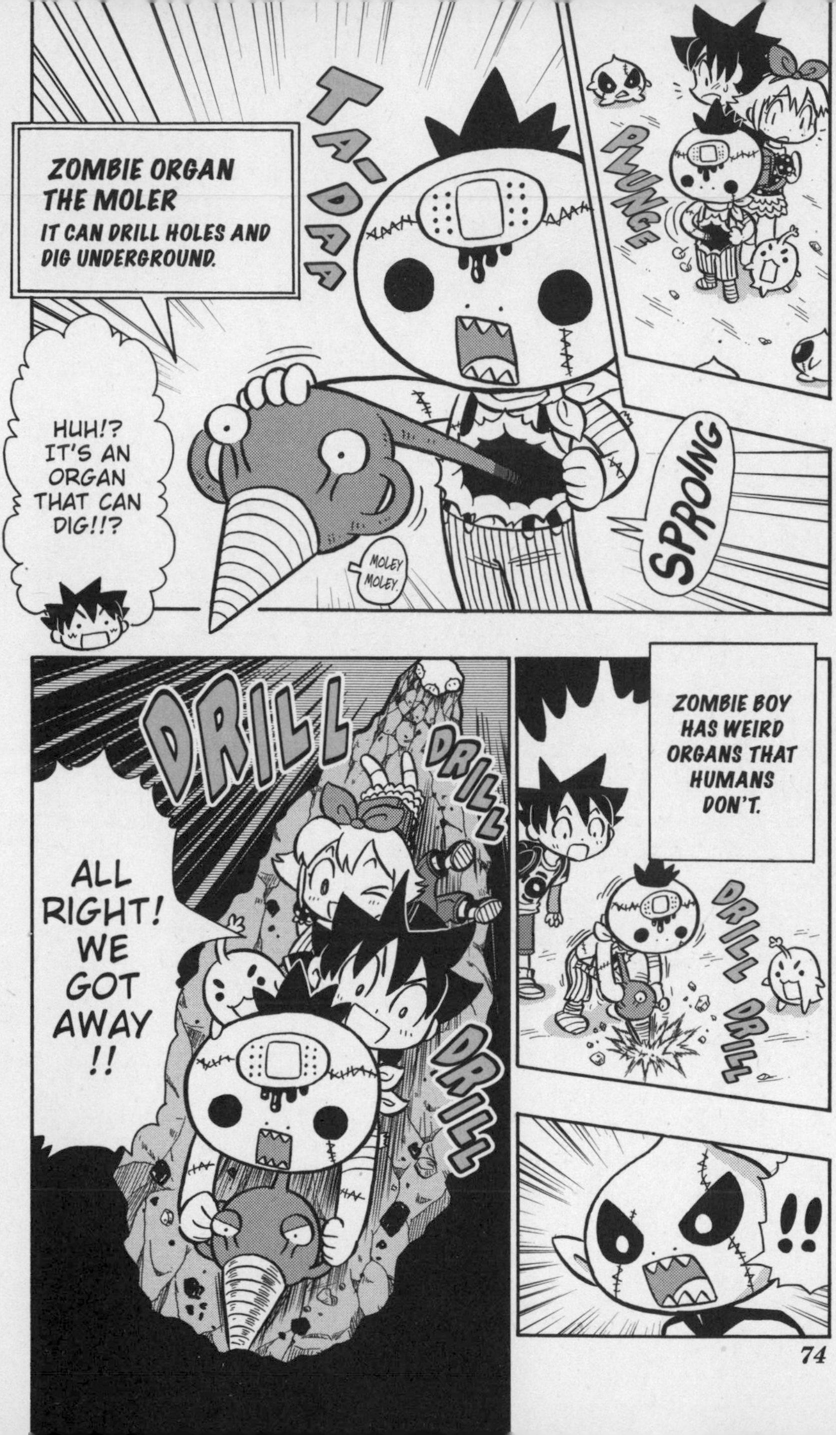

PLUNGE
TA-DAA
ZOMBIE ORGAN
THE MOLER
IT CAN DRILL HOLES AND DIG UNDERGROUND.
SPROING
MOLEY MOLEY.
HUH!? IT'S AN ORGAN THAT CAN DIG!!?
ZOMBIE BOY HAS WEIRD ORGANS THAT HUMANS DON'T.
DRILL DRILL DRILL
!!
DRILL
DRILL
DRILL
ALL RIGHT! WE GOT AWAY!!

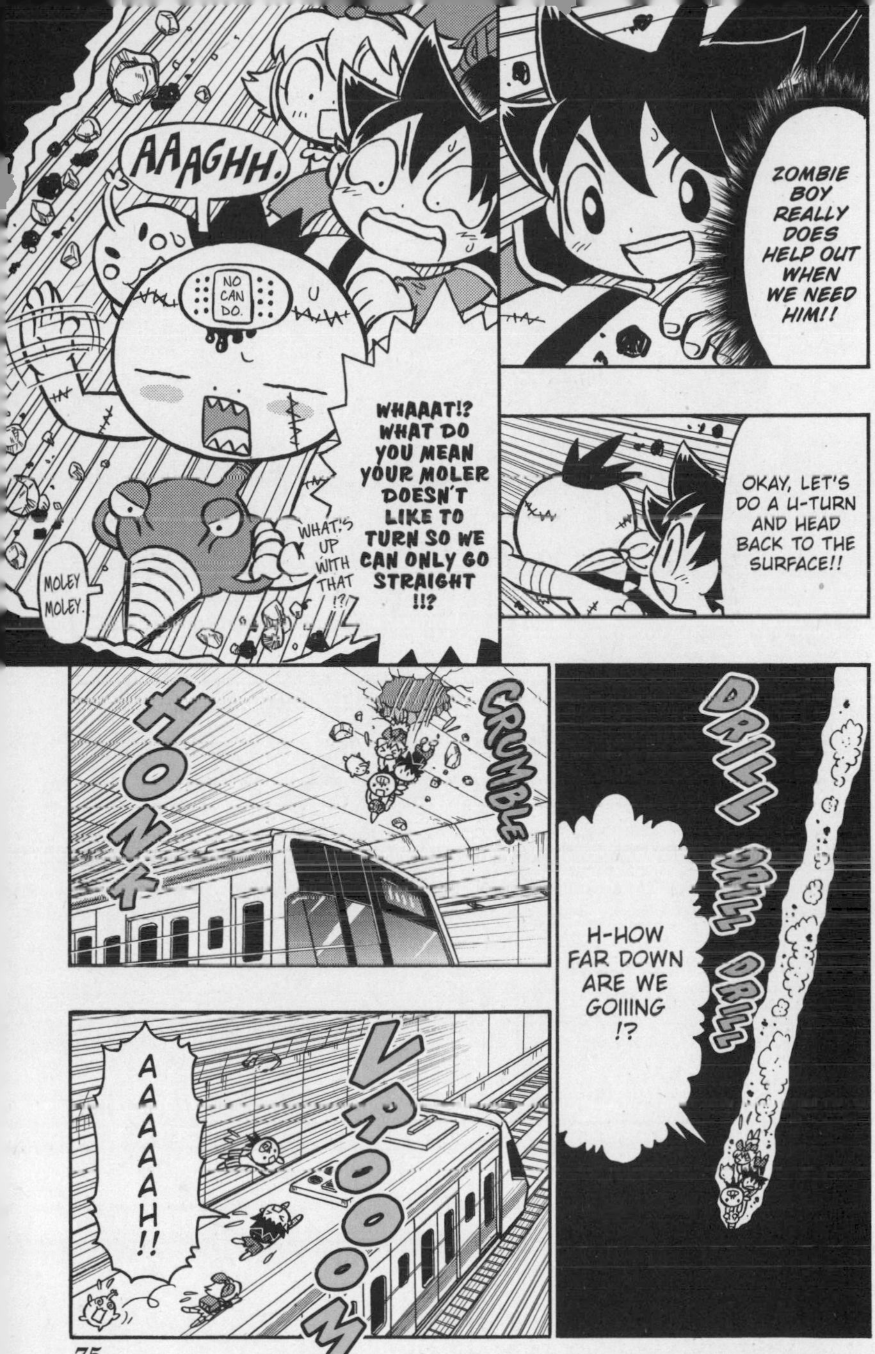
ZOMBIE BOY REALLY DOES HELP OUT WHEN WE NEED HIM!!
OKAY, LET'S DO A U-TURN AND HEAD BACK TO THE SURFACE!!
AAAGHH.
NO CAN DO.
WHAAAT!? WHAT DO YOU MEAN YOUR MOLER DOESN'T LIKE TO TURN SO WE CAN ONLY GO STRAIGHT!!?
WHAT'S UP WITH THAT!?
MOLEY MOLEY.
DRILL DRILL DRILL
H-HOW FAR DOWN ARE WE GOIIING!?
CRUMBLE
HONK
VROOOOM
AAAAAAH!!

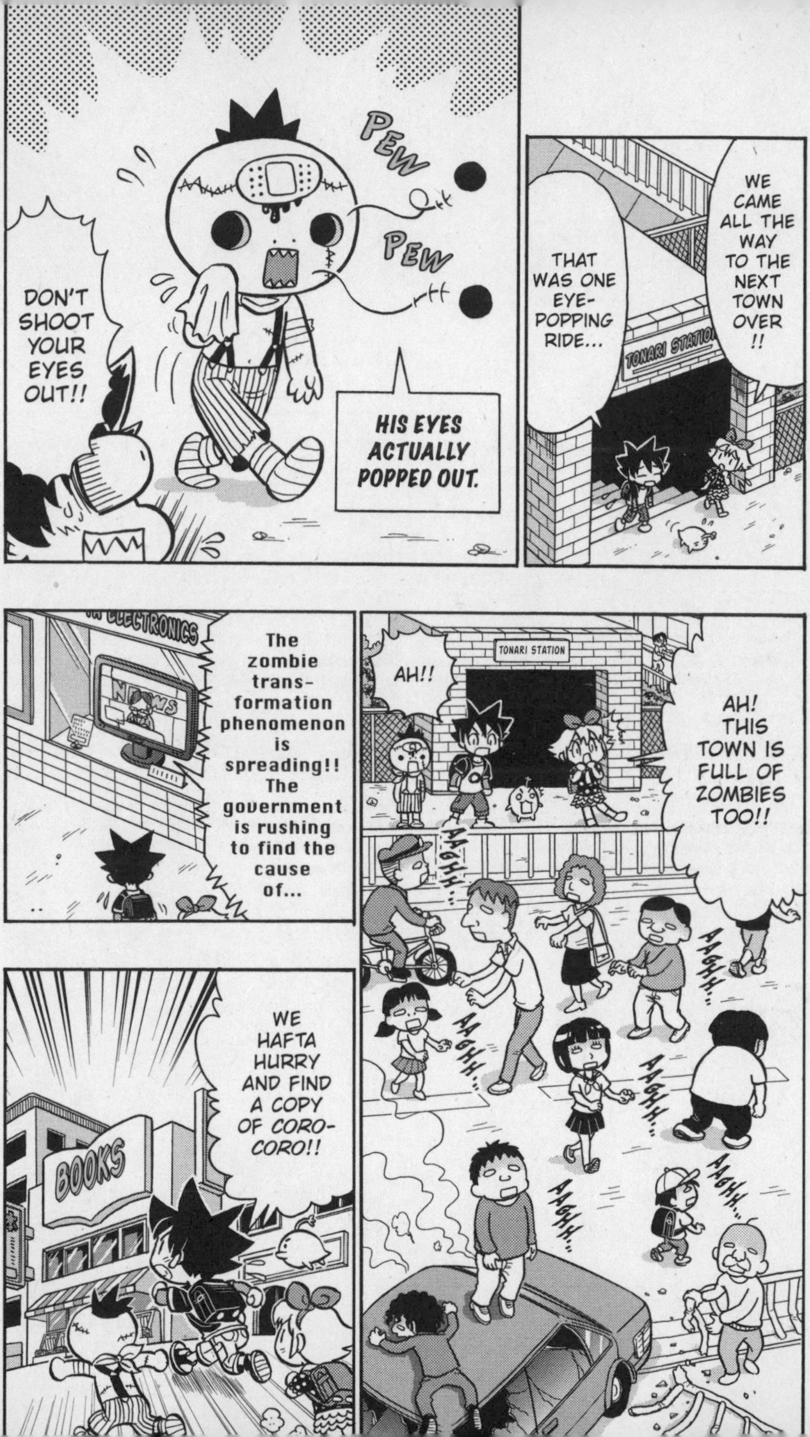

WE CAME ALL THE WAY TO THE NEXT TOWN OVER!!
THAT WAS ONE EYE-POPPING RIDE...
TONARI STATION
PEW
PEW
DON'T SHOOT YOUR EYES OUT!!
HIS EYES ACTUALLY POPPED OUT.
TONARI STATION
AH! THIS TOWN IS FULL OF ZOMBIES TOO!!
AH!!
AAGHH...
AAGHH...
AAGHH...
AAGHH...
AAGHH...
AAGHH...
AAGHH...
ELECTRONICS
NEWS
The zombie transformation phenomenon is spreading!! The government is rushing to find the cause of...
WE HAFTA HURRY AND FIND A COPY OF CORO-CORO!!
BOOKS

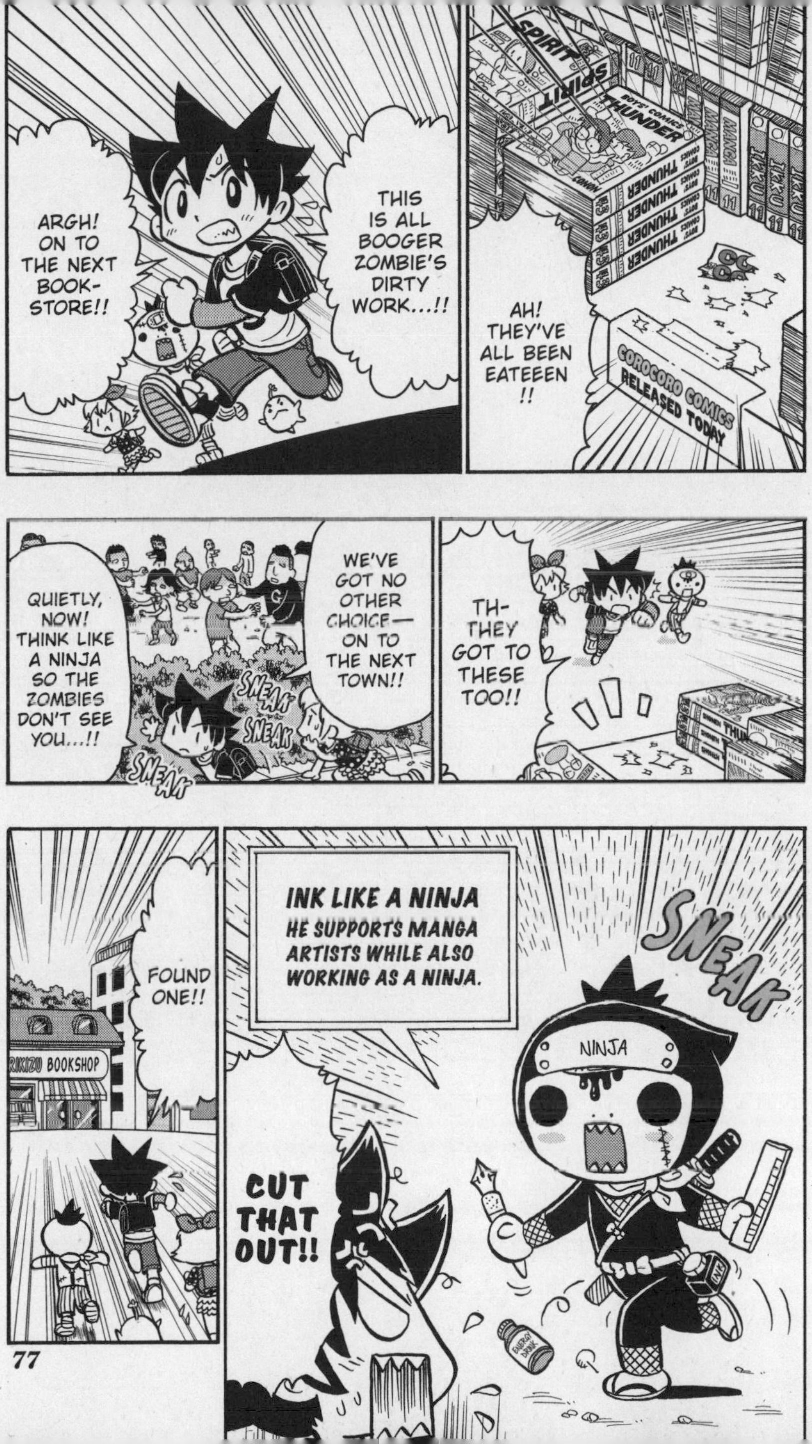
AH! THEY'VE ALL BEEN EATEEEN!!
COROCORO COMICS RELEASED TODAY
THIS IS ALL BOOGER ZOMBIE'S DIRTY WORK...!!
ARGH! ON TO THE NEXT BOOK-STORE!!
TH-THEY GOT TO THESE TOO!!
WE'VE GOT NO OTHER CHOICE— ON TO THE NEXT TOWN!!
QUIETLY, NOW! THINK LIKE A NINJA SO THE ZOMBIES DON'T SEE YOU...!!
SNEAK SNEAK SNEAK
INK LIKE A NINJA
HE SUPPORTS MANGA ARTISTS WHILE ALSO WORKING AS A NINJA.
SNEAK
NINJA
CUT THAT OUT!!
FOUND ONE!!
RIKIZU BOOKSHOP

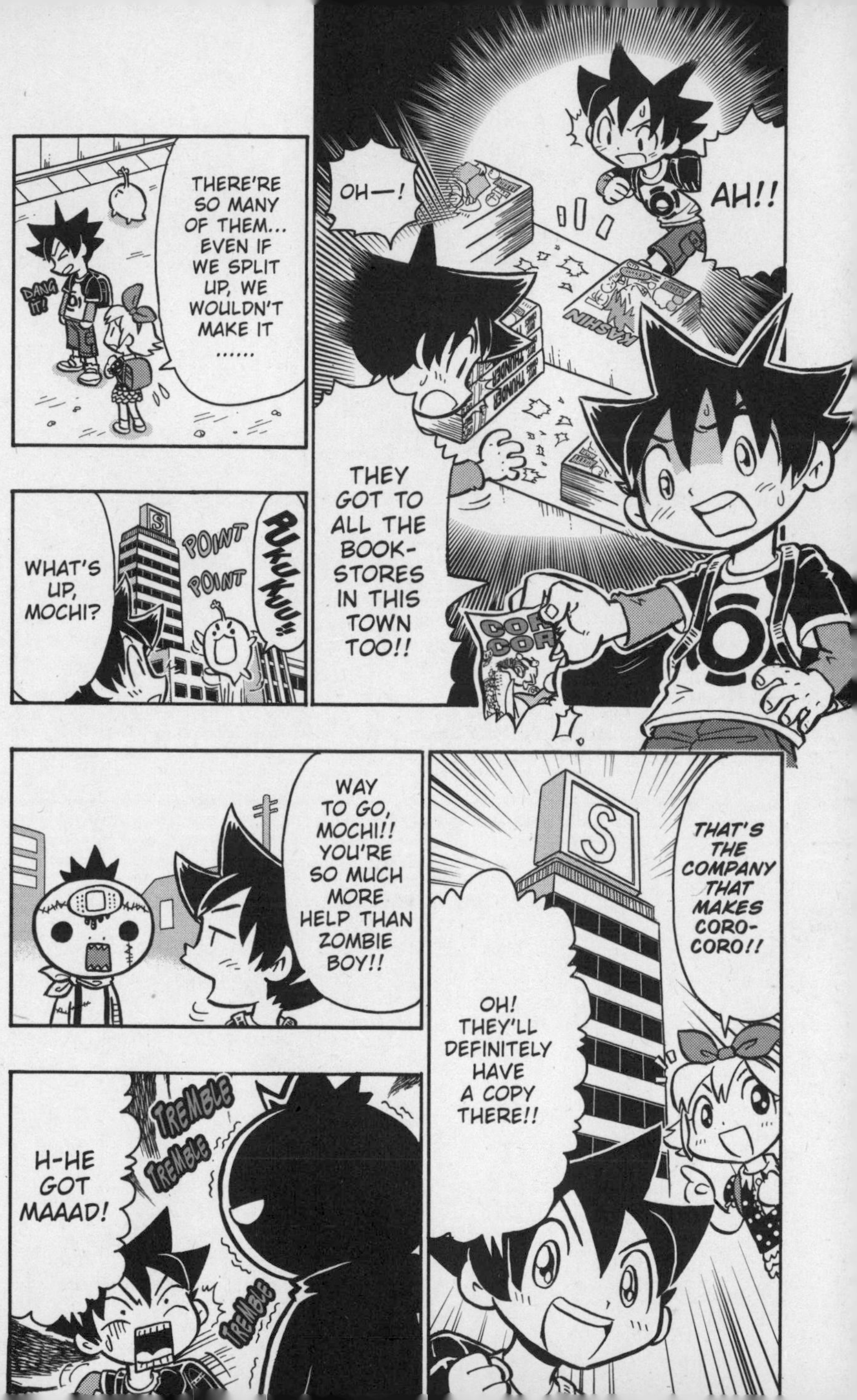
AH!!
OH—!
KASHIN
THUNDER
THUNDER
CORO CORO
THEY GOT TO ALL THE BOOK-STORES IN THIS TOWN TOO!!
THERE'RE SO MANY OF THEM... EVEN IF WE SPLIT UP, WE WOULDN'T MAKE IT ......
DANG IT!
PUKUKUU!!
POINT
POINT
WHAT'S UP, MOCHI?
THAT'S THE COMPANY THAT MAKES CORO-CORO!!
OH! THEY'LL DEFINITELY HAVE A COPY THERE!!
WAY TO GO, MOCHI!! YOU'RE SO MUCH MORE HELP THAN ZOMBIE BOY!!
TREMBLE
TREMBLE
H-HE GOT MAAAD!
TREMBLE

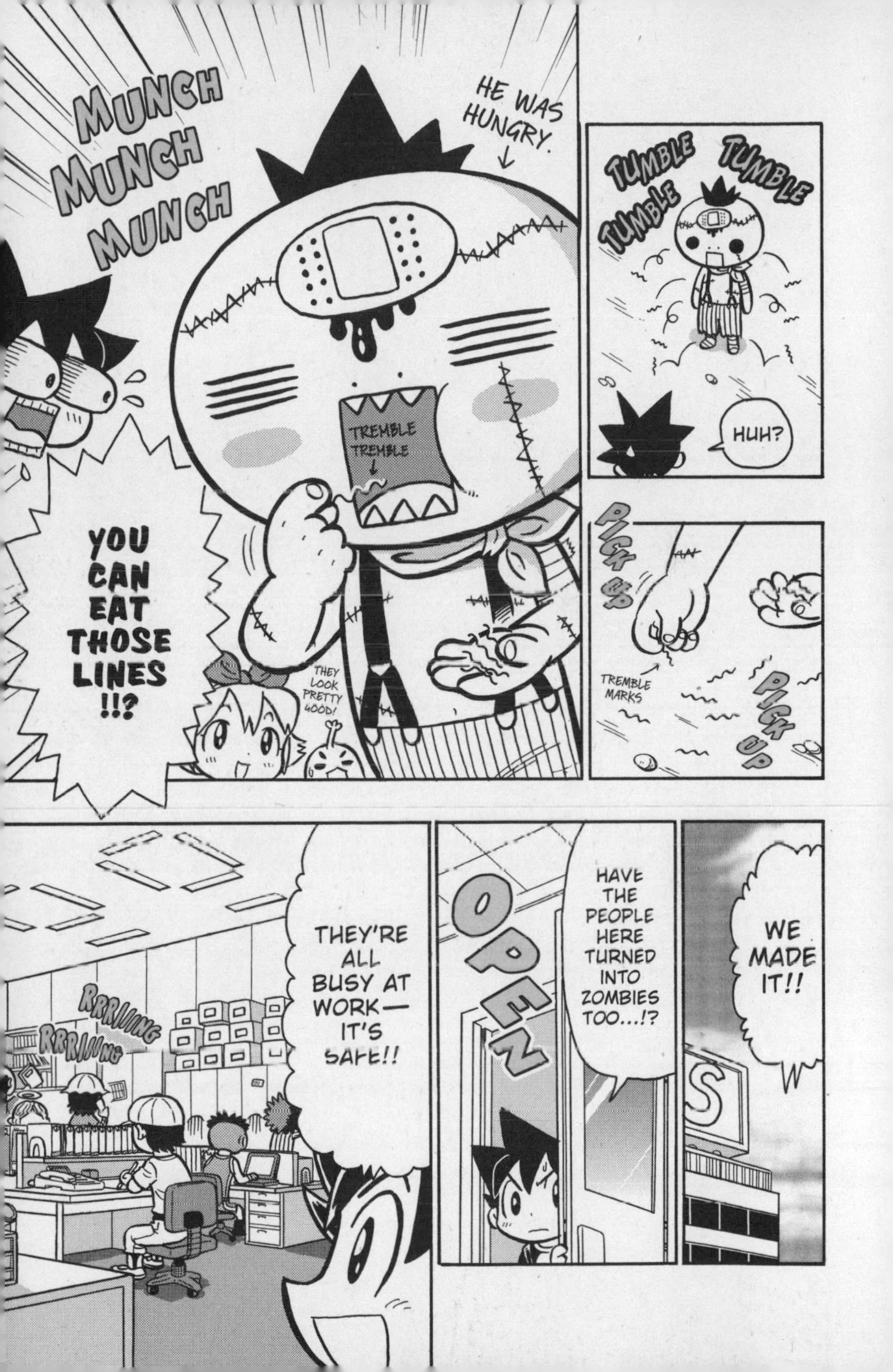
TUMBLE TUMBLE
TUMBLE
HUH?
PICK UP
TREMBLE MARKS
PICK UP
HE WAS HUNGRY.
MUNCH
MUNCH
MUNCH
TREMBLE TREMBLE
YOU CAN EAT THOSE LINES!!?
THEY LOOK PRETTY GOOD!
WE MADE IT!!
HAVE THE PEOPLE HERE TURNED INTO ZOMBIES TOO...!?
OPEN
THEY'RE ALL BUSY AT WORK— IT'S SAFE!!
RRRIIING
RRRIIING

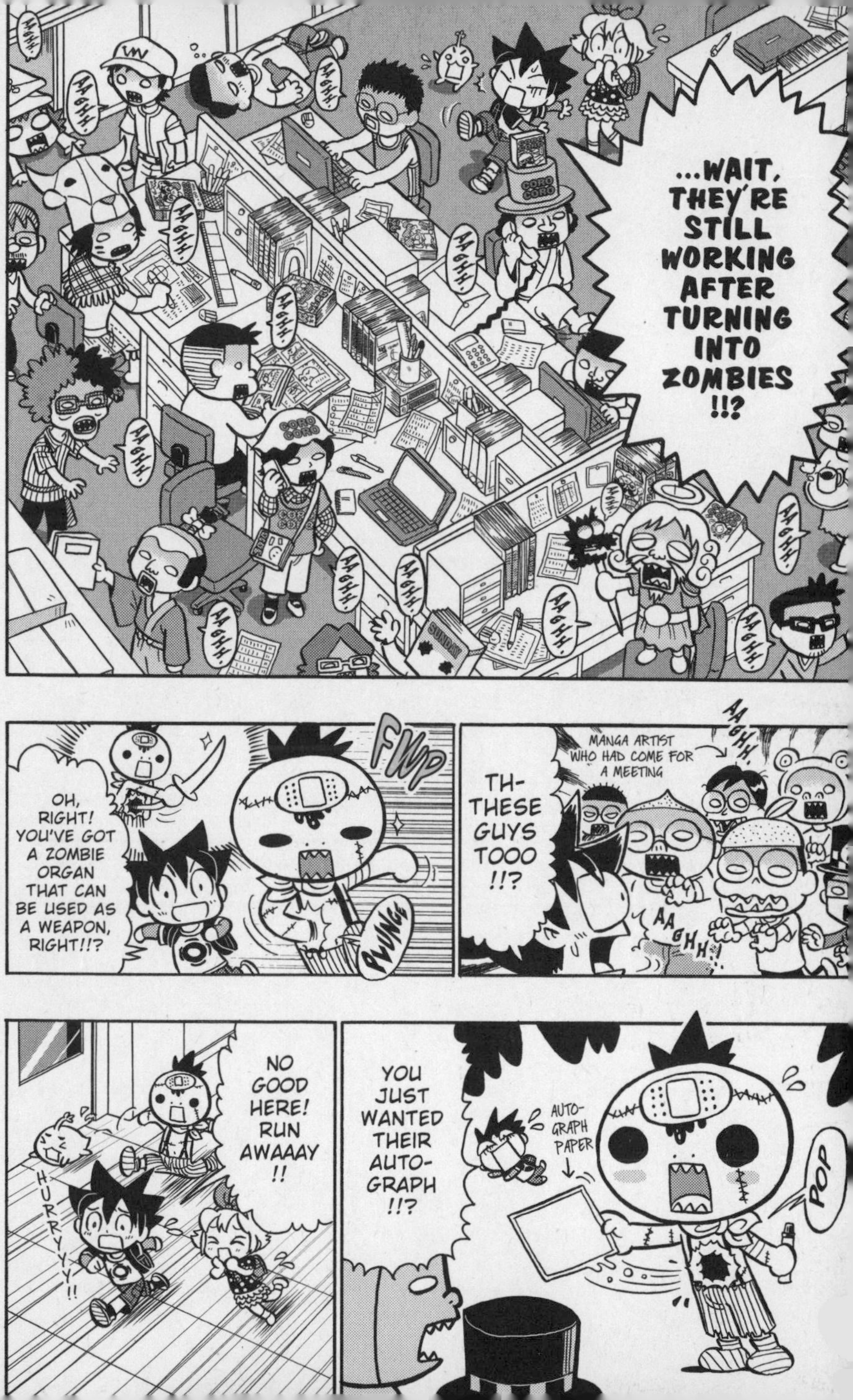
...WAIT, THEY'RE STILL WORKING AFTER TURNING INTO ZOMBIES!!?
AAGHH.
AAGHH.
AAGHH.
AAGHH.
AAGHH.
AAGHH.
AAGHH.
AAGHH.
AAGHH.
AAGHH.
AAGHH.
AAGHH.
AAGHH.
MANGA ARTIST WHO HAD COME FOR A MEETING
TH-THESE GUYS TOOO!!?
AAGHH!
FWP
OH, RIGHT! YOU'VE GOT A ZOMBIE ORGAN THAT CAN BE USED AS A WEAPON, RIGHT!!?
PLUNGE
POP
AUTO-GRAPH PAPER
YOU JUST WANTED THEIR AUTO-GRAPH!!?
NO GOOD HERE! RUN AWAAAY!!
HURRYYY!!

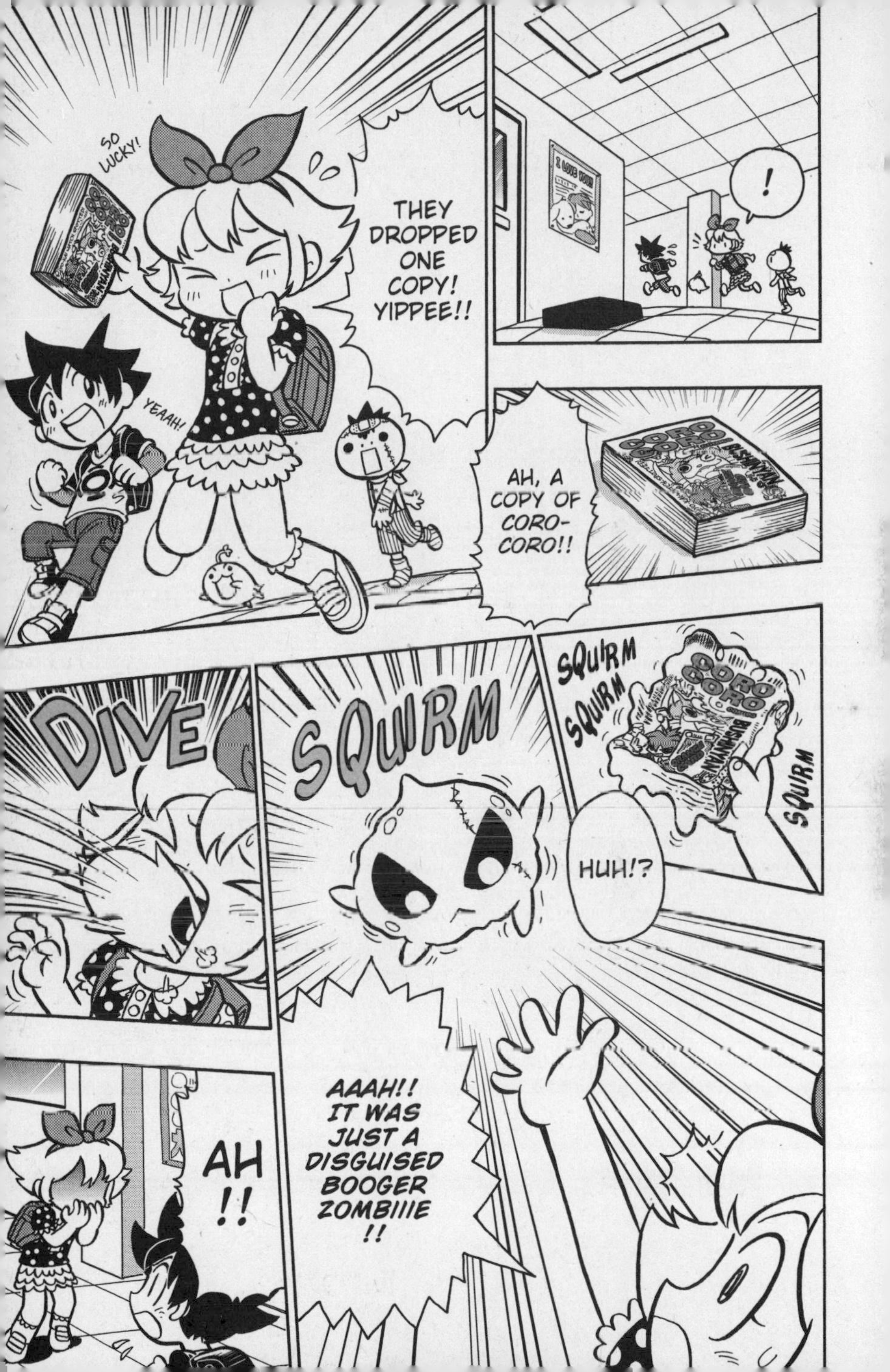
!
AH, A COPY OF CORO-CORO!!
THEY DROPPED ONE COPY! YIPPEE!!
SO LUCKY!
YEAAH!
SQUIRM
SQUIRM
SQUIRM
HUH!?
SQUIRM
AAAH!! IT WAS JUST A DISGUISED BOOGER ZOMBIIIE!!
DIVE
AH!!

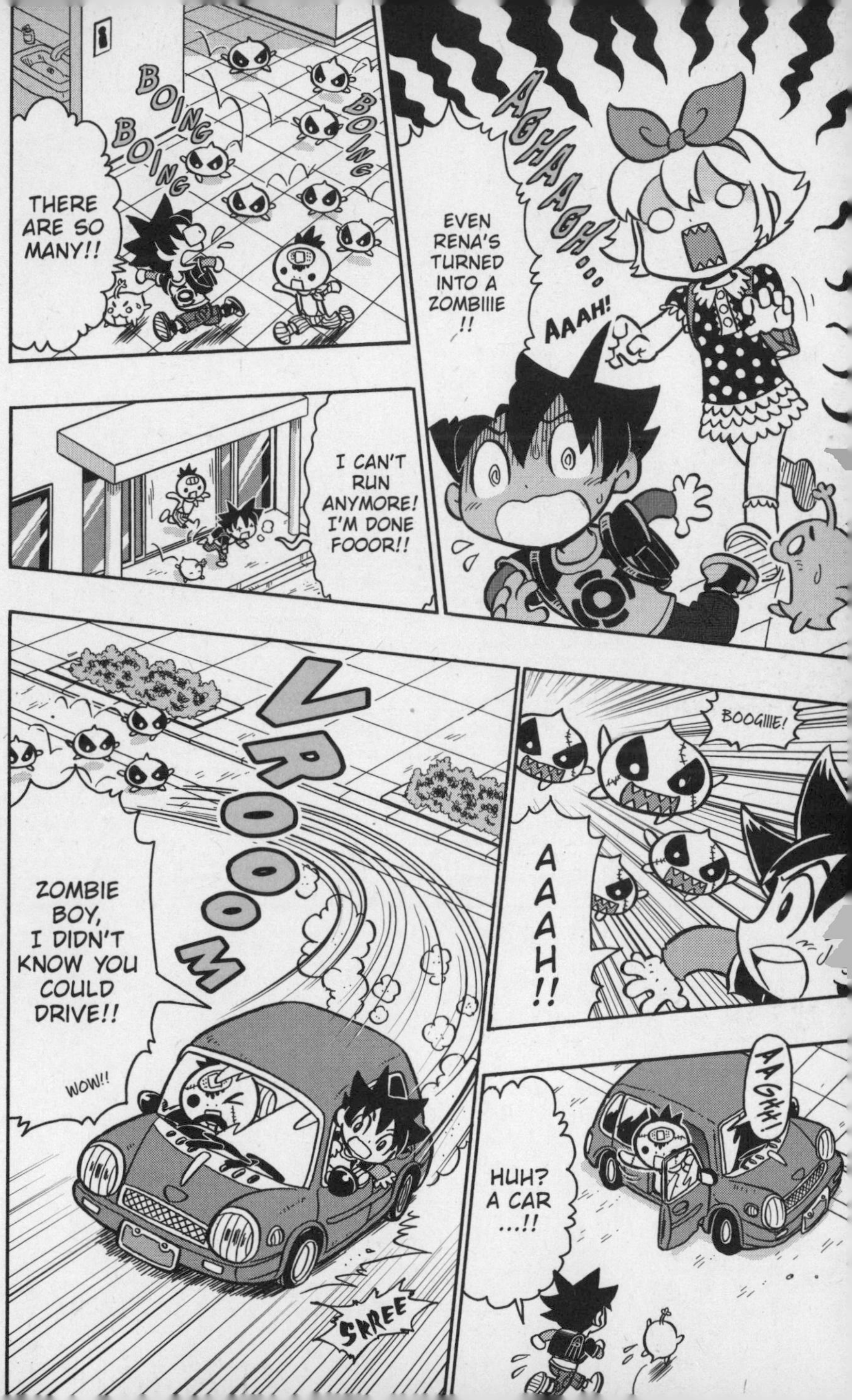
AGHAAGH...
EVEN RENA'S TURNED INTO A ZOMBIIIE!!
AAAH!
BOING BOING BOING
THERE ARE SO MANY!!
I CAN'T RUN ANYMORE! I'M DONE FOOOR!!
BOOGIIIE!
AAAAH!!
AAGHH!
HUH? A CAR ...!!
VROOOOOM
ZOMBIE BOY, I DIDN'T KNOW YOU COULD DRIVE!!
WOW!!
SKREE

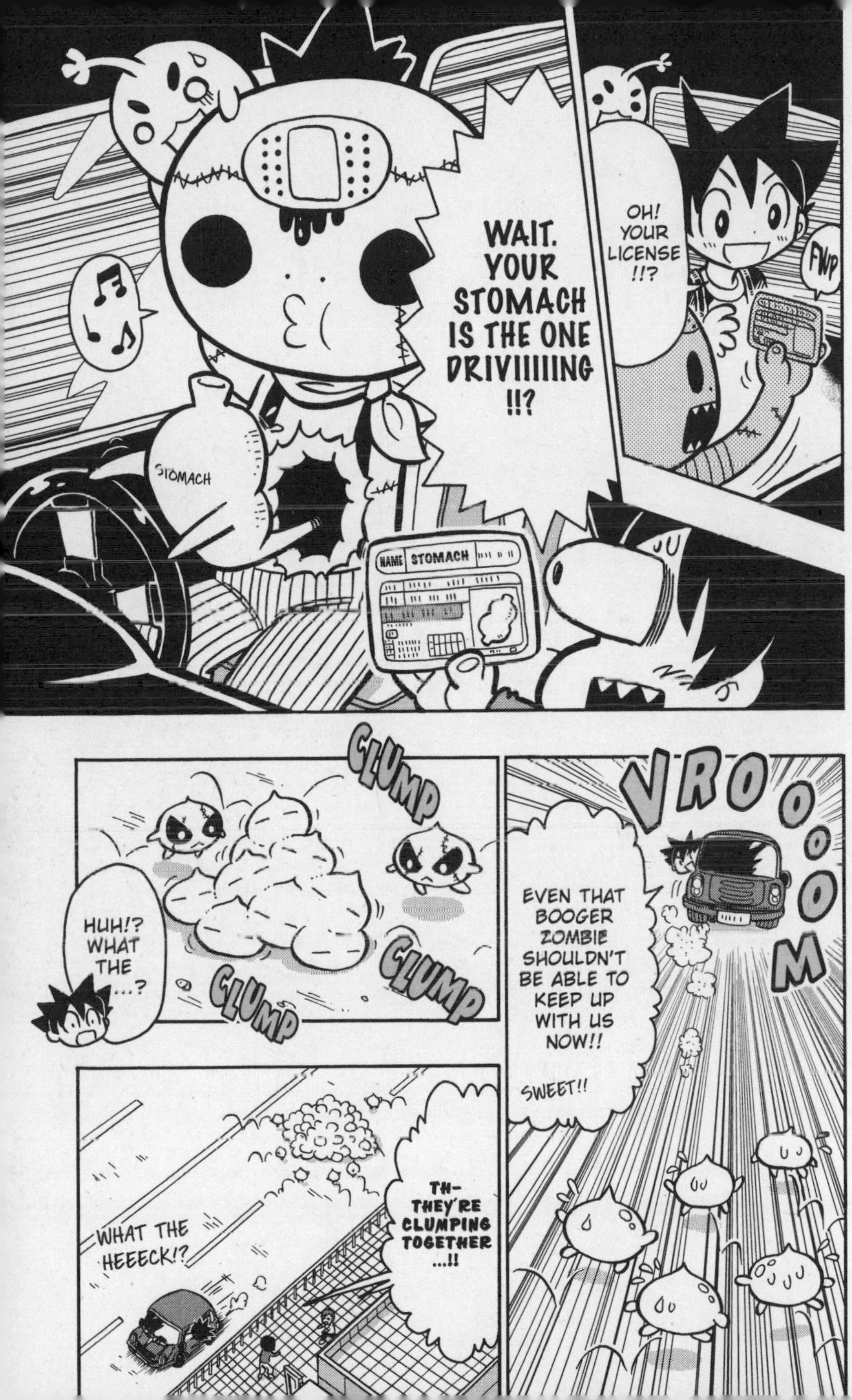
OH! YOUR LICENSE !!?
FWP
WAIT. YOUR STOMACH IS THE ONE DRIVIIIIING !!?
STOMACH
NAME STOMACH
VROOOOOM
EVEN THAT BOOGER ZOMBIE SHOULDN'T BE ABLE TO KEEP UP WITH US NOW!!
SWEET!!
CLUMP
CLUMP
CLUMP
HUH!? WHAT THE ...?
TH- THEY'RE CLUMPING TOGETHER ...!!
WHAT THE HEEECK!?

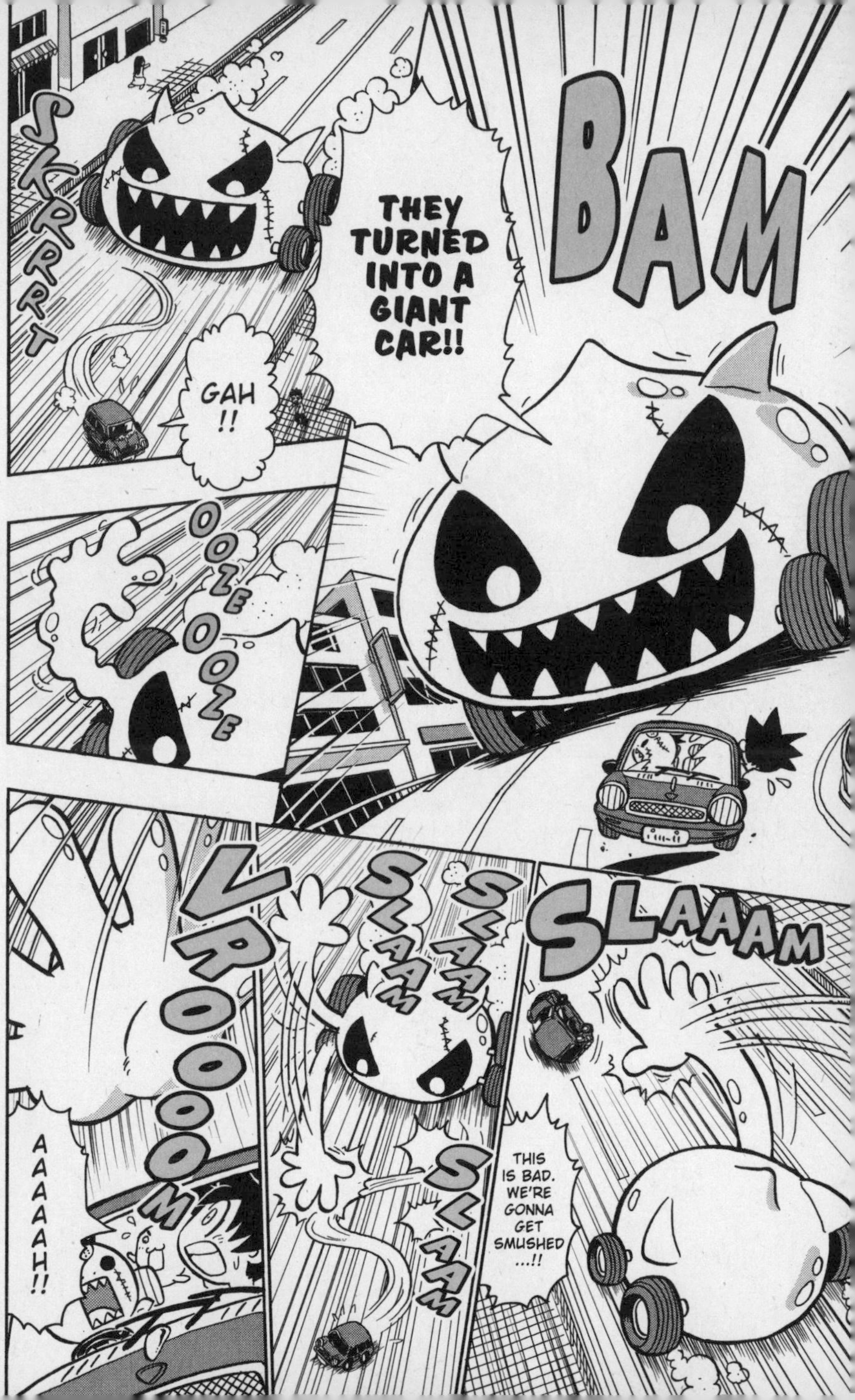
BAM
THEY TURNED INTO A GIANT CAR!!
SKRRRT
GAH!!
OOZE OOZE
SLAAAM
THIS IS BAD. WE'RE GONNA GET SMUSHED ...!!
SLAAAM SLAAM
SLAAM
VROOOOOM
AAAAAAH!!

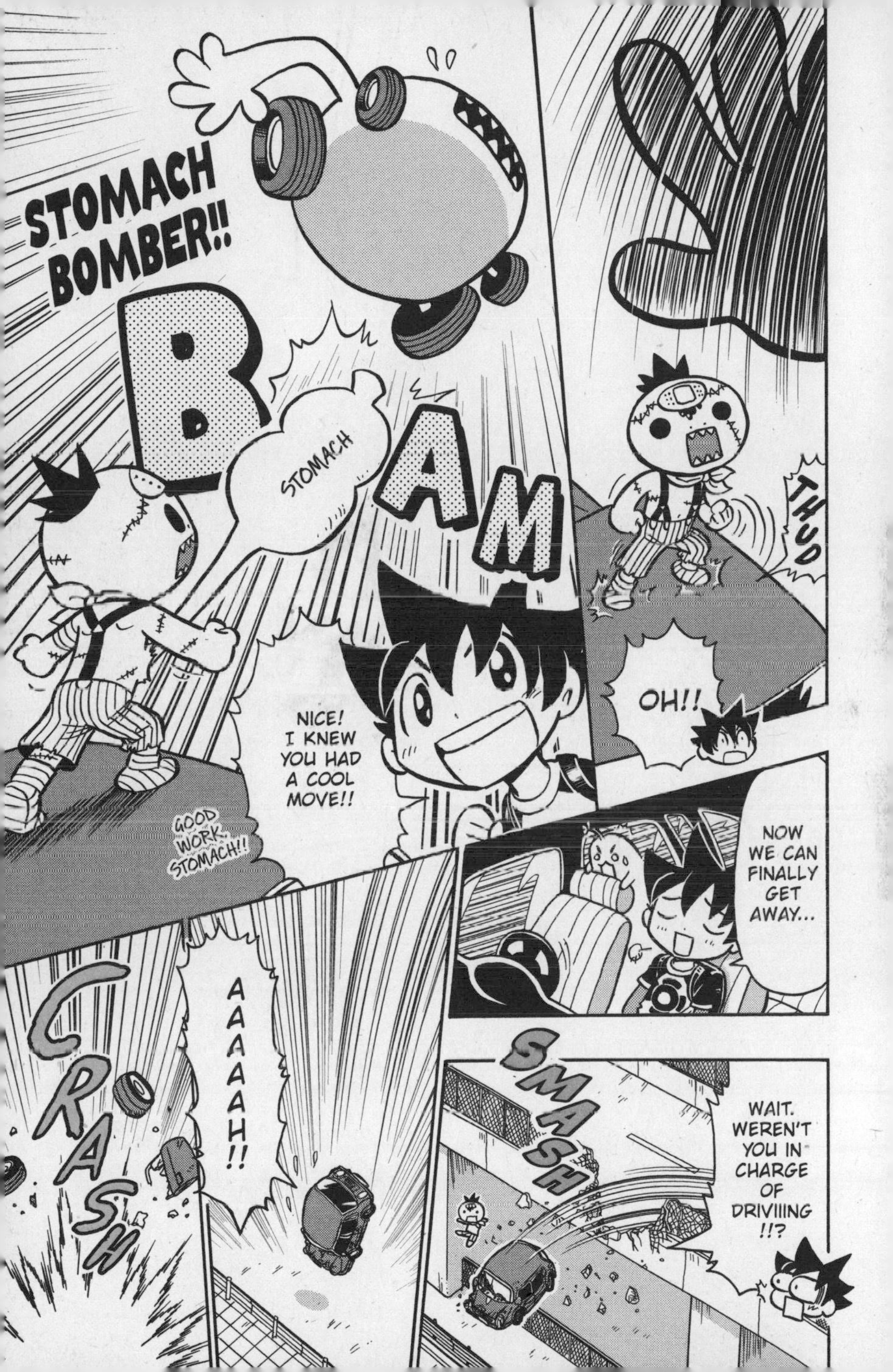
THUD
OH!!
STOMACH BOMBER!!
BAM
STOMACH
NICE! I KNEW YOU HAD A COOL MOVE!!
GOOD WORK, STOMACH!!
NOW WE CAN FINALLY GET AWAY...
SMASH
WAIT. WEREN'T YOU IN CHARGE OF DRIVIIING!!?
AAAAAAAH!!
CRASH

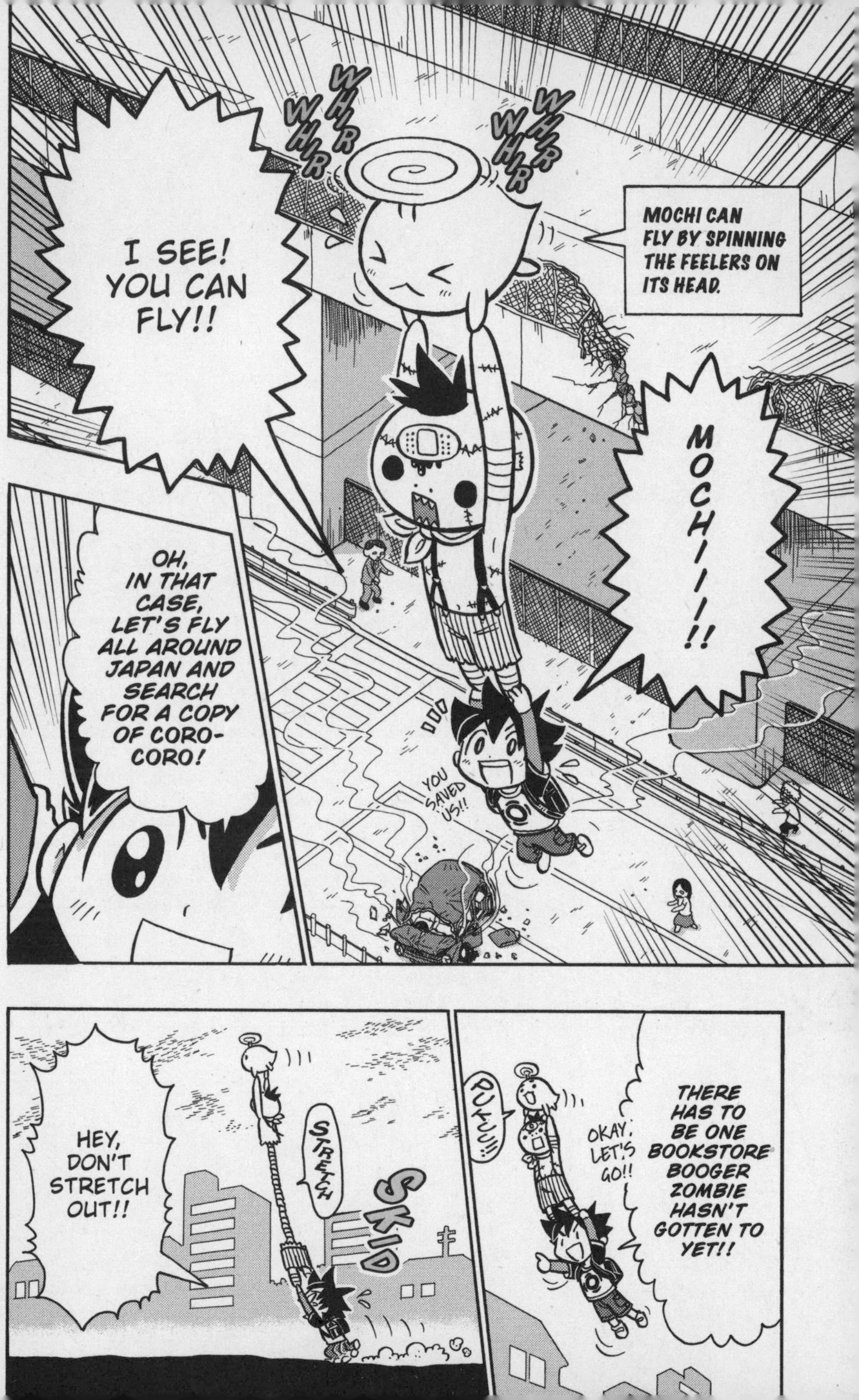
WHIR WHIR
MOCHI CAN FLY BY SPINNING THE FEELERS ON ITS HEAD.
WHIR WHIR
I SEE! YOU CAN FLY!!
MOCHI!!!!
YOU SAVED US!!
OH, IN THAT CASE, LET'S FLY ALL AROUND JAPAN AND SEARCH FOR A COPY OF CORO-CORO!
THERE HAS TO BE ONE BOOKSTORE BOOGER ZOMBIE HASN'T GOTTEN TO YET!!
OKAY. LET'S GO!!
PUKU!!
SKID
STRETCH
HEY, DON'T STRETCH OUT!!

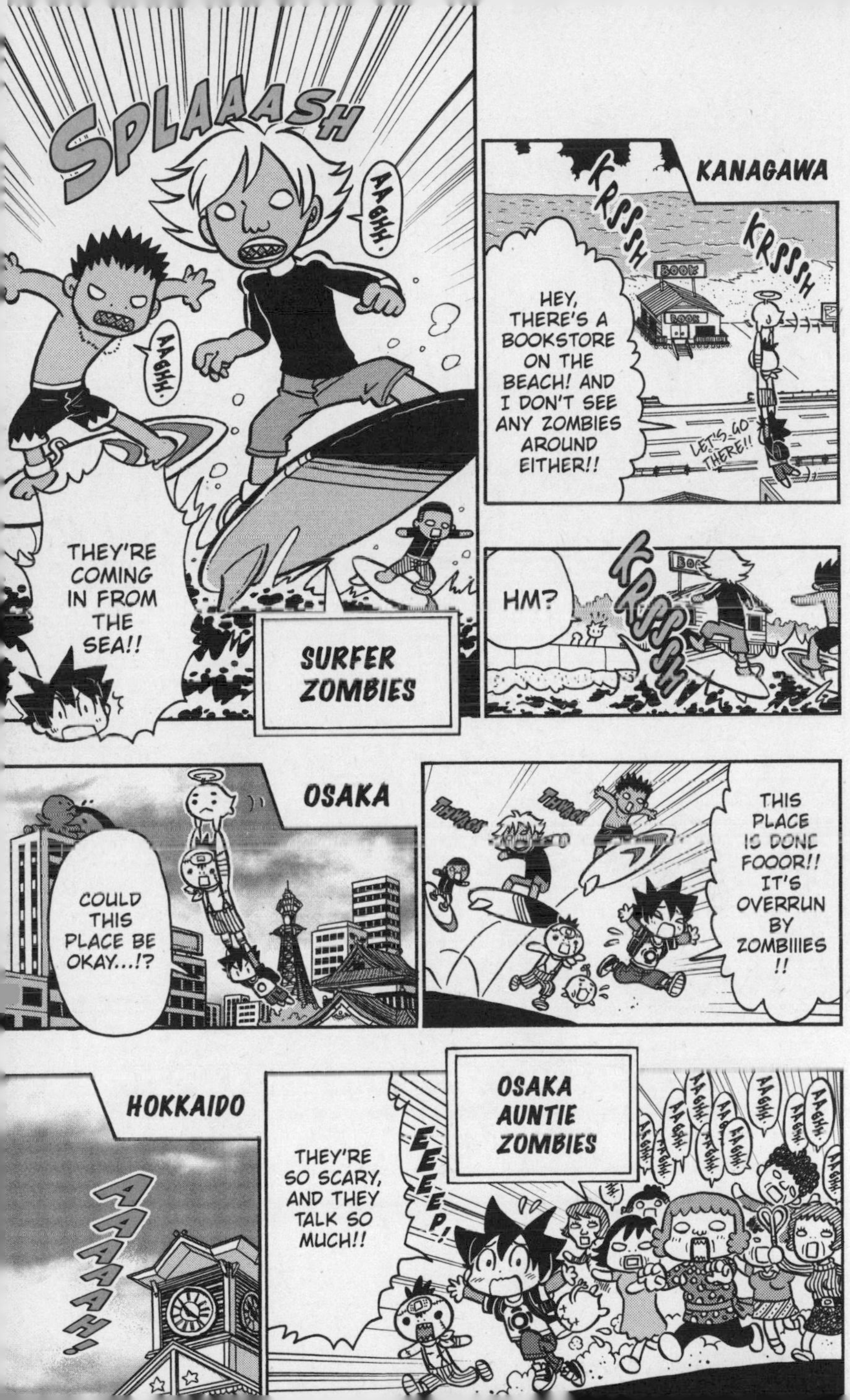
KANAGAWA
KRSSSH
KRSSSH
BOOK
HEY, THERE'S A BOOKSTORE ON THE BEACH! AND I DON'T SEE ANY ZOMBIES AROUND EITHER!!
LET'S GO THERE!!
KRSSSH
HM?
SPLAAASH
AAGHH.
AAGHH.
THEY'RE COMING IN FROM THE SEA!!
SURFER ZOMBIES
THWACK
THWACK
THIS PLACE IS DONE FOOOR!! IT'S OVERRUN BY ZOMBIIIES!!
OSAKA
COULD THIS PLACE BE OKAY...!?
OSAKA AUNTIE ZOMBIES
AAGHH.
AAGHH.
AAGHH.
AAGHH.
EEEEP!
THEY'RE SO SCARY, AND THEY TALK SO MUCH!!
HOKKAIDO
AAAAAAH!

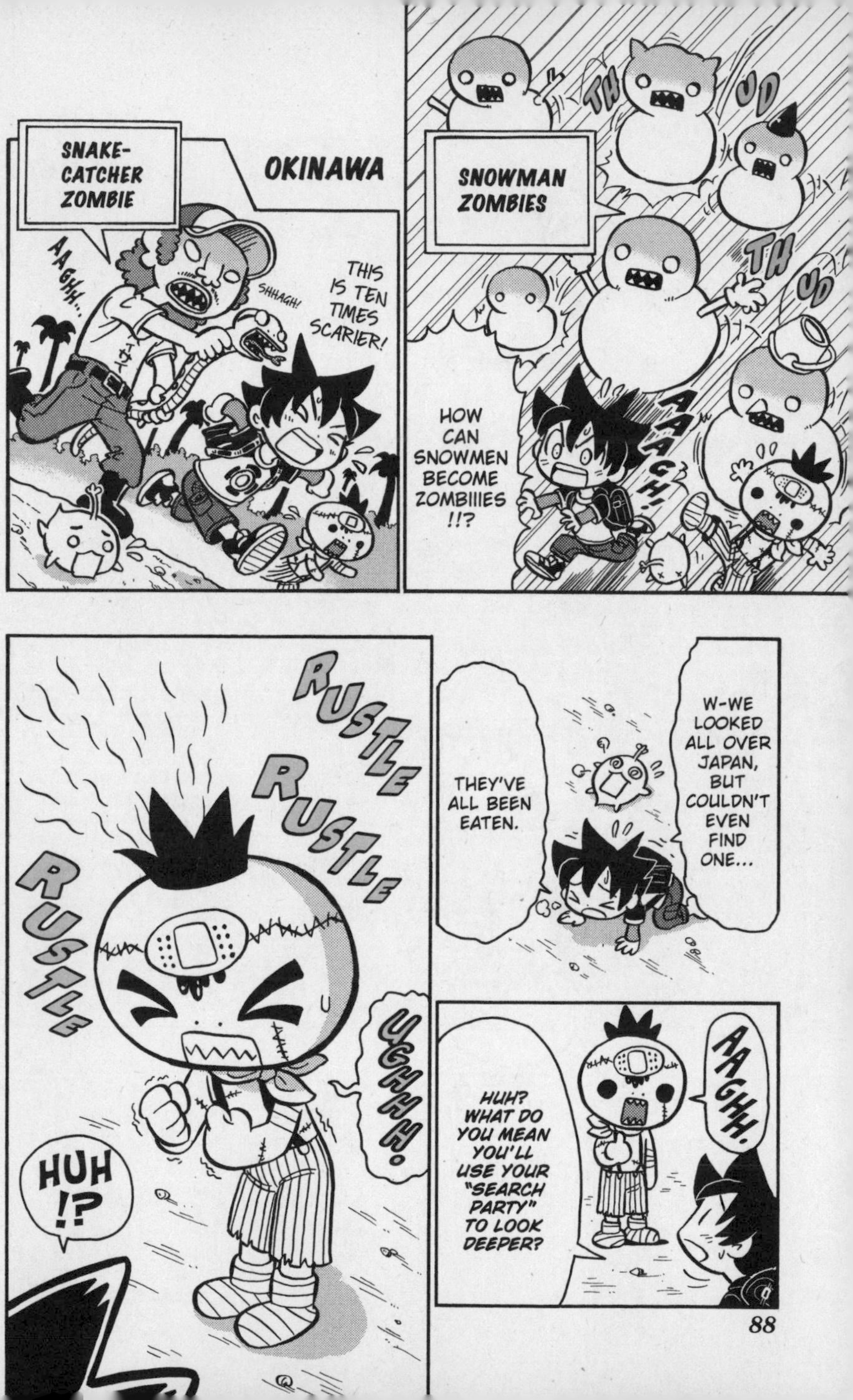
SNOWMAN ZOMBIES
TH UD
TH UD
AAAGH!
HOW CAN SNOWMEN BECOME ZOMBIIIES!!?
OKINAWA
SNAKE-CATCHER ZOMBIE
AAGHH...
SHHAGH!
THIS IS TEN TIMES SCARIER!
W-WE LOOKED ALL OVER JAPAN, BUT COULDN'T EVEN FIND ONE...
THEY'VE ALL BEEN EATEN.
AAGHH.
HUH? WHAT DO YOU MEAN YOU'LL USE YOUR "SEARCH PARTY" TO LOOK DEEPER?
RUSTLE
RUSTLE
RUSTLE
UGHHHH!
HUH!?

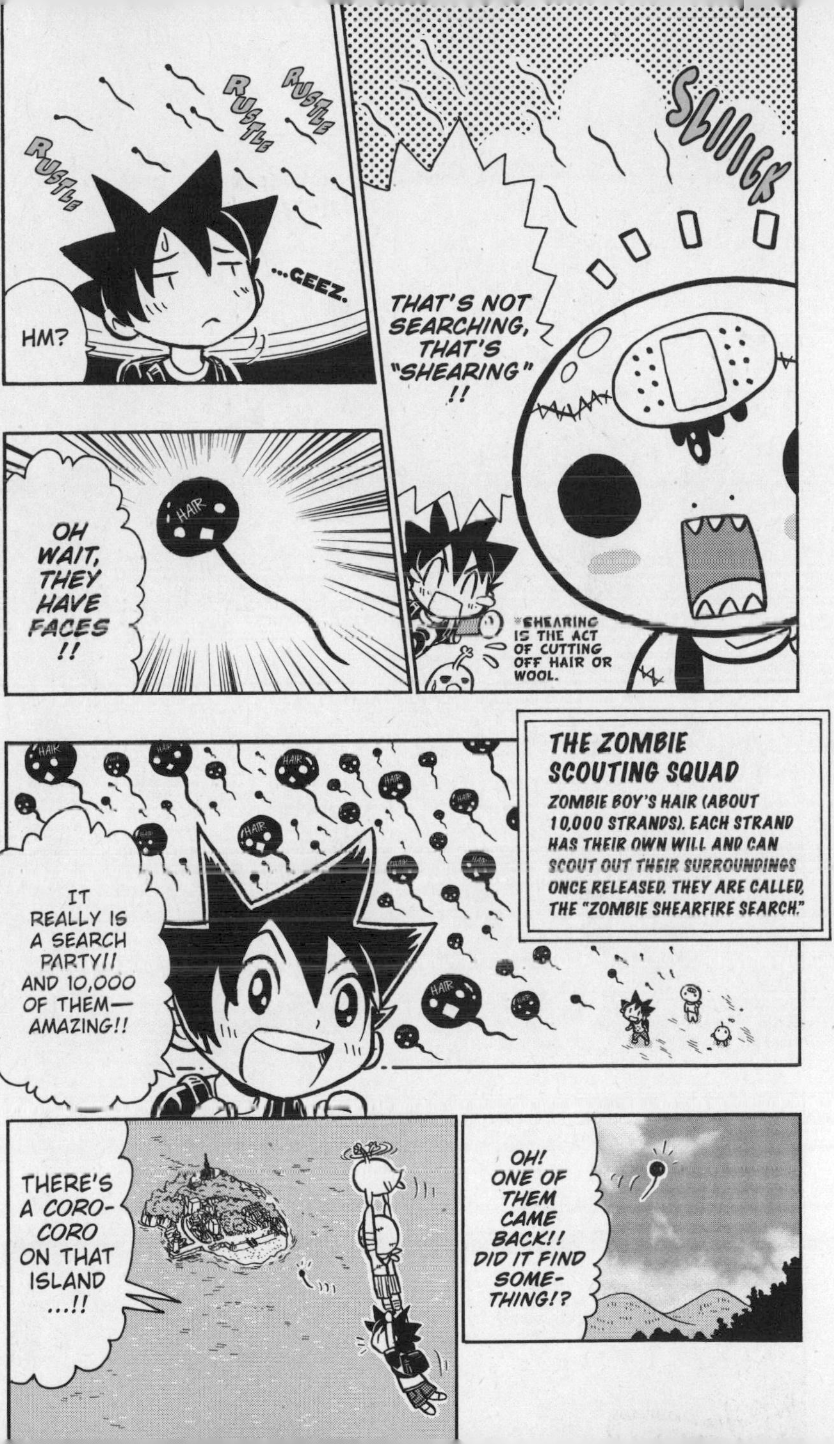
SLIIICK
THAT'S NOT SEARCHING, THAT'S "SHEARING"!!
*SHEARING IS THE ACT OF CUTTING OFF HAIR OR WOOL.
RUSTLE
RUSTLE
RUSTLE
...GEEZ.
HM?
HAIR
OH WAIT, THEY HAVE FACES!!
THE ZOMBIE SCOUTING SQUAD
ZOMBIE BOY'S HAIR (ABOUT 10,000 STRANDS). EACH STRAND HAS THEIR OWN WILL AND CAN SCOUT OUT THEIR SURROUNDINGS ONCE RELEASED. THEY ARE CALLED THE "ZOMBIE SHEARFIRE SEARCH."
IT REALLY IS A SEARCH PARTY!! AND 10,000 OF THEM—AMAZING!!
OH! ONE OF THEM CAME BACK!! DID IT FIND SOME-THING!?
THERE'S A CORO-CORO ON THAT ISLAND ...!!

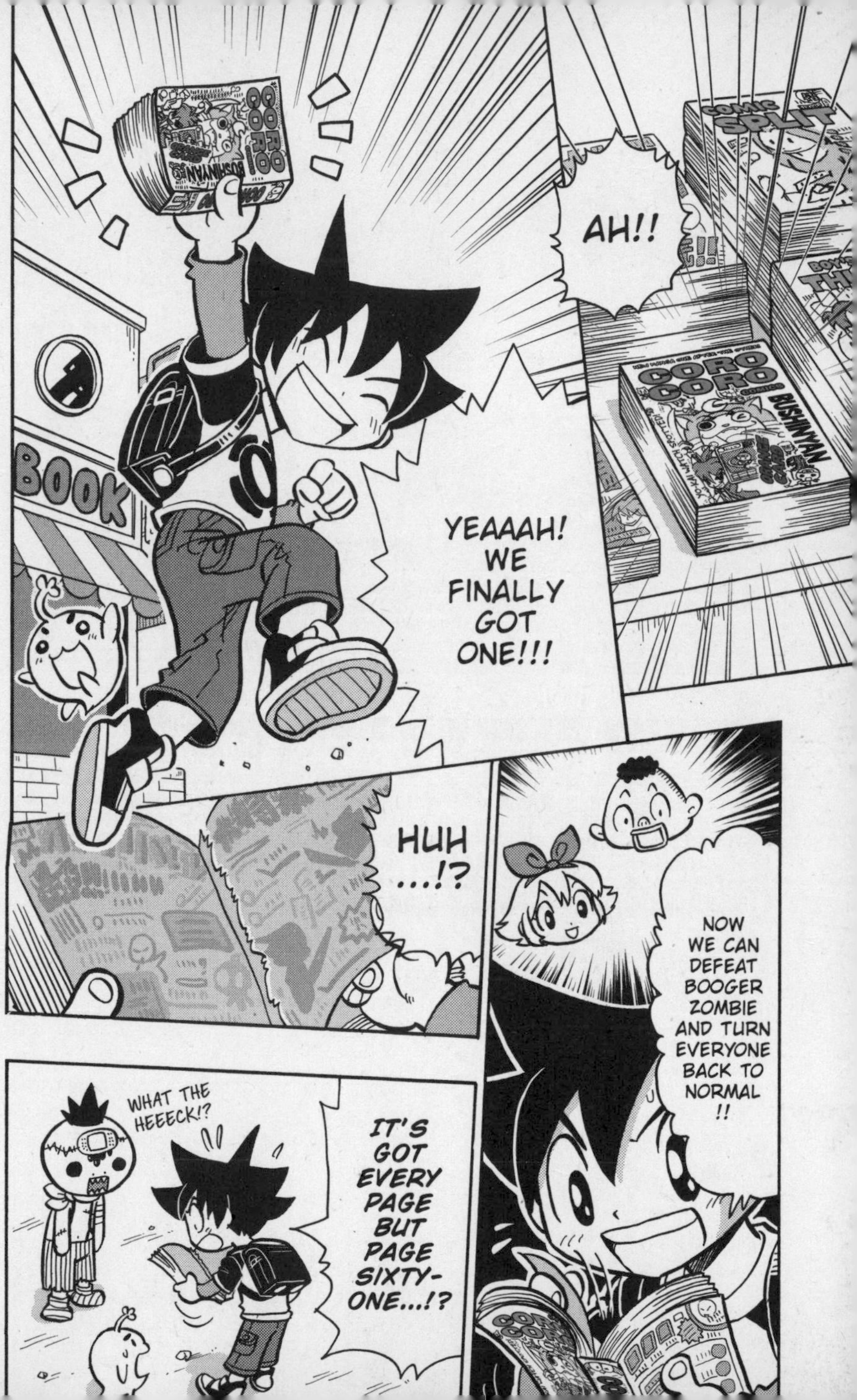

COMIC SPLIT
CORO CORO COMICS
BUSHINYAN
AH!!
BOOK
YEAAAH! WE FINALLY GOT ONE!!!
NOW WE CAN DEFEAT BOOGER ZOMBIE AND TURN EVERYONE BACK TO NORMAL!!
HUH...!?
IT'S GOT EVERY PAGE BUT PAGE SIXTY-ONE...!?
WHAT THE HEEECK!?

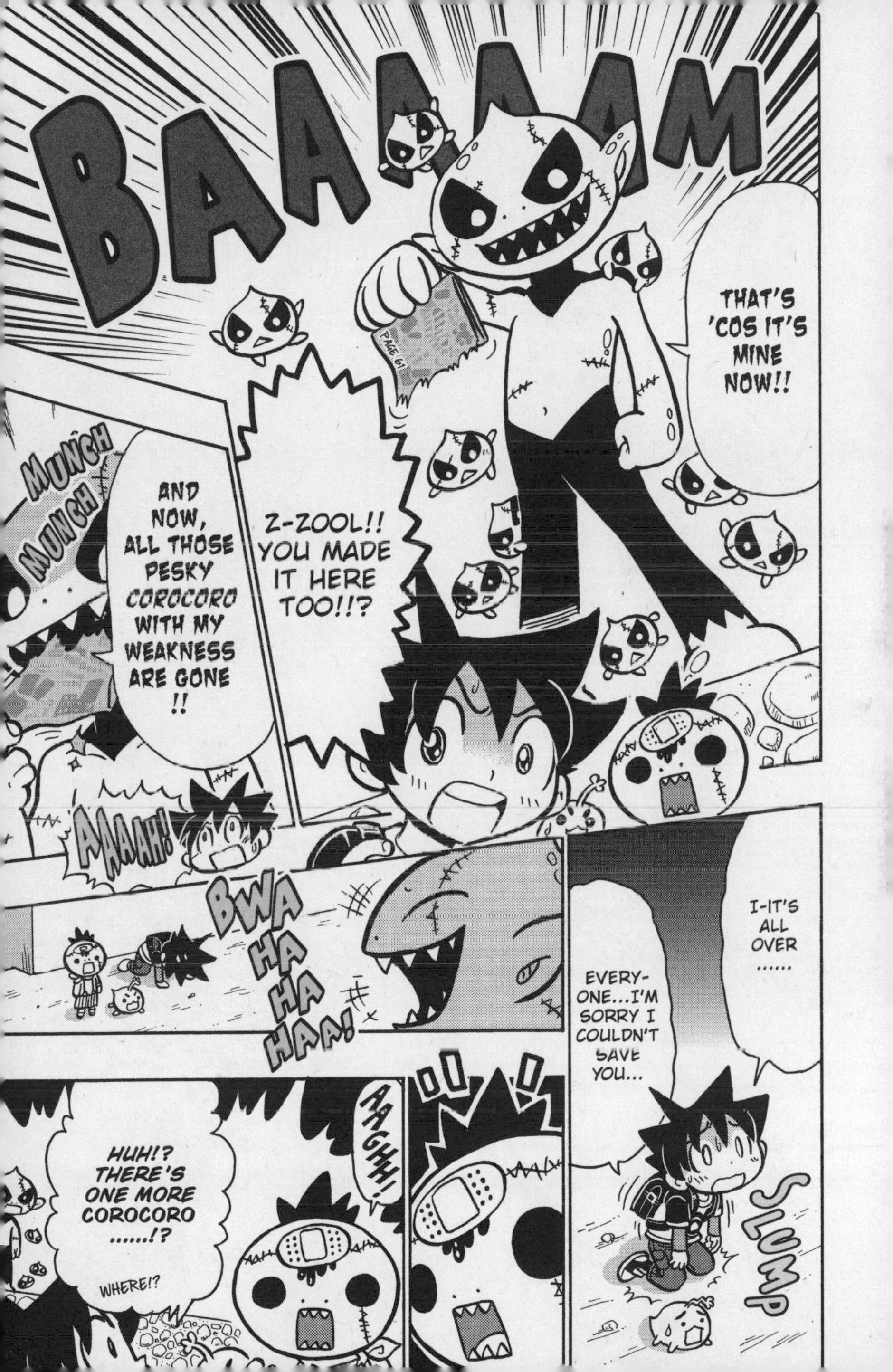
BAAAAAM
THAT'S 'COS IT'S MINE NOW!!
PAGE 61
Z-ZOOL!! YOU MADE IT HERE TOO!!?
AND NOW, ALL THOSE PESKY COROCORO WITH MY WEAKNESS ARE GONE!!
MUNCH MUNCH
AAAAH!
I-IT'S ALL OVER ......
EVERY-ONE...I'M SORRY I COULDN'T SAVE YOU...
SLUMP
BWA HA HA HA HAA!
!!
AAGHH!
HUH!? THERE'S ONE MORE COROCORO ......!?
WHERE!?

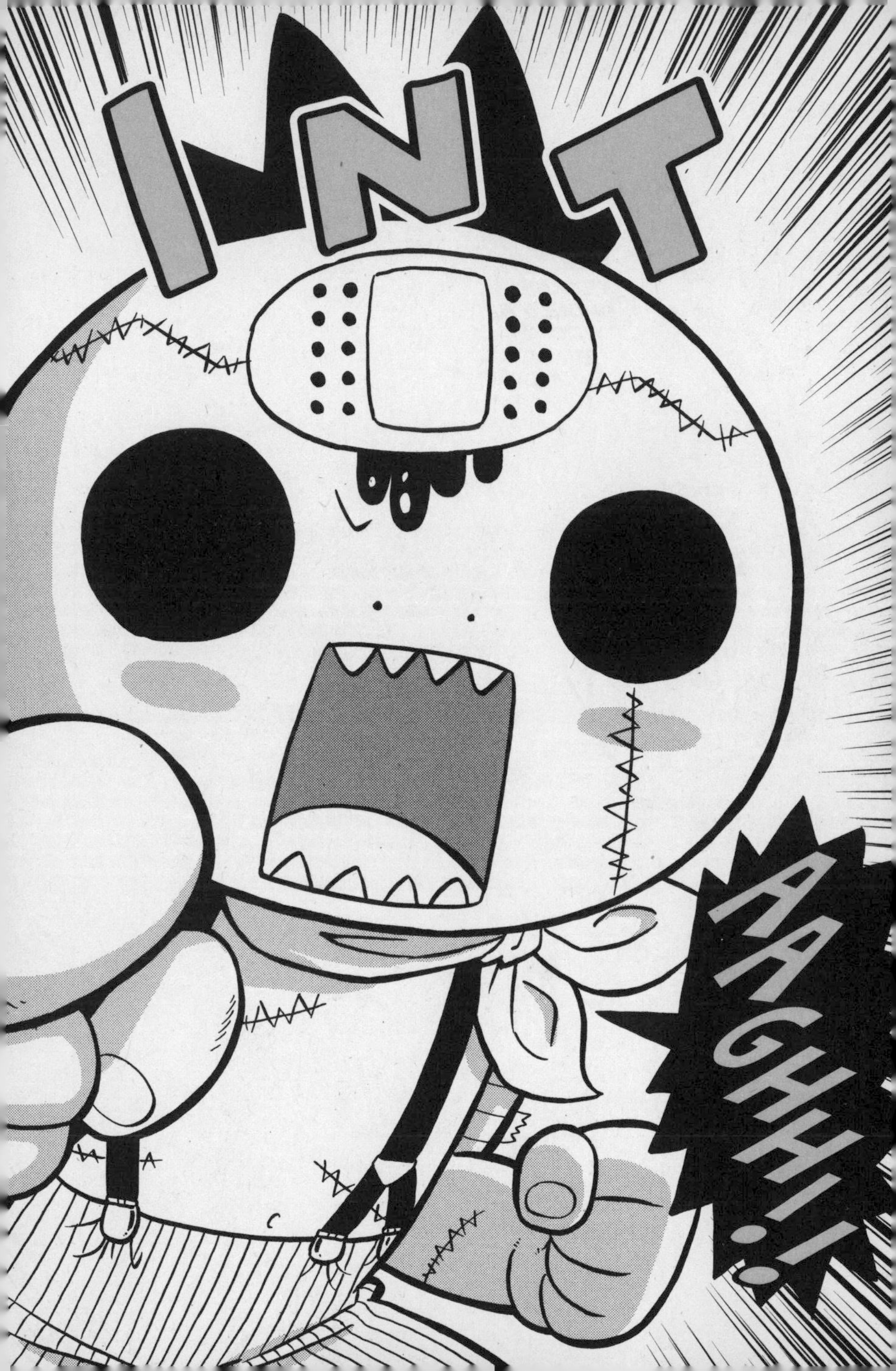
INT
AAGHH!!

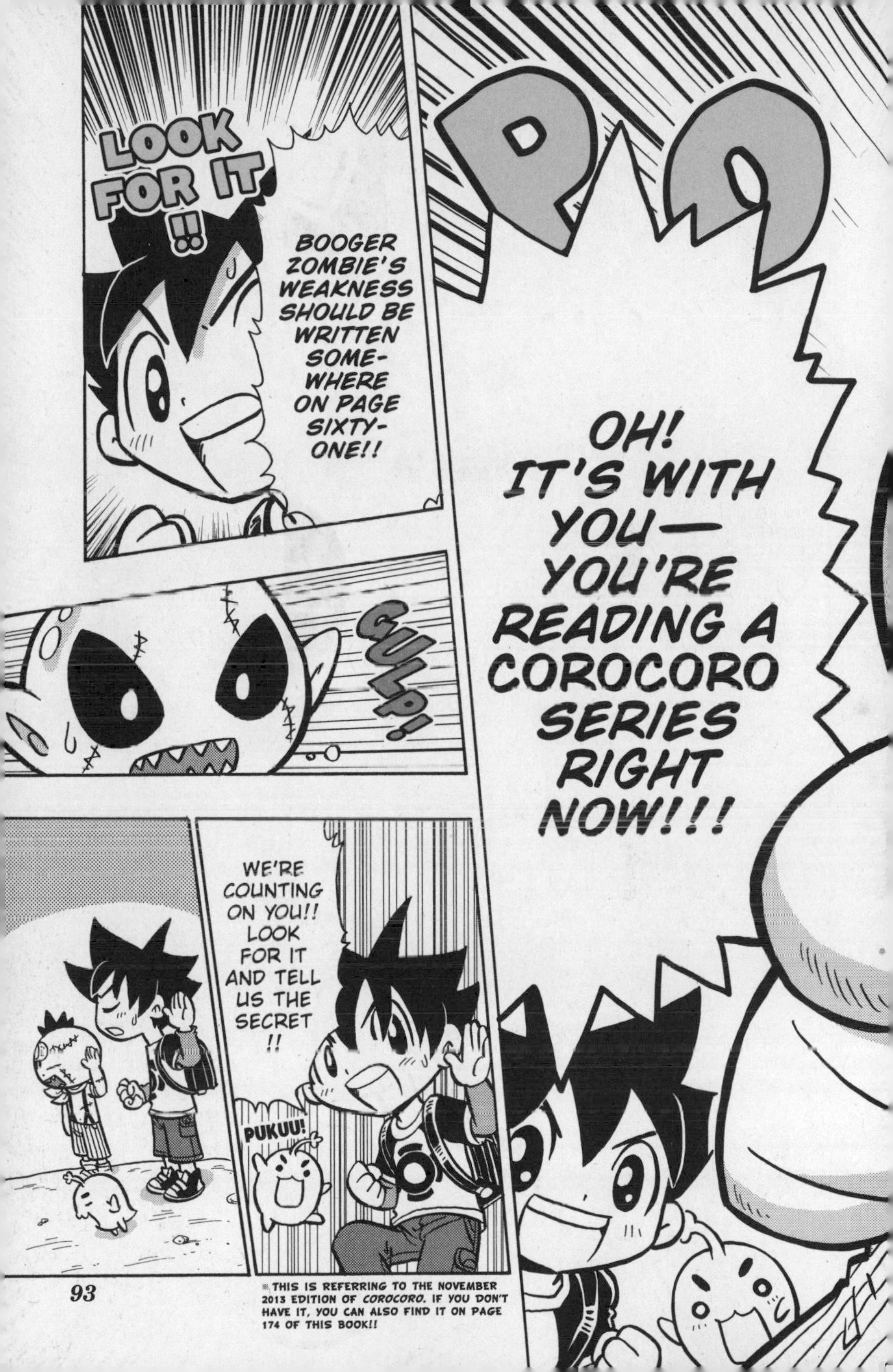
OH! IT'S WITH YOU— YOU'RE READING A COROCORO SERIES RIGHT NOW!!!
LOOK FOR IT!!
BOOGER ZOMBIE'S WEAKNESS SHOULD BE WRITTEN SOMEWHERE ON PAGE SIXTY-ONE!!
GULP!
WE'RE COUNTING ON YOU!! LOOK FOR IT AND TELL US THE SECRET!!
PUKUU!

※THIS IS REFERRING TO THE NOVEMBER 2013 EDITION OF *COROCORO*. IF YOU DON'T HAVE IT, YOU CAN ALSO FIND IT ON PAGE 174 OF THIS BOOK!!

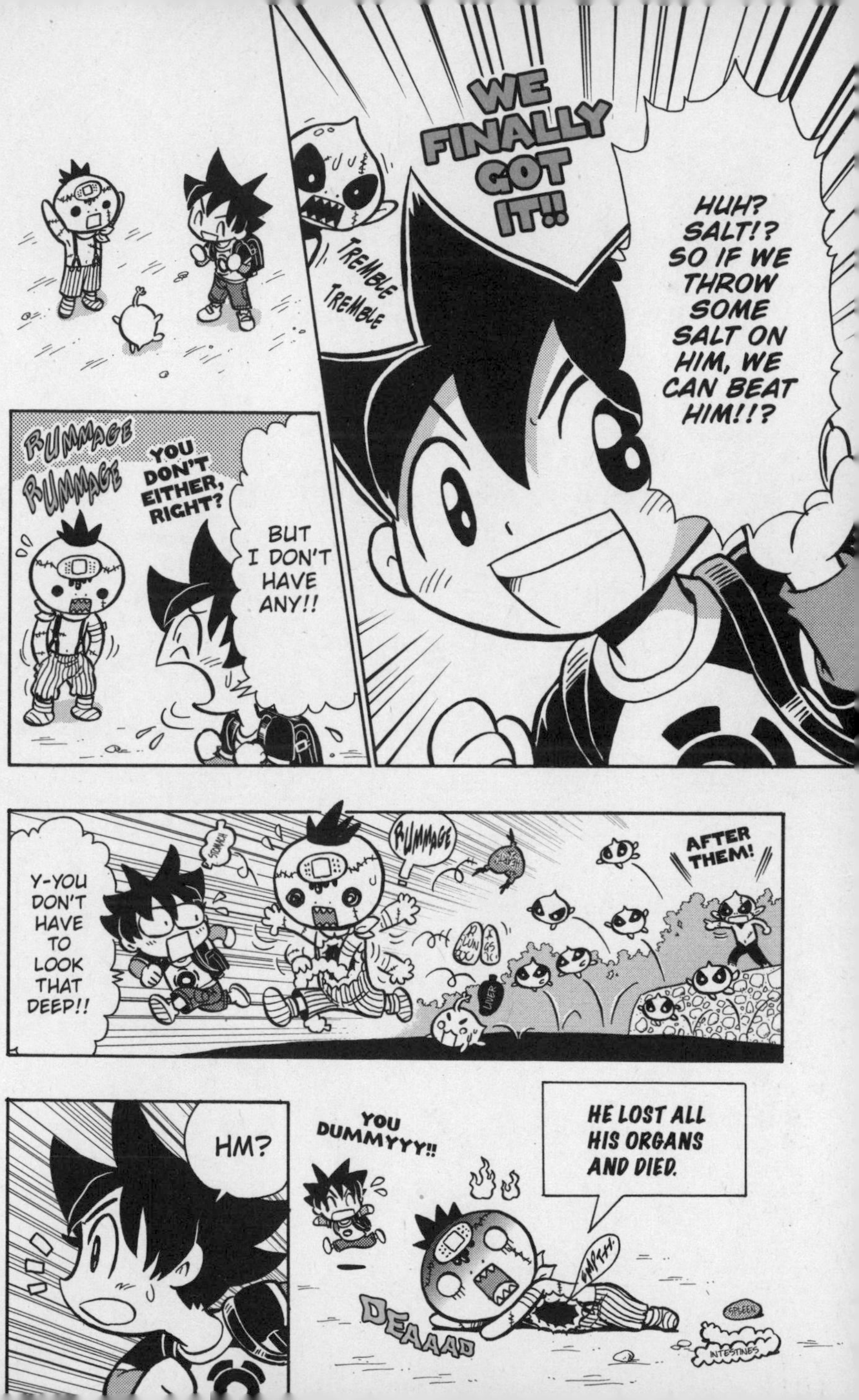
HUH? SALT!? SO IF WE THROW SOME SALT ON HIM, WE CAN BEAT HIM!!?
WE FINALLY GOT IT!!
TREMBLE TREMBLE
YOU DON'T EITHER, RIGHT?
BUT I DON'T HAVE ANY!!
RUMMAGE RUMMAGE
AFTER THEM!
RUMMAGE
STOMACH
LIVER
Y-YOU DON'T HAVE TO LOOK THAT DEEP!!
HE LOST ALL HIS ORGANS AND DIED.
YOU DUMMYYY!!
DEAAAD
SPLEEN
INTESTINES
HM?

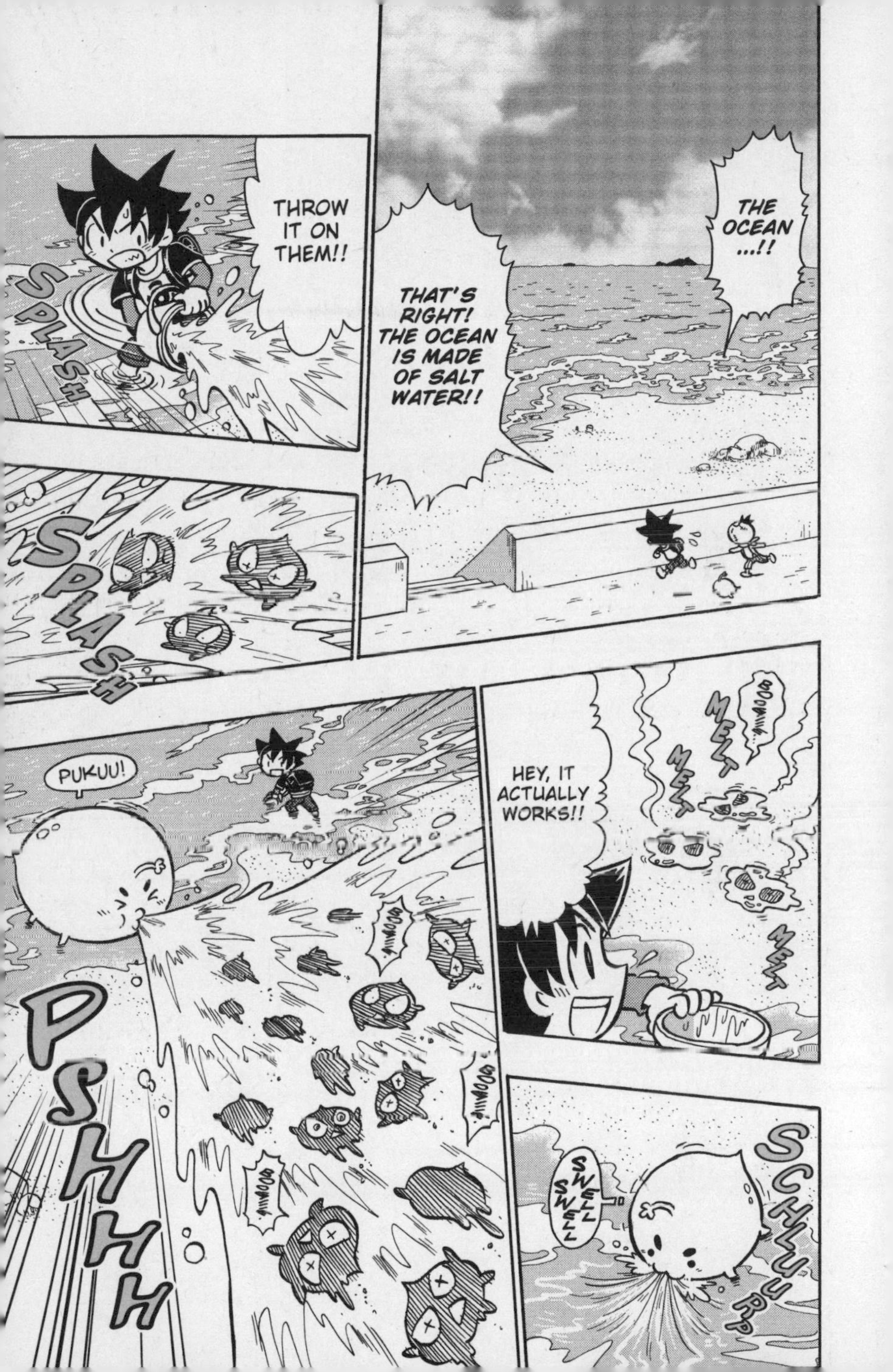
THE OCEAN ...!!
THAT'S RIGHT! THE OCEAN IS MADE OF SALT WATER!!
THROW IT ON THEM!!
SPLASH
SPLASH
HEY, IT ACTUALLY WORKS!!
MELT
MELT
MELT
SCHLURP
SWELL SWELL
PUKUU!
PSHHHH

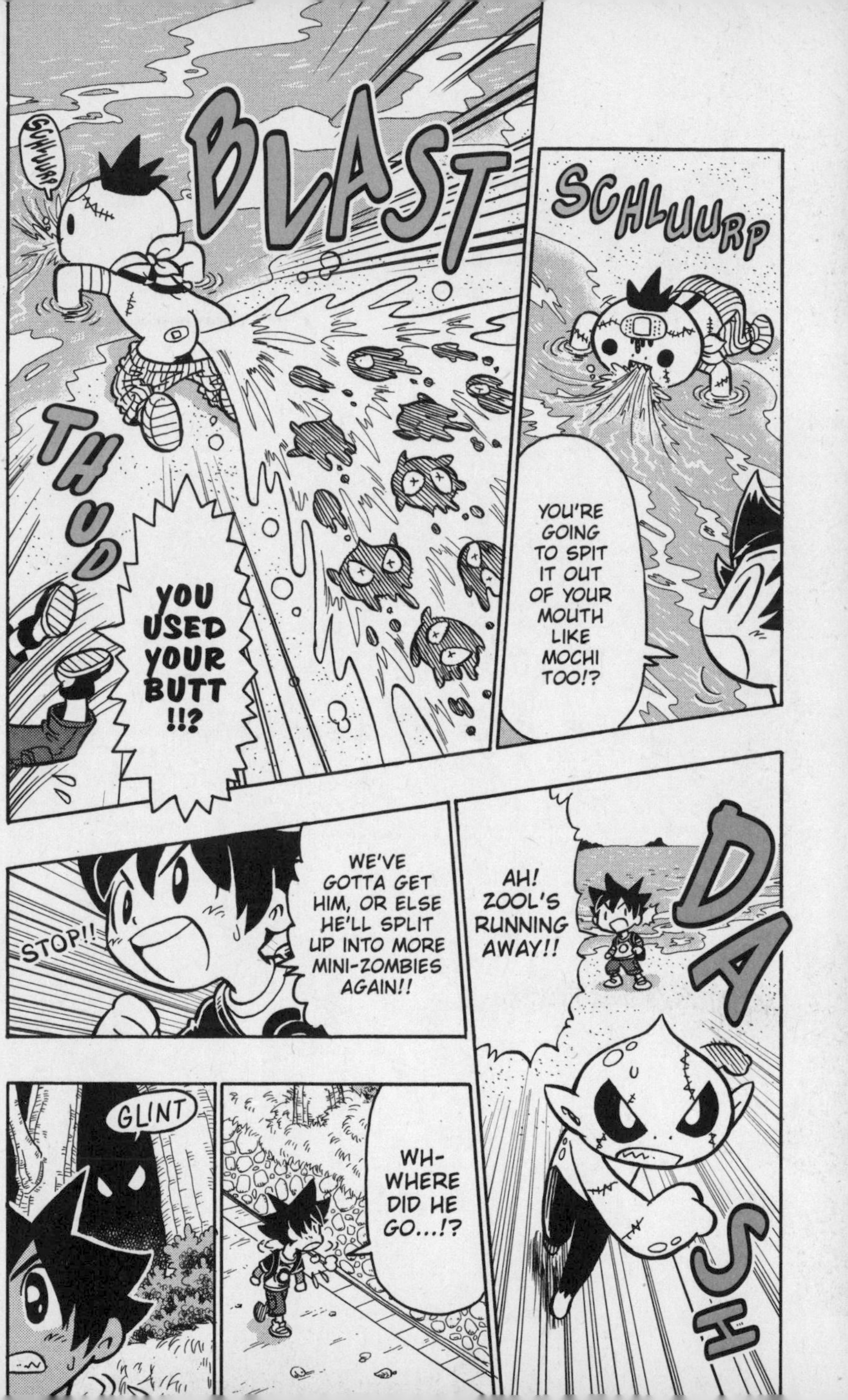
SCHLUURP
YOU'RE GOING TO SPIT IT OUT OF YOUR MOUTH LIKE MOCHI TOO!?
SCHLUURP?
BLAST
THUD
YOU USED YOUR BUTT!!?
DA
AH! ZOOL'S RUNNING AWAY!!
SH
WE'VE GOTTA GET HIM, OR ELSE HE'LL SPLIT UP INTO MORE MINI-ZOMBIES AGAIN!!
STOP!!
WH-WHERE DID HE GO...!?
GLINT

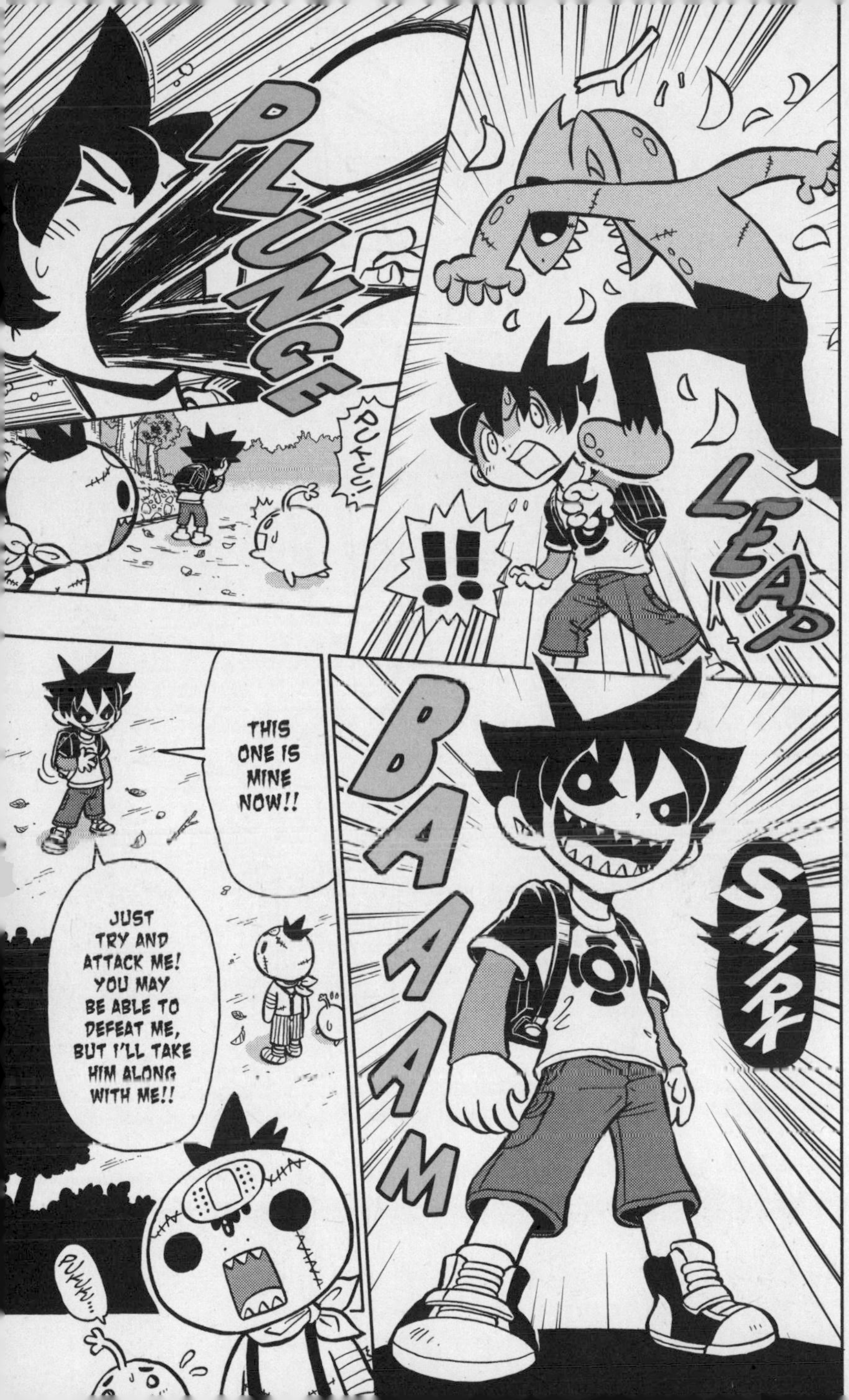
!!
LEAP
PLUNGE
PUKUU!
BAAAM
SMIRK
THIS ONE IS MINE NOW!!
JUST TRY AND ATTACK ME! YOU MAY BE ABLE TO DEFEAT ME, BUT I'LL TAKE HIM ALONG WITH ME!!
PUKUKU...

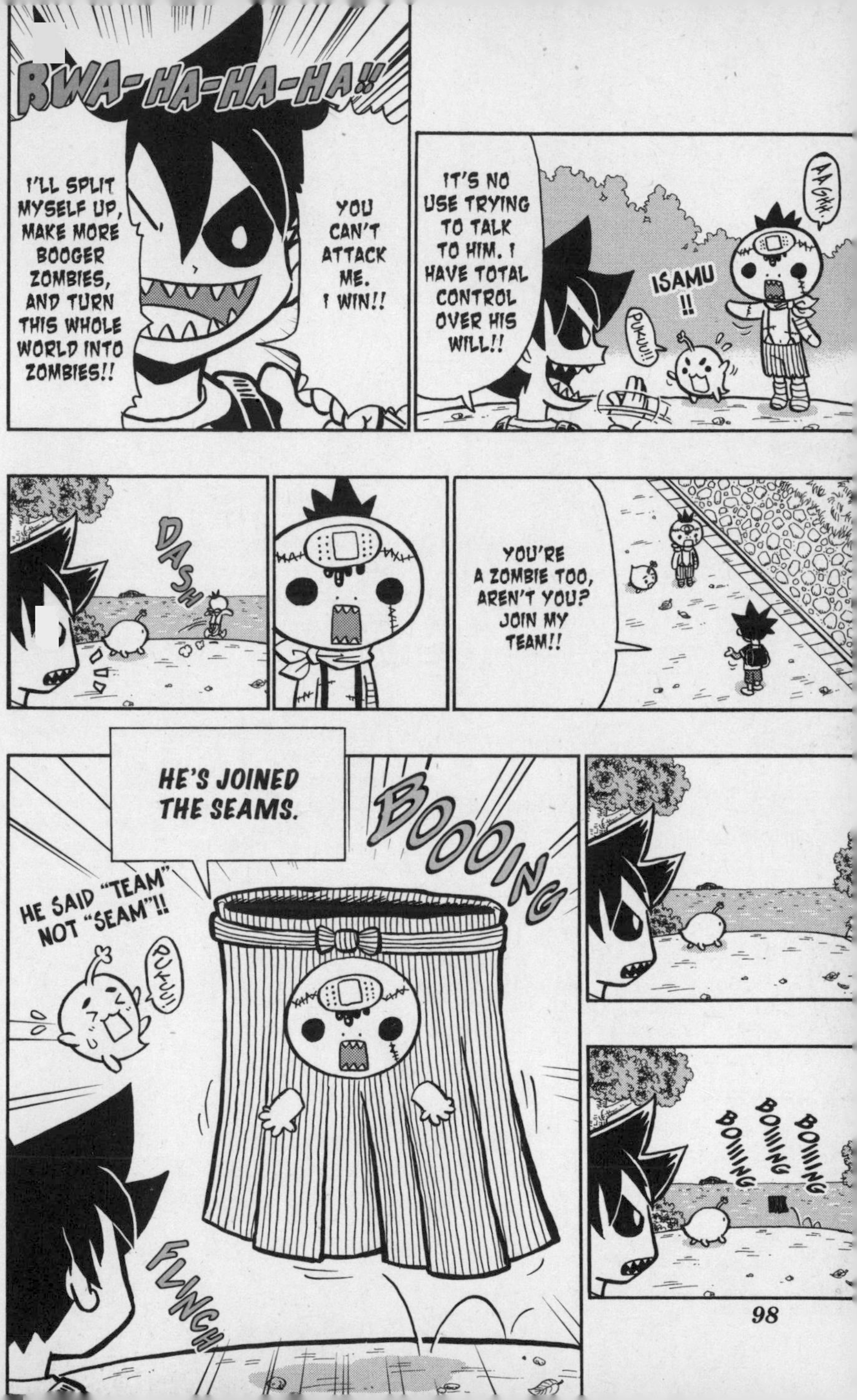

AAGHK.
ISAMU!!
IT'S NO USE TRYING TO TALK TO HIM. I HAVE TOTAL CONTROL OVER HIS WILL!!
PUKUU!!
BWA-HA-HA-HA!!
YOU CAN'T ATTACK ME. I WIN!!
I'LL SPLIT MYSELF UP, MAKE MORE BOOGER ZOMBIES, AND TURN THIS WHOLE WORLD INTO ZOMBIES!!
YOU'RE A ZOMBIE TOO, AREN'T YOU? JOIN MY TEAM!!
DASH
BOIIIING
BOIIIING
BOIIIING
BOOOING
HE'S JOINED THE SEAMS.
HE SAID "TEAM" NOT "SEAM"!!
PUKUU!!
FLINCH

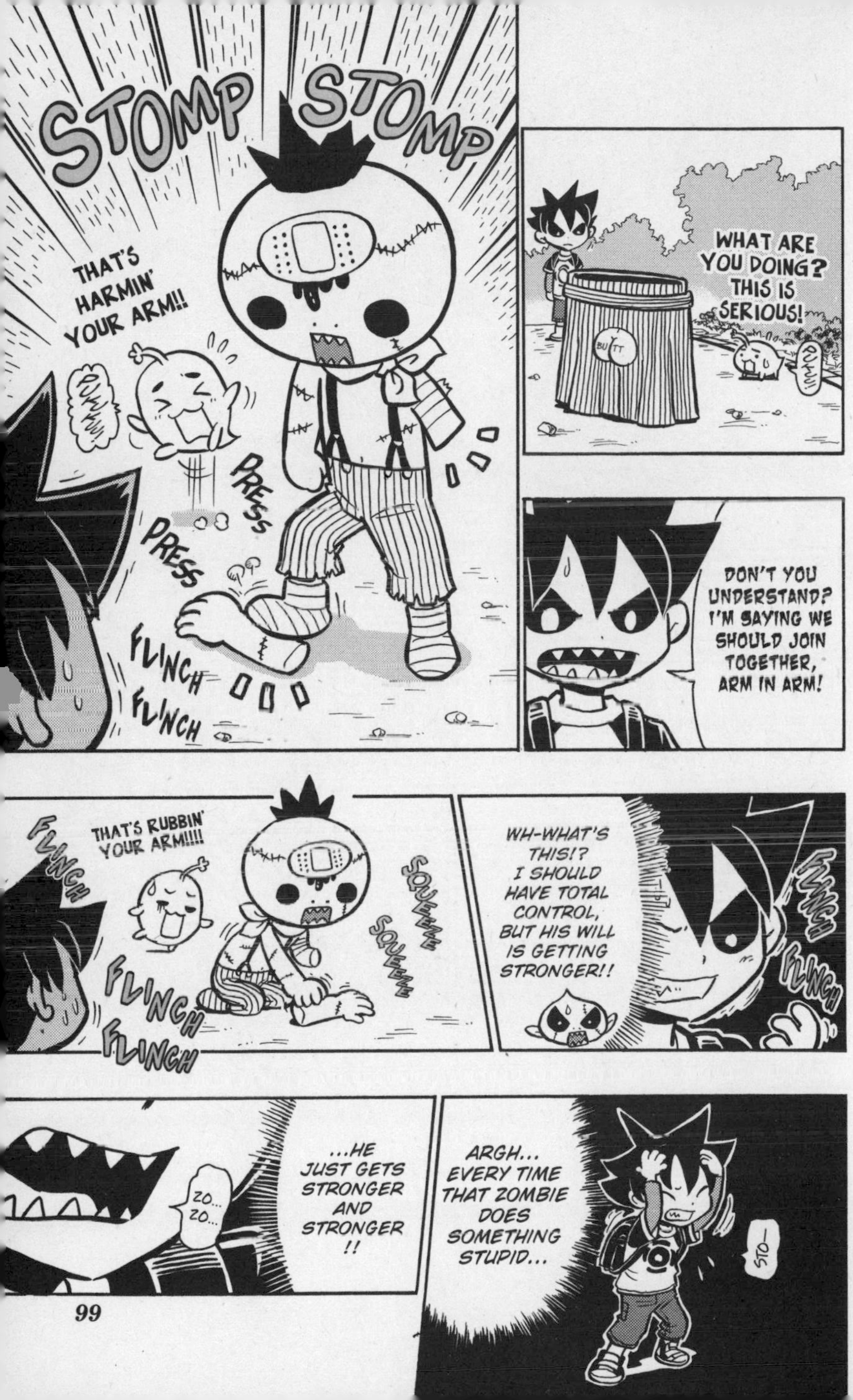

WHAT ARE YOU DOING? THIS IS SERIOUS!
BUTT
DON'T YOU UNDERSTAND? I'M SAYING WE SHOULD JOIN TOGETHER, ARM IN ARM!
STOMP STOMP
THAT'S HARMIN' YOUR ARM!!
PRESS
PRESS
FLINCH
FLINCH
WH-WHAT'S THIS!? I SHOULD HAVE TOTAL CONTROL, BUT HIS WILL IS GETTING STRONGER!!
FLINCH
FLINCH
THAT'S RUBBIN' YOUR ARM!!!!
SQUEEEZE
SQUEEEZE
FLINCH
FLINCH
FLINCH
ARGH... EVERY TIME THAT ZOMBIE DOES SOMETHING STUPID...
STO—
...HE JUST GETS STRONGER AND STRONGER!!
ZO... ZO...

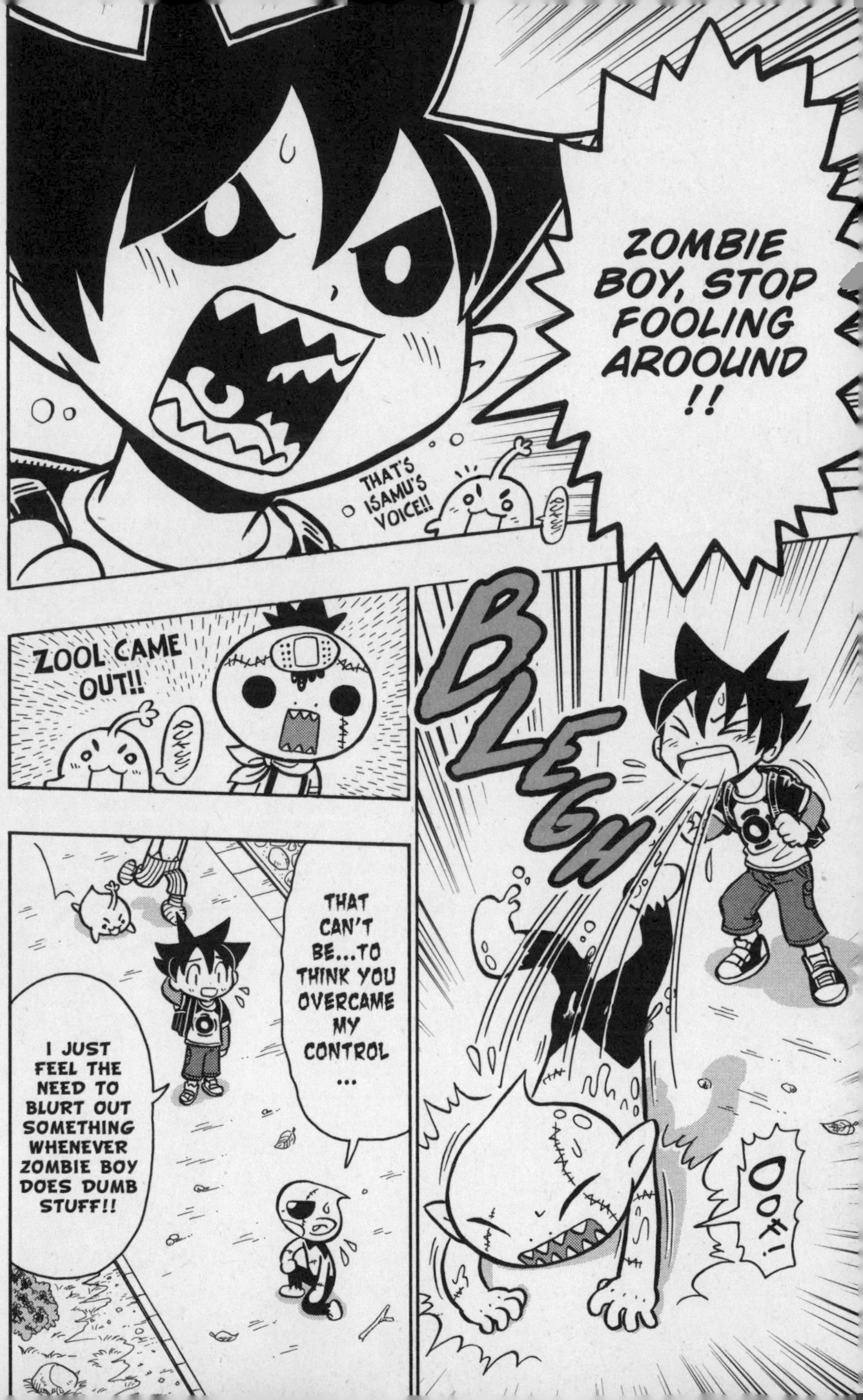
ZOMBIE BOY, STOP FOOLING AROOUND!!
THAT'S ISAMU'S VOICE!!
BLEGH
OOF!
ZOOL CAME OUT!!
THAT CAN'T BE...TO THINK YOU OVERCAME MY CONTROL...
I JUST FEEL THE NEED TO BLURT OUT SOMETHING WHENEVER ZOMBIE BOY DOES DUMB STUFF!!

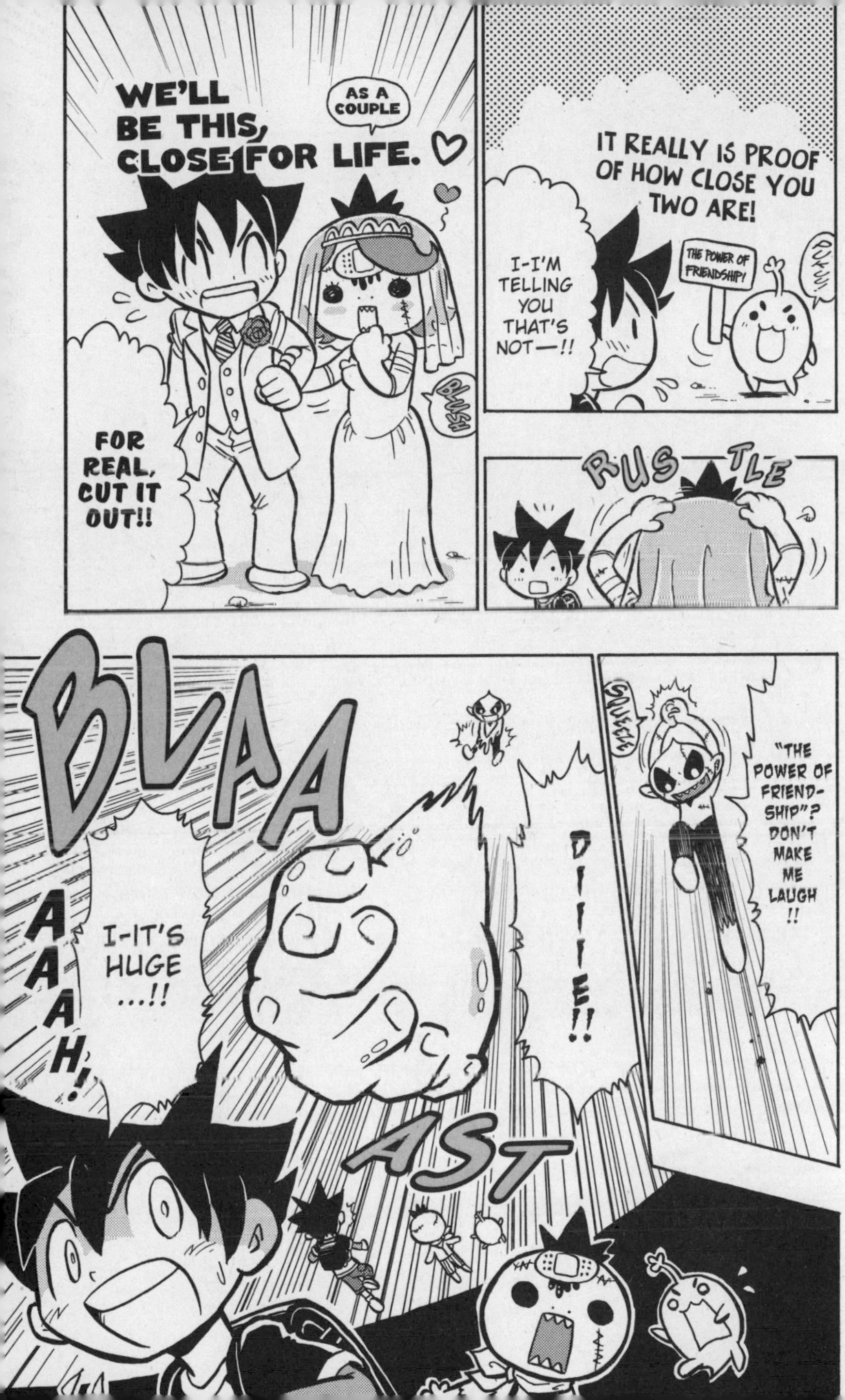
IT REALLY IS PROOF OF HOW CLOSE YOU TWO ARE!
THE POWER OF FRIENDSHIP!
PUKYU!
I-I'M TELLING YOU THAT'S NOT—!!
RUSTLE
WE'LL BE THIS, CLOSE FOR LIFE. ♡
AS A COUPLE
BLUSH
FOR REAL, CUT IT OUT!!
SQUEEZE
"THE POWER OF FRIEND-SHIP"? DON'T MAKE ME LAUGH!!
DIIIIE!!
BLAAAST
I-IT'S HUGE...!!
AAAAH!

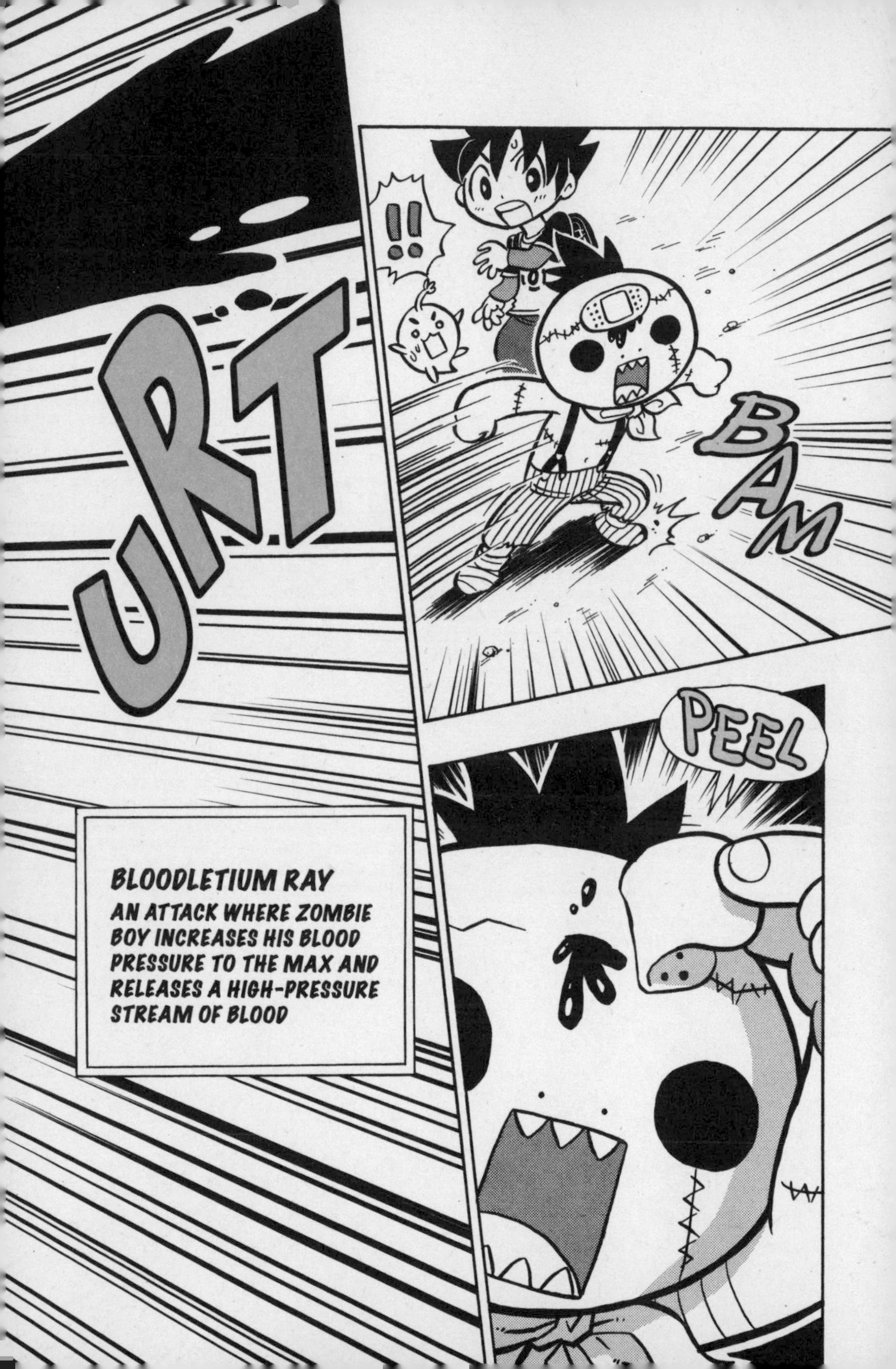
!!
BAM
PEEL
URT
BLOODLETIUM RAY
AN ATTACK WHERE ZOMBIE BOY INCREASES HIS BLOOD PRESSURE TO THE MAX AND RELEASES A HIGH-PRESSURE STREAM OF BLOOD

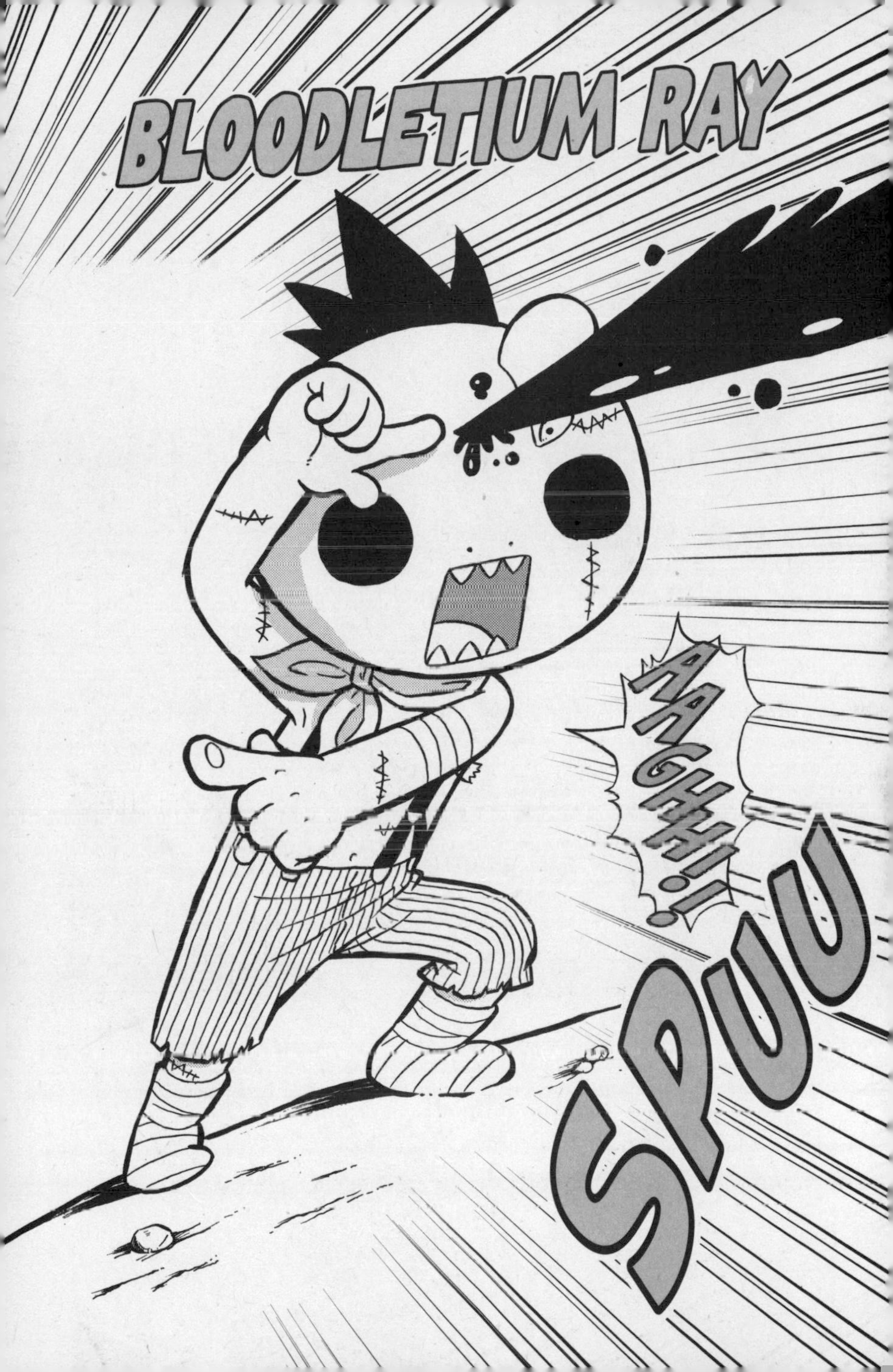
BLOODLETIUM RAY
AAGH!!!
SPUU

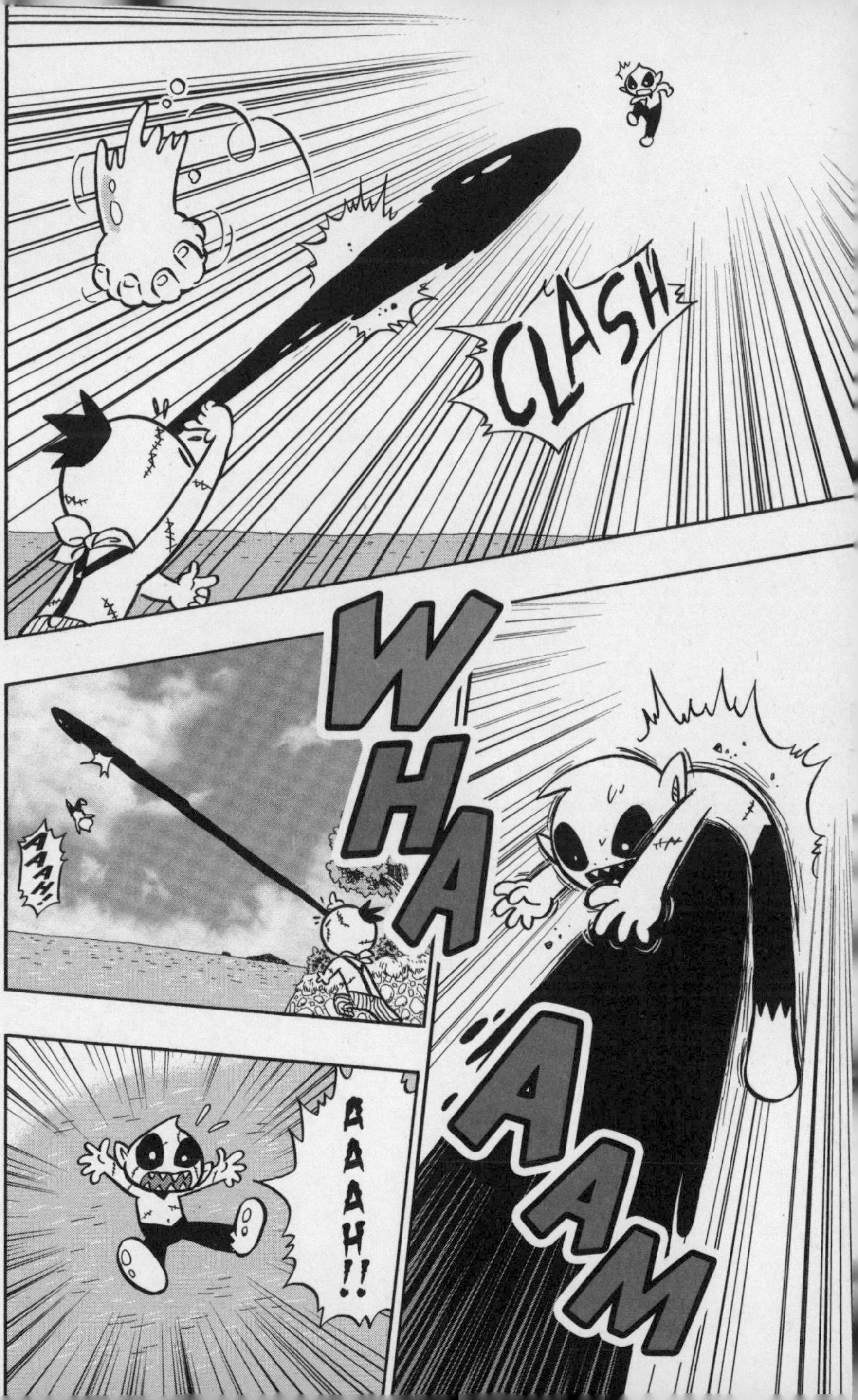

CLASH
WHAAAAM
AAAAH!
AAAAH!!

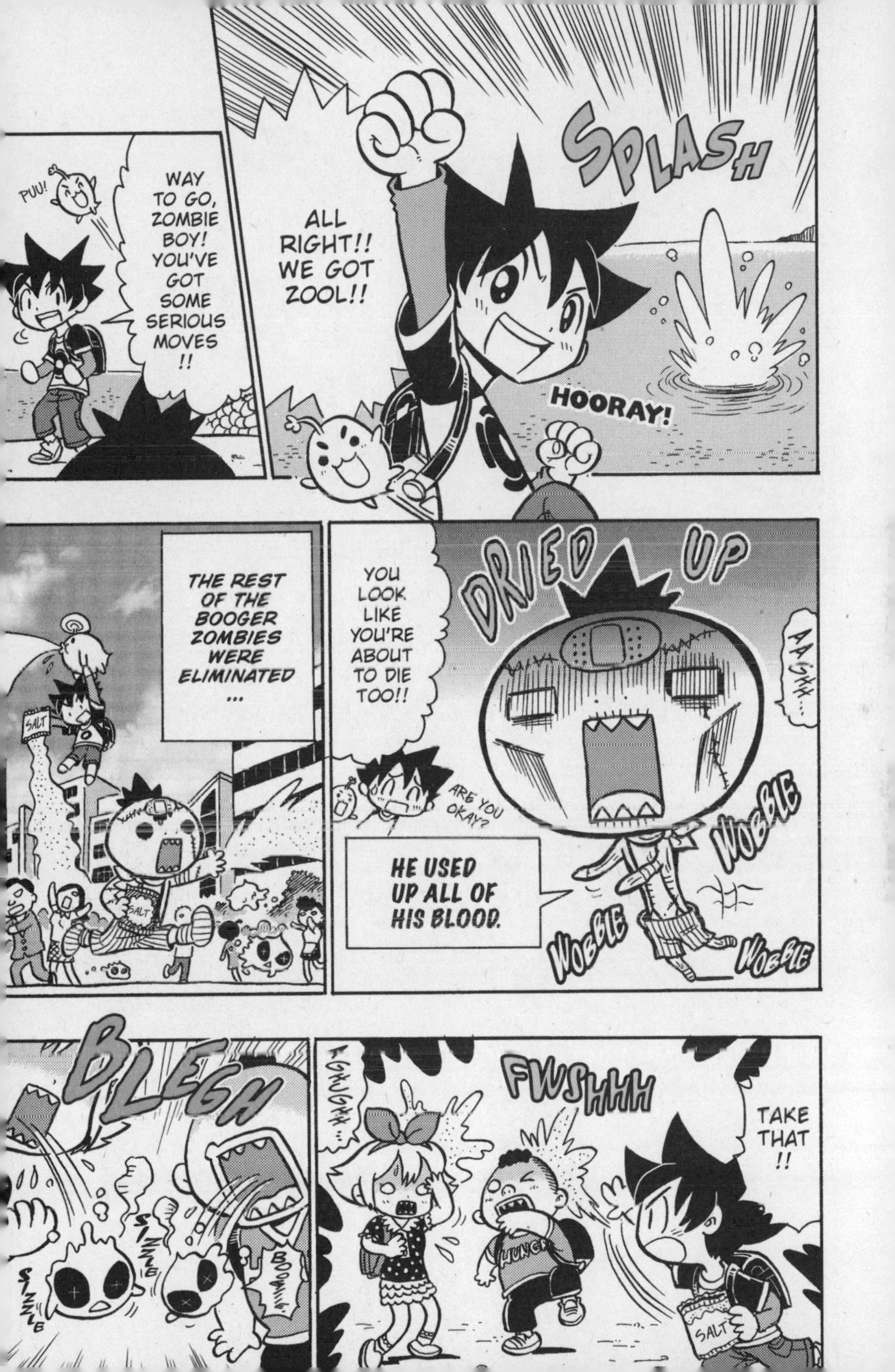

SPLASH
ALL RIGHT!! WE GOT ZOOL!!
HOORAY!
PUU!
WAY TO GO, ZOMBIE BOY! YOU'VE GOT SOME SERIOUS MOVES !!
DRIED UP
AAGHH...
YOU LOOK LIKE YOU'RE ABOUT TO DIE TOO!!
ARE YOU OKAY?
WOBBLE
WOBBLE
WOBBLE
HE USED UP ALL OF HIS BLOOD.
THE REST OF THE BOOGER ZOMBIES WERE ELIMINATED ...
SALT
SALT
TAKE THAT !!
FWSHHH
SALT
BLEGH
SIZZLE
SIZZLE

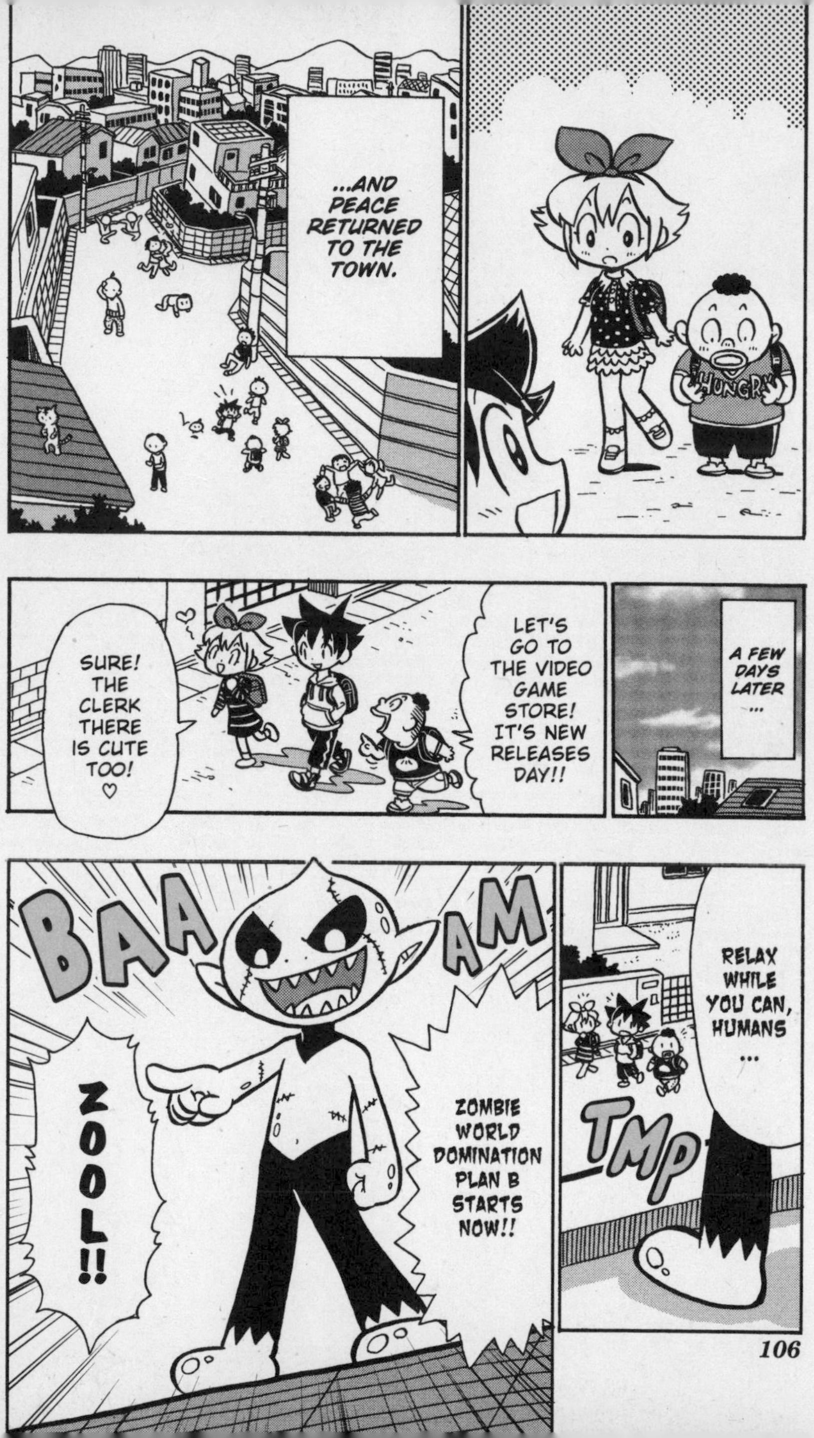
...AND PEACE RETURNED TO THE TOWN.
A FEW DAYS LATER ...
LET'S GO TO THE VIDEO GAME STORE! IT'S NEW RELEASES DAY!!
SURE! THE CLERK THERE IS CUTE TOO! ♡
TMP
RELAX WHILE YOU CAN, HUMANS ...
BAAAM
ZOMBIE WORLD DOMINATION PLAN B STARTS NOW!!
ZOOL!!

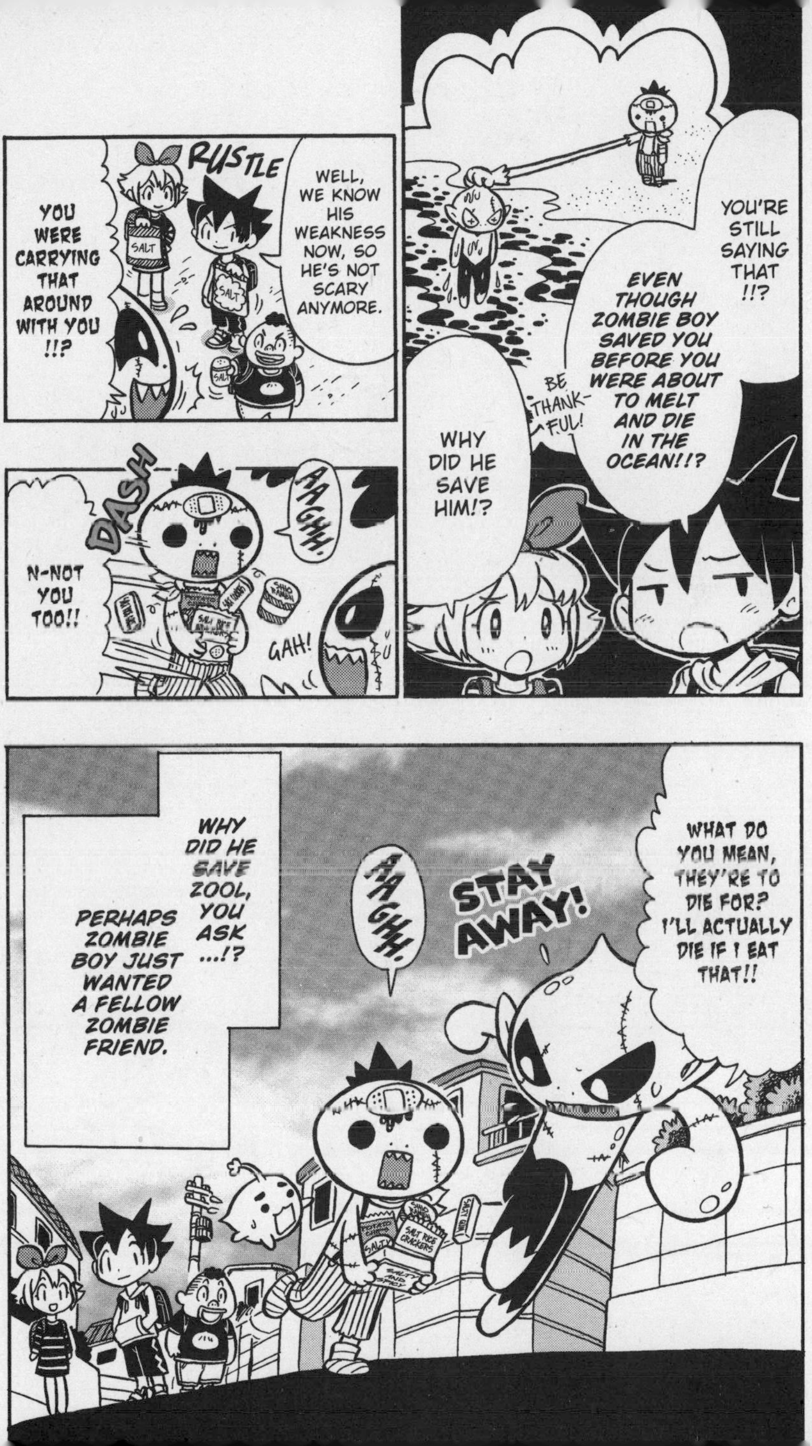
YOU'RE STILL SAYING THAT !!?
EVEN THOUGH ZOMBIE BOY SAVED YOU BEFORE YOU WERE ABOUT TO MELT AND DIE IN THE OCEAN!!?
BE THANKFUL!
WHY DID HE SAVE HIM!?
RUSTLE
WELL, WE KNOW HIS WEAKNESS NOW, SO HE'S NOT SCARY ANYMORE.
SALT
SALT
SALT
YOU WERE CARRYING THAT AROUND WITH YOU !!?
AAGHH.
DASH
N-NOT YOU TOO!!
GAH!
WHAT DO YOU MEAN, THEY'RE TO DIE FOR? I'LL ACTUALLY DIE IF I EAT THAT!!
STAY AWAY!
AAGHH.
WHY DID HE SAVE ZOOL, YOU ASK ...!?
PERHAPS ZOMBIE BOY JUST WANTED A FELLOW ZOMBIE FRIEND.
SALT RICE CRACKERS
SALTY AND SPICY

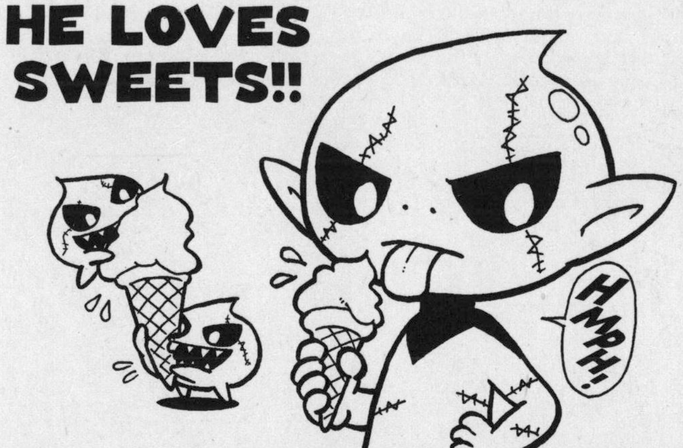
HE LOVES SWEETS!!
HMPH!

THE BATTLE'Z ON!

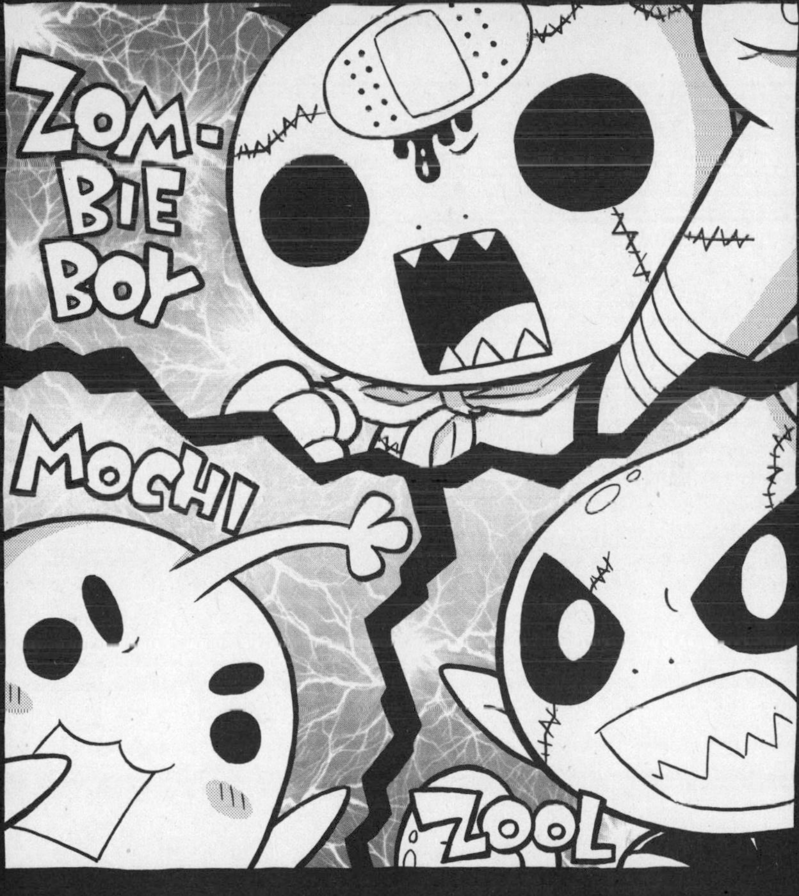
ZOM-BIE BOY
MOCHI
ZOOL

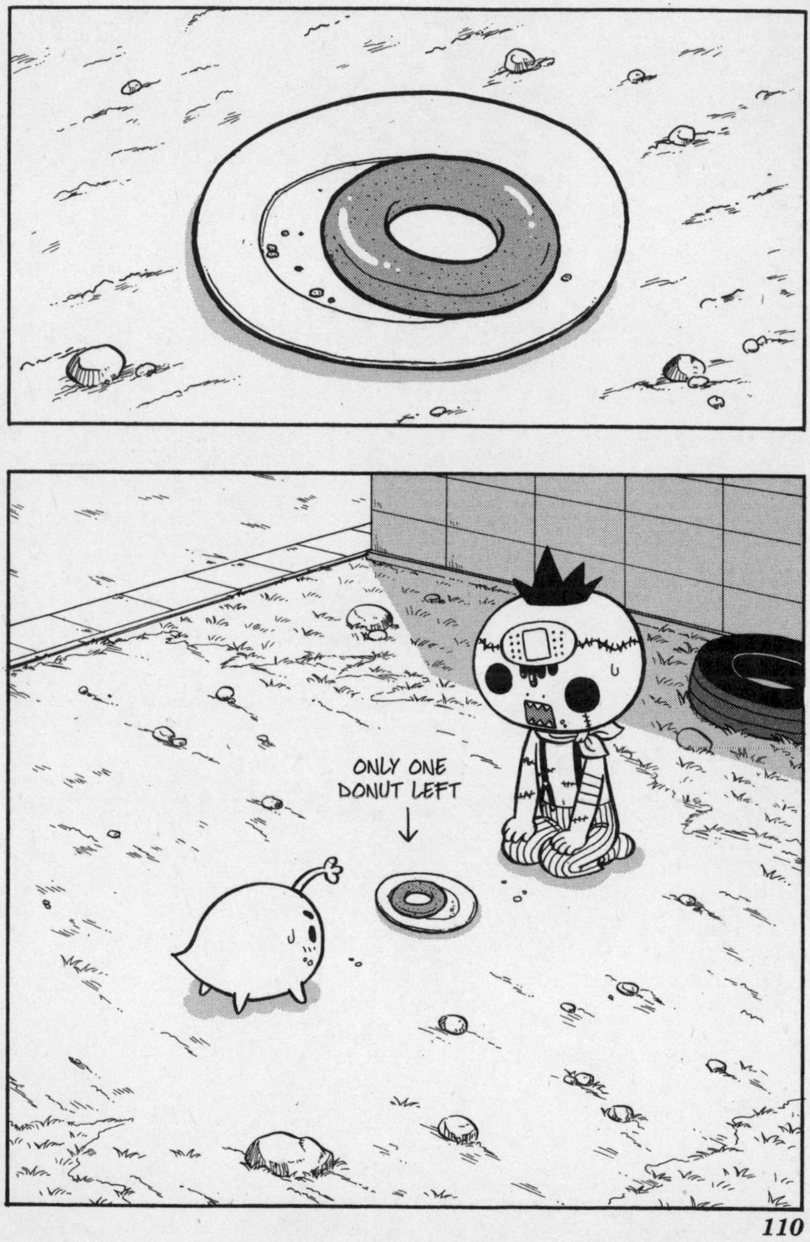
ONLY ONE
DONUT LEFT

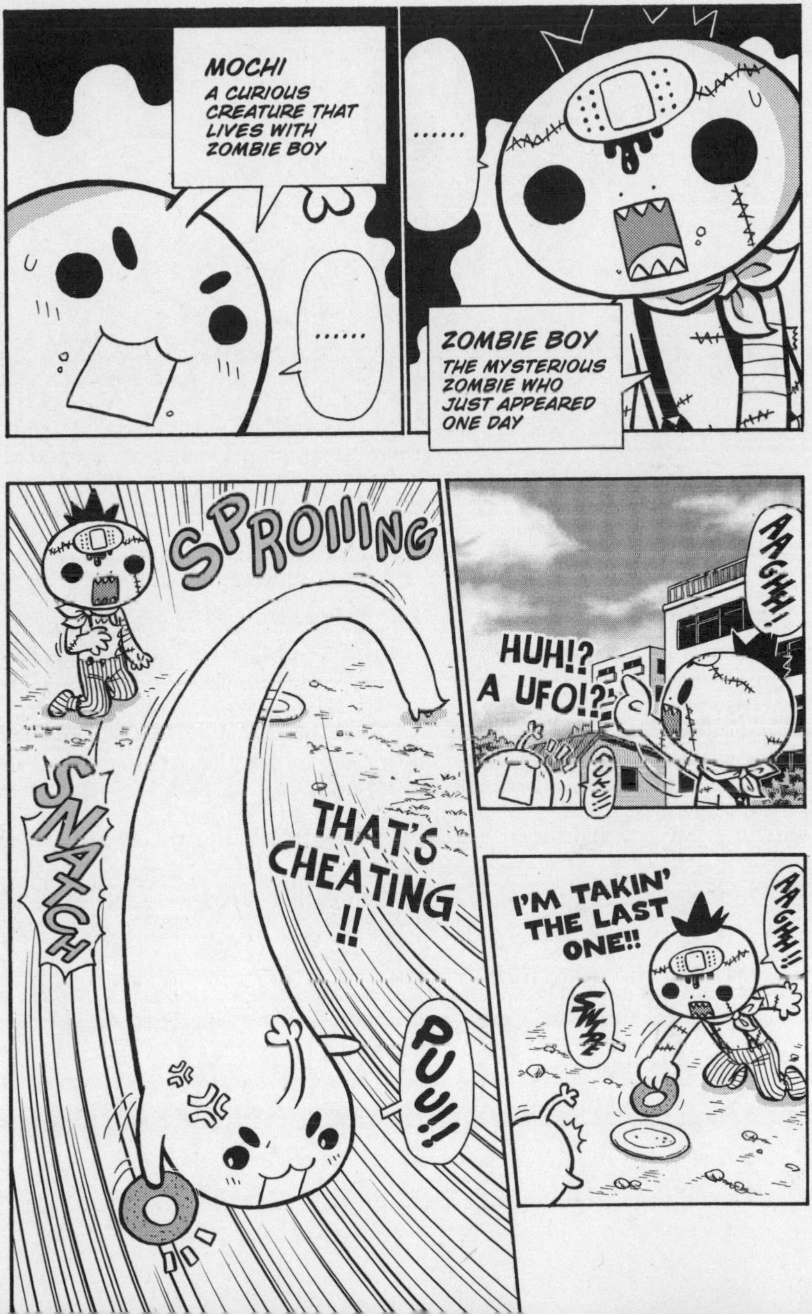
......
ZOMBIE BOY
THE MYSTERIOUS ZOMBIE WHO JUST APPEARED ONE DAY
MOCHI
A CURIOUS CREATURE THAT LIVES WITH ZOMBIE BOY
......
AAGHH!
HUH!? A UFO!?
UKK!!
AAGHH!!
I'M TAKIN' THE LAST ONE!!
SPROIIING
THAT'S CHEATING!!
SNATCH
PUU!!

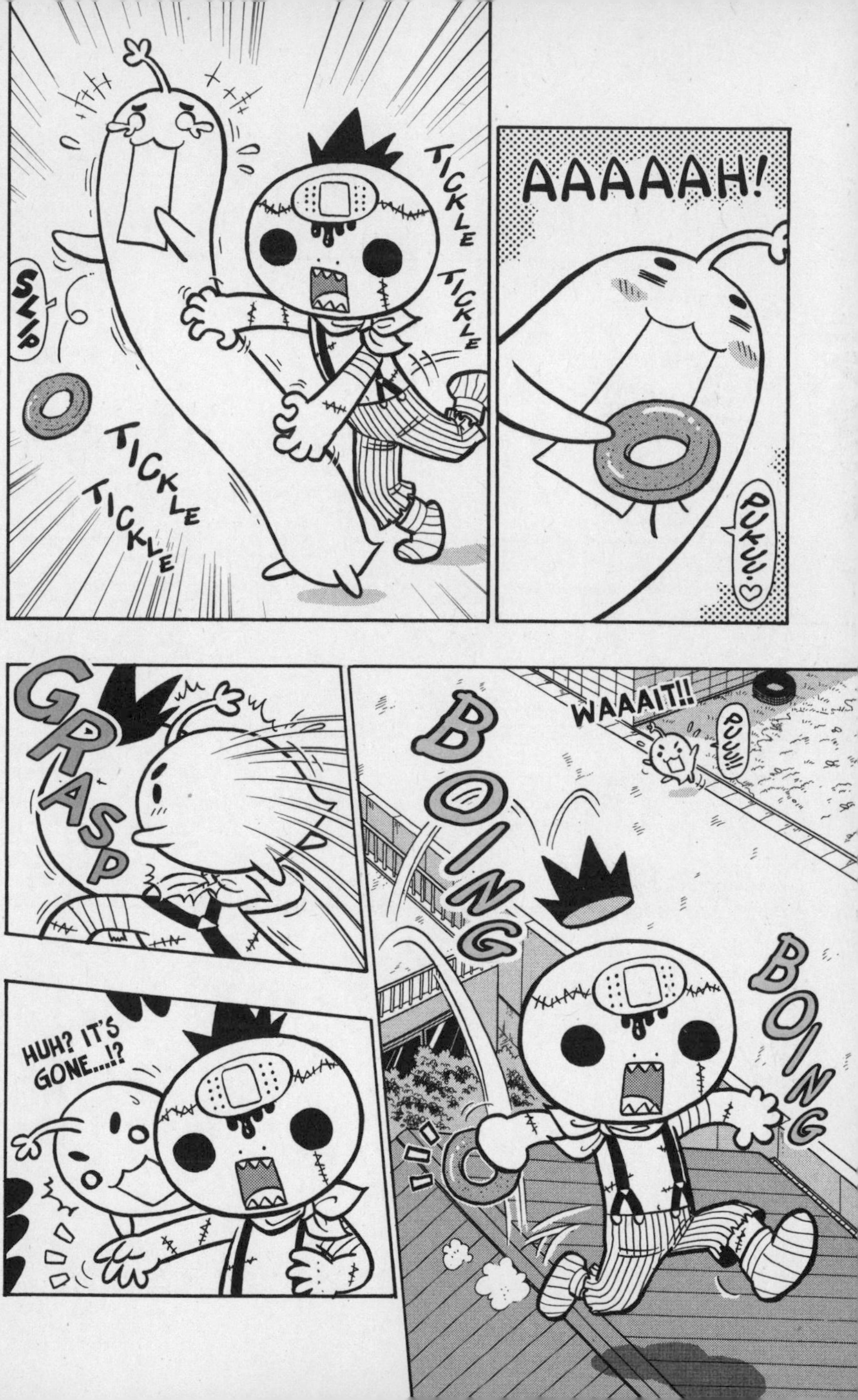
AAAAAH!
PUKUU♡
TICKLE TICKLE
SLIP
TICKLE TICKLE
WAAAIT!!
PUUU!!
BOING
BOING
GRASP
HUH? IT'S GONE...!?

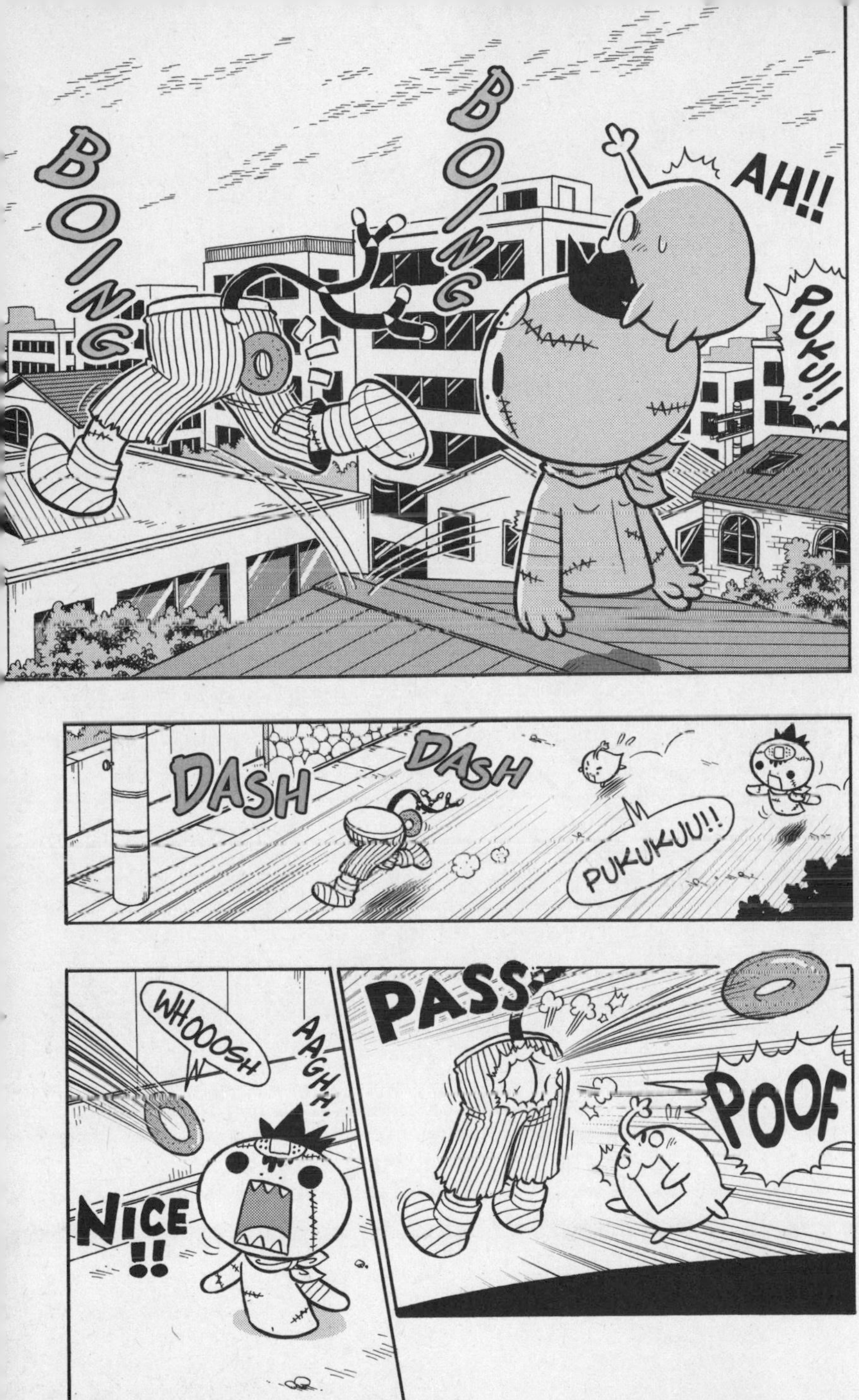
AH!!
PUKU!!
BOING
BOING
PUKUKUU!!
DASH
DASH
PASS
POOF
WHOOOSH
AAGHH
NICE!!

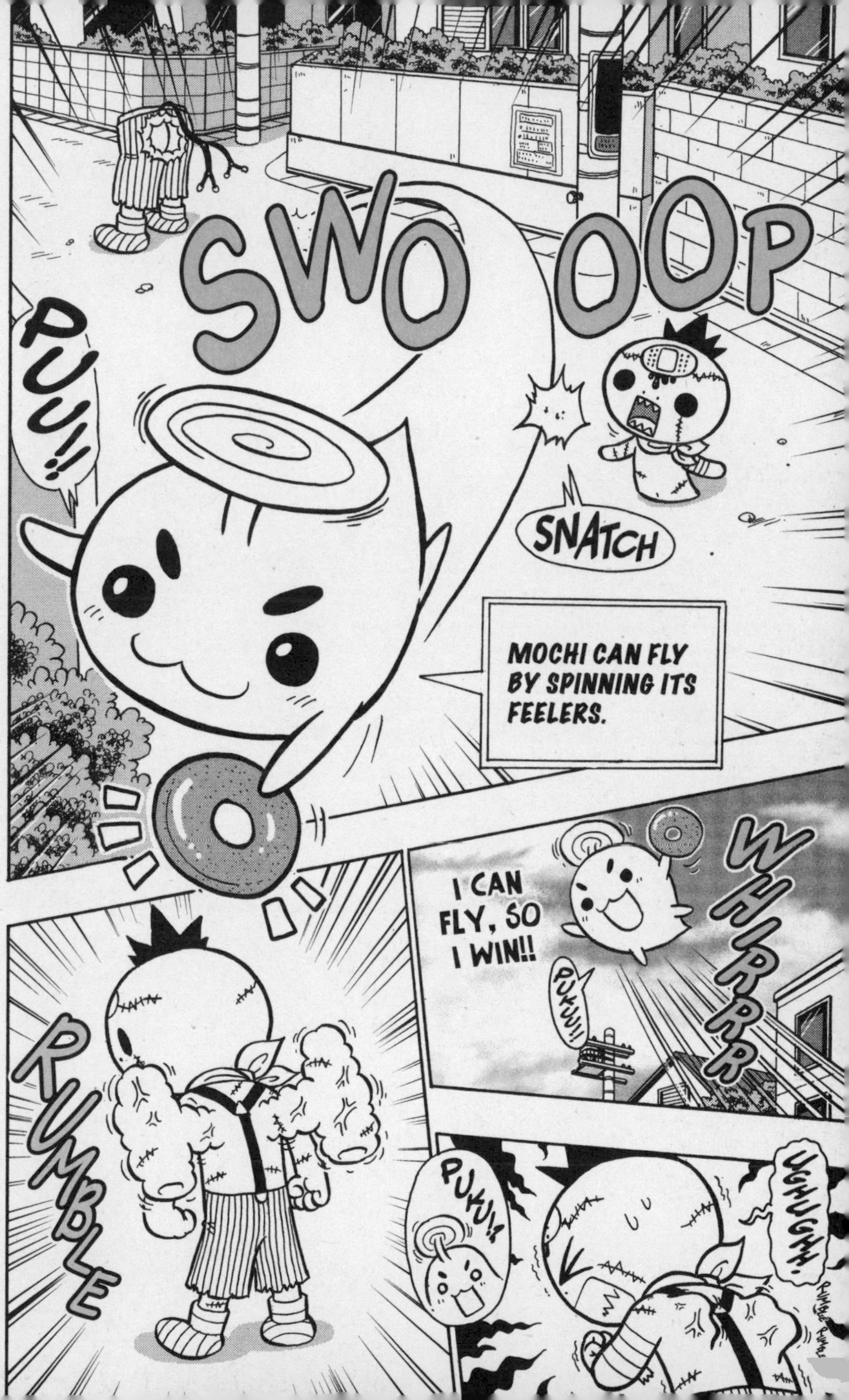
SWOOOP
SNATCH
MOCHI CAN FLY BY SPINNING ITS FEELERS.
PUU!!
WHIRRR
I CAN FLY, SO I WIN!!
PUKU!!
UGHUGHH.
RUMBLE RUMBLE
PUKU!!
RUMBLE

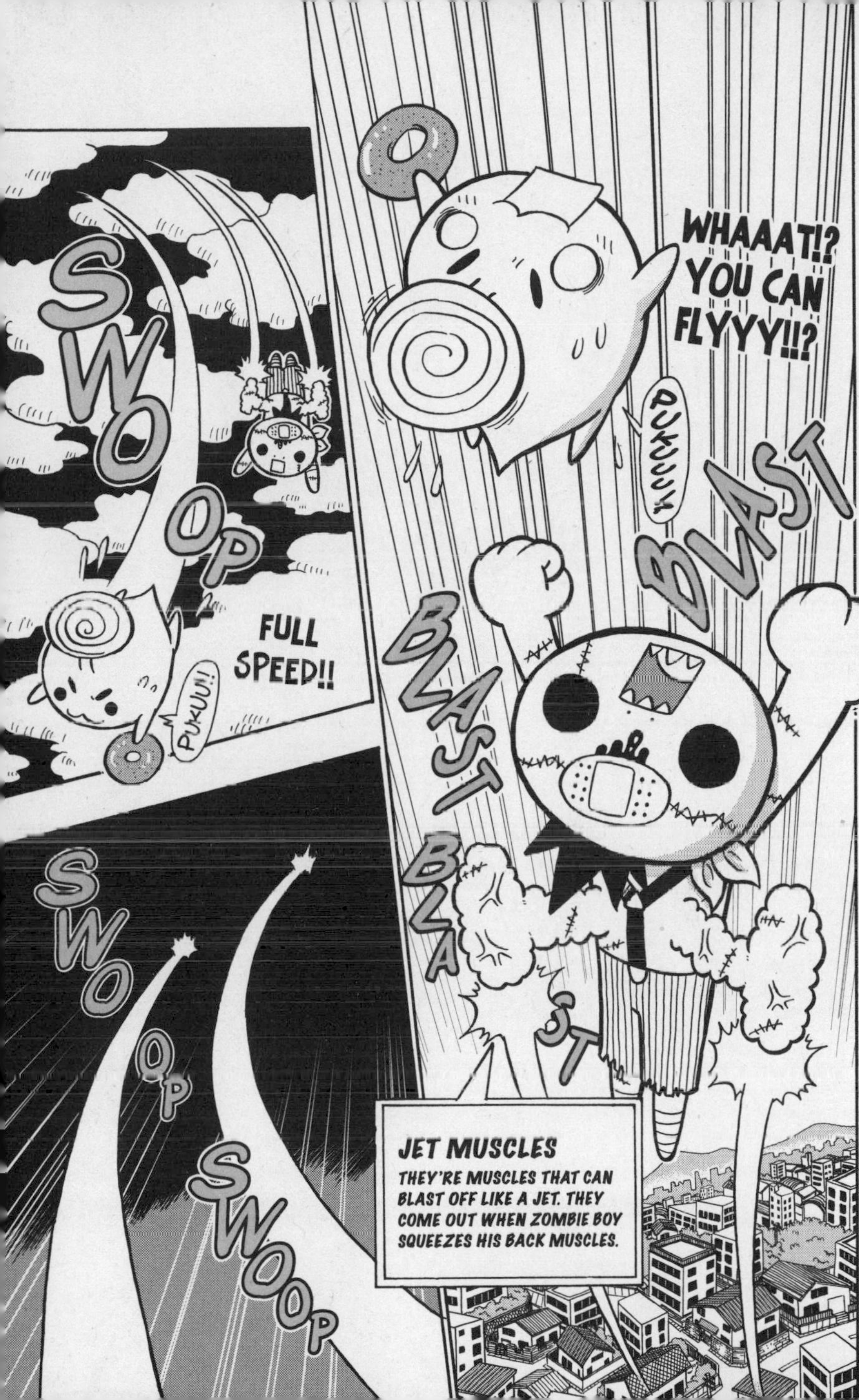
WHAAAT!? YOU CAN FLYYY!!?
PUKUUUU
BLAST
BLAST BLAST BLAST
JET MUSCLES
THEY'RE MUSCLES THAT CAN BLAST OFF LIKE A JET. THEY COME OUT WHEN ZOMBIE BOY SQUEEZES HIS BACK MUSCLES.
SWOOP
FULL SPEED!!
PUKUU!
SWOOP
SWOOP

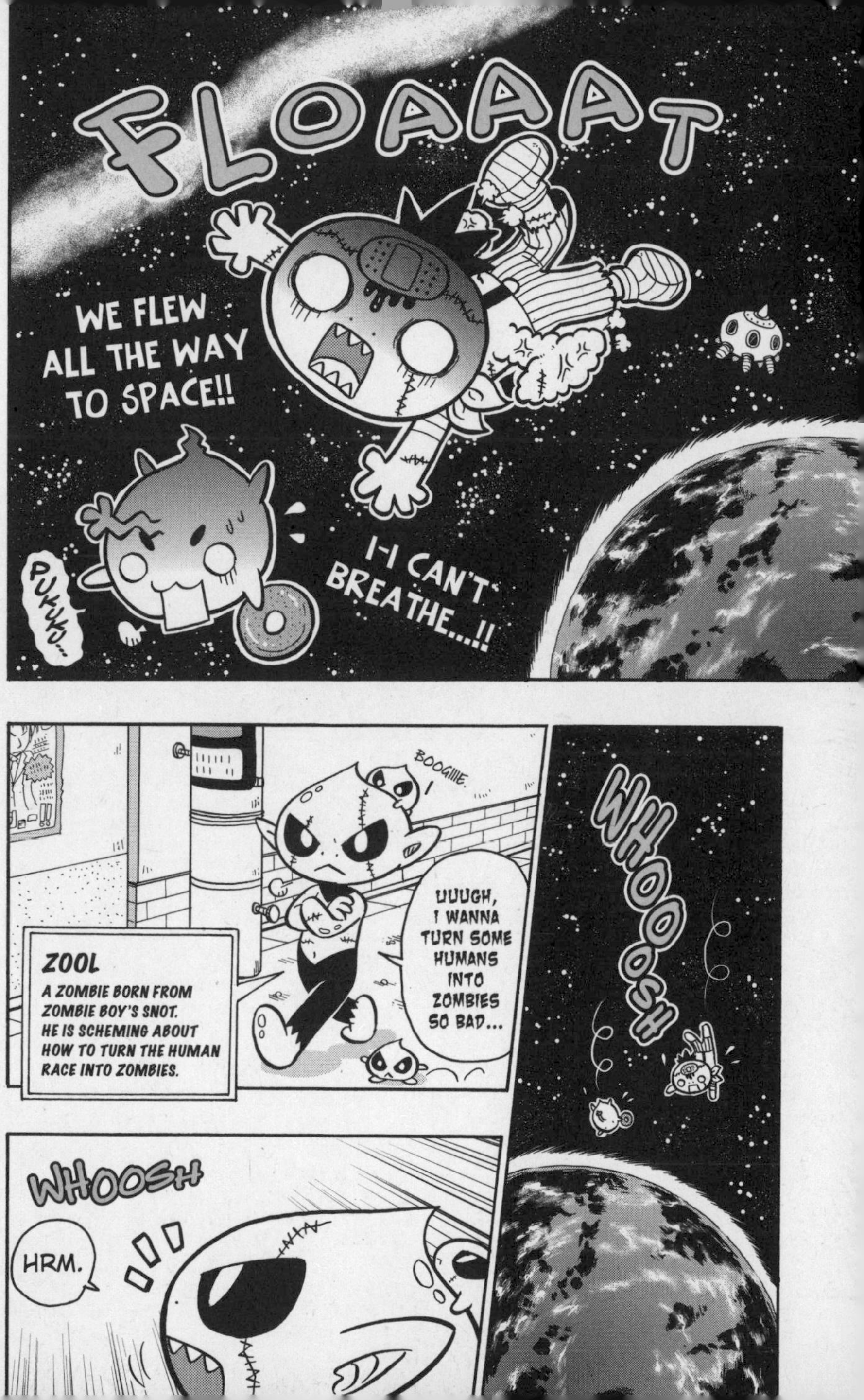
FLOAAAT
WE FLEW ALL THE WAY TO SPACE!!
I-I CAN'T BREATHE...!!
PUKUKU...
WHOOOOSH
BOOGIIIE.
UUUGH, I WANNA TURN SOME HUMANS INTO ZOMBIES SO BAD...
ZOOL
A ZOMBIE BORN FROM ZOMBIE BOY'S SNOT. HE IS SCHEMING ABOUT HOW TO TURN THE HUMAN RACE INTO ZOMBIES.
WHOOSH
HRM.

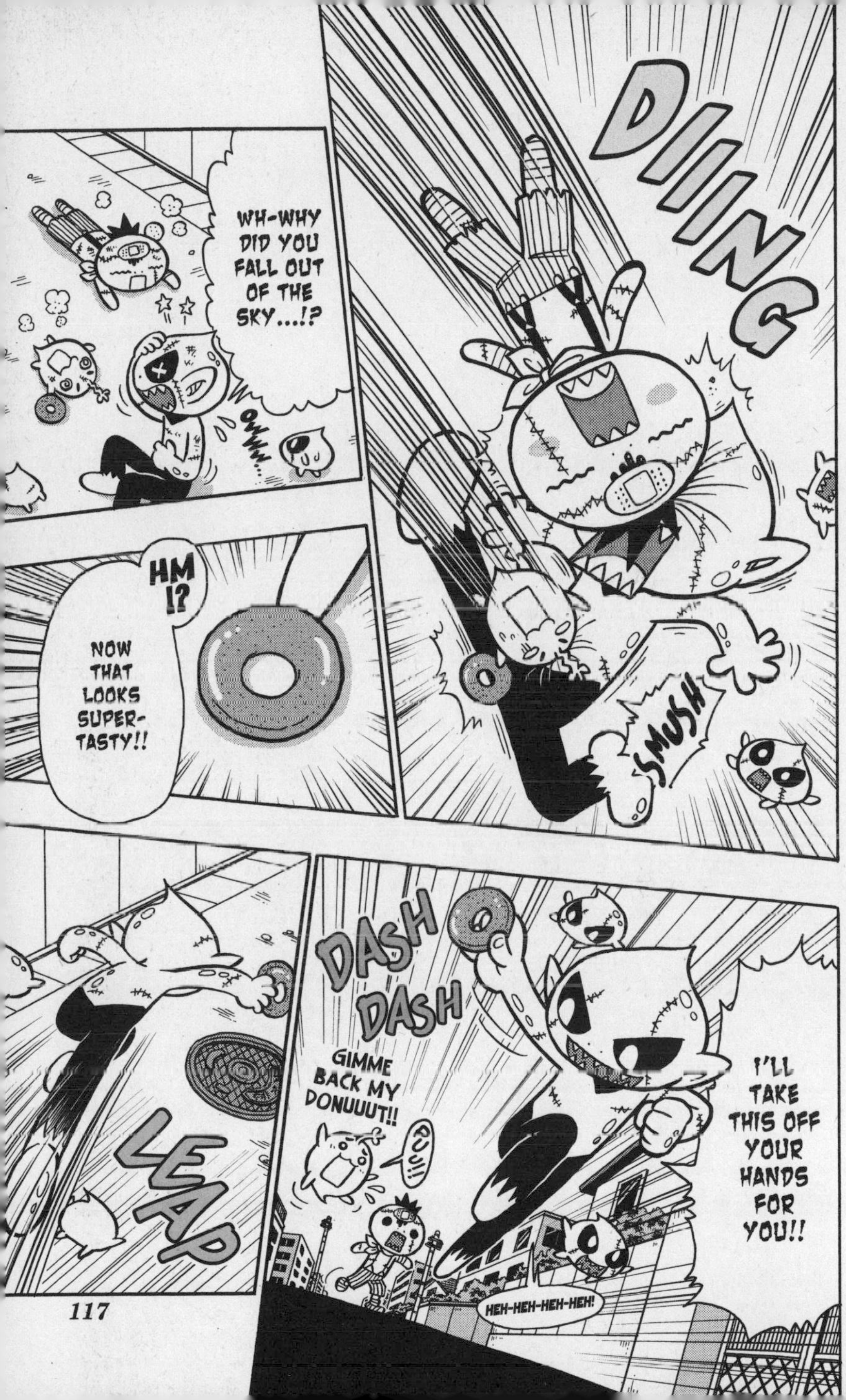
DIIING
SMUSH
WH-WHY DID YOU FALL OUT OF THE SKY...!?
OWWW...
HM !?
NOW THAT LOOKS SUPER-TASTY!!
I'LL TAKE THIS OFF YOUR HANDS FOR YOU!!
DASH DASH
GIMME BACK MY DONUUUT!!
HEH-HEH-HEH-HEH!
LEAP

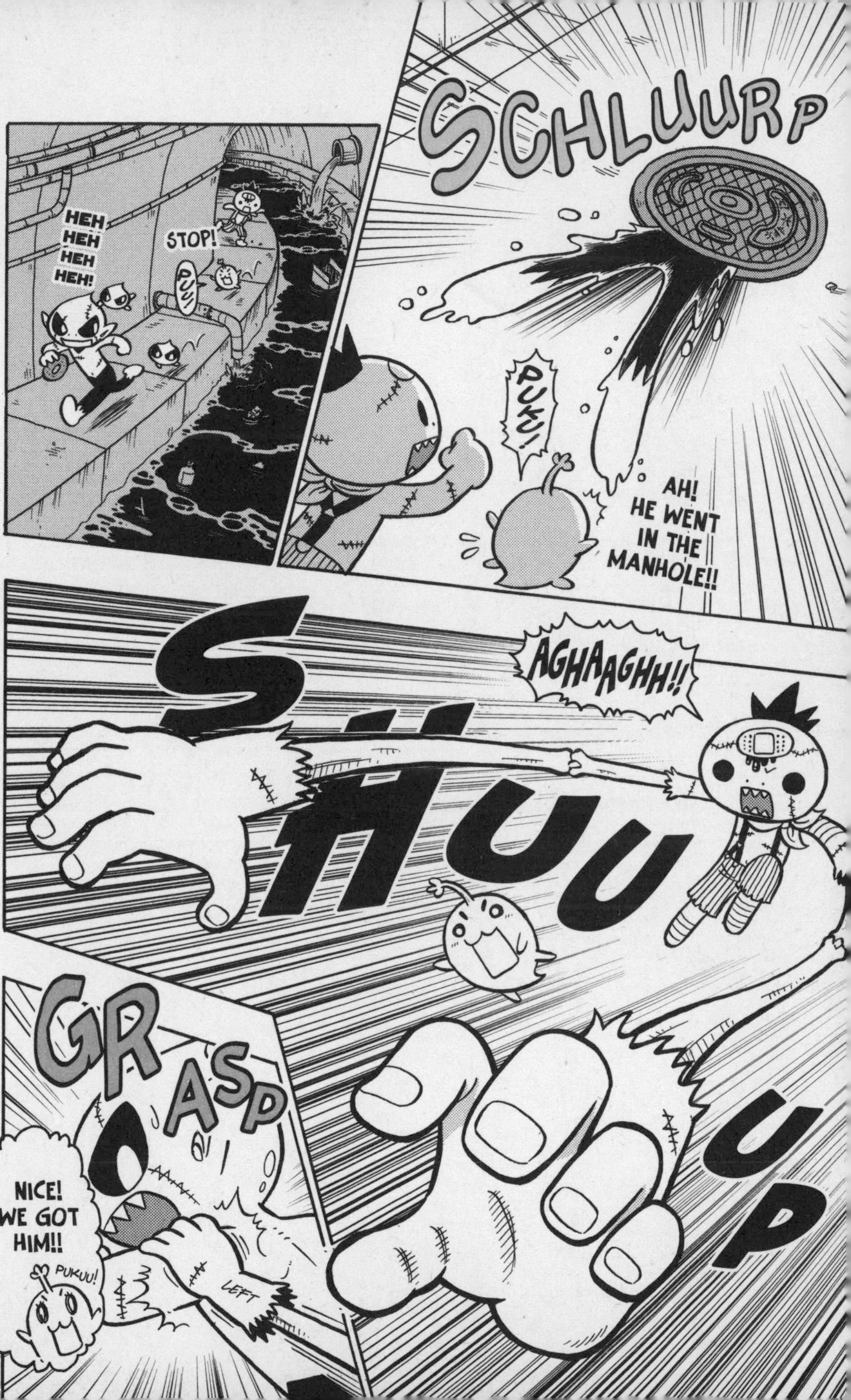
SCHLUURP
PUKU!
AH! HE WENT IN THE MANHOLE!!
HEH HEH HEH HEH!
STOP!
SHHUU
AGHAAGHH!!
GRASP
UP
NICE! WE GOT HIM!!
PUKUU!
LEFT

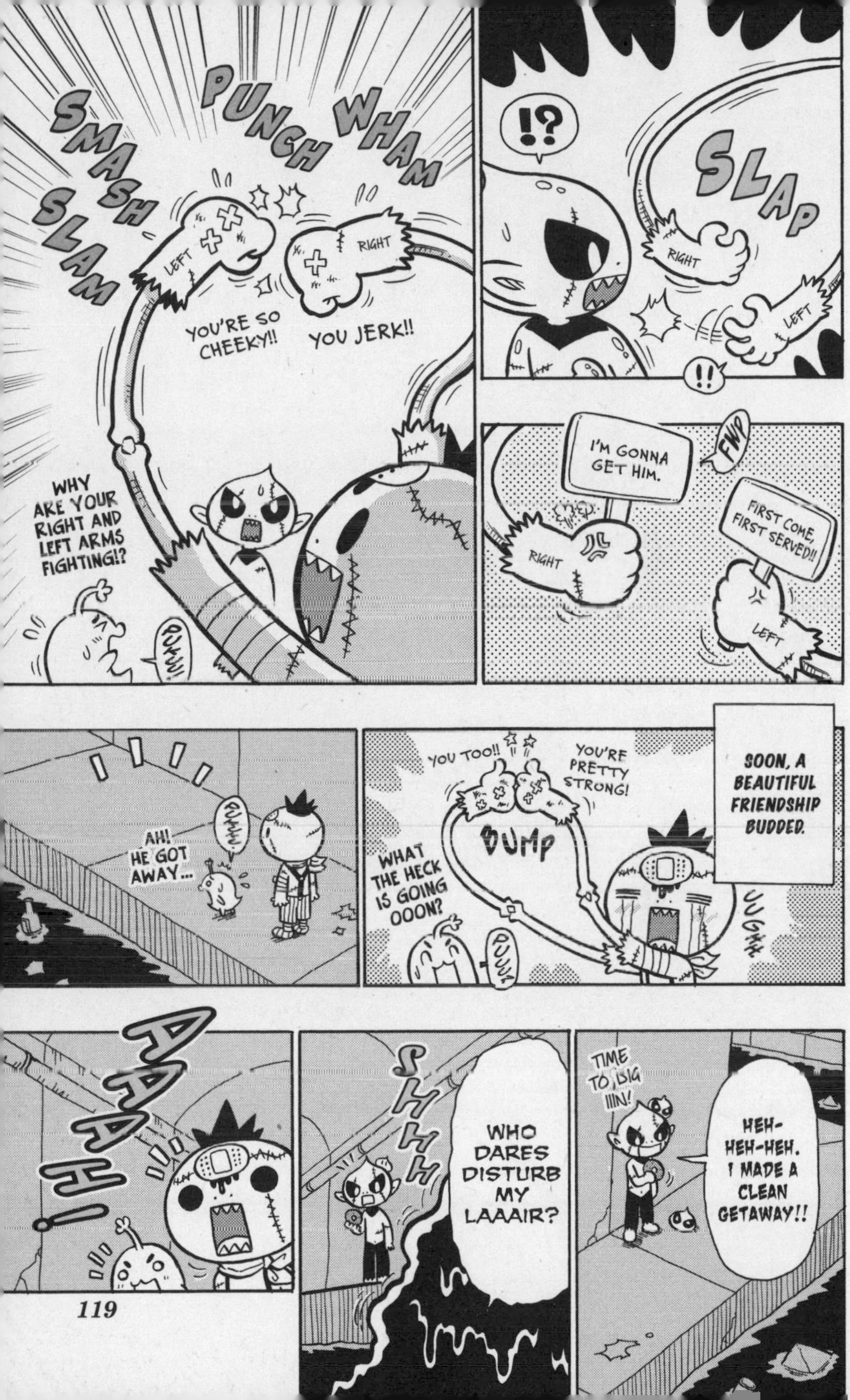

!?
SLAP
RIGHT
LEFT
!!
I'M GONNA GET HIM.
FWP
FIRST COME, FIRST SERVED!!
RIGHT
LEFT
SMASH
SLAM
PUNCH
WHAM
LEFT
RIGHT
YOU'RE SO CHEEKY!!
YOU JERK!!
WHY ARE YOUR RIGHT AND LEFT ARMS FIGHTING!?
PUKUU
SOON, A BEAUTIFUL FRIENDSHIP BUDDED.
YOU'RE PRETTY STRONG!
YOU TOO!!
DUMP
UGH
WHAT THE HECK IS GOING OOON?
PUUU
PUKUU
AH! HE GOT AWAY...
TIME TO DIG IIIN!
HEH-HEH-HEH. I MADE A CLEAN GETAWAY!!
SHHH
WHO DARES DISTURB MY LAAAIR?
AAAH!

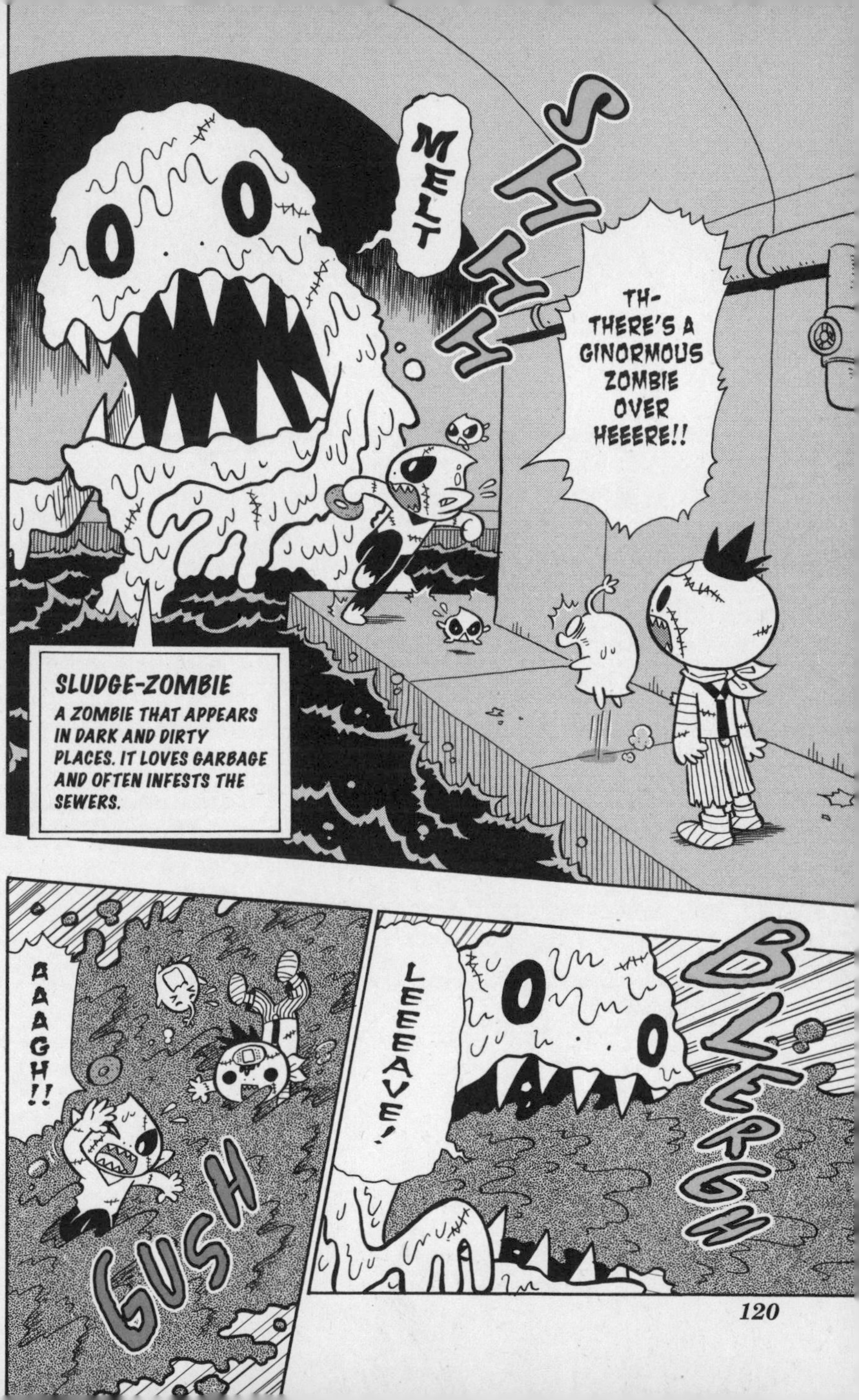
SHHHH
MELT
TH- THERE'S A GINORMOUS ZOMBIE OVER HEEERE!!
SLUDGE-ZOMBIE
A ZOMBIE THAT APPEARS IN DARK AND DIRTY PLACES. IT LOVES GARBAGE AND OFTEN INFESTS THE SEWERS.
BLERGH
LEEEAVE!
AAAAGH!!
GUSH

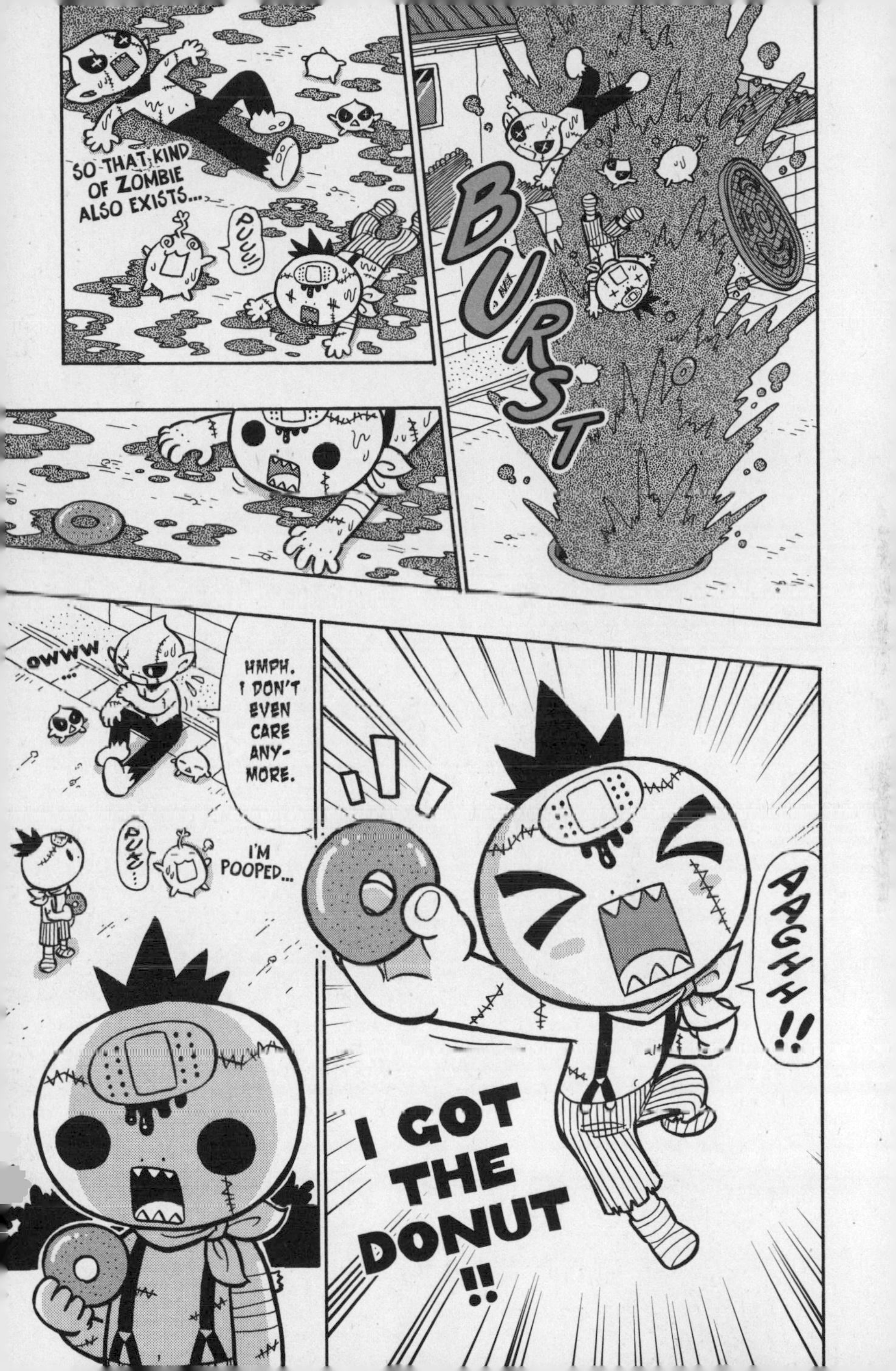
BURST
SO THAT KIND OF ZOMBIE ALSO EXISTS...
PUUU!
!!!
AAGHH!!
I GOT THE DONUT!!
HMPH. I DON'T EVEN CARE ANYMORE.
OWWW...
I'M POOPED...
PUKU...

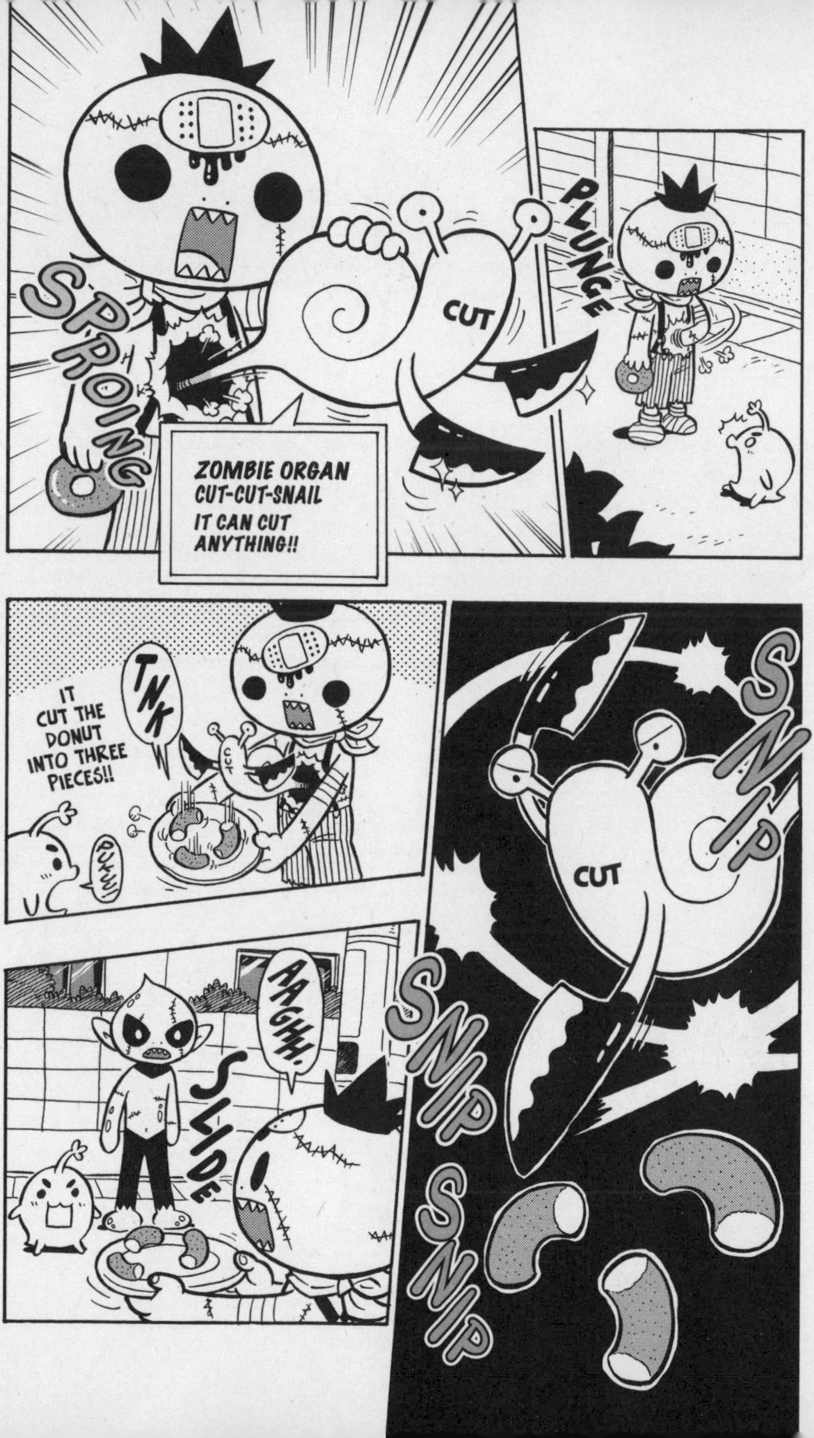
PLUNGE
CUT
SPROING
ZOMBIE ORGAN CUT-CUT-SNAIL
IT CAN CUT ANYTHING!!
SNIP
CUT
SNIP SNIP SNIP
TNK
CUT
IT CUT THE DONUT INTO THREE PIECES!!
QUKU!
AAGHH!
SLIDE

LET'S ALL ENJOY IT TOGETHER!!

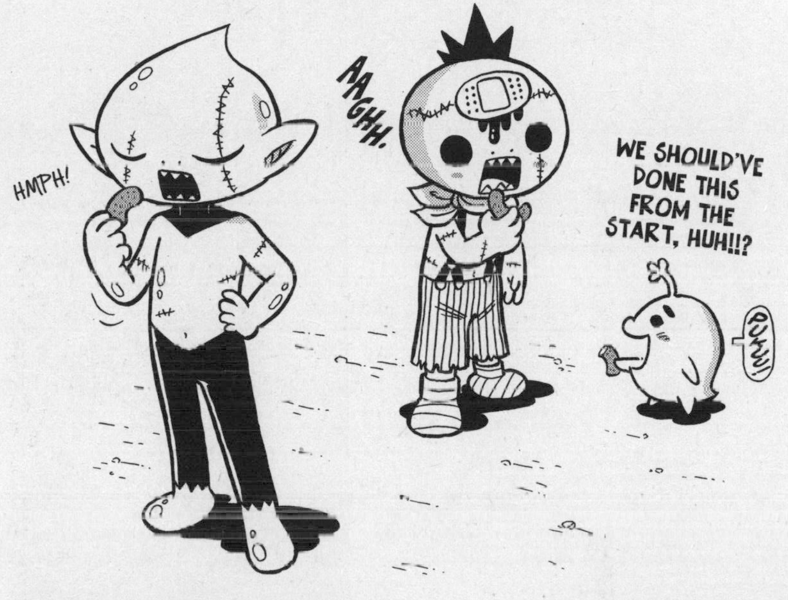
WE SHOULD'VE DONE THIS FROM THE START, HUH!!?
PUKU!
AAGHH.
HMPH!

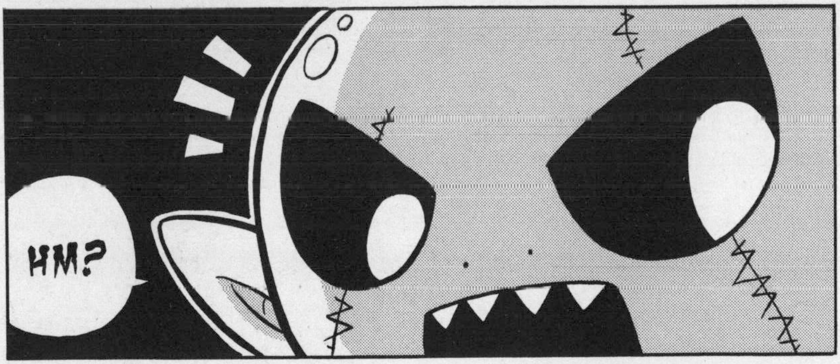
HM?

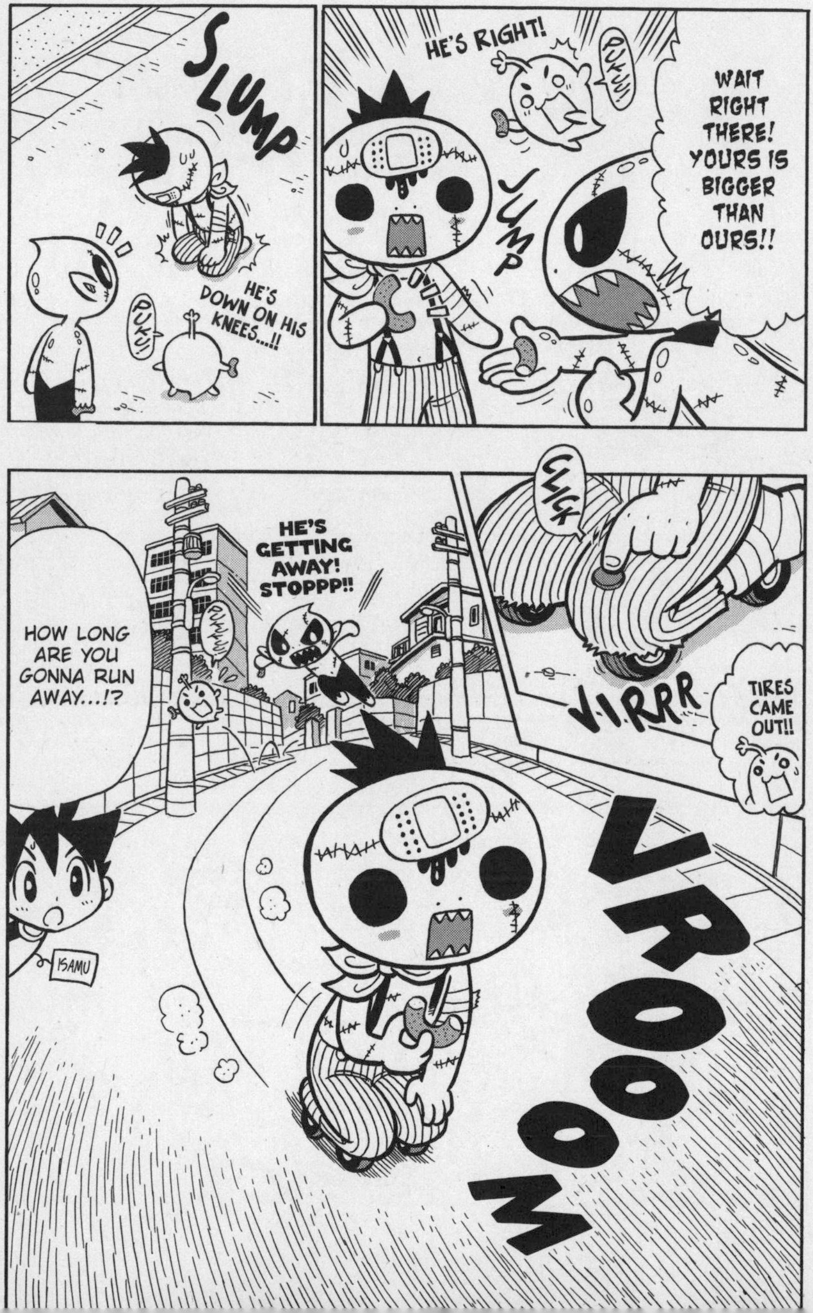
HE'S RIGHT!
PUKUU!
WAIT RIGHT THERE! YOURS IS BIGGER THAN OURS!!
JUMP
SLUMP
HE'S DOWN ON HIS KNEES...!!
PUKU
CLICK
VIRRR
TIRES CAME OUT!!
HE'S GETTING AWAY! STOPPP!!
HOW LONG ARE YOU GONNA RUN AWAY...!?
ISAMU
VROOOOM

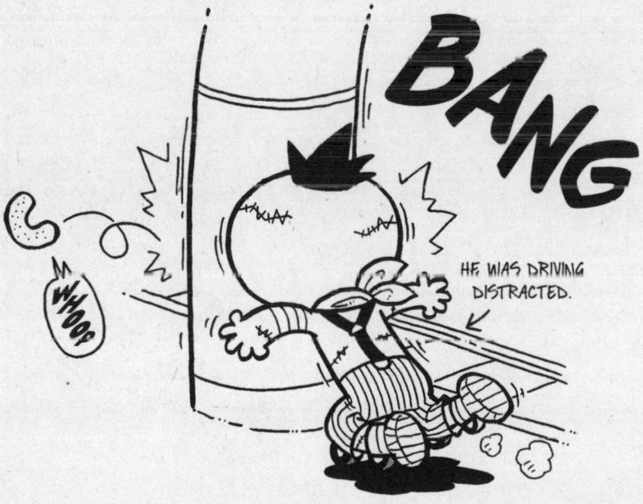
BANG
WHOOPS
HE WAS DRIVING DISTRACTED.

MEETING THE MYTERIOUZ SPACE PIRATE!

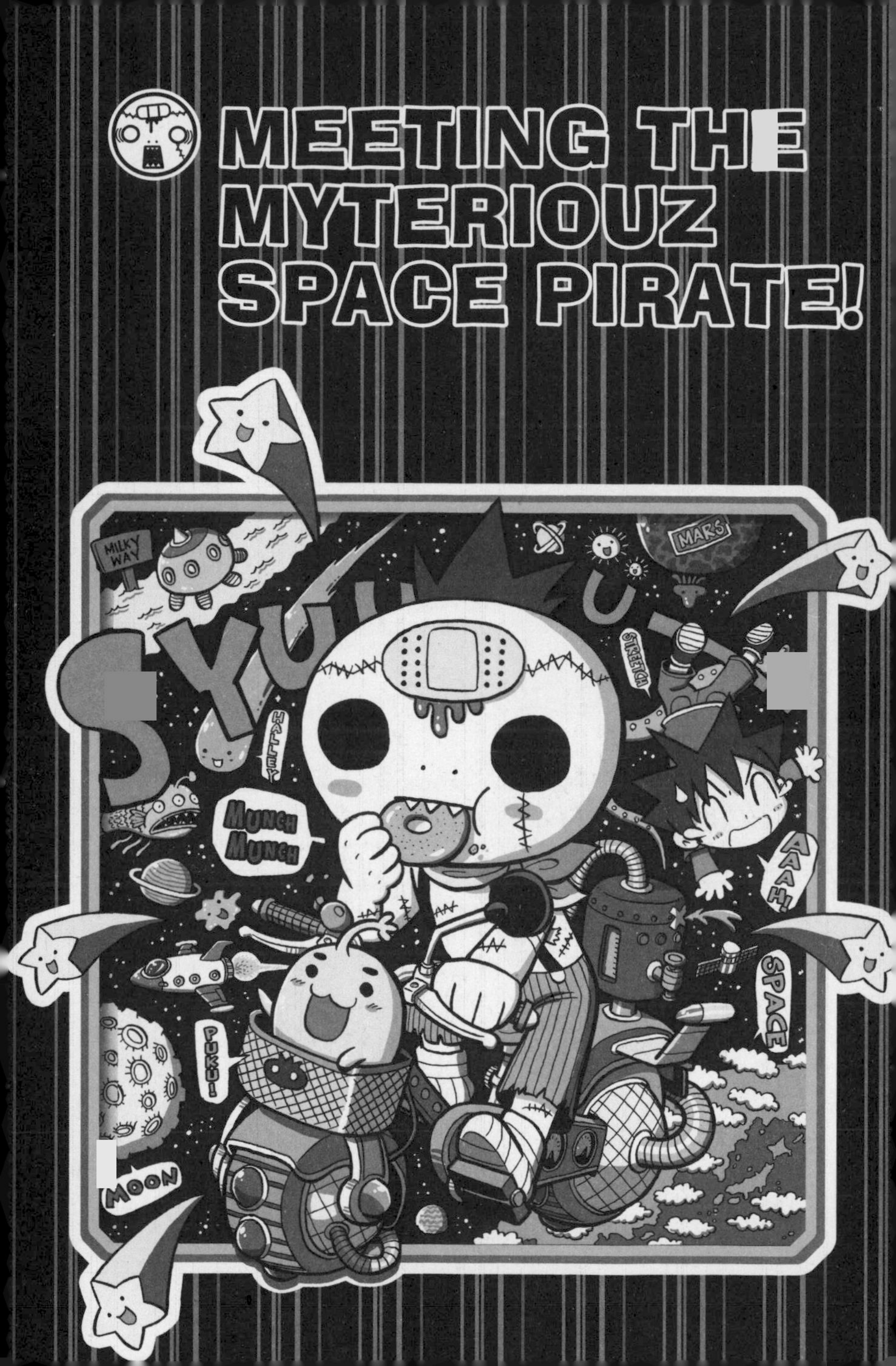
MILKY WAY
MARS
HALLEY
MUNCH MUNCH
AAAH!
SPACE
PUKU!
MOON

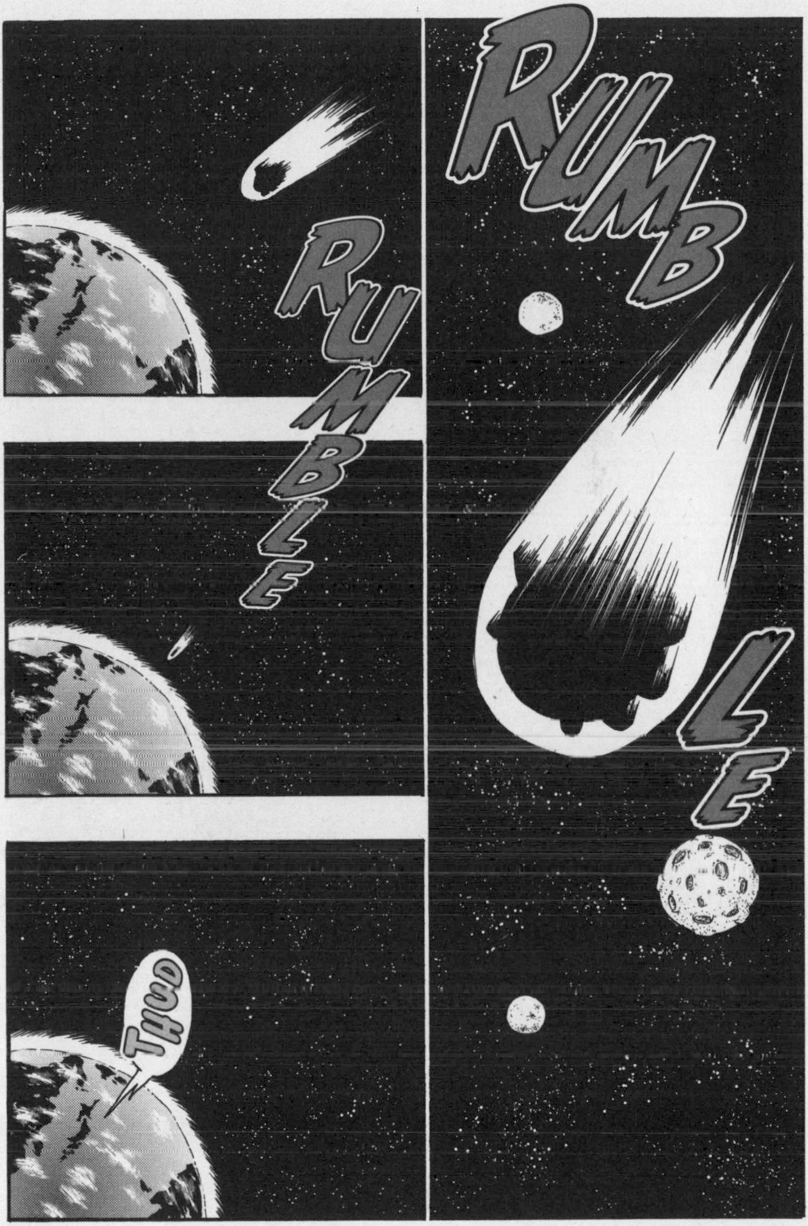
RUMBLE
RUMBLE
THUD

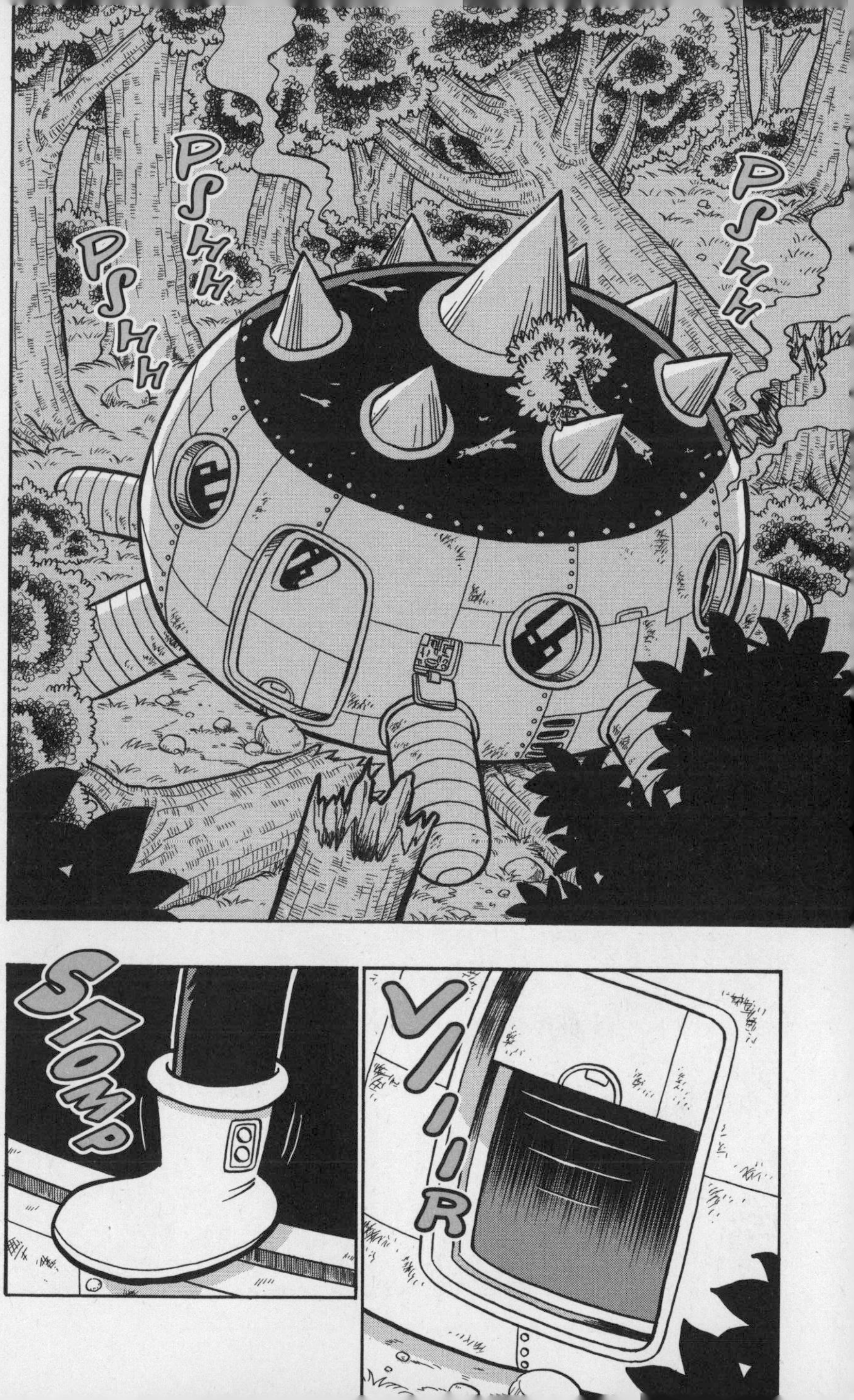
PSHH
PSHH
PSHH
VIIR
STOMP

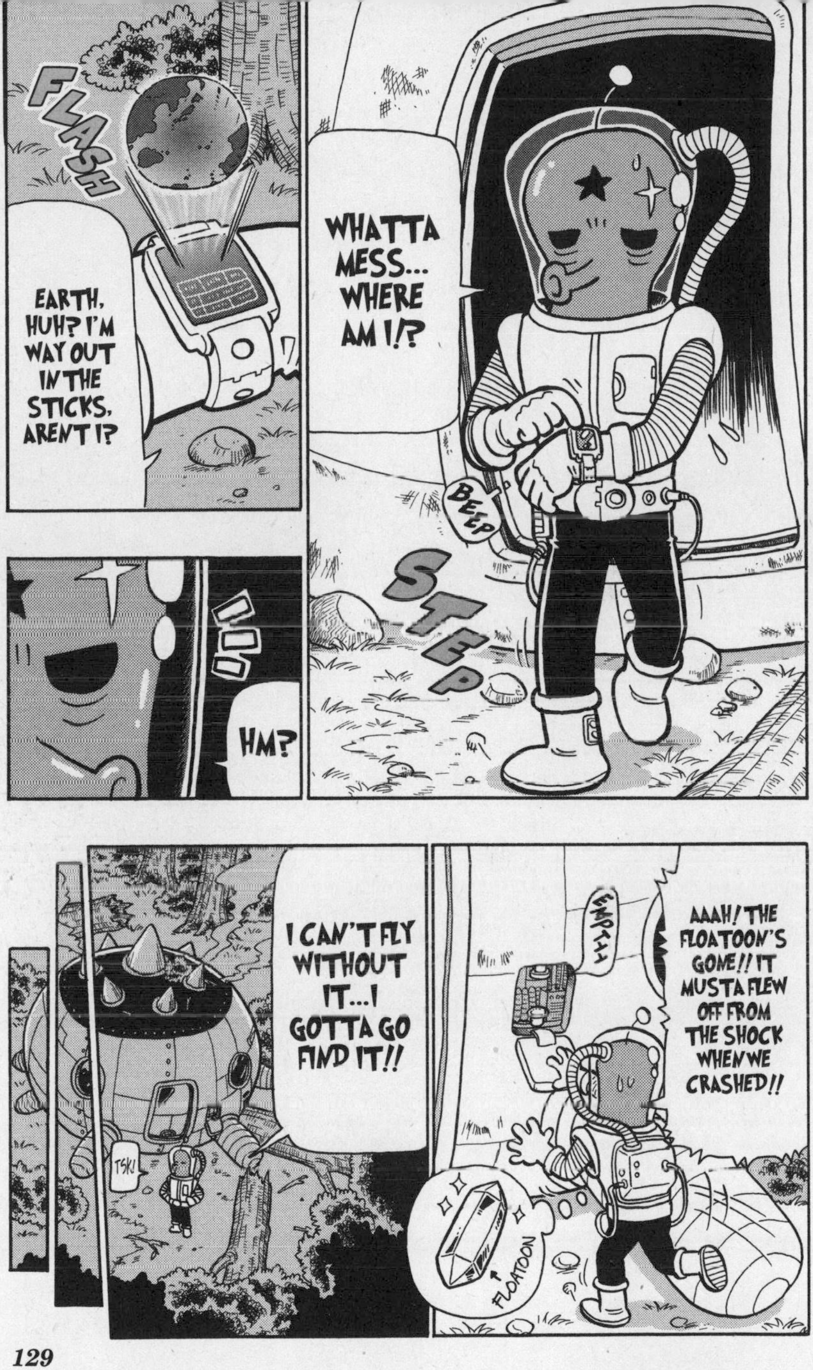
WHATTA MESS... WHERE AM I!?
BEEP
STEP
FLASH
EARTH, HUH? I'M WAY OUT IN THE STICKS, AREN'T I?
HM?
AAAH! THE FLOATOON'S GONE!! IT MUSTA FLEW OFF FROM THE SHOCK WHEN WE CRASHED!!
EMPTY
FLOATOON
I CAN'T FLY WITHOUT IT...I GOTTA GO FIND IT!!
TSK!

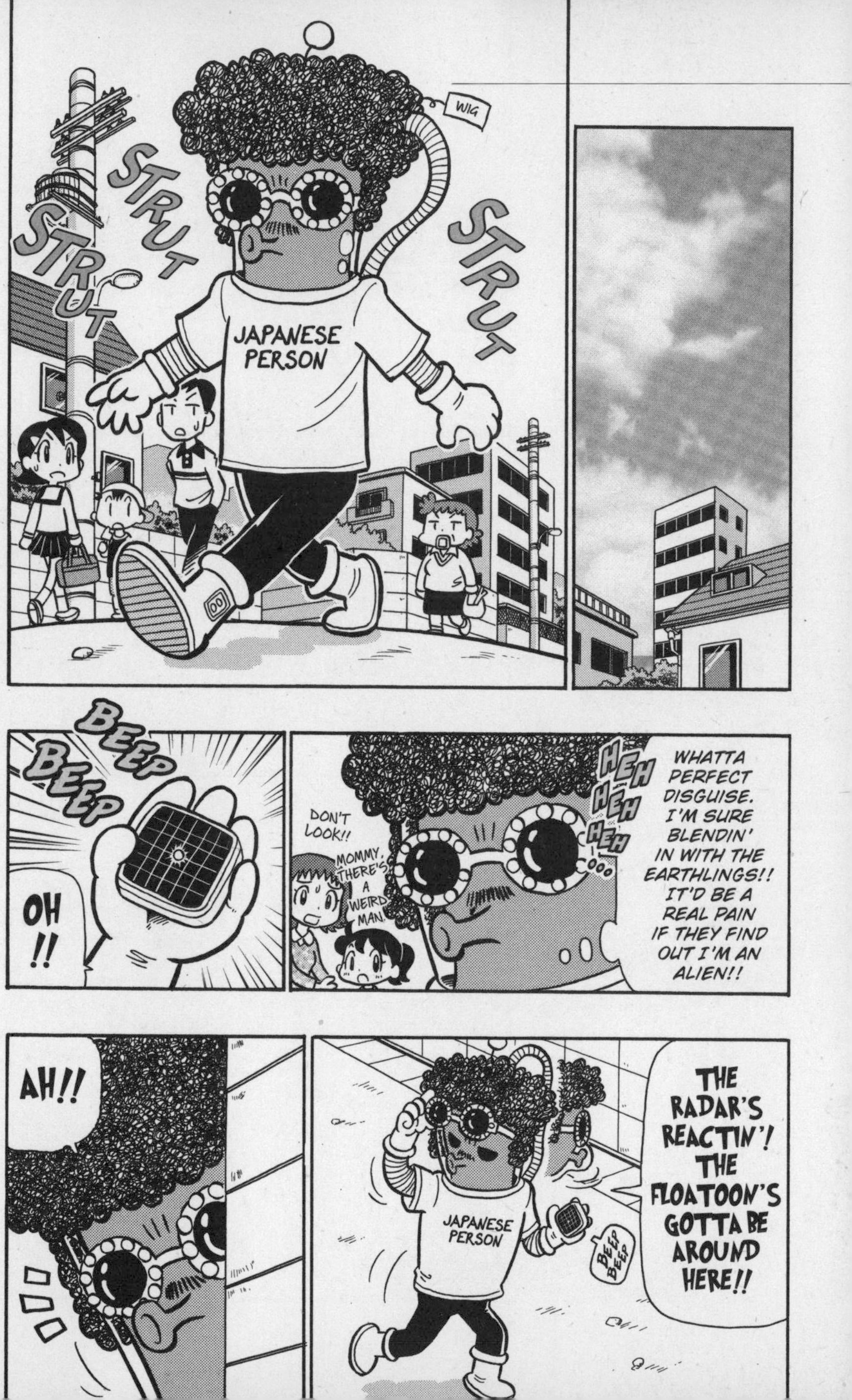
STRUT
STRUT
STRUT
WIG
JAPANESE PERSON
HEH HEH HEH
WHATTA PERFECT DISGUISE. I'M SURE BLENDIN' IN WITH THE EARTHLINGS!! IT'D BE A REAL PAIN IF THEY FIND OUT I'M AN ALIEN!!
DON'T LOOK!!
MOMMY, THERE'S A WEIRD MAN.
BEEP BEEP
OH!!
THE RADAR'S REACTIN'! THE FLOATOON'S GOTTA BE AROUND HERE!!
BEEP BEEP
JAPANESE PERSON
AH!!

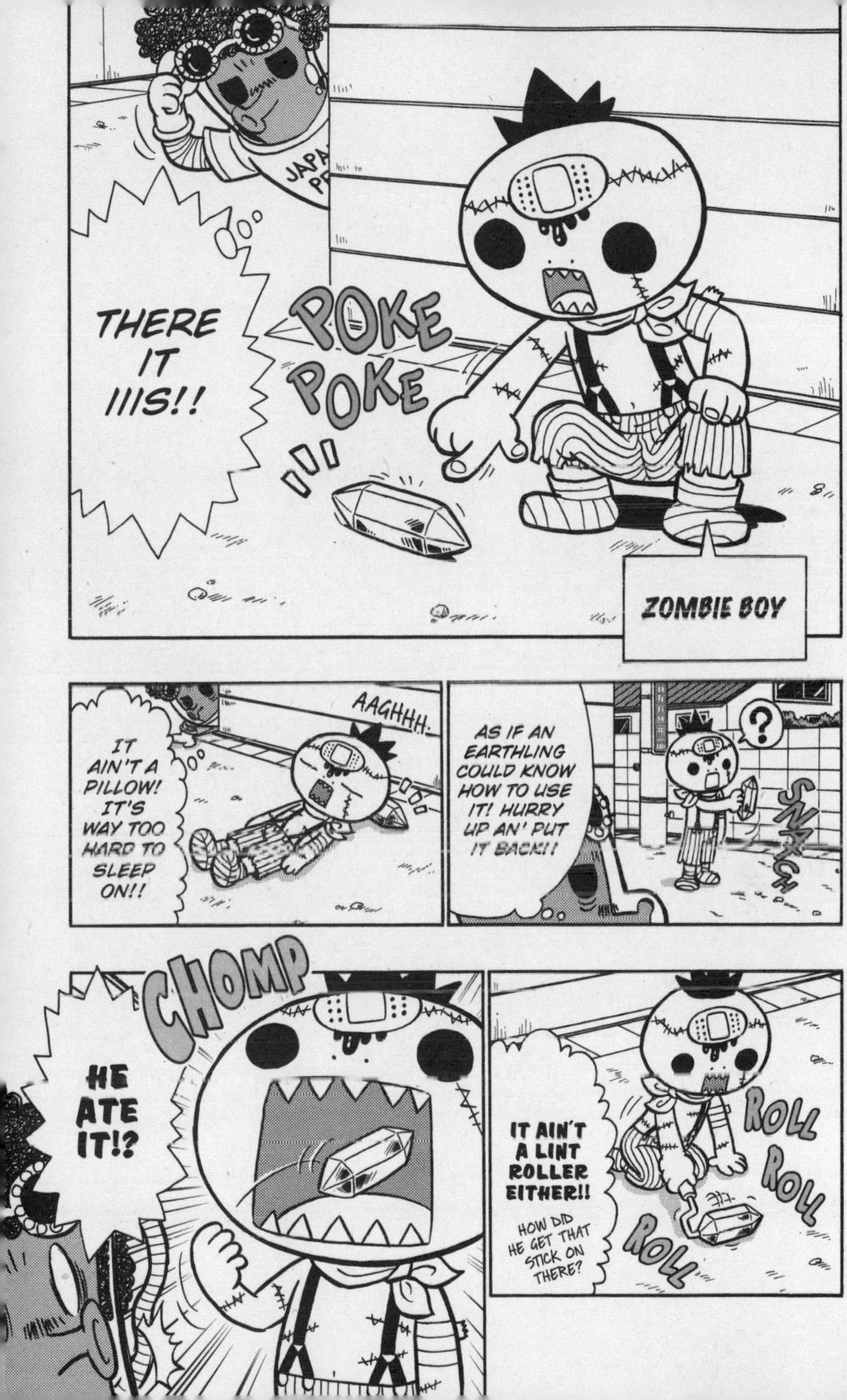
THERE IT IIIS!!
POKE POKE
ZOMBIE BOY
AS IF AN EARTHLING COULD KNOW HOW TO USE IT! HURRY UP AN' PUT IT BACK!!
?
SNATCH
AAGHHH.
IT AIN'T A PILLOW! IT'S WAY TOO HARD TO SLEEP ON!!
IT AIN'T A LINT ROLLER EITHER!!
HOW DID HE GET THAT STICK ON THERE?
ROLL ROLL ROLL
CHOMP
HE ATE IT!?

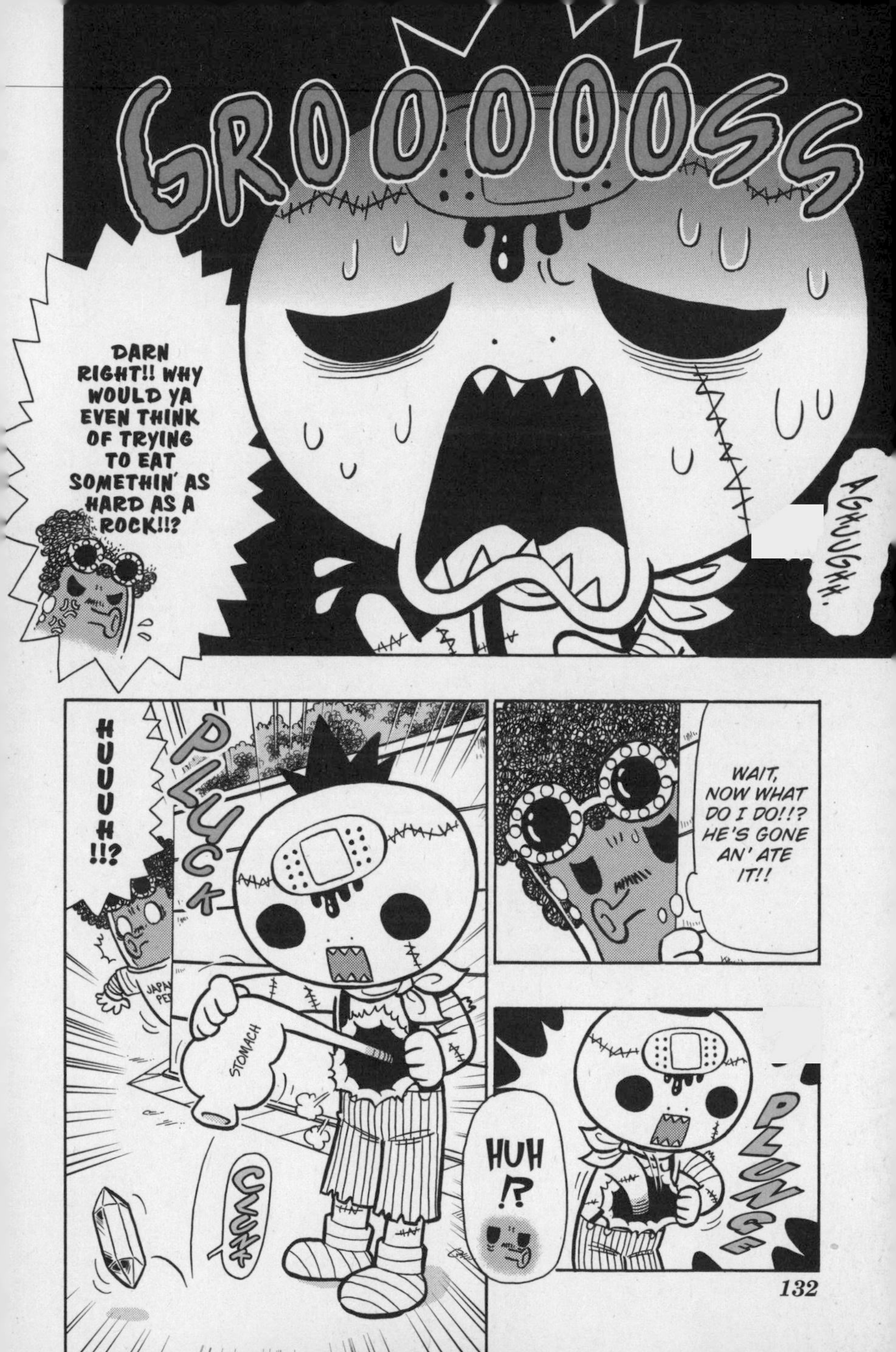
GROOOOOSS
AGHUUGHH.
DARN RIGHT!! WHY WOULD YA EVEN THINK OF TRYING TO EAT SOMETHIN' AS HARD AS A ROCK!!?
WAIT, NOW WHAT DO I DO!!? HE'S GONE AN' ATE IT!!
PLUNGE
HUH !?
HUUUUH!!?
PLUCK
STOMACH
CLUNK

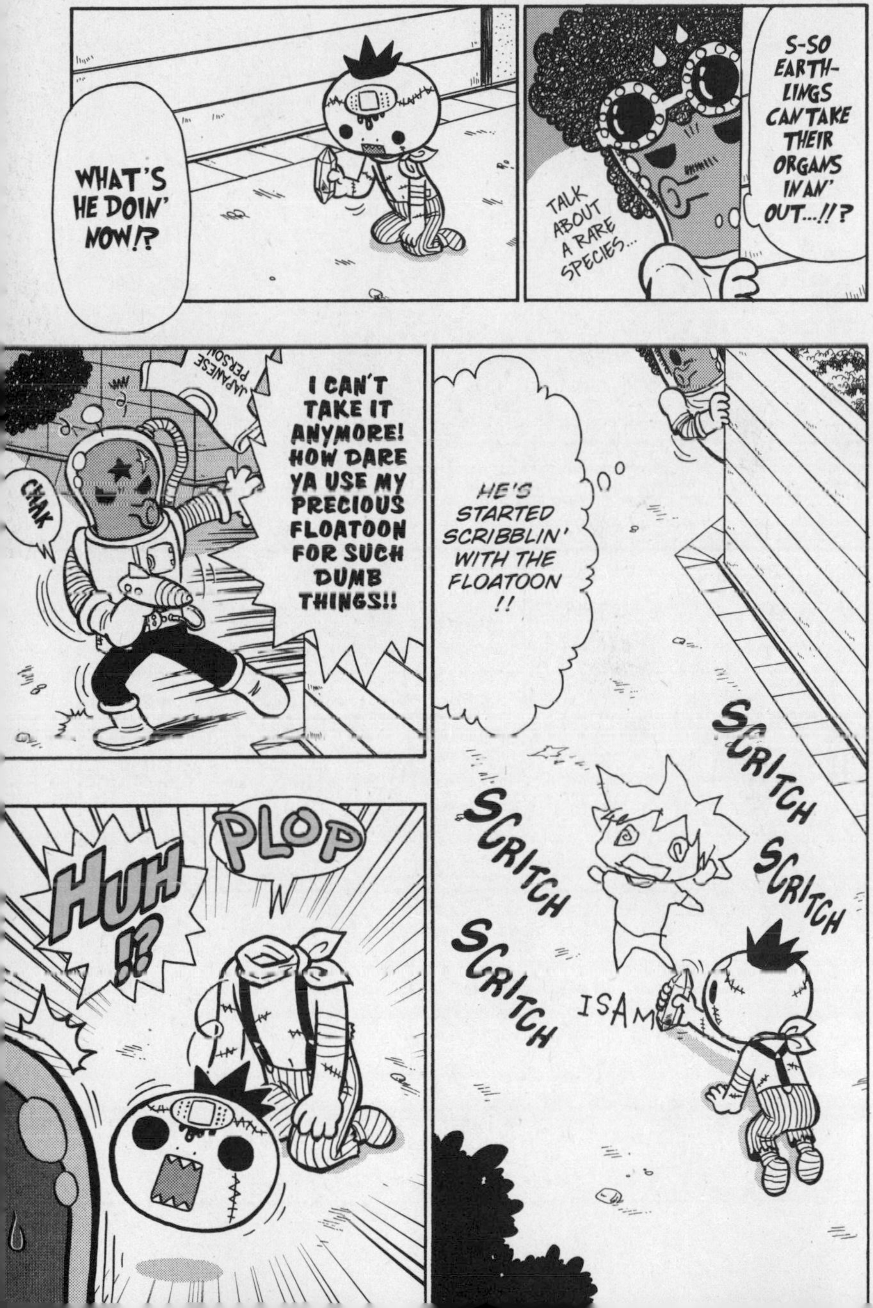
S-SO EARTH-LINGS CAN TAKE THEIR ORGANS IN AN' OUT...!!?
TALK ABOUT A RARE SPECIES...
WHAT'S HE DOIN' NOW!?
HE'S STARTED SCRIBBLIN' WITH THE FLOATOON !!
SCRITCH
SCRITCH
SCRITCH
SCRITCH
ISAM
JAPANESE PERSON
I CAN'T TAKE IT ANYMORE! HOW DARE YA USE MY PRECIOUS FLOATOON FOR SUCH DUMB THINGS!!
CHAK
PLOP
HUH !?

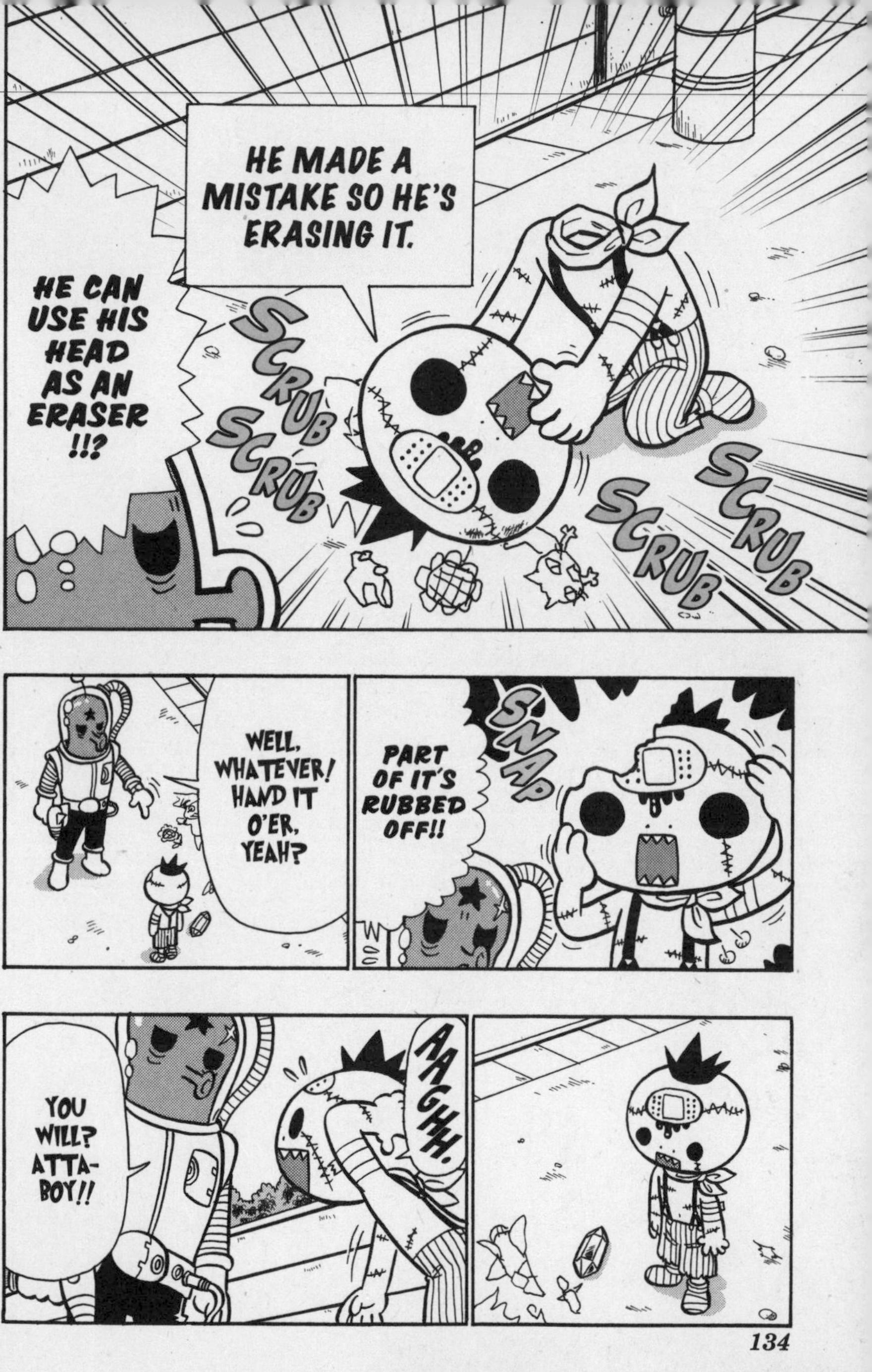
HE MADE A MISTAKE SO HE'S ERASING IT.
SCRUB SCRUB
SCRUB SCRUB
HE CAN USE HIS HEAD AS AN ERASER !!?
SNAP
PART OF IT'S RUBBED OFF!!
WELL, WHATEVER! HAND IT O'ER, YEAH?
AAGHH.
YOU WILL? ATTA-BOY!!

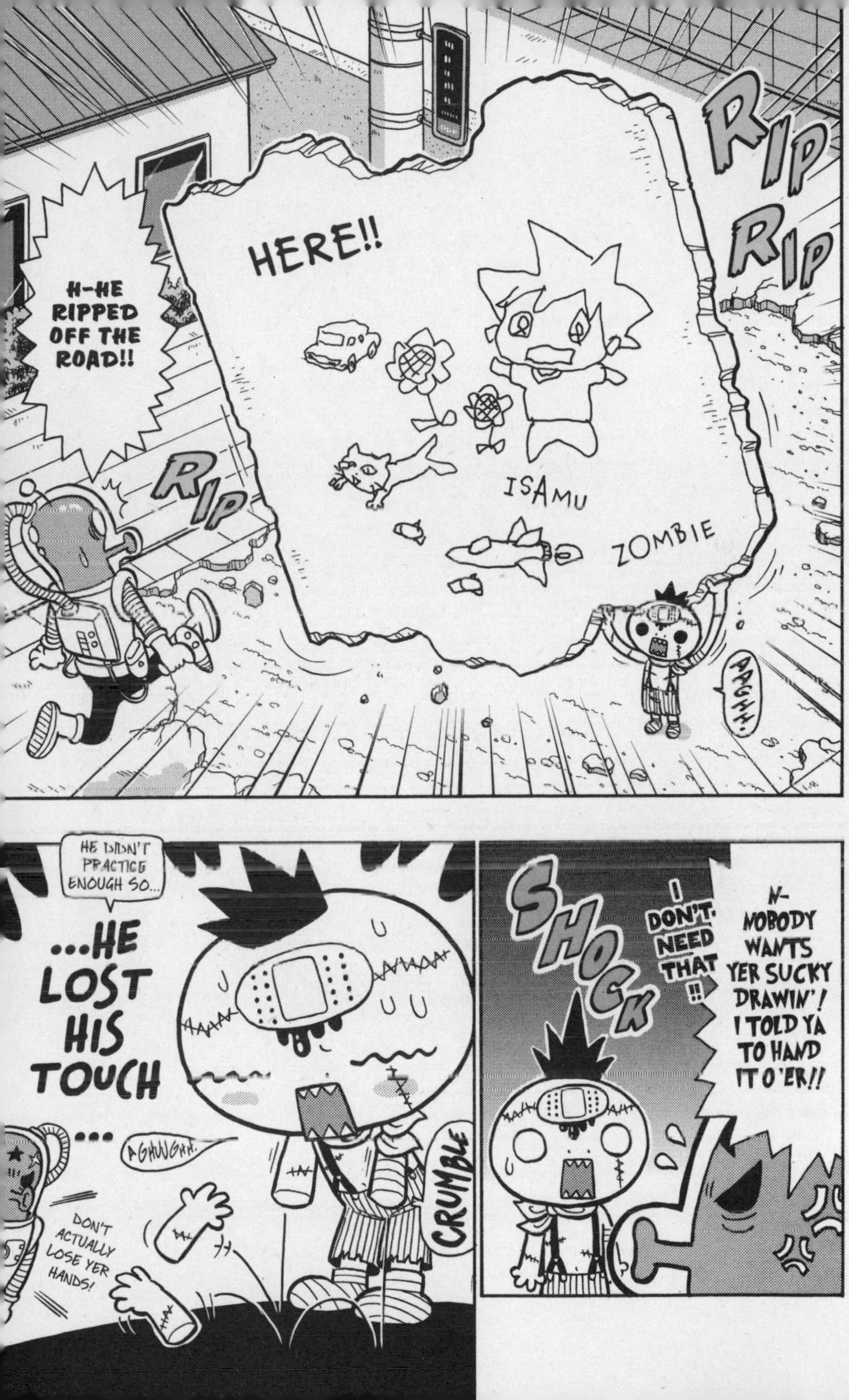
RIP RIP
HERE!!
ISAMU
ZOMBIE
H-HE RIPPED OFF THE ROAD!!
RIP
ARGHH.
N-NOBODY WANTS YER SUCKY DRAWIN'! I TOLD YA TO HAND IT O'ER!!
I DON'T NEED THAT!!
SHOCK
HE DIDN'T PRACTICE ENOUGH SO...
...HE LOST HIS TOUCH...
CRUMBLE
AGHUGHH.
DON'T ACTUALLY LOSE YER HANDS!

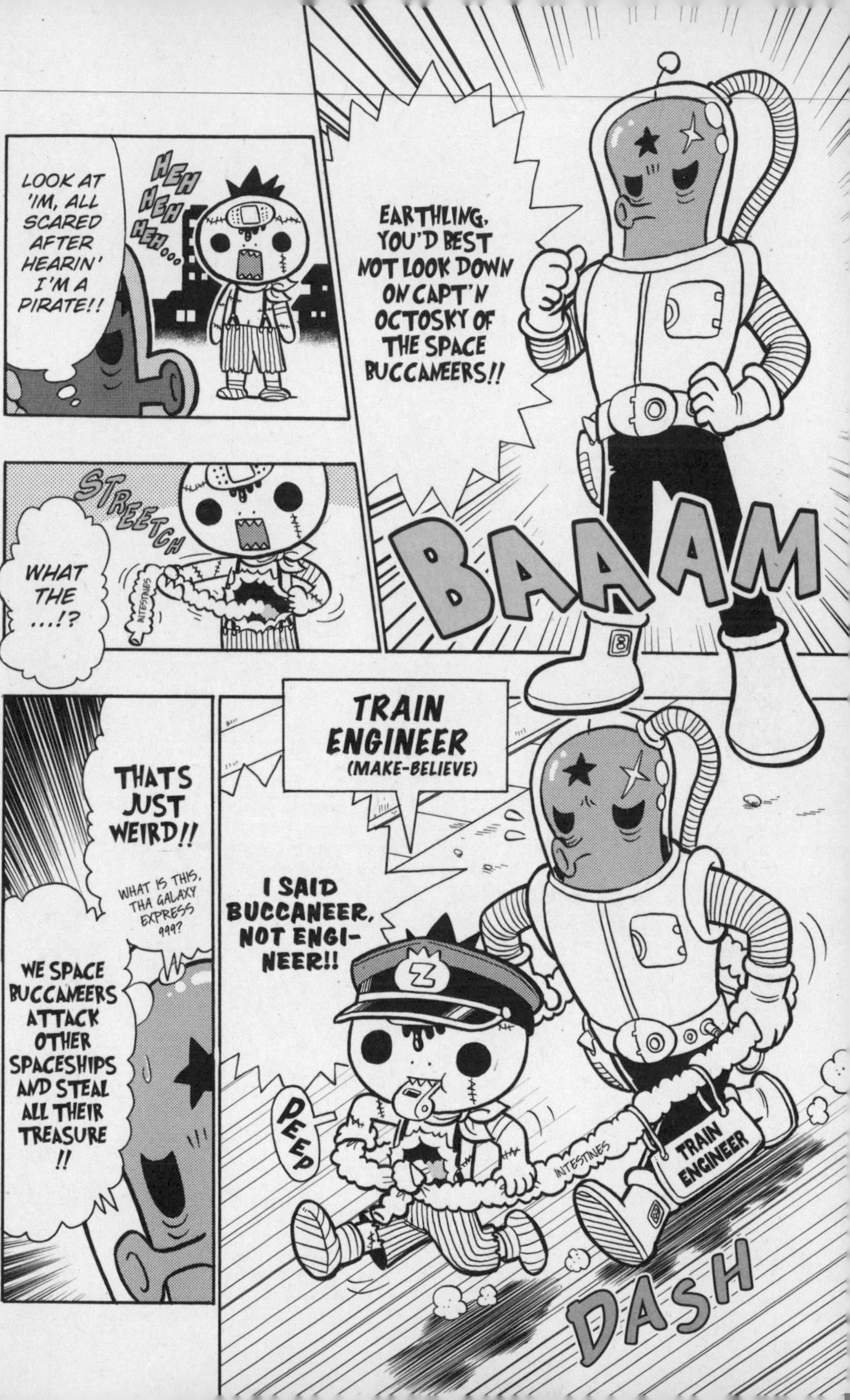
EARTHLING, YOU'D BEST NOT LOOK DOWN ON CAPT'N OCTOSKY OF THE SPACE BUCCANEERS!!
BAAAM
HEH HEH HEH...
LOOK AT 'IM, ALL SCARED AFTER HEARIN' I'M A PIRATE!!
STREEETCH
WHAT THE ...!?
INTESTINES
TRAIN ENGINEER (MAKE-BELIEVE)
I SAID BUCCANEER, NOT ENGI-NEER!!
PEEP
INTESTINES
TRAIN ENGINEER
DASH
THATS JUST WEIRD!!
WHAT IS THIS, THA GALAXY EXPRESS 999?
WE SPACE BUCCANEERS ATTACK OTHER SPACESHIPS AND STEAL ALL THEIR TREASURE !!

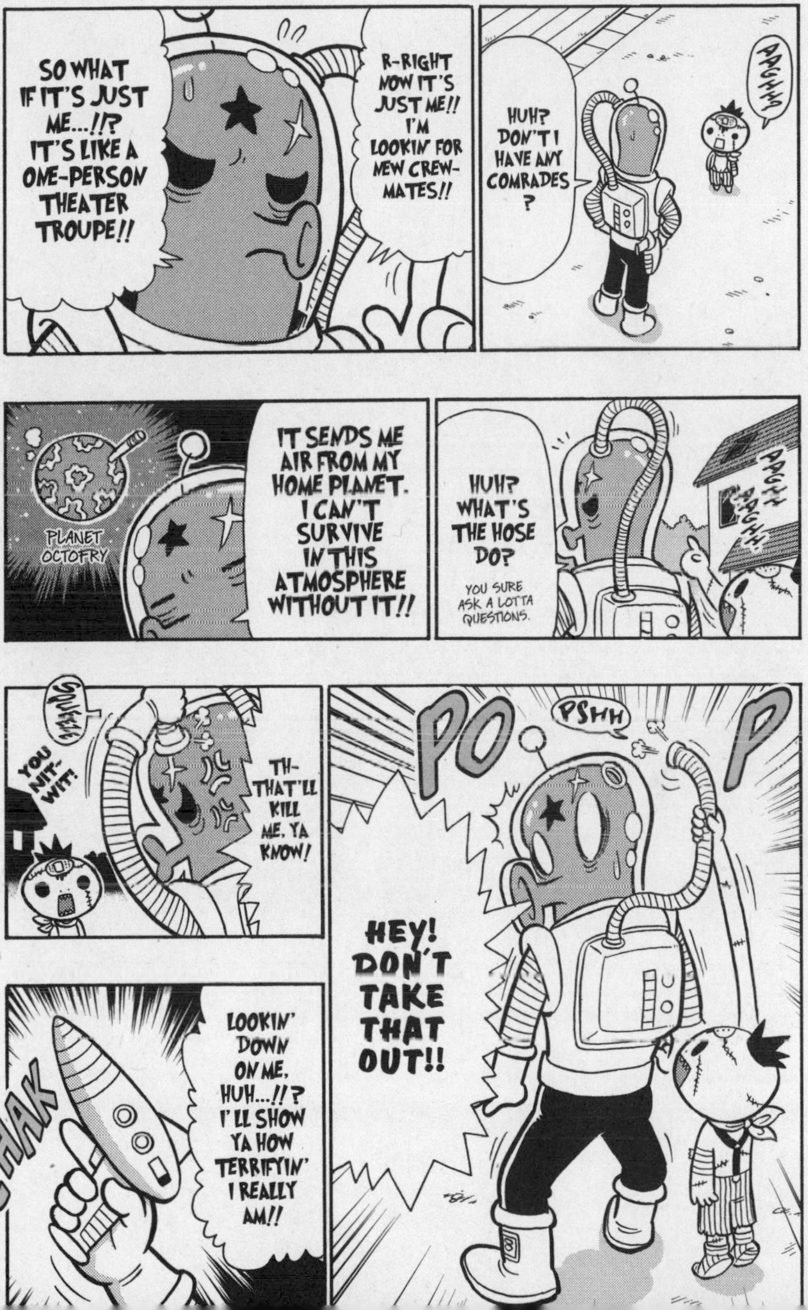
HUH? DON'T I HAVE ANY COMRADES?
ARGHHH
R-RIGHT NOW IT'S JUST ME!! I'M LOOKIN' FOR NEW CREW-MATES!!
SO WHAT IF IT'S JUST ME...!!? IT'S LIKE A ONE-PERSON THEATER TROUPE!!
ARGHH ARGHH
HUH? WHAT'S THE HOSE DO?
YOU SURE ASK A LOTTA QUESTIONS.
IT SENDS ME AIR FROM MY HOME PLANET. I CAN'T SURVIVE IN THIS ATMOSPHERE WITHOUT IT!!
PLANET OCTOFRY
POP
PSHH
HEY! DON'T TAKE THAT OUT!!
SQUEEZE
TH-THAT'LL KILL ME, YA KNOW!
YOU NITWIT!
LOOKIN' DOWN ON ME, HUH...!!? I'LL SHOW YA HOW TERRIFYIN' I REALLY AM!!
CHAK

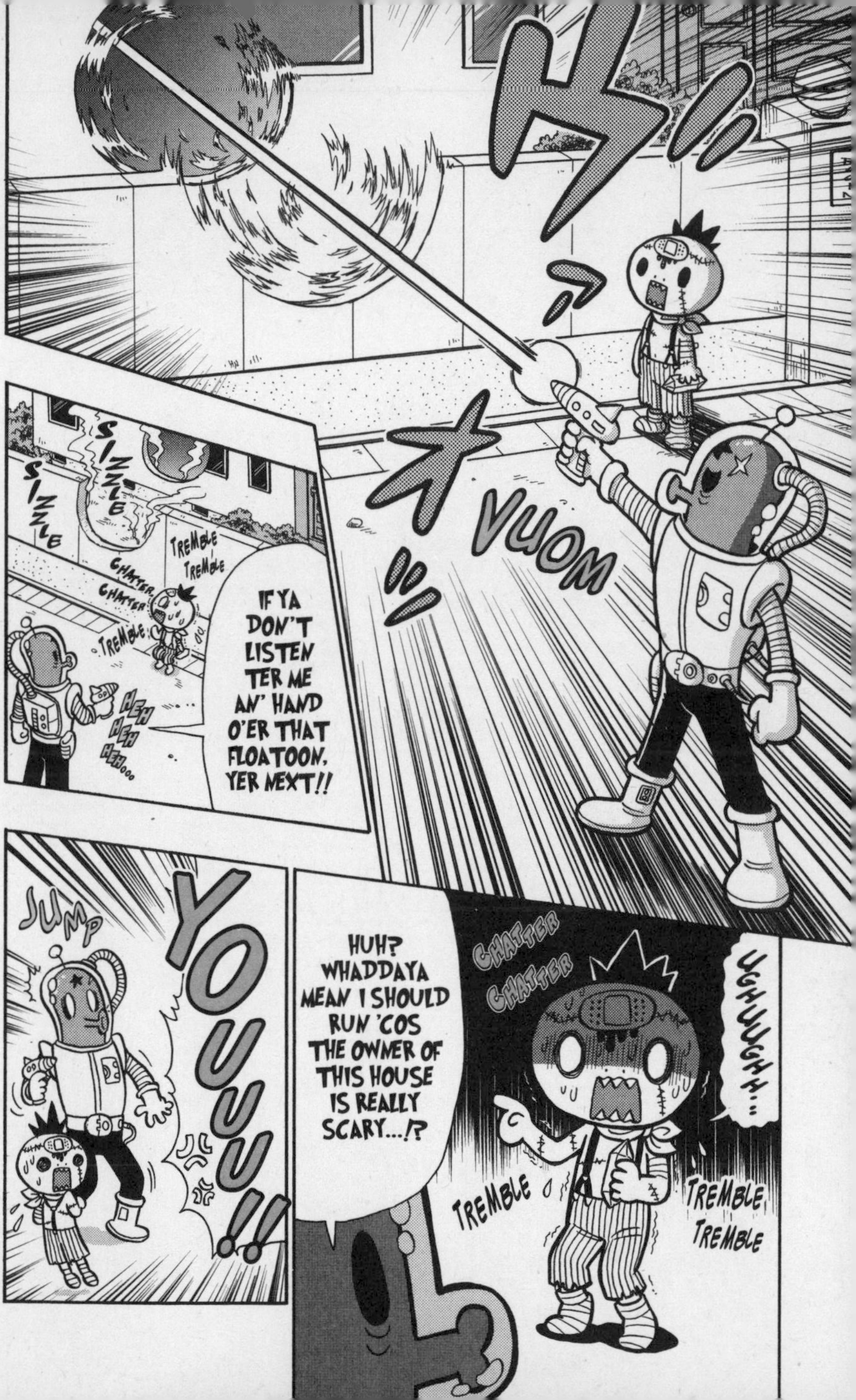
VUOM
SIZZLE
SIZZLE
TREMBLE TREMBLE
CHATTER CHATTER
TREMBLE
IF YA DON'T LISTEN TER ME AN' HAND O'ER THAT FLOATOON, YER NEXT!!
HEH HEH HEH...
HUH? WHADDAYA MEAN I SHOULD RUN 'COS THE OWNER OF THIS HOUSE IS REALLY SCARY...!?
CHATTER CHATTER
UGHUUGHH...
TREMBLE
TREMBLE TREMBLE
YOUUUU!!
JUMP

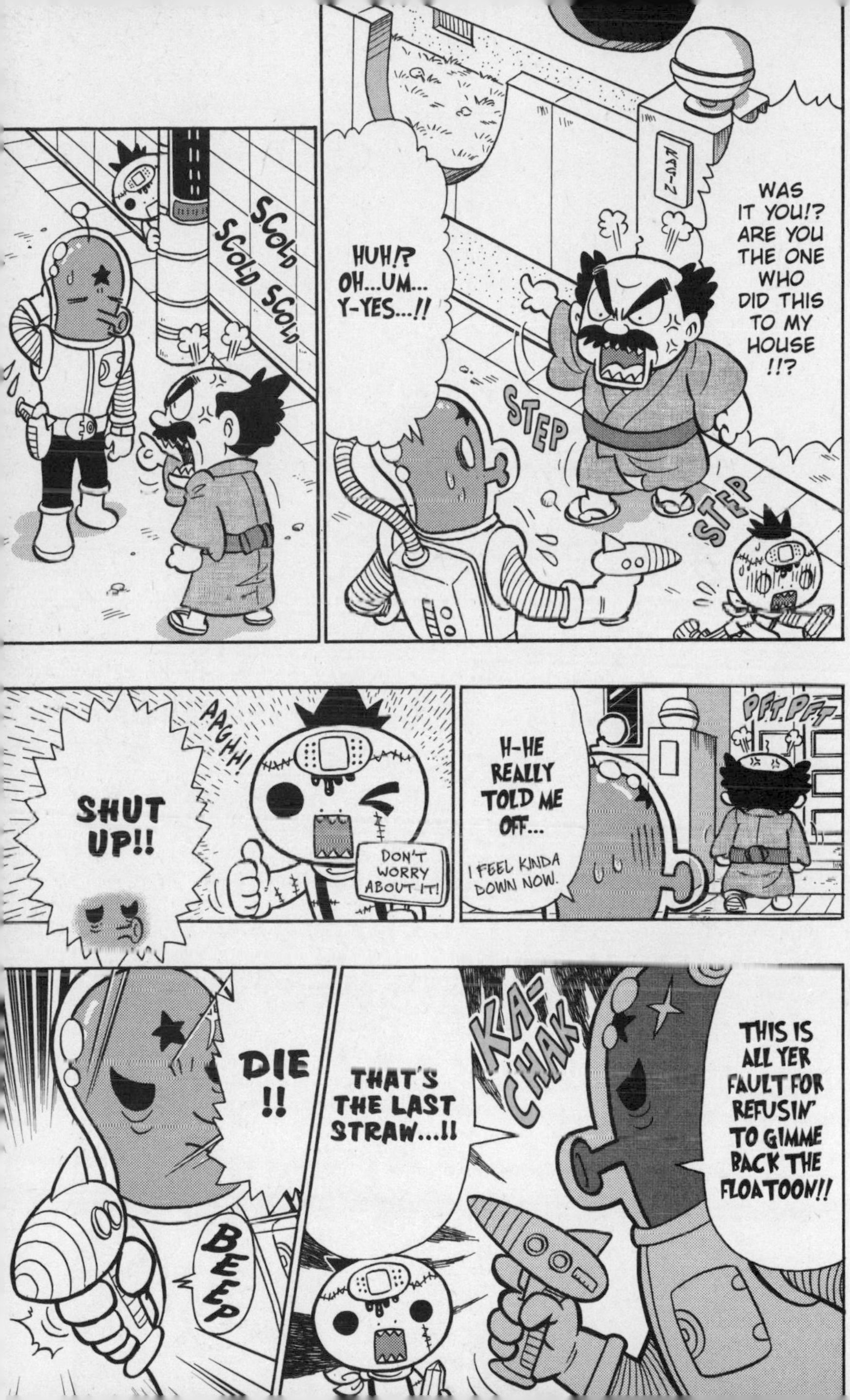
WAS IT YOU!? ARE YOU THE ONE WHO DID THIS TO MY HOUSE !!?
HUH!? OH...UM... Y-YES...!!
STEP
STEP
SCOLD SCOLD SCOLD SCOLD
PFT PFT
H-HE REALLY TOLD ME OFF...
I FEEL KINDA DOWN NOW.
AAGHH!
DON'T WORRY ABOUT IT!
SHUT UP!!
KA-CHAK
THIS IS ALL YER FAULT FOR REFUSIN' TO GIMME BACK THE FLOATOON!!
THAT'S THE LAST STRAW...!!
DIE !!
BEEP

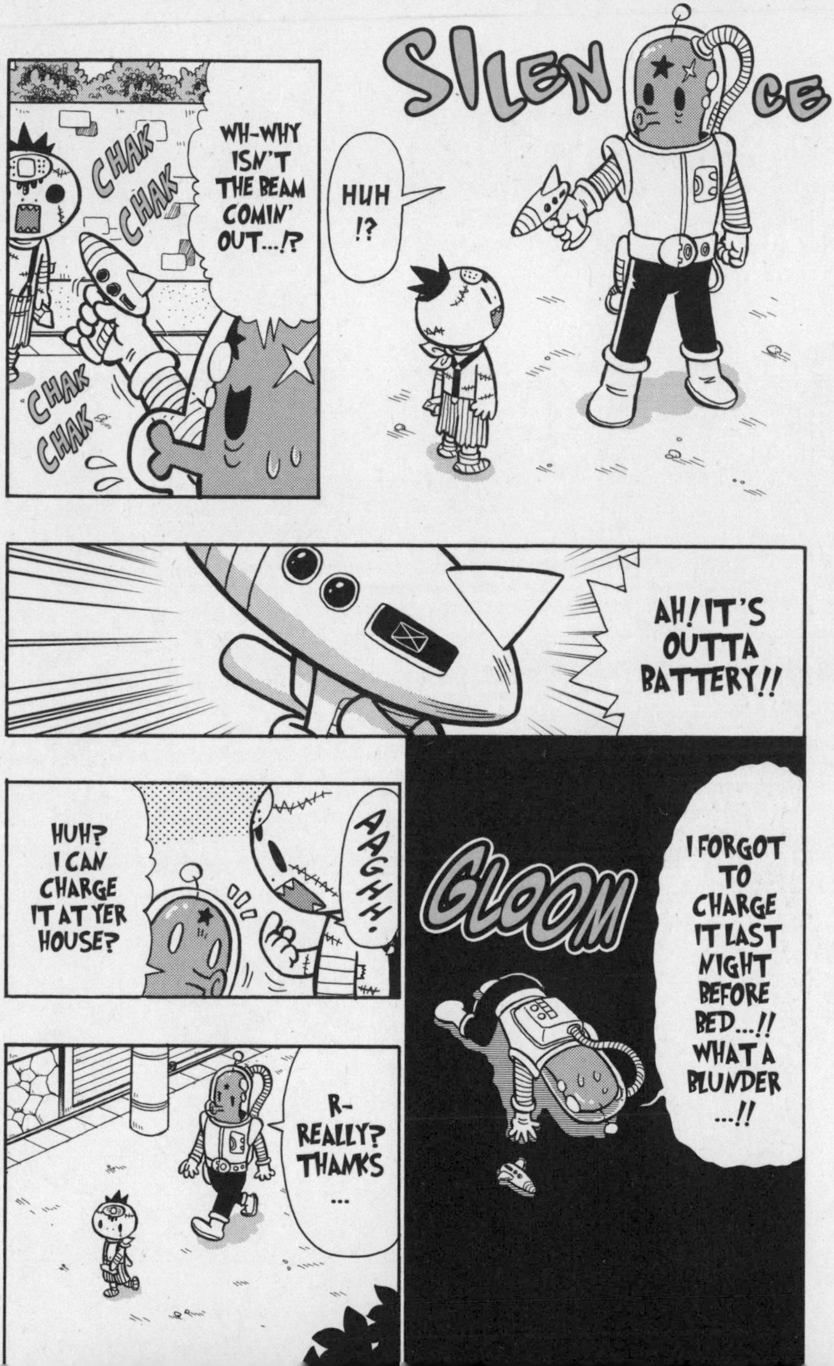
SILENCE
HUH !?
WH-WHY ISN'T THE BEAM COMIN' OUT...!?
CHAK CHAK
CHAK CHAK
AH! IT'S OUTTA BATTERY!!
GLOOM
I FORGOT TO CHARGE IT LAST NIGHT BEFORE BED...!! WHAT A BLUNDER ...!!
AAGHH.
HUH? I CAN CHARGE IT AT YER HOUSE?
R-REALLY? THANKS ...

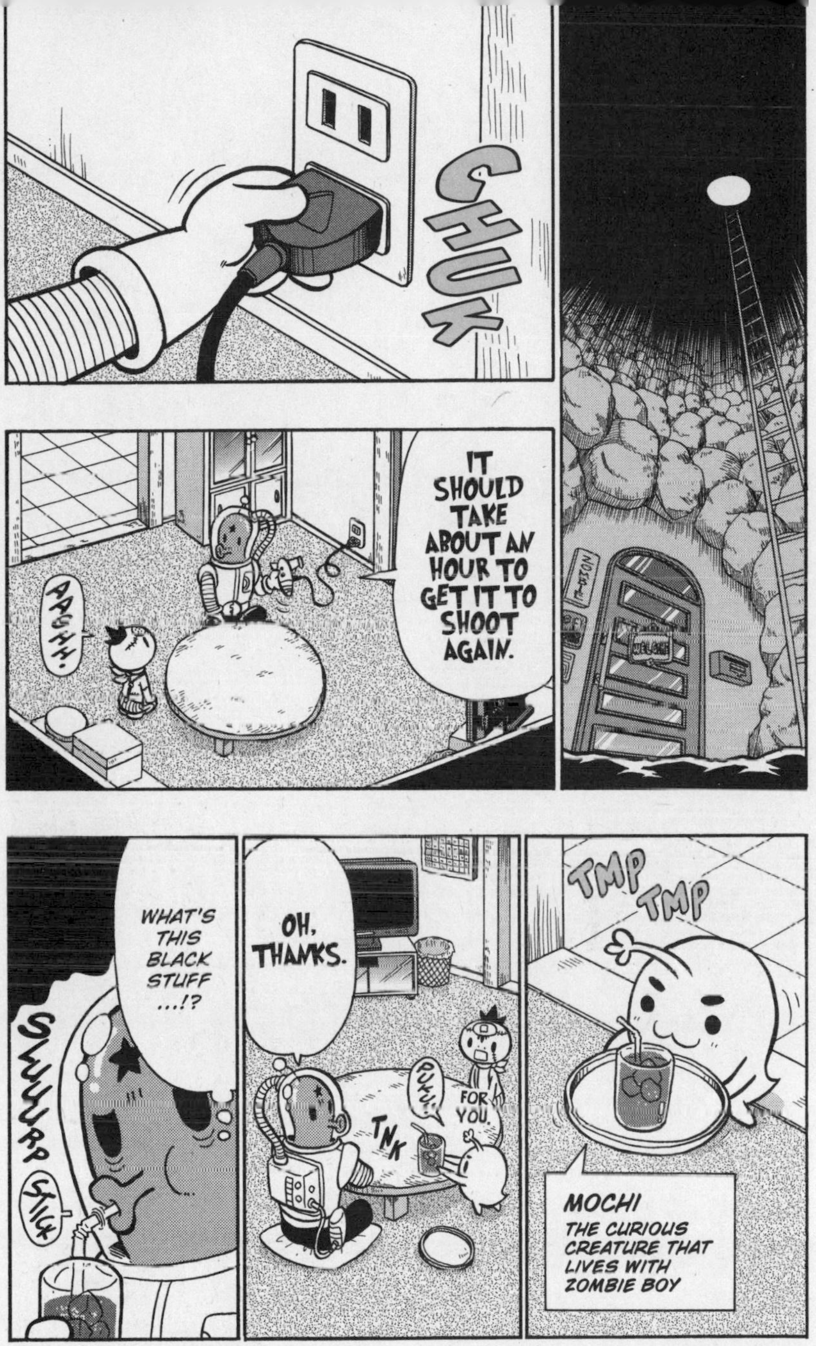
ZOMBIE
CHUK
IT SHOULD TAKE ABOUT AN HOUR TO GET IT TO SHOOT AGAIN.
AAGHH.
TMP TMP
MOCHI
THE CURIOUS CREATURE THAT LIVES WITH ZOMBIE BOY
OH, THANKS.
FOR YOU.
PUKU.
TNK
WHAT'S THIS BLACK STUFF ...!?
SWUUURP
STICK

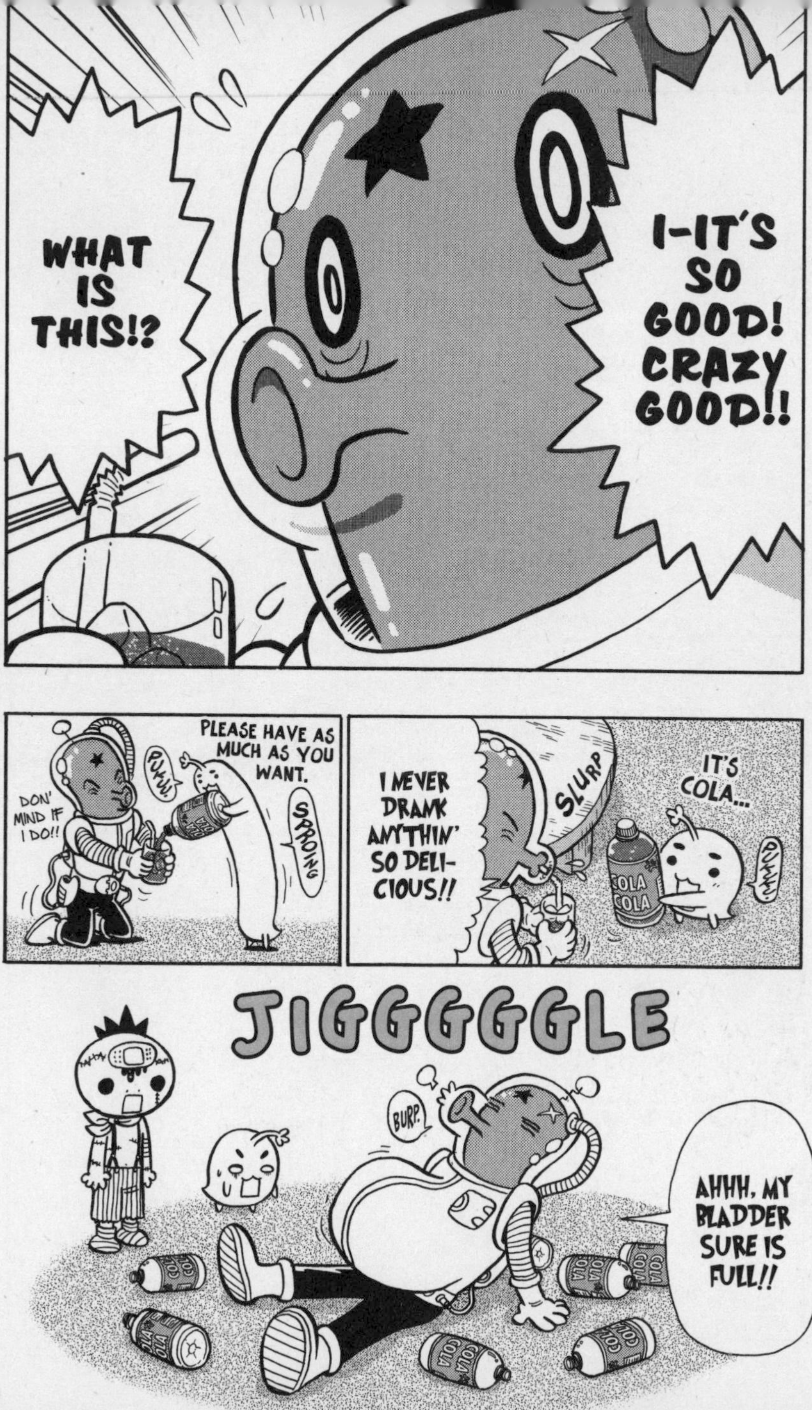
I-IT'S SO GOOD! CRAZY GOOD!!
WHAT IS THIS!?
IT'S COLA...
SLURP
COLA COLA
I NEVER DRANK ANYTHIN' SO DELI-CIOUS!!
PLEASE HAVE AS MUCH AS YOU WANT.
SPROING
DON' MIND IF I DO!!
JIGGGGGLE
AHHH, MY BLADDER SURE IS FULL!!
BURP.

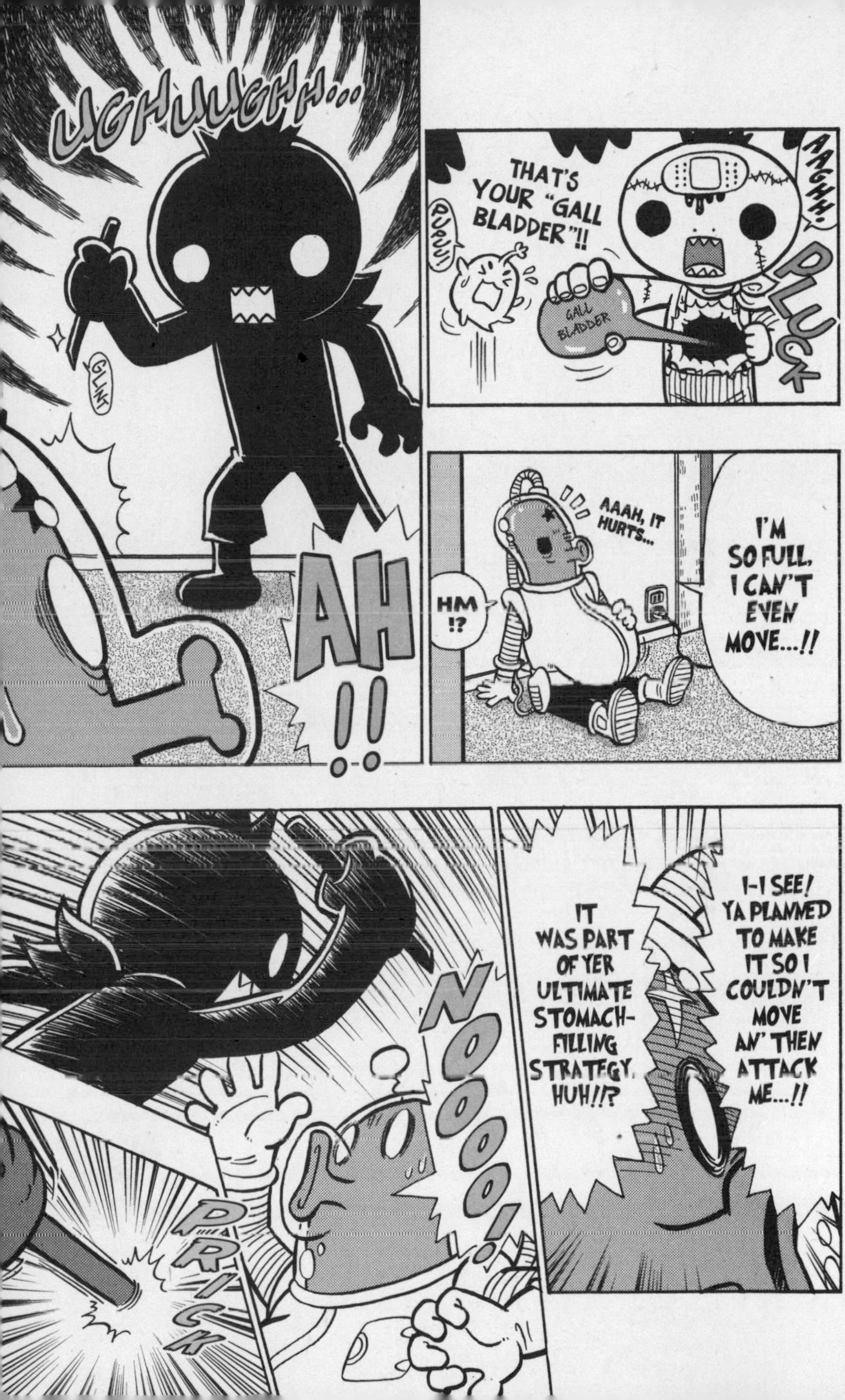
AAGHH!
PLUCK
THAT'S YOUR "GALL BLADDER"!!
PUPUU
GALL BLADDER
I'M SO FULL, I CAN'T EVEN MOVE...!!
AAAH, IT HURTS...
HM !?
UGHUUGHH...
GLINT
AH!!
I-I SEE! YA PLANNED TO MAKE IT SO I COULDN'T MOVE AN' THEN ATTACK ME...!!
IT WAS PART OF YER ULTIMATE STOMACH-FILLING STRATEGY, HUH!!?
NOOOOO!
PRICK

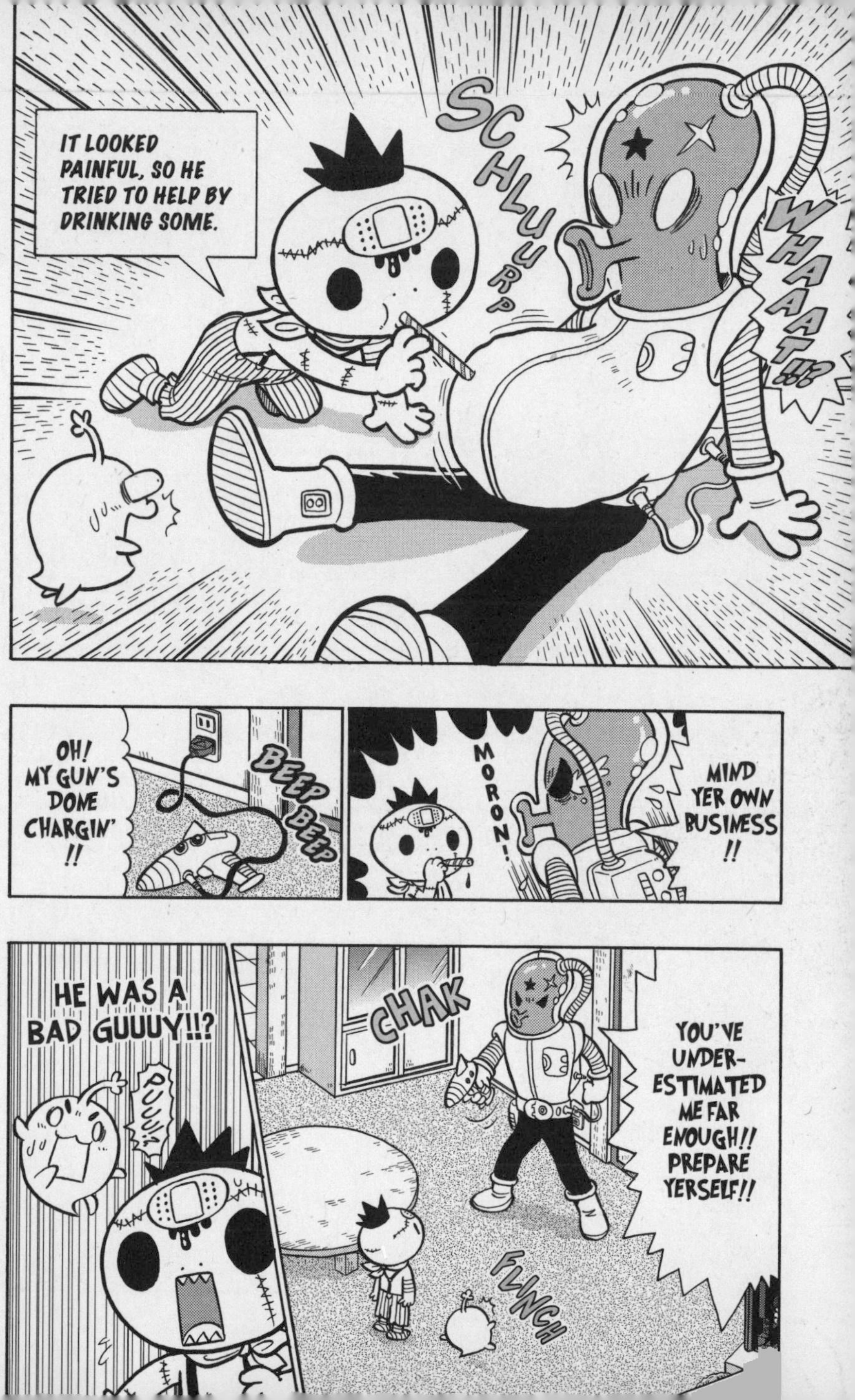
WHAAAT!!?
SCHLUURP
IT LOOKED PAINFUL, SO HE TRIED TO HELP BY DRINKING SOME.
MIND YER OWN BUSINESS!!
MORON!
OH! MY GUN'S DONE CHARGIN'!!
BEEP BEEP
YOU'VE UNDER-ESTIMATED ME FAR ENOUGH!! PREPARE YERSELF!!
CHAK
FLINCH
HE WAS A BAD GUUUY!!?
PUUU!?

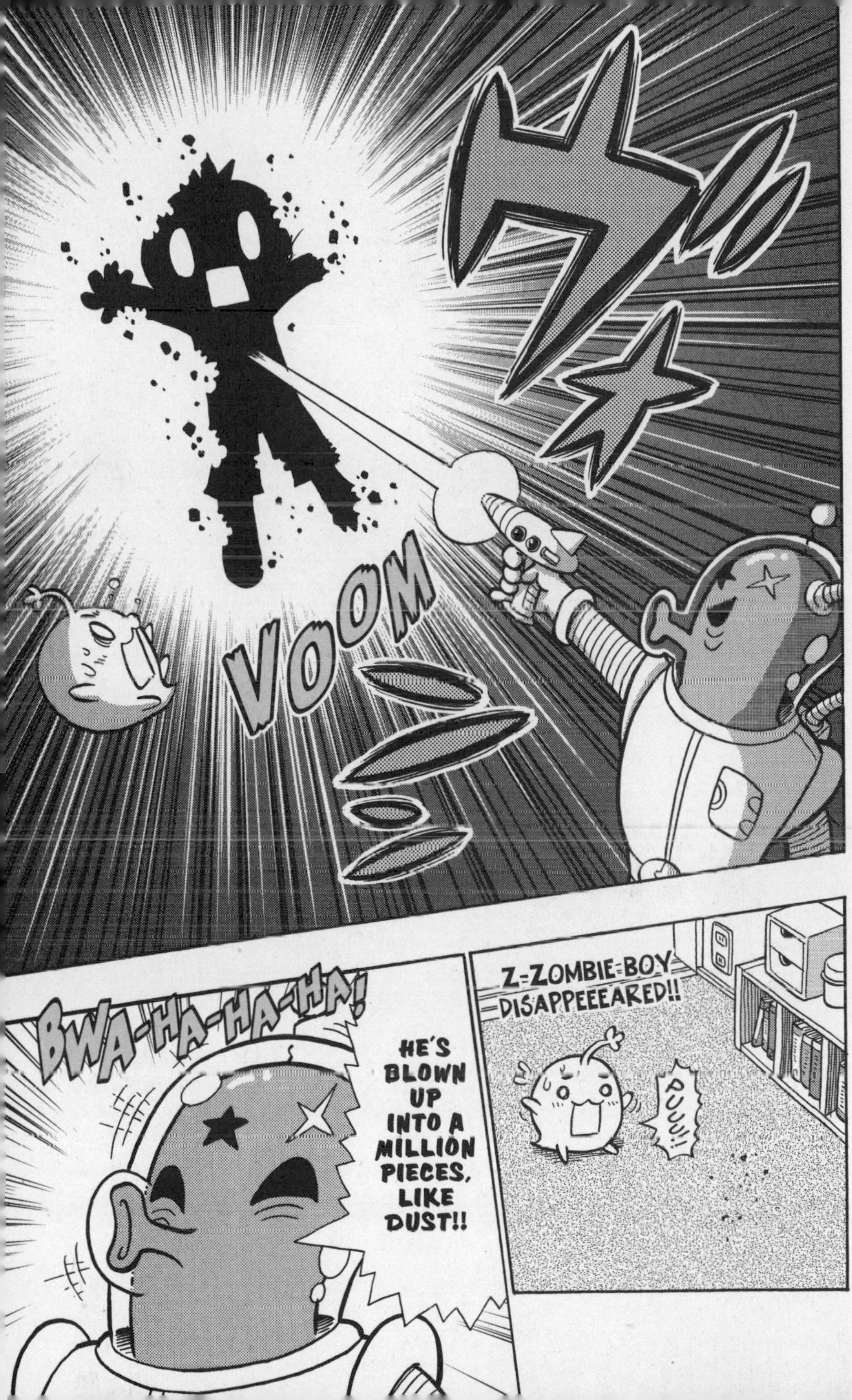
VOOM
Z-ZOMBIE-BOY DISAPPEEEARED!!
PUUU!!
BWA-HA-HA-HA!
HE'S BLOWN UP INTO A MILLION PIECES, LIKE DUST!!

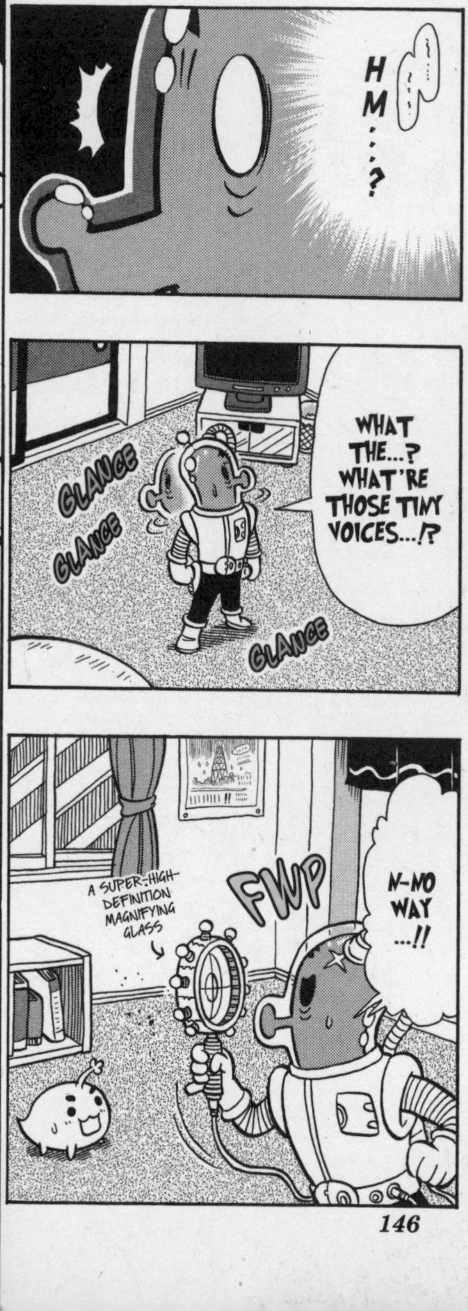
HM...?
WHAT THE...? WHAT'RE THOSE TINY VOICES...!?
GLANCE
GLANCE
GLANCE
N-NO WAY ...!!
FWP
A SUPER-HIGH-DEFINITION MAGNIFYING GLASS

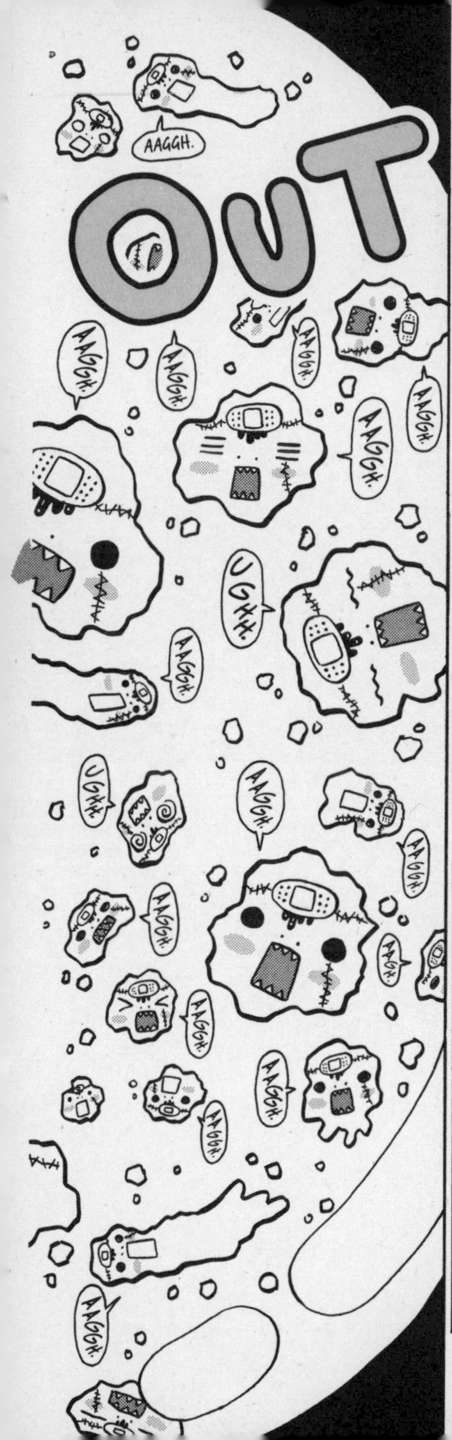
AAGGH.
OUT
AAGGH.
AAGGH.
AAGGH.
AAGGH.
AAGGH.
UGHH.
AAGGH.
UGHH.
AAGGH.
AAGGH.
AAGGH.
AAGGH.
AAGGH.
AAGGH.
AAGGH.
AAGGH.

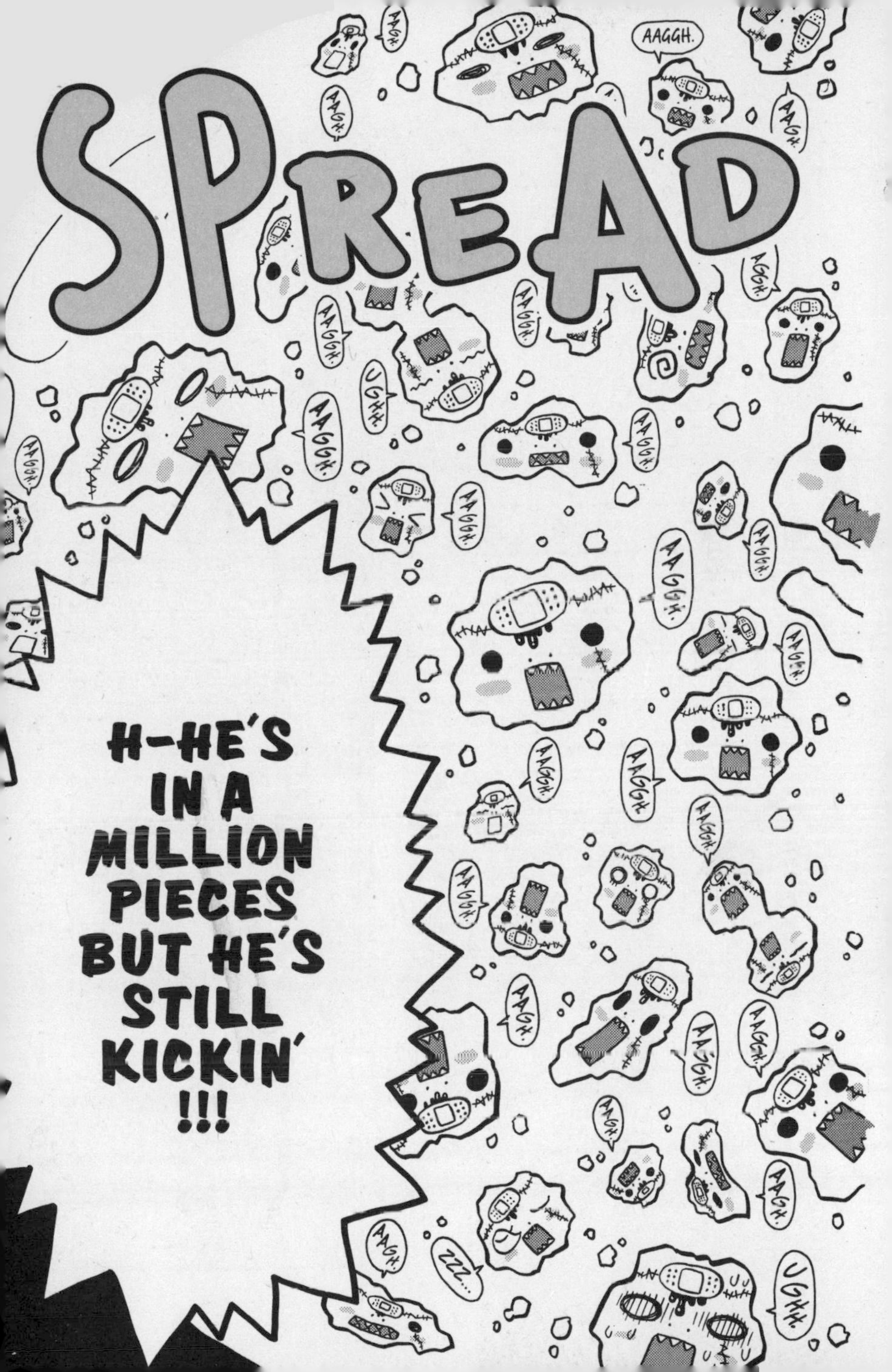

SPREAD
AAGGH.
AAGH.
AAGGH.
AAGH.
AAGGH.
UGHH.
AAGGH.
AAGGH.
AAGGH.
AAGH.
AAGGH.
AAGGH.
AAGGH.
AAGGH.
AAGH.
AAGGH.
AAGGH.
AAGH.
UGHH.
ZZZ...
AAGH.
H-HE'S IN A MILLION PIECES BUT HE'S STILL KICKIN' !!!

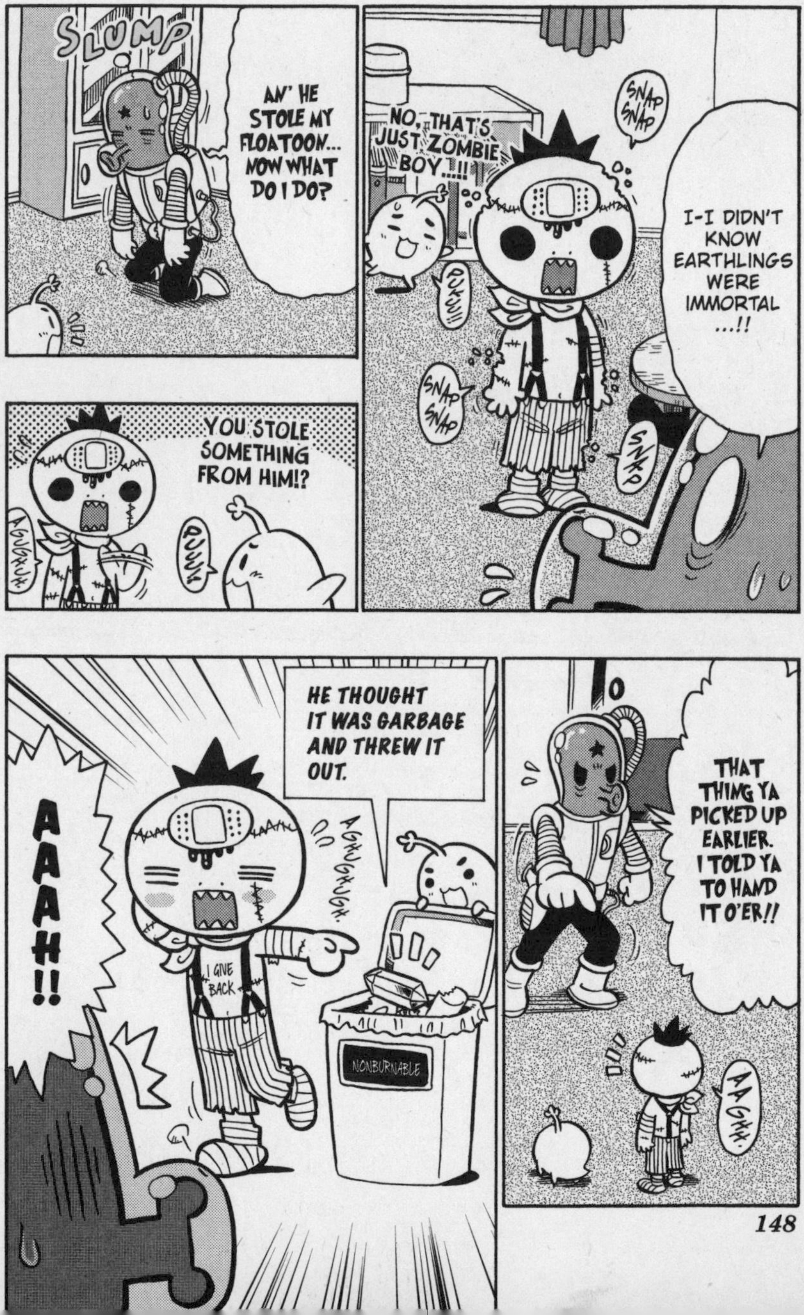

SNAP SNAP
I-I DIDN'T KNOW EARTHLINGS WERE IMMORTAL ...!!
NO, THAT'S JUST ZOMBIE BOY...!!!
SNAP SNAP
SNAP
SLUMP
AN' HE STOLE MY FLOATOON... NOW WHAT DO I DO?
YOU STOLE SOMETHING FROM HIM!?
THAT THING YA PICKED UP EARLIER. I TOLD YA TO HAND IT O'ER!!
HE THOUGHT IT WAS GARBAGE AND THREW IT OUT.
I GIVE BACK
NONBURNABLE
AAAAH!!

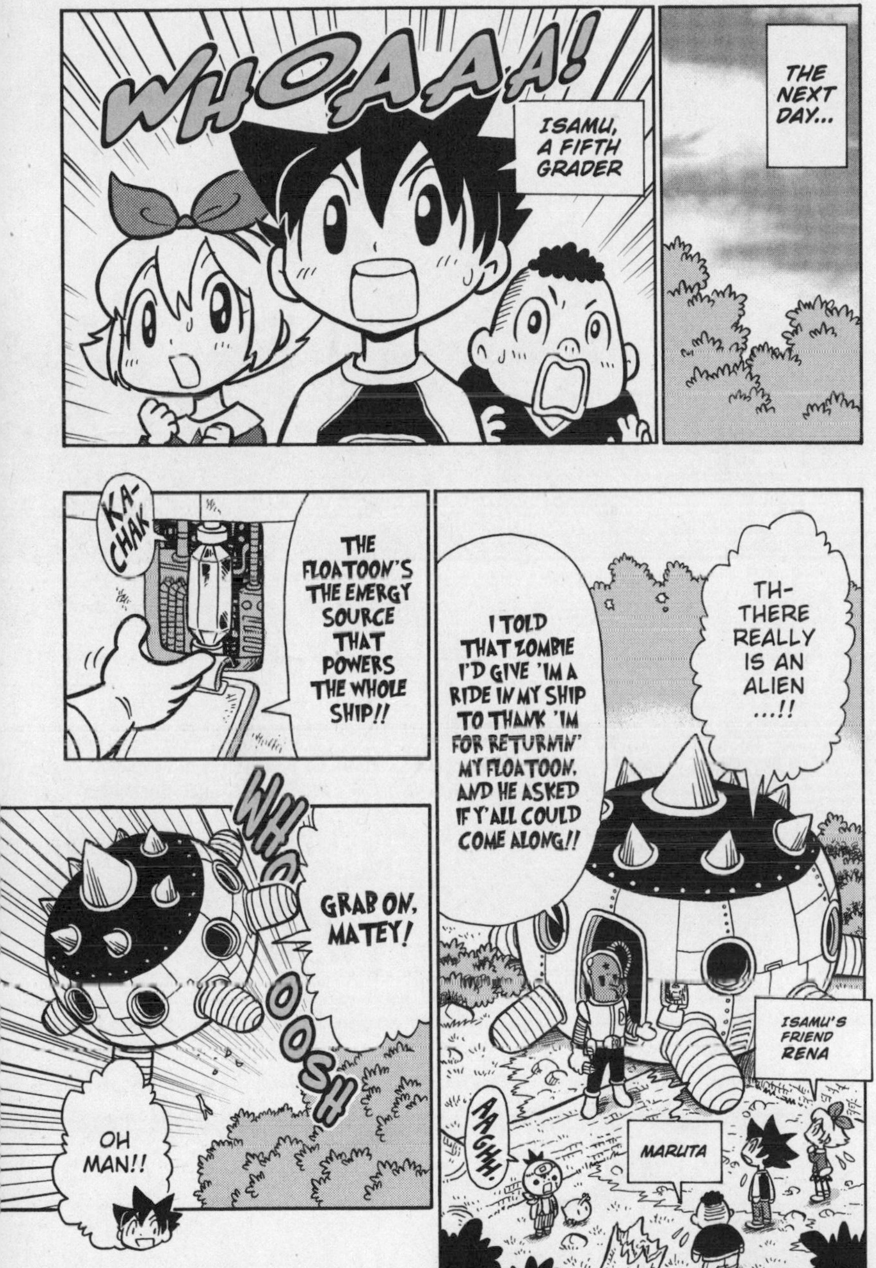
THE NEXT DAY...
WHOAAAA!
ISAMU, A FIFTH GRADER
TH-THERE REALLY IS AN ALIEN ...!!
I TOLD THAT ZOMBIE I'D GIVE 'IM A RIDE IN MY SHIP TO THANK 'IM FOR RETURNIN' MY FLOATOON, AND HE ASKED IF Y'ALL COULD COME ALONG!!
ISAMU'S FRIEND RENA
MARUTA
AAGHH.
KA-CHAK
THE FLOATOON'S THE ENERGY SOURCE THAT POWERS THE WHOLE SHIP!!
WHOOOOSH
GRAB ON, MATEY!
OH MAN!!

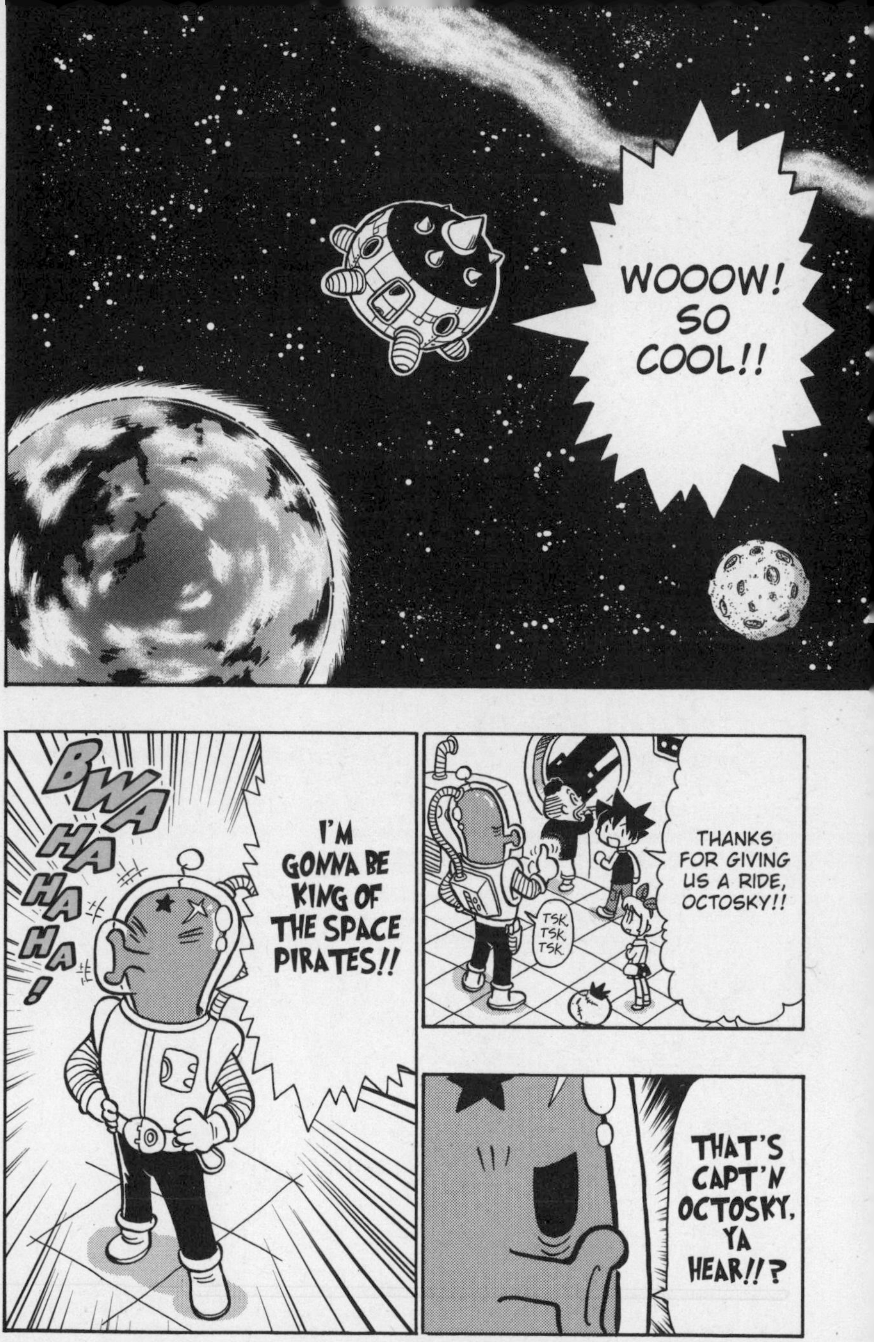
WOOOW! SO COOL!!
THANKS FOR GIVING US A RIDE, OCTOSKY!!
TSK. TSK. TSK.
THAT'S CAPT'N OCTOSKY, YA HEAR!!?
BWAHAHAHAHA!
I'M GONNA BE KING OF THE SPACE PIRATES!!

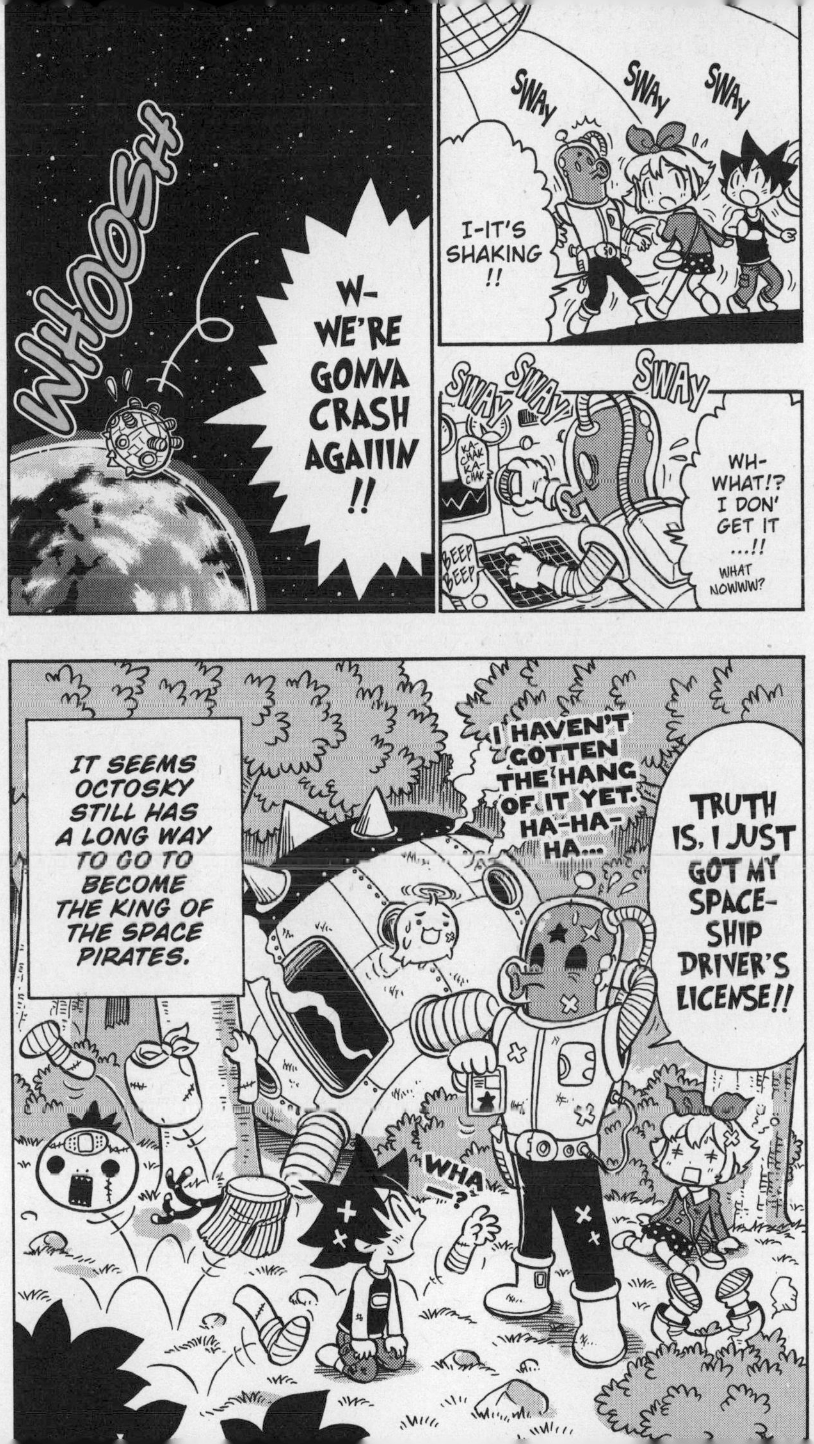
SWAY
SWAY
SWAY
I-IT'S SHAKING !!
SWAY
SWAY
SWAY
KA-CHAK KA-CHAK
BEEP BEEP
WH-WHAT!? I DON' GET IT ...!!
WHAT NOWWW?
WHOOSH
W-WE'RE GONNA CRASH AGAIIIN !!
TRUTH IS, I JUST GOT MY SPACE-SHIP DRIVER'S LICENSE!!
I HAVEN'T GOTTEN THE HANG OF IT YET. HA-HA-HA...
IT SEEMS OCTOSKY STILL HAS A LONG WAY TO GO TO BECOME THE KING OF THE SPACE PIRATES.
WHA—?

EARTH AIN'T TOO BAD!!
YUUUM!
PIZZA BUN
CONVENIENCE STORE
COLA

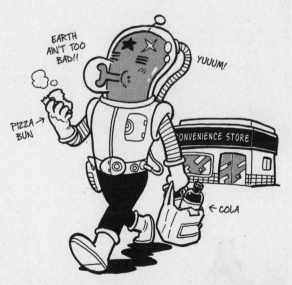

ZOMBIE BOY SETZ UP SHOP!

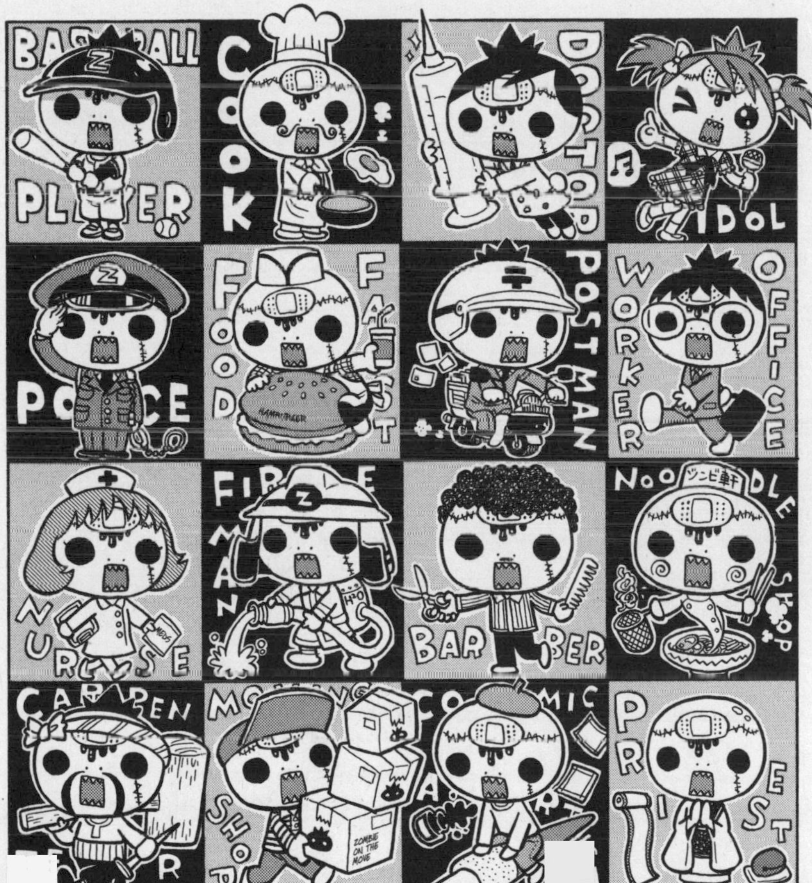
IDOL
DOCTOR
COOK
OFFICE WORKER
POSTMAN
FAST FOOD
HAMBURGER
ゾンビ軒
BARBER
H2O
MEDS
PRIEST
ZOMBIE ON THE MOVE

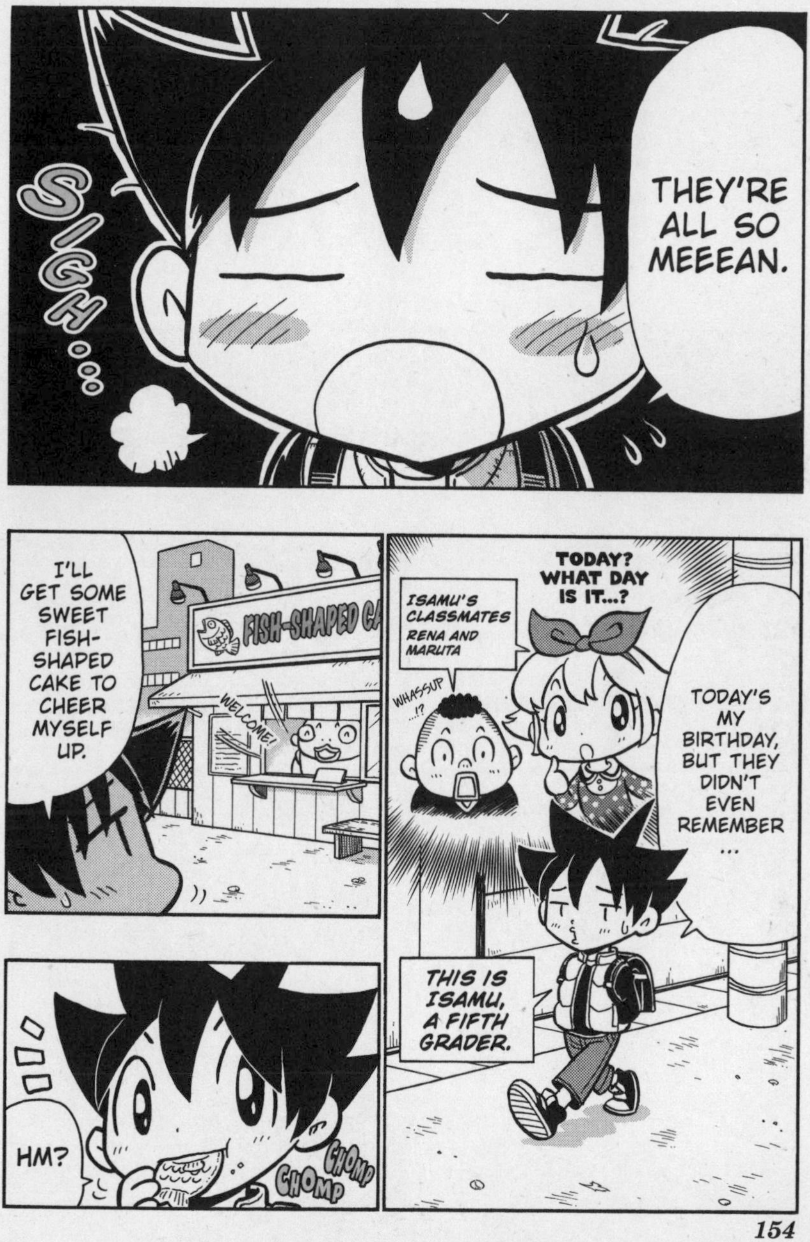
SIGH...
THEY'RE ALL SO MEEEAN.
TODAY? WHAT DAY IS IT...?
ISAMU'S CLASSMATES RENA AND MARUTA
WHASSUP ...!?
TODAY'S MY BIRTHDAY, BUT THEY DIDN'T EVEN REMEMBER ...
THIS IS ISAMU, A FIFTH GRADER.
I'LL GET SOME SWEET FISH-SHAPED CAKE TO CHEER MYSELF UP.
FISH-SHAPED CA
WELCOME!
HM?
CHOMP
CHOMP

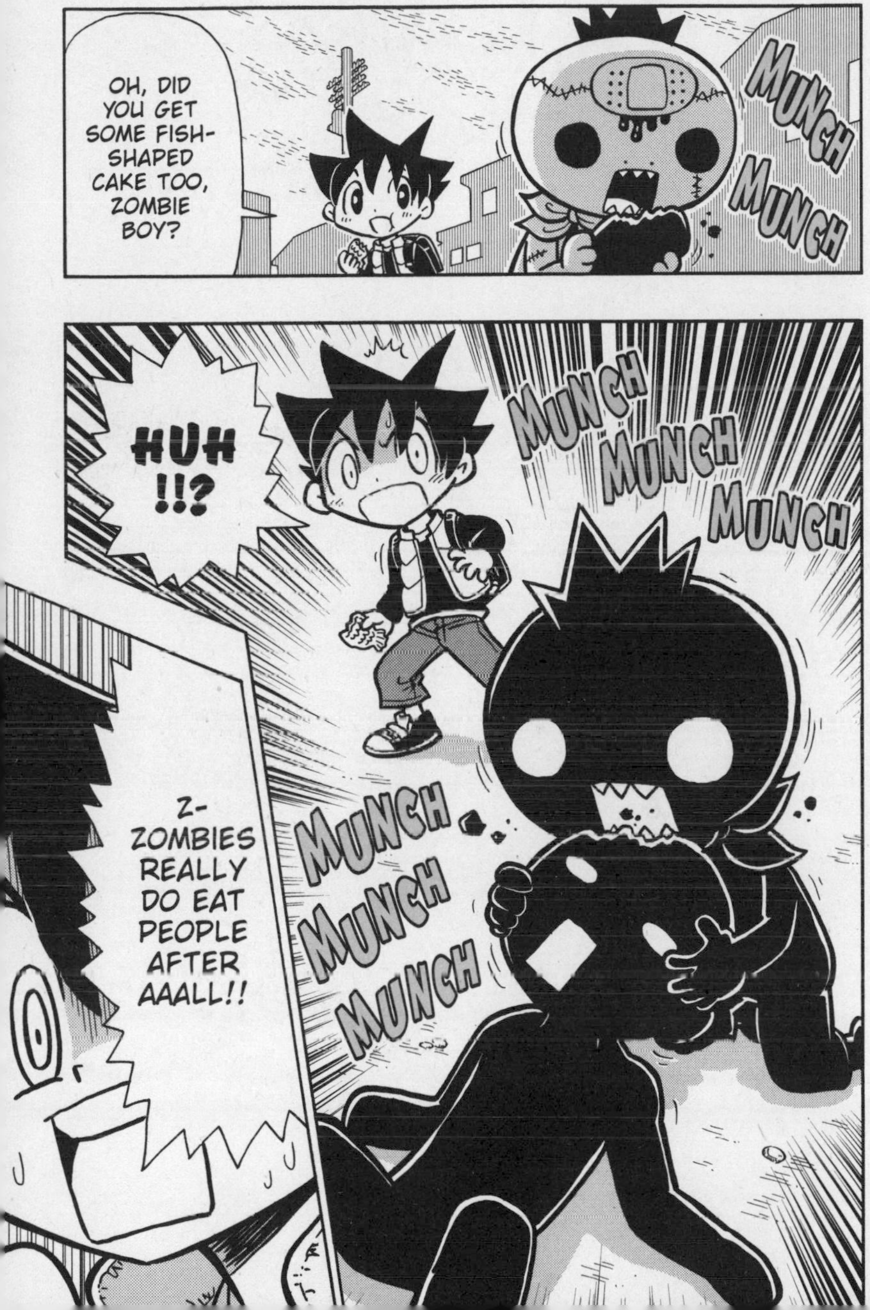
MUNCH MUNCH
OH, DID YOU GET SOME FISH-SHAPED CAKE TOO, ZOMBIE BOY?
MUNCH MUNCH MUNCH
HUH !!?
MUNCH MUNCH MUNCH
Z-ZOMBIES REALLY DO EAT PEOPLE AFTER AAALL!!

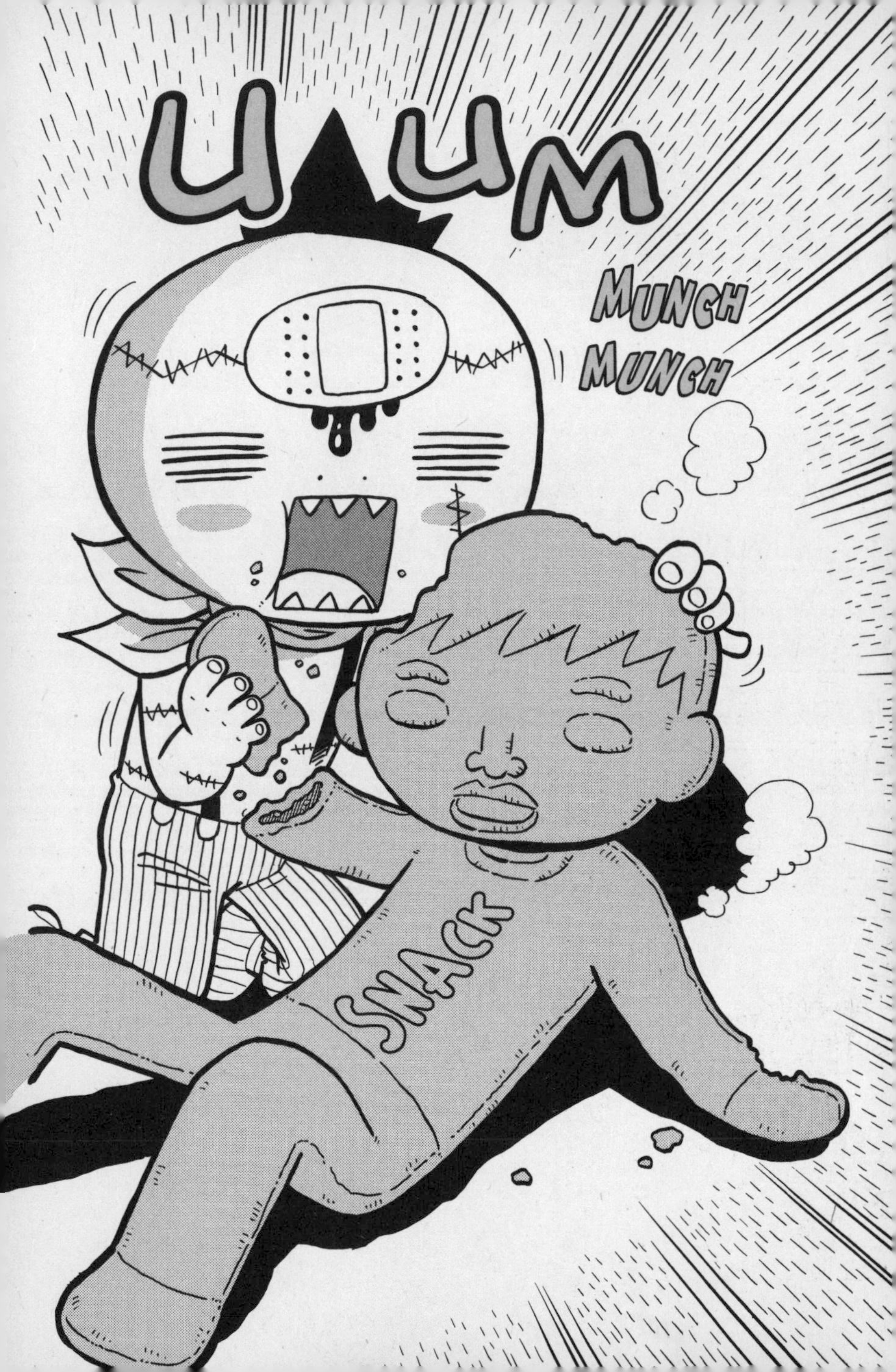
UMUM
MUNCH
MUNCH
SNACK

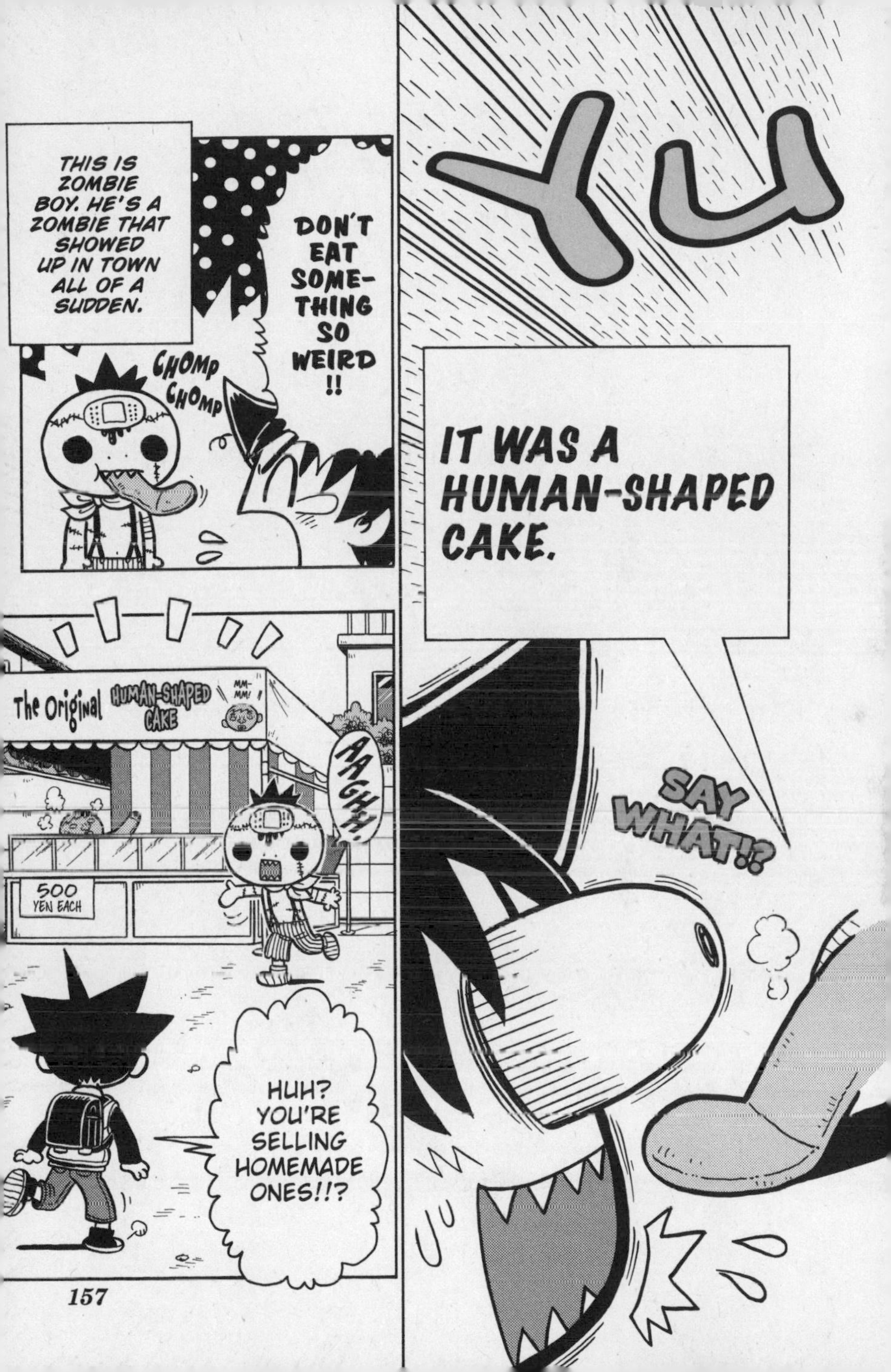
YU
IT WAS A HUMAN-SHAPED CAKE.
SAY WHAT!?
THIS IS ZOMBIE BOY. HE'S A ZOMBIE THAT SHOWED UP IN TOWN ALL OF A SUDDEN.
DON'T EAT SOMETHING SO WEIRD!!
CHOMP CHOMP
The Original HUMAN-SHAPED CAKE
MM-MM!
AAGHH!
500 YEN EACH
HUH? YOU'RE SELLING HOMEMADE ONES!!?

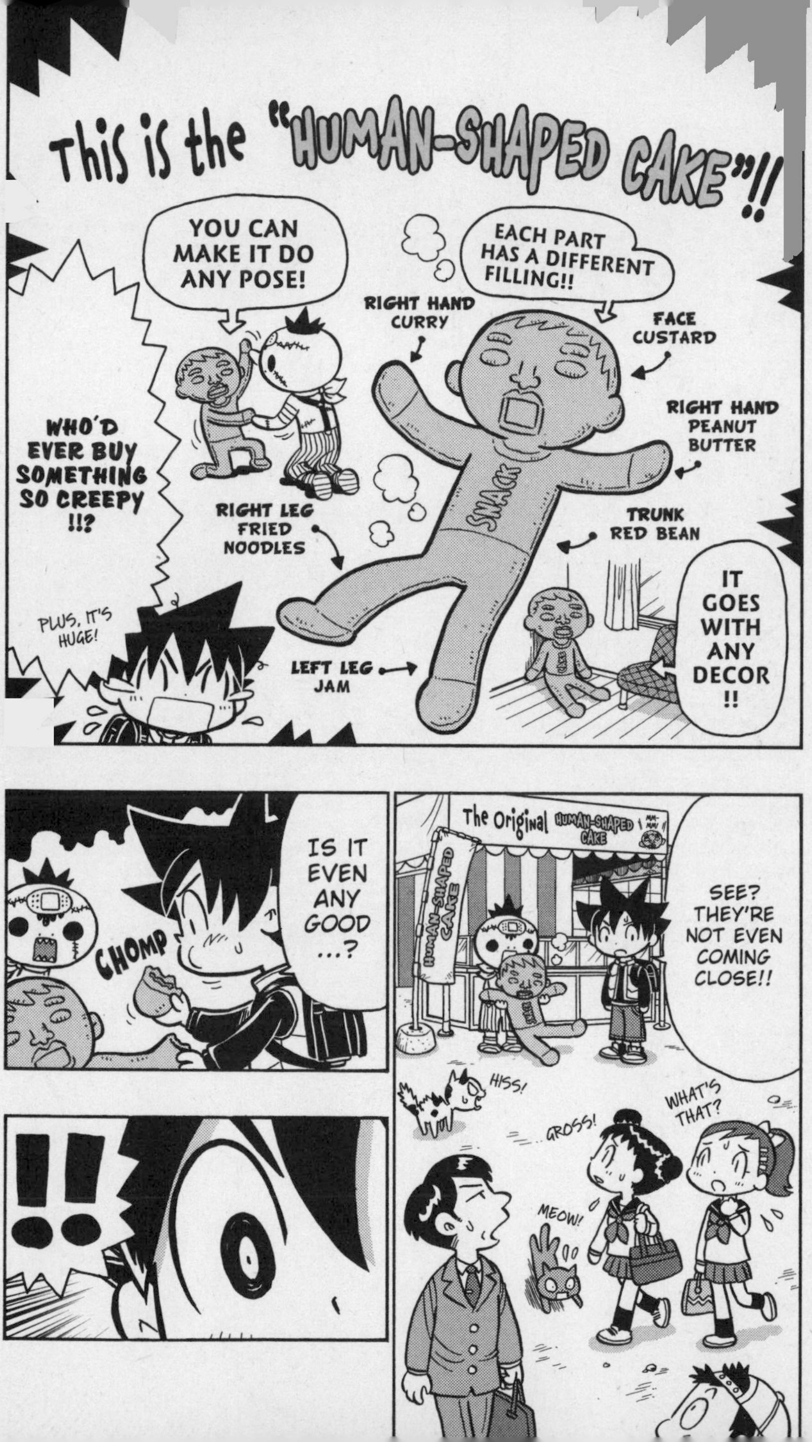
This is the "HUMAN-SHAPED CAKE"!!
EACH PART HAS A DIFFERENT FILLING!!
FACE CUSTARD
RIGHT HAND CURRY
RIGHT HAND PEANUT BUTTER
TRUNK RED BEAN
RIGHT LEG FRIED NOODLES
IT GOES WITH ANY DECOR!!
LEFT LEG JAM
YOU CAN MAKE IT DO ANY POSE!
WHO'D EVER BUY SOMETHING SO CREEPY!!?
PLUS, IT'S HUGE!
The Original HUMAN-SHAPED CAKE
MAN-MAN
HUMAN-SHAPED CAKE
SEE? THEY'RE NOT EVEN COMING CLOSE!!
HISS!
WHAT'S THAT?
...GROSS!
MEOW!
IS IT EVEN ANY GOOD...?
CHOMP
!!

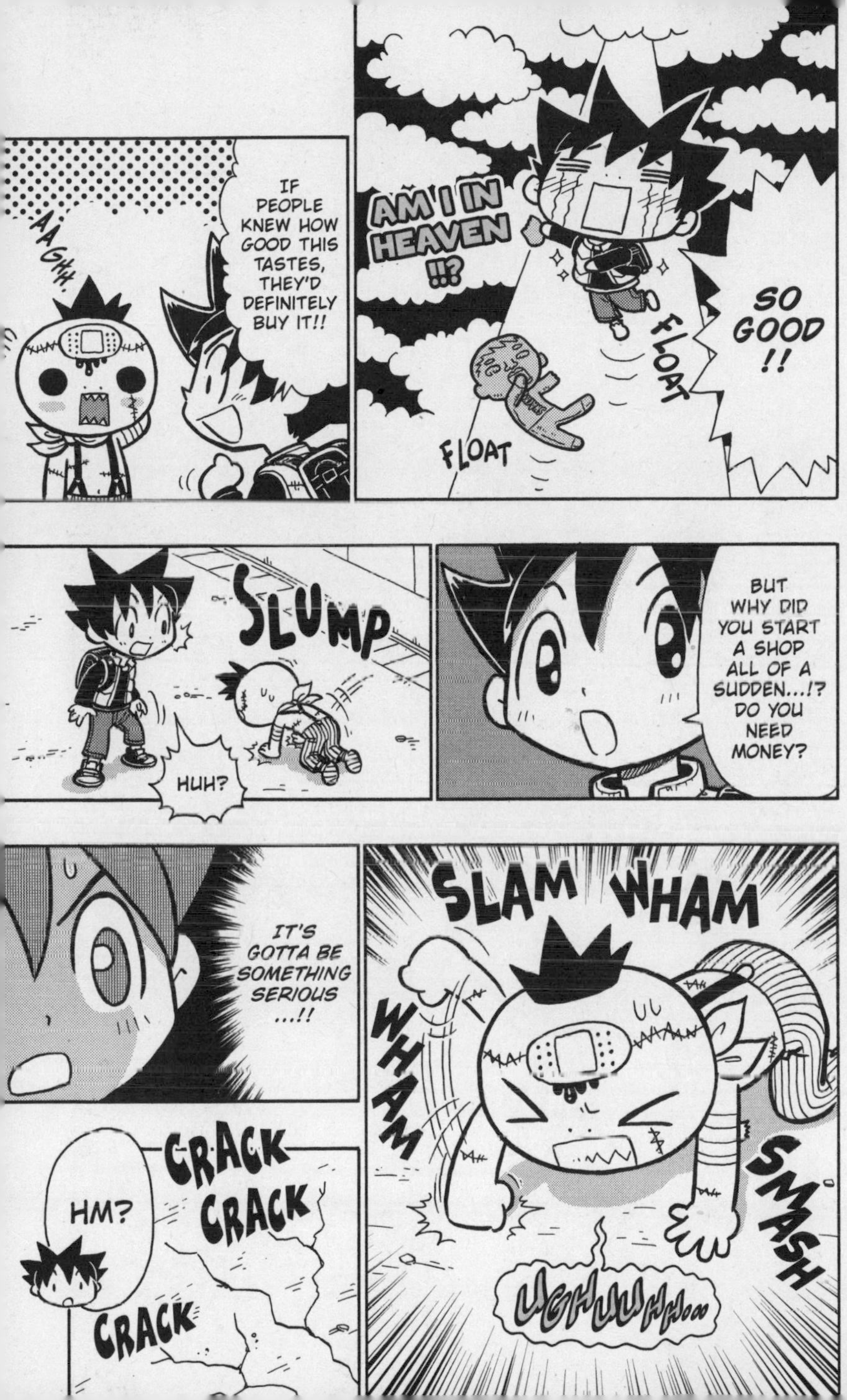
AM I IN HEAVEN !!?
SO GOOD !!
FLOAT
FLOAT
IF PEOPLE KNEW HOW GOOD THIS TASTES, THEY'D DEFINITELY BUY IT!!
AAGHH.
BUT WHY DID YOU START A SHOP ALL OF A SUDDEN...!? DO YOU NEED MONEY?
SLUMP
HUH?
SLAM
WHAM
WHAM
SMASH
UGHUUHH...
IT'S GOTTA BE SOMETHING SERIOUS ...!!
HM?
CRACK
CRACK
CRACK

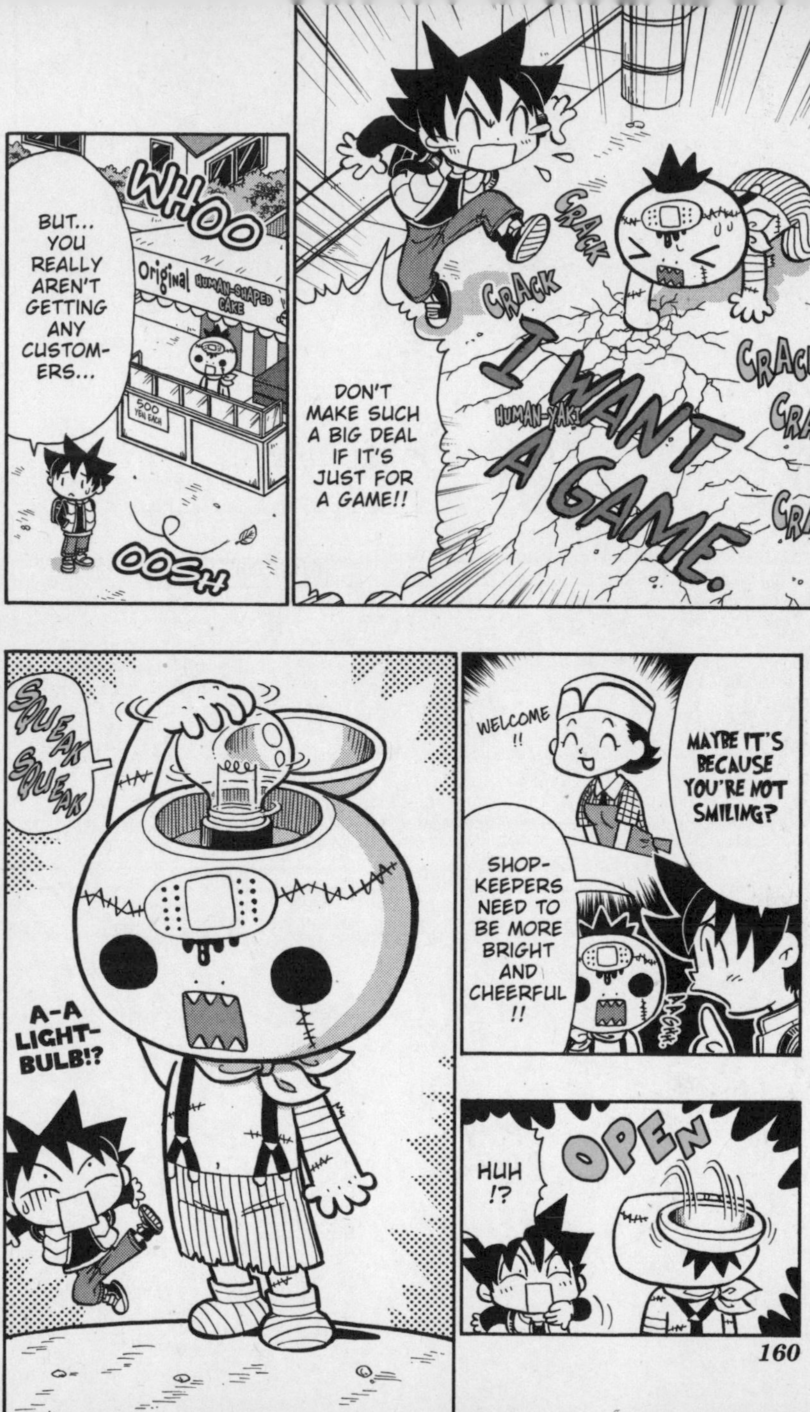
CRACK
CRACK
DON'T MAKE SUCH A BIG DEAL IF IT'S JUST FOR A GAME!!
HUMAN-YAKI
I WANT A GAME.
CRACK
CRACK
CRACK
WHOO
BUT... YOU REALLY AREN'T GETTING ANY CUSTOMERS...
Original HUMAN-SHAPED CAKE
500 YEN EACH
OOSH
WELCOME!!
MAYBE IT'S BECAUSE YOU'RE NOT SMILING?
SHOP-KEEPERS NEED TO BE MORE BRIGHT AND CHEERFUL!!
OPEN
HUH!?
SQUEAK SQUEAK
A-A LIGHT-BULB!?

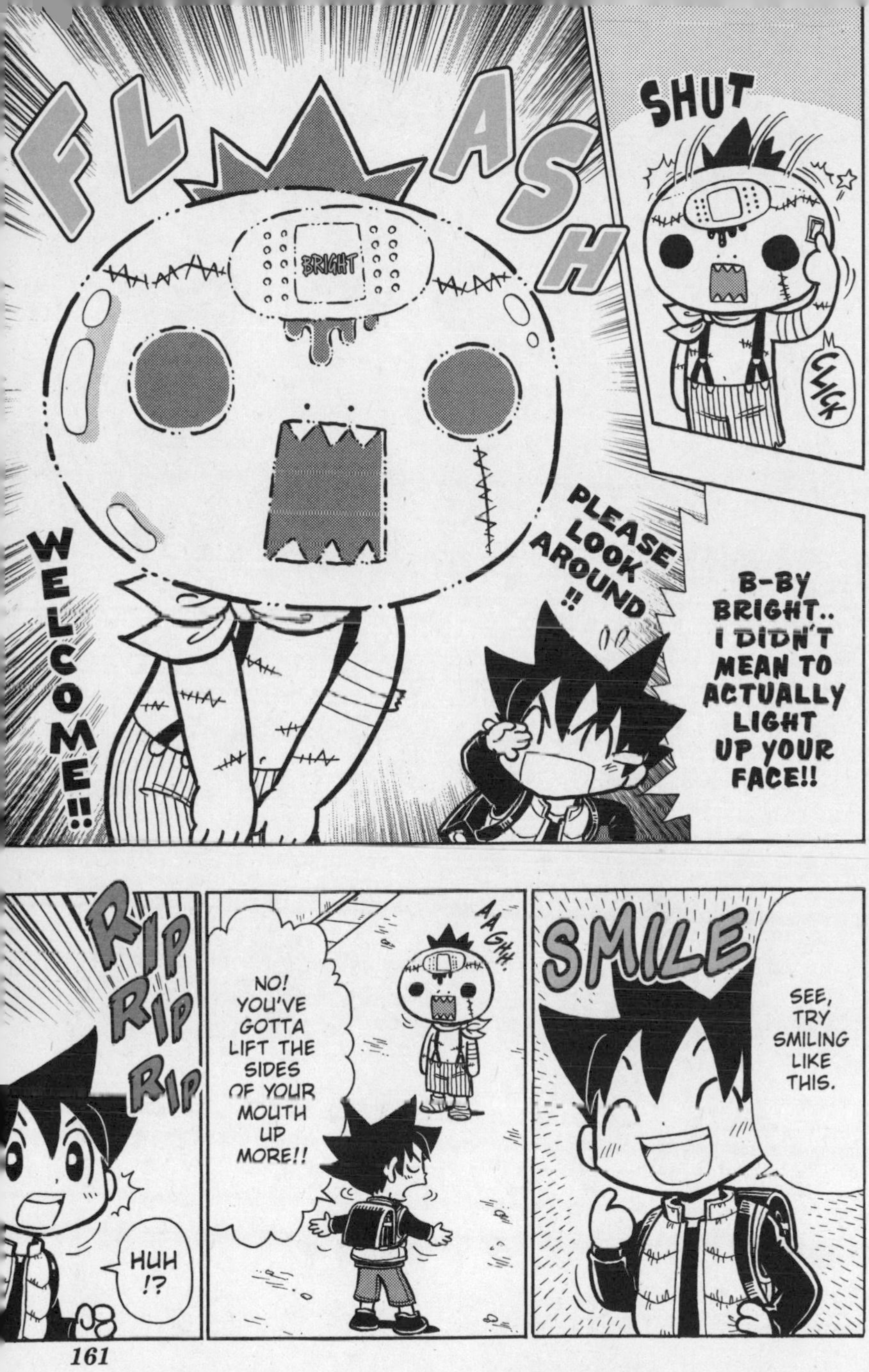
SHUT
CLICK
FLASH
BRIGHT
WELCOME!!
PLEASE LOOK AROUND!!
B-BY BRIGHT.. I DIDN'T MEAN TO ACTUALLY LIGHT UP YOUR FACE!!
SMILE
SEE, TRY SMILING LIKE THIS.
AAGHH
NO! YOU'VE GOTTA LIFT THE SIDES OF YOUR MOUTH UP MORE!!
RIP RIP RIP
HUH !?

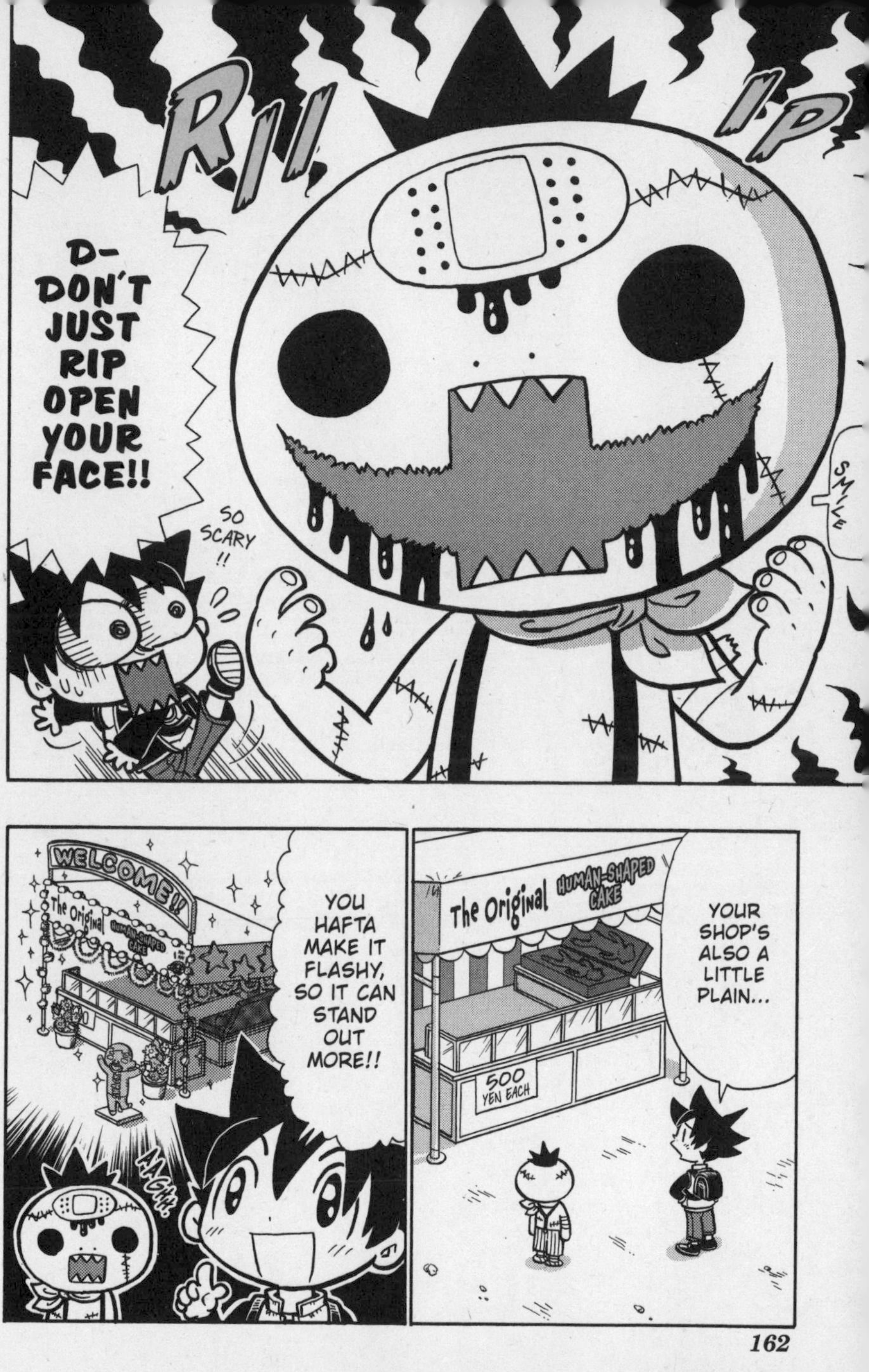
RIIIP
SMILE
D-DON'T JUST RIP OPEN YOUR FACE!!
SO SCARY!!
YOUR SHOP'S ALSO A LITTLE PLAIN...
The Original HUMAN-SHAPED CAKE
500 YEN EACH
YOU HAFTA MAKE IT FLASHY, SO IT CAN STAND OUT MORE!!
WELCOME!!
The Original HUMAN-SHAPED CAKE
AAGH!!

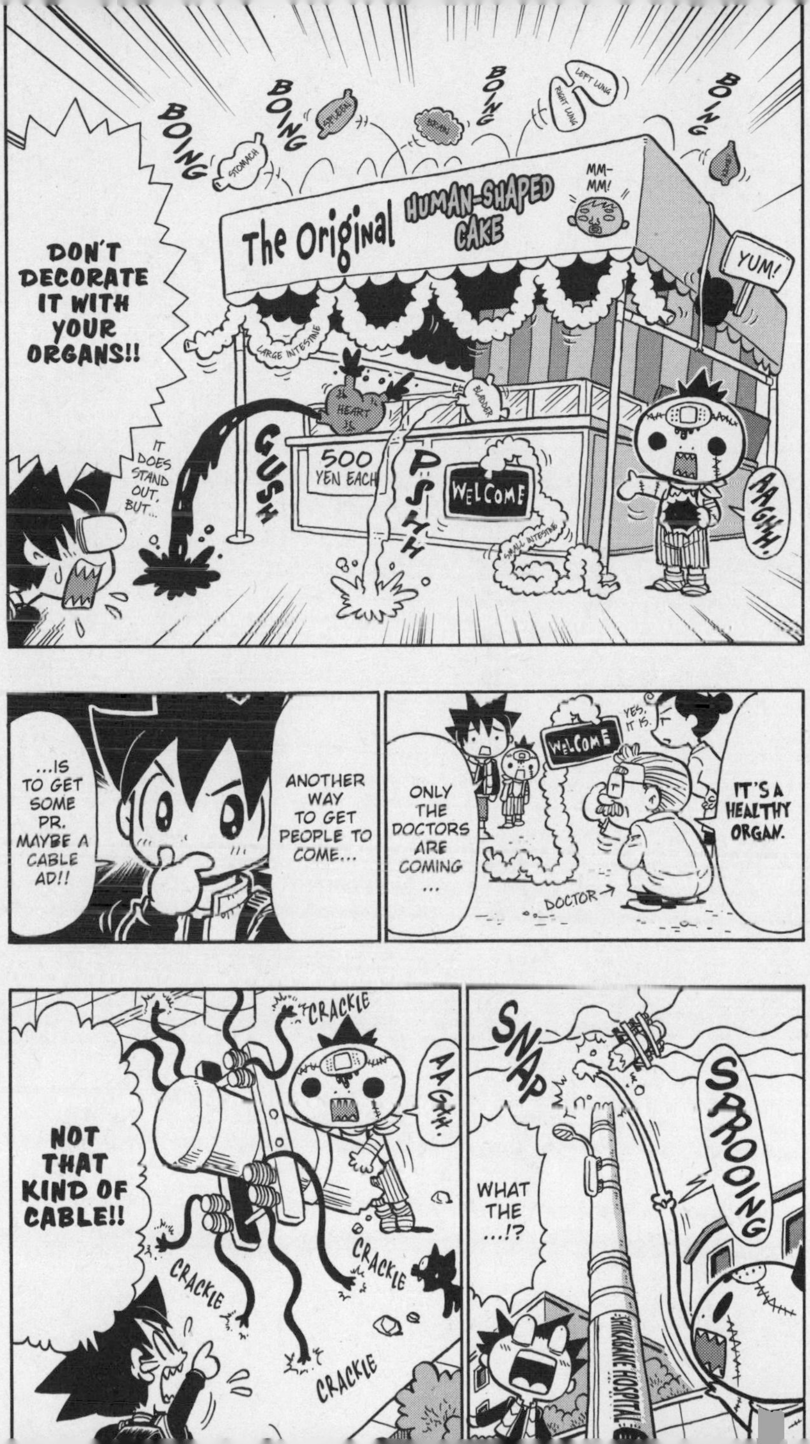
BOING
LEFT LUNG
RIGHT LUNG
BOING
BRAIN
SPLEEN
BOING
STOMACH
BOING
MM-MM!
YUM!
The Original HUMAN-SHAPED CAKE
DON'T DECORATE IT WITH YOUR ORGANS!!
LARGE INTESTINE
BLADDER
HEART
AAGHH.
SMALL INTESTINE
WELCOME
PSHHH
500 YEN EACH
GUSH
IT DOES STAND OUT, BUT...
IT'S A HEALTHY ORGAN.
YES, IT IS.
WELCOME
ONLY THE DOCTORS ARE COMING ...
DOCTOR→
ANOTHER WAY TO GET PEOPLE TO COME...
...IS TO GET SOME PR. MAYBE A CABLE AD!!
SPROOING
SNAP
WHAT THE ...!?
SHIKABANE HOSPITAL
CRACKLE
AAGHH.
NOT THAT KIND OF CABLE!!
CRACKLE
CRACKLE
CRACKLE

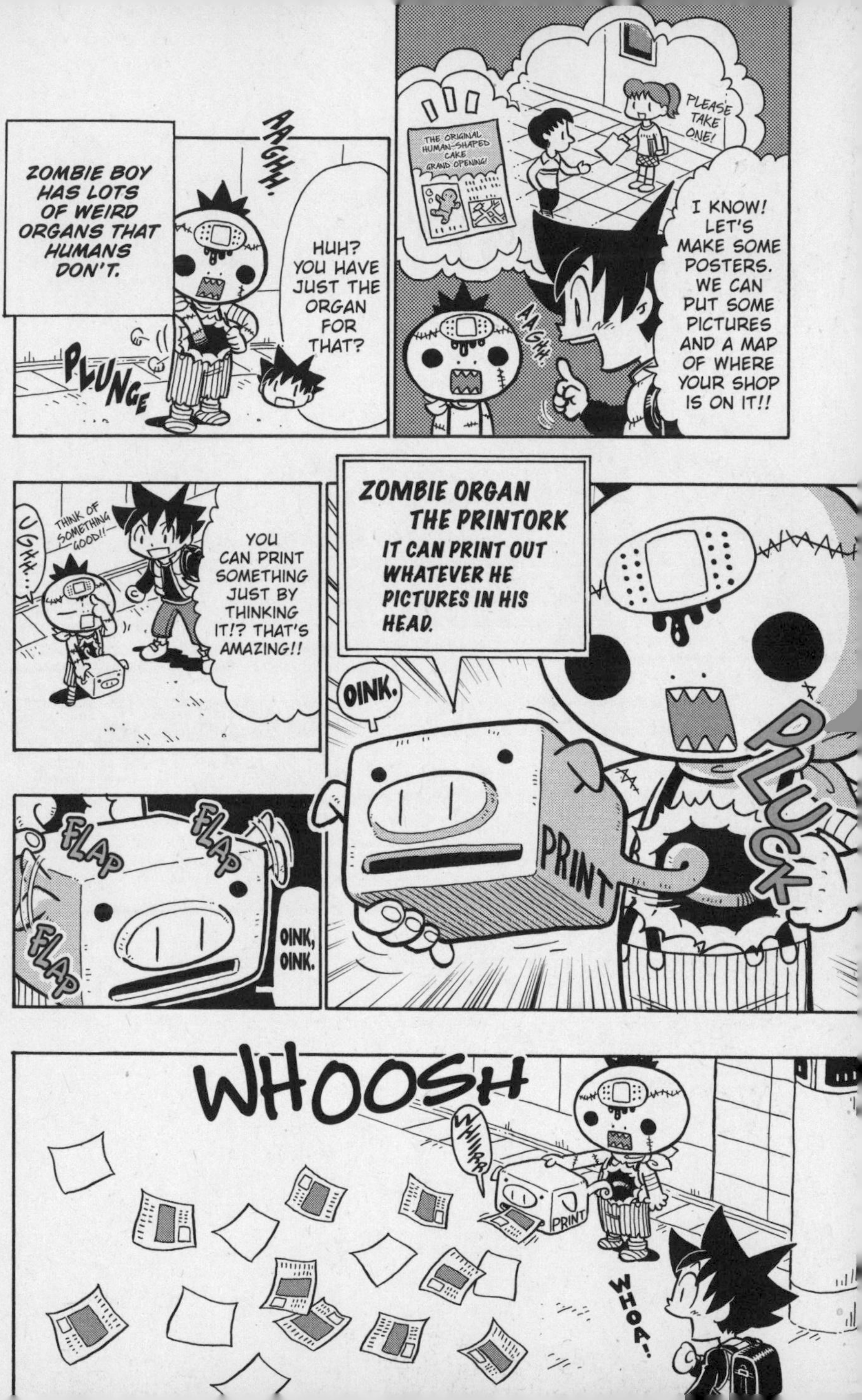
PLEASE TAKE ONE!
THE ORIGINAL HUMAN-SHAPED CAKE GRAND OPENING!
I KNOW! LET'S MAKE SOME POSTERS. WE CAN PUT SOME PICTURES AND A MAP OF WHERE YOUR SHOP IS ON IT!!
AAGHH.
AAGHH.
HUH? YOU HAVE JUST THE ORGAN FOR THAT?
ZOMBIE BOY HAS LOTS OF WEIRD ORGANS THAT HUMANS DON'T.
PLUNGE
ZOMBIE ORGAN THE PRINTORK
IT CAN PRINT OUT WHATEVER HE PICTURES IN HIS HEAD.
PLUCK
OINK.
PRINT
YOU CAN PRINT SOMETHING JUST BY THINKING IT!? THAT'S AMAZING!!
THINK OF SOMETHING GOOD!!
UGHH...
FLAP
FLAP
FLAP
OINK, OINK.
WHOOSH
WHIRR
PRINT
WHOA!

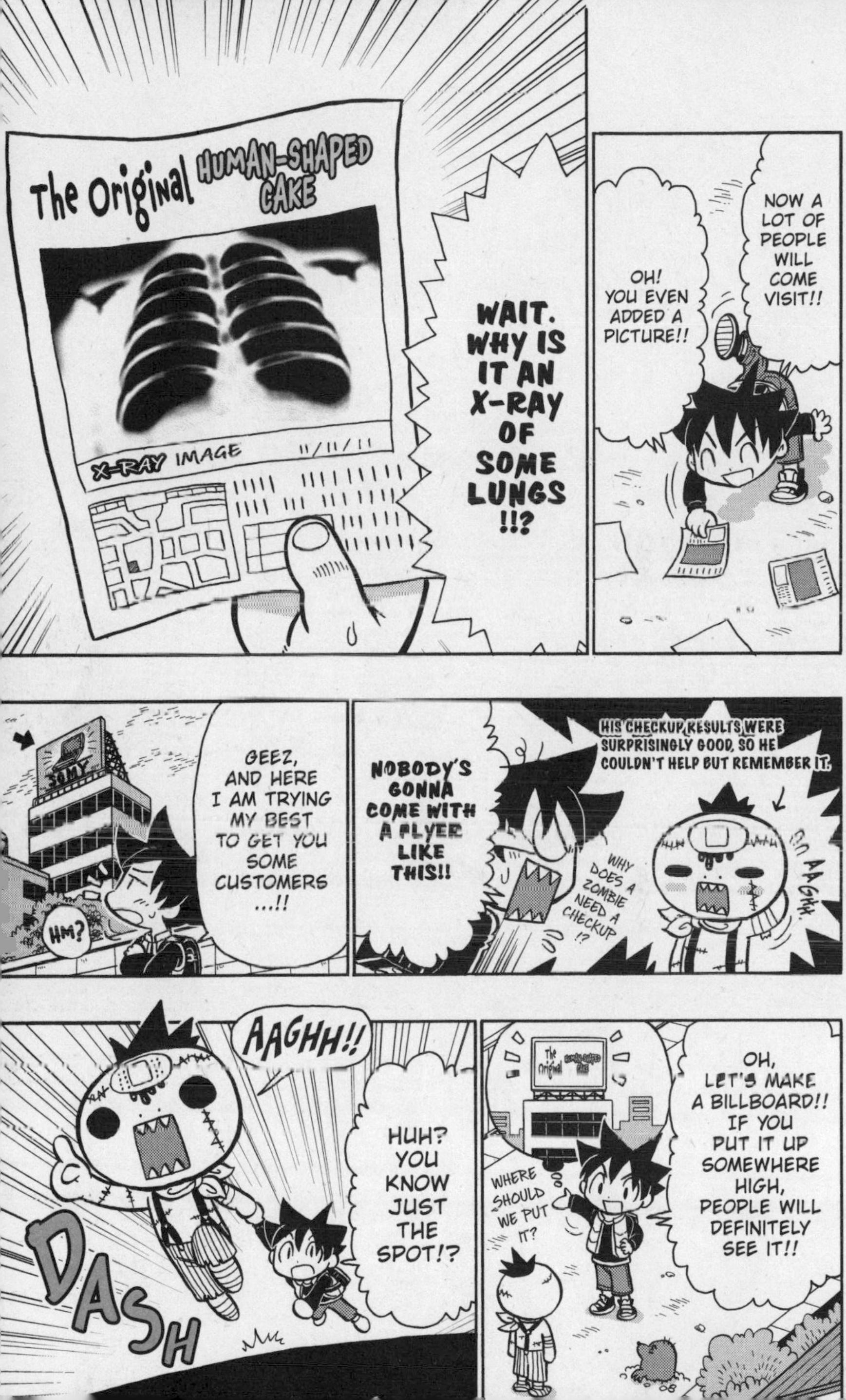
NOW A LOT OF PEOPLE WILL COME VISIT!!
OH! YOU EVEN ADDED A PICTURE!!
The Original HUMAN-SHAPED CAKE
X-RAY IMAGE
WAIT. WHY IS IT AN X-RAY OF SOME LUNGS!!?
HIS CHECKUP RESULTS WERE SURPRISINGLY GOOD, SO HE COULDN'T HELP BUT REMEMBER IT.
AAGHH.
WHY DOES A ZOMBIE NEED A CHECKUP!?
NOBODY'S GONNA COME WITH A FLYER LIKE THIS!!
GEEZ, AND HERE I AM TRYING MY BEST TO GET YOU SOME CUSTOMERS...!!
HM?
OH, LET'S MAKE A BILLBOARD!! IF YOU PUT IT UP SOMEWHERE HIGH, PEOPLE WILL DEFINITELY SEE IT!!
The Original
WHERE SHOULD WE PUT IT?
AAGHH!!
HUH? YOU KNOW JUST THE SPOT!?
DASH

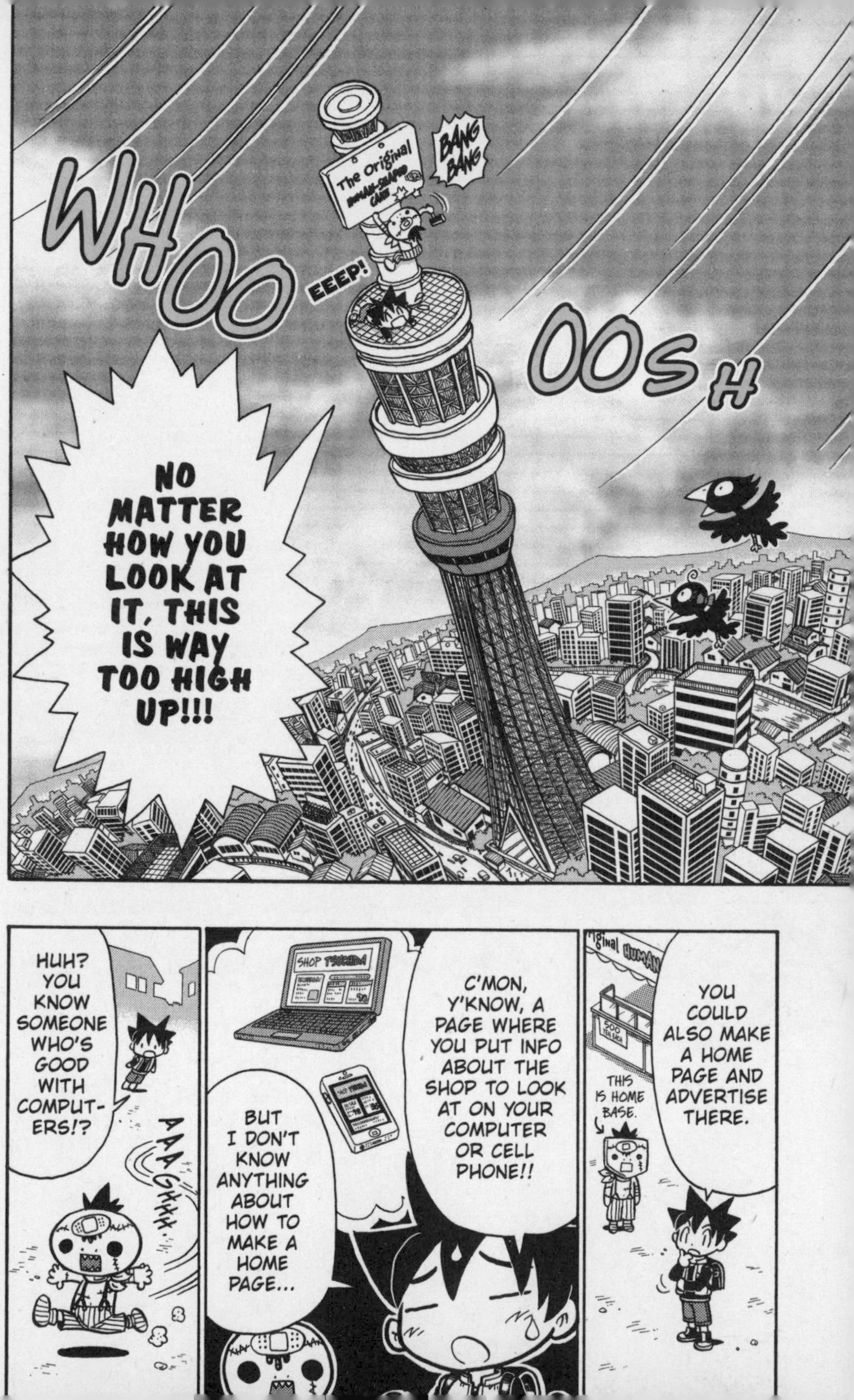
The Original HUMAN-SHAPED CAKE
BANG BANG
WHOOOOSH
EEEP!
NO MATTER HOW YOU LOOK AT IT, THIS IS WAY TOO HIGH UP!!!
Original HUMAN
YOU COULD ALSO MAKE A HOME PAGE AND ADVERTISE THERE.
THIS IS HOME BASE.
SHOP TSUCHIDA
C'MON, Y'KNOW, A PAGE WHERE YOU PUT INFO ABOUT THE SHOP TO LOOK AT ON YOUR COMPUTER OR CELL PHONE!!
BUT I DON'T KNOW ANYTHING ABOUT HOW TO MAKE A HOME PAGE...
HUH? YOU KNOW SOMEONE WHO'S GOOD WITH COMPUTERS!?
AAAGHHH

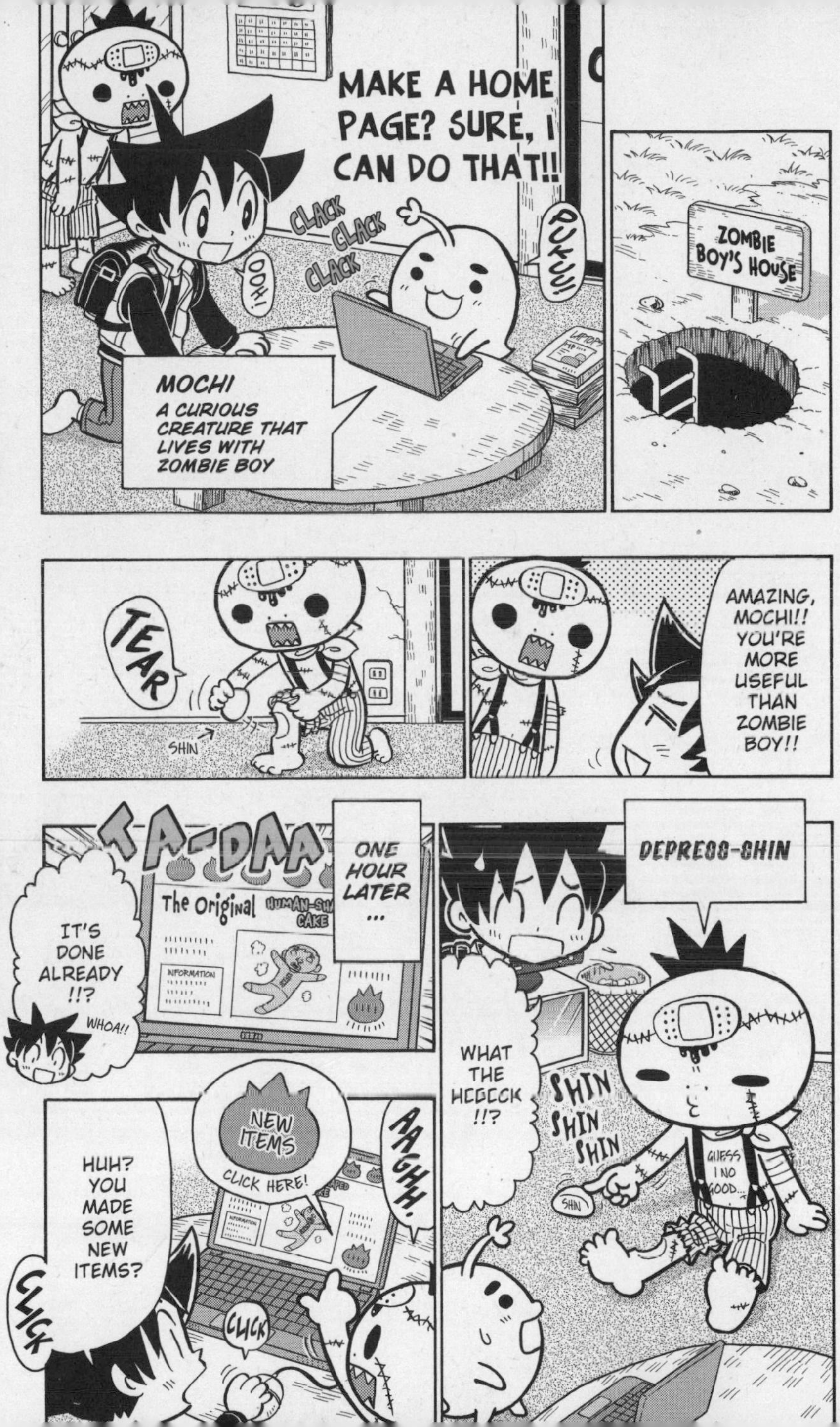
ZOMBIE BOY'S HOUSE
MAKE A HOME PAGE? SURE, I CAN DO THAT!!
PUKUU!
CLACK CLACK CLACK
OOH!
MOCHI
A CURIOUS CREATURE THAT LIVES WITH ZOMBIE BOY
AMAZING, MOCHI!! YOU'RE MORE USEFUL THAN ZOMBIE BOY!!
TEAR
SHIN
DEPRESS-SHIN
WHAT THE HECCCK!!?
SHIN SHIN SHIN
GUESS I NO GOOD...
SHIN
ONE HOUR LATER...
TA-DAA
The Original
CAKE
INFORMATION
IT'S DONE ALREADY!!?
WHOA!!
AAGHH!
NEW ITEMS
CLICK HERE!
HUH? YOU MADE SOME NEW ITEMS?
CLICK
CLICK

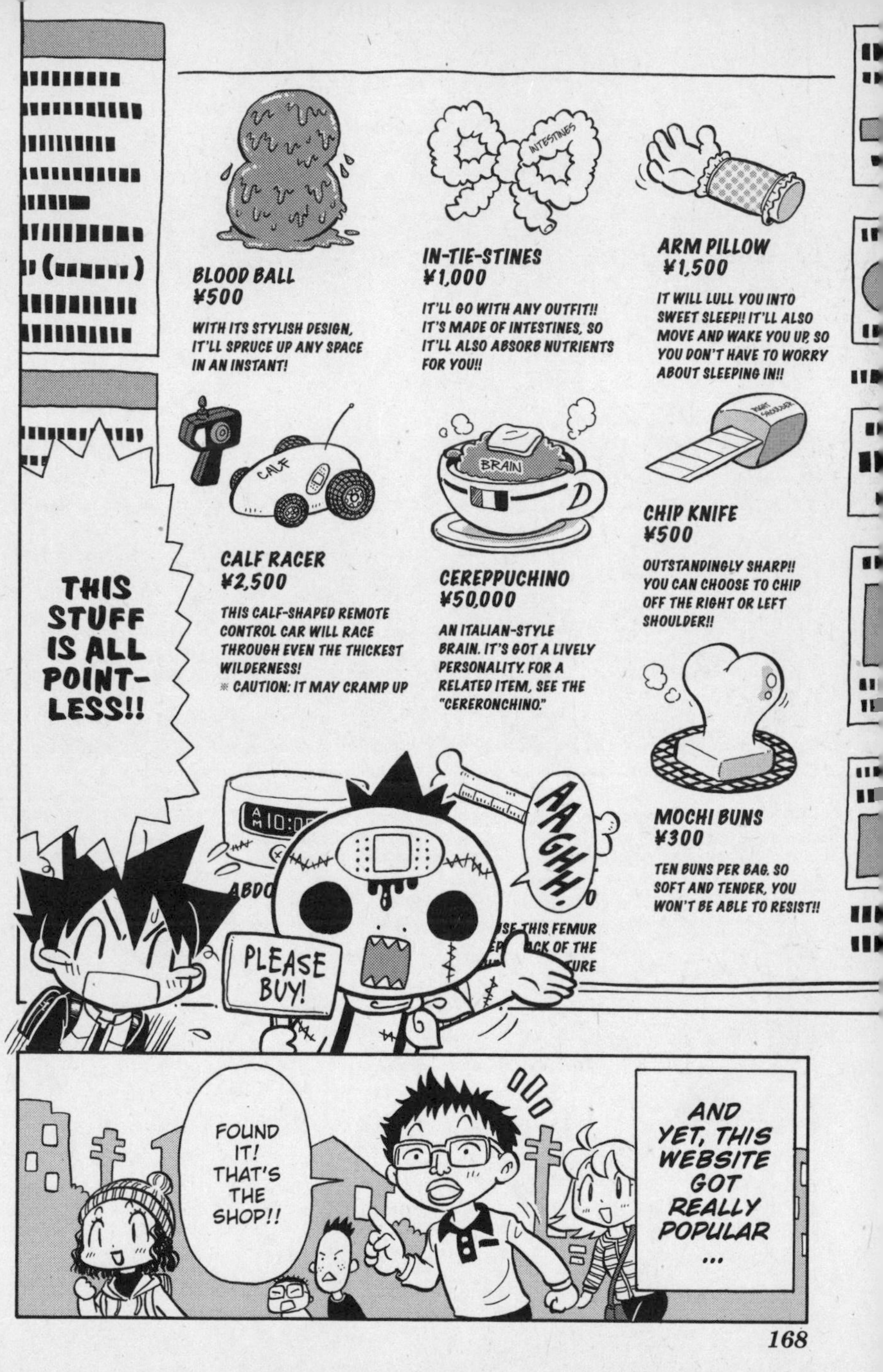

ARM PILLOW
¥1,500
IT WILL LULL YOU INTO SWEET SLEEP!! IT'LL ALSO MOVE AND WAKE YOU UP, SO YOU DON'T HAVE TO WORRY ABOUT SLEEPING IN!!
INTESTINES
IN-TIE-STINES
¥1,000
IT'LL GO WITH ANY OUTFIT!! IT'S MADE OF INTESTINES, SO IT'LL ALSO ABSORB NUTRIENTS FOR YOU!!
BLOOD BALL
¥500
WITH ITS STYLISH DESIGN, IT'LL SPRUCE UP ANY SPACE IN AN INSTANT!
CHIP KNIFE
¥500
OUTSTANDINGLY SHARP!! YOU CAN CHOOSE TO CHIP OFF THE RIGHT OR LEFT SHOULDER!!
BRAIN
CEREPPUCHINO
¥50,000
AN ITALIAN-STYLE BRAIN. IT'S GOT A LIVELY PERSONALITY. FOR A RELATED ITEM, SEE THE "CERERONCHINO."
CALF
CALF RACER
¥2,500
THIS CALF-SHAPED REMOTE CONTROL CAR WILL RACE THROUGH EVEN THE THICKEST WILDERNESS!
※ CAUTION: IT MAY CRAMP UP
MOCHI BUNS
¥300
TEN BUNS PER BAG. SO SOFT AND TENDER, YOU WON'T BE ABLE TO RESIST!!
AAGHH!
THIS STUFF IS ALL POINTLESS!!
PLEASE BUY!
AND YET, THIS WEBSITE GOT REALLY POPULAR...
FOUND IT! THAT'S THE SHOP!!

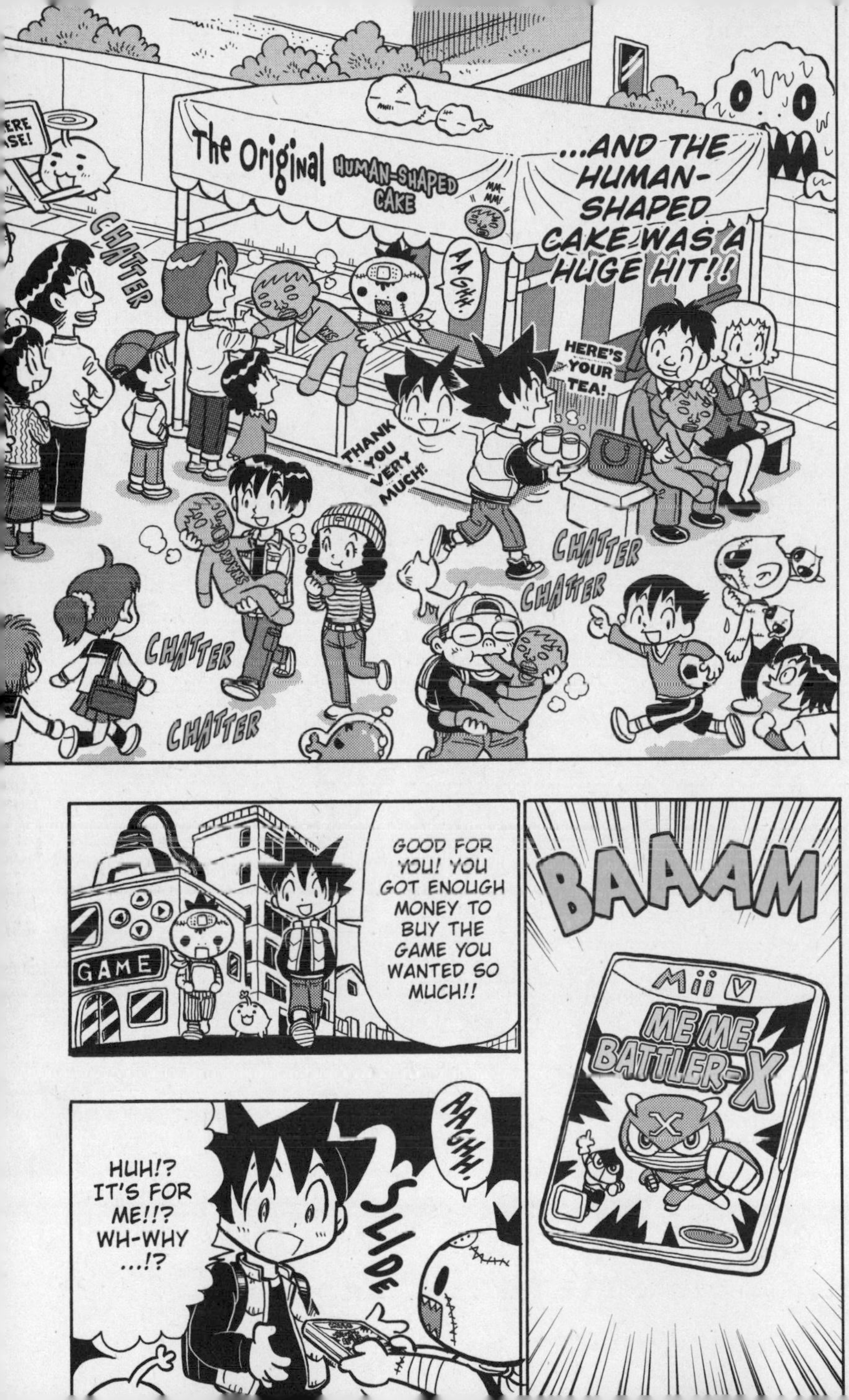
...AND THE HUMAN-SHAPED CAKE WAS A HUGE HIT!!
The Original HUMAN-SHAPED CAKE
MM-MM!
AAGHH.
HERE'S YOUR TEA!
THANK YOU VERY MUCH!
CHATTER
CHATTER
CHATTER
CHATTER
CHATTER
BAAAM
Mii V
ME ME BATTLER-X
GOOD FOR YOU! YOU GOT ENOUGH MONEY TO BUY THE GAME YOU WANTED SO MUCH!!
GAME
AAGHH.
SLIDE
HUH!? IT'S FOR ME!!? WH-WHY ...!?

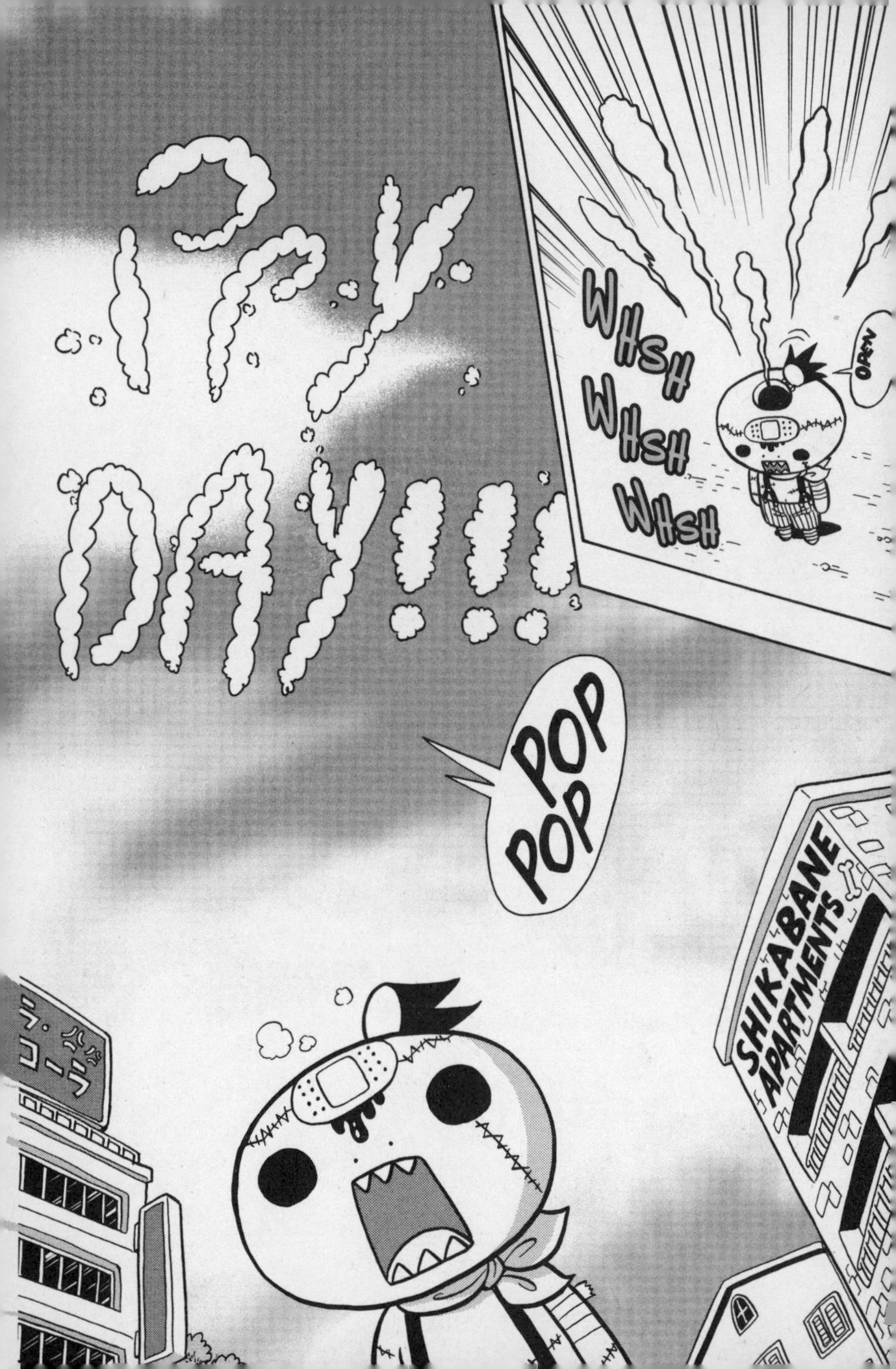
OPEN
WHSH
WHSH
WHSH
PAY DAY!!!
POP POP
SHIKABANE APARTMENTS

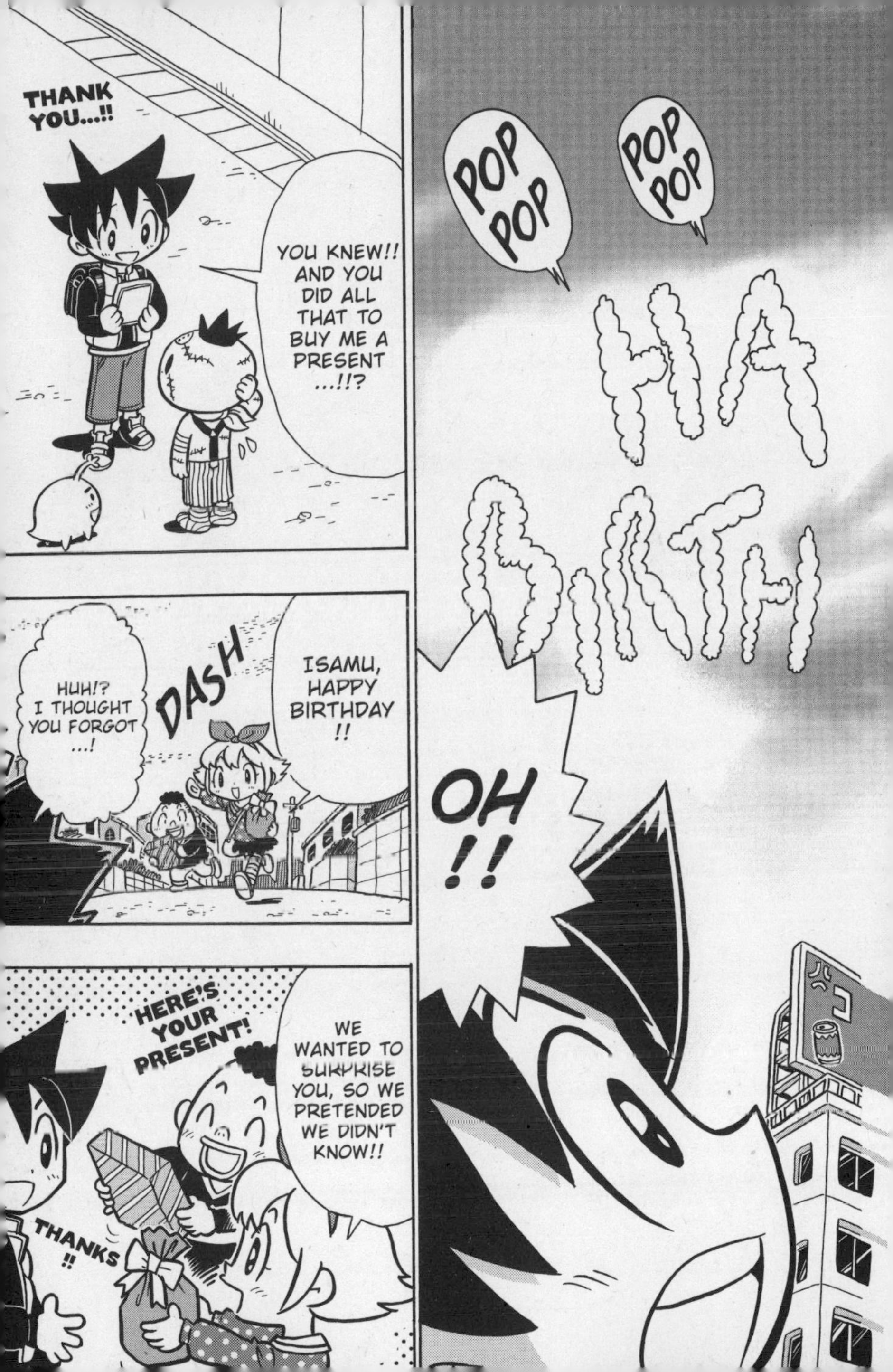
POP POP
POP POP
HA
BIRTH
OH!!
YOU KNEW!! AND YOU DID ALL THAT TO BUY ME A PRESENT ...!!?
THANK YOU...!!
ISAMU, HAPPY BIRTHDAY!!
DASH
HUH!? I THOUGHT YOU FORGOT ...!
WE WANTED TO SURPRISE YOU, SO WE PRETENDED WE DIDN'T KNOW!!
HERE'S YOUR PRESENT!
THANKS!!

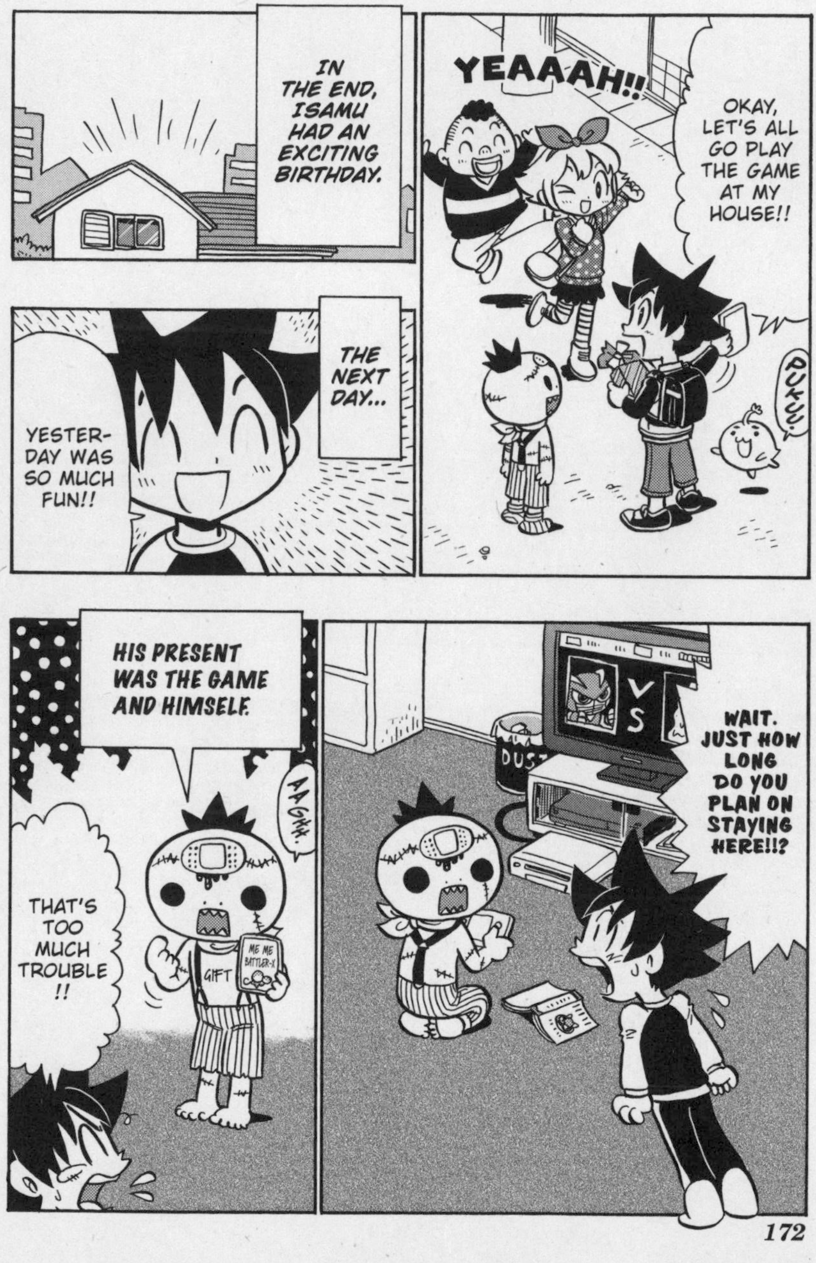
YEAAAH!!
OKAY, LET'S ALL GO PLAY THE GAME AT MY HOUSE!!
PUKUU.
IN THE END, ISAMU HAD AN EXCITING BIRTHDAY.
THE NEXT DAY...
YESTER-DAY WAS SO MUCH FUN!!
WAIT. JUST HOW LONG DO YOU PLAN ON STAYING HERE!!?
DUST
VS
HIS PRESENT WAS THE GAME AND HIMSELF.
AAGHH.
GIFT
ME ME BATTLER-X
THAT'S TOO MUCH TROUBLE!!

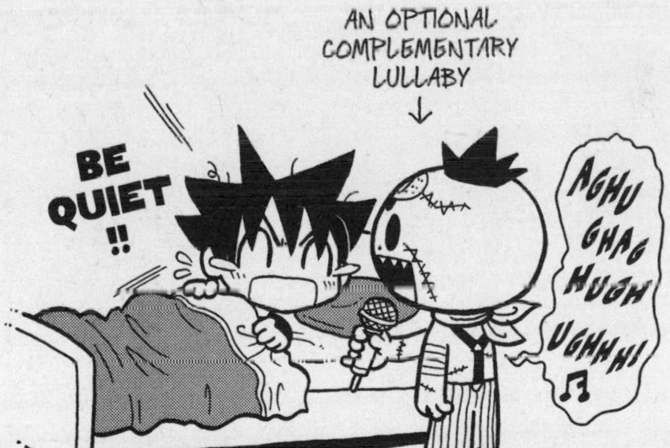
AN OPTIONAL COMPLEMENTARY LULLABY
AGHU GHAG HUGH UGHHH! ♫
BE QUIET!!

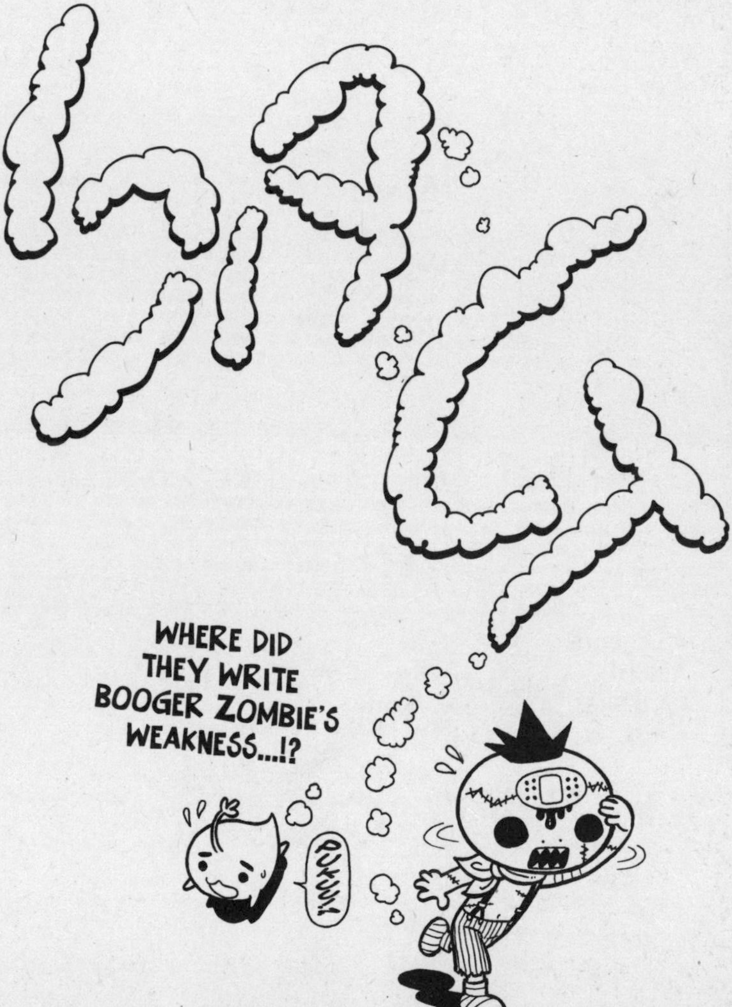
WHERE DID THEY WRITE BOOGER ZOMBIE'S WEAKNESS...!?
PUKUU!

TROUBLE ON THE STREETZ!

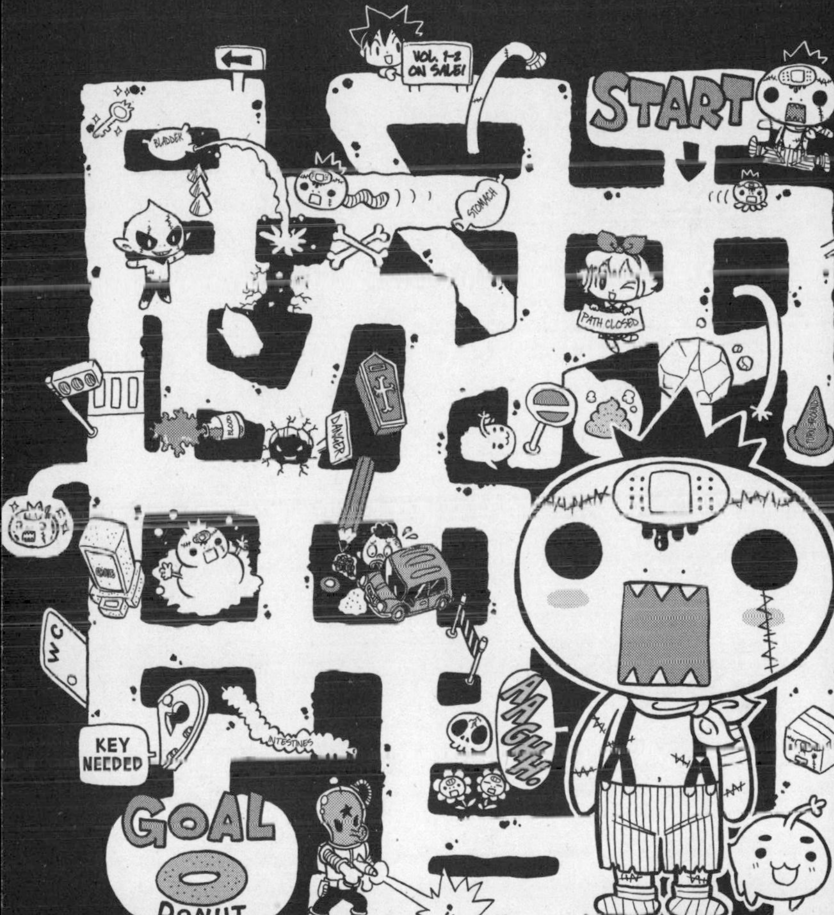
VOL. 1-2 ON SALE!
START
BLADDER
STOMACH
PATH CLOSED
BLOOD
DANGER
TURN AROUND
WC
KEY NEEDED
INTESTINES
AAGGH!
GOAL
DONUT

INSTRUCTIONS: YOU CAN ONLY TAKE EACH ROAD ONCE. YOU NEED TO PICK UP A KEY TO GET THROUGH THE "KEY NEEDED" GATE.

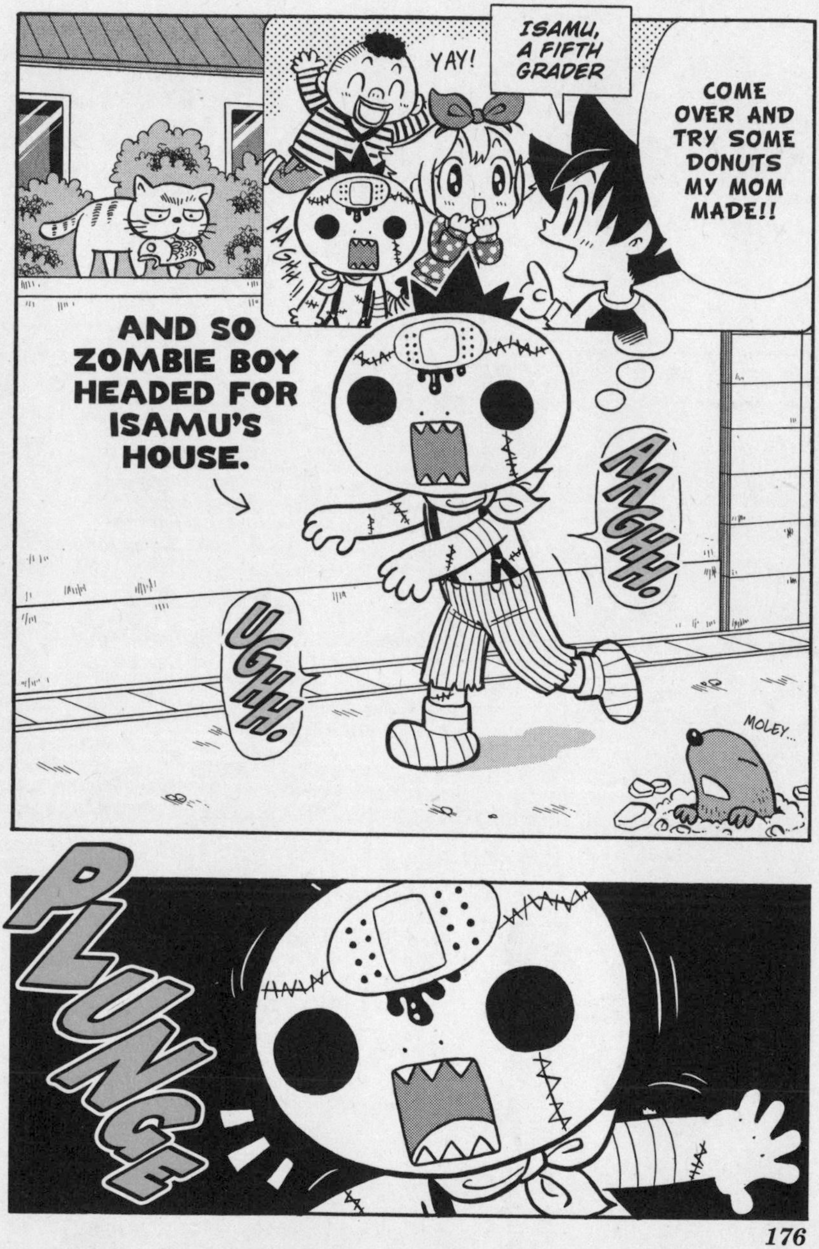
COME OVER AND TRY SOME DONUTS MY MOM MADE!!
ISAMU, A FIFTH GRADER
YAY!
AAGHH!!
AND SO ZOMBIE BOY HEADED FOR ISAMU'S HOUSE.
AAGHH.
UGHH.
MOLEY...
PLUNGE

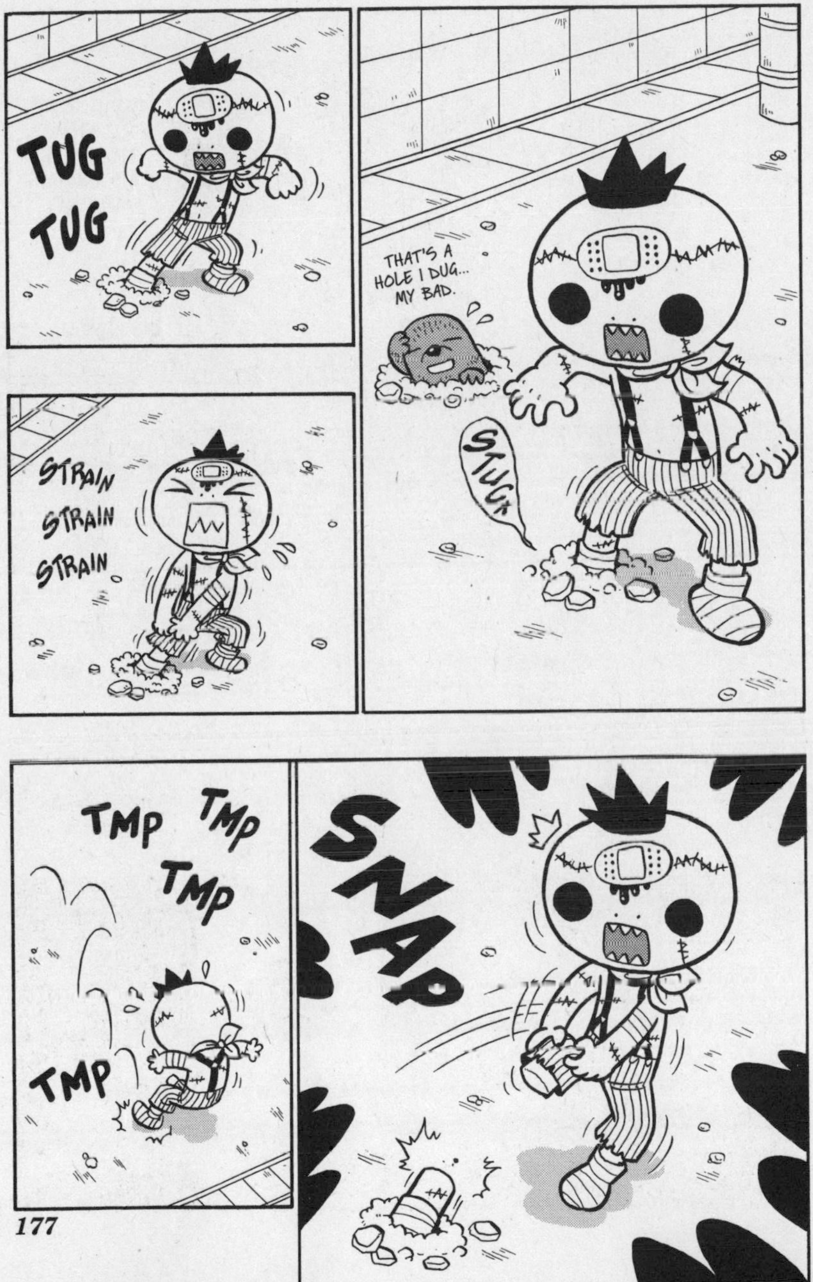
THAT'S A HOLE I DUG... MY BAD.
STUCK
TUG TUG
STRAIN STRAIN STRAIN
SNAP
TMP TMP TMP TMP

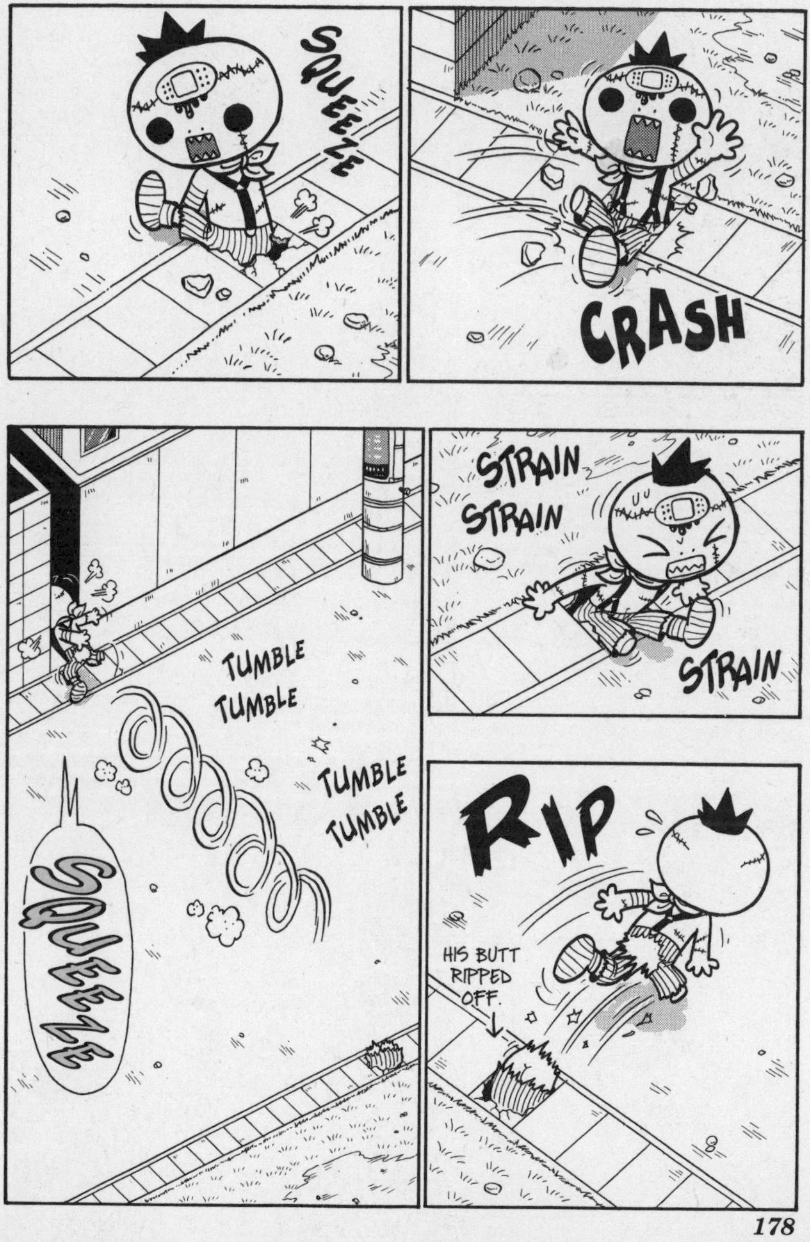
CRASH
SQUEEZE
STRAIN
STRAIN
STRAIN
RIP
HIS BUTT RIPPED OFF.
TUMBLE TUMBLE
TUMBLE TUMBLE
SQUEEZE

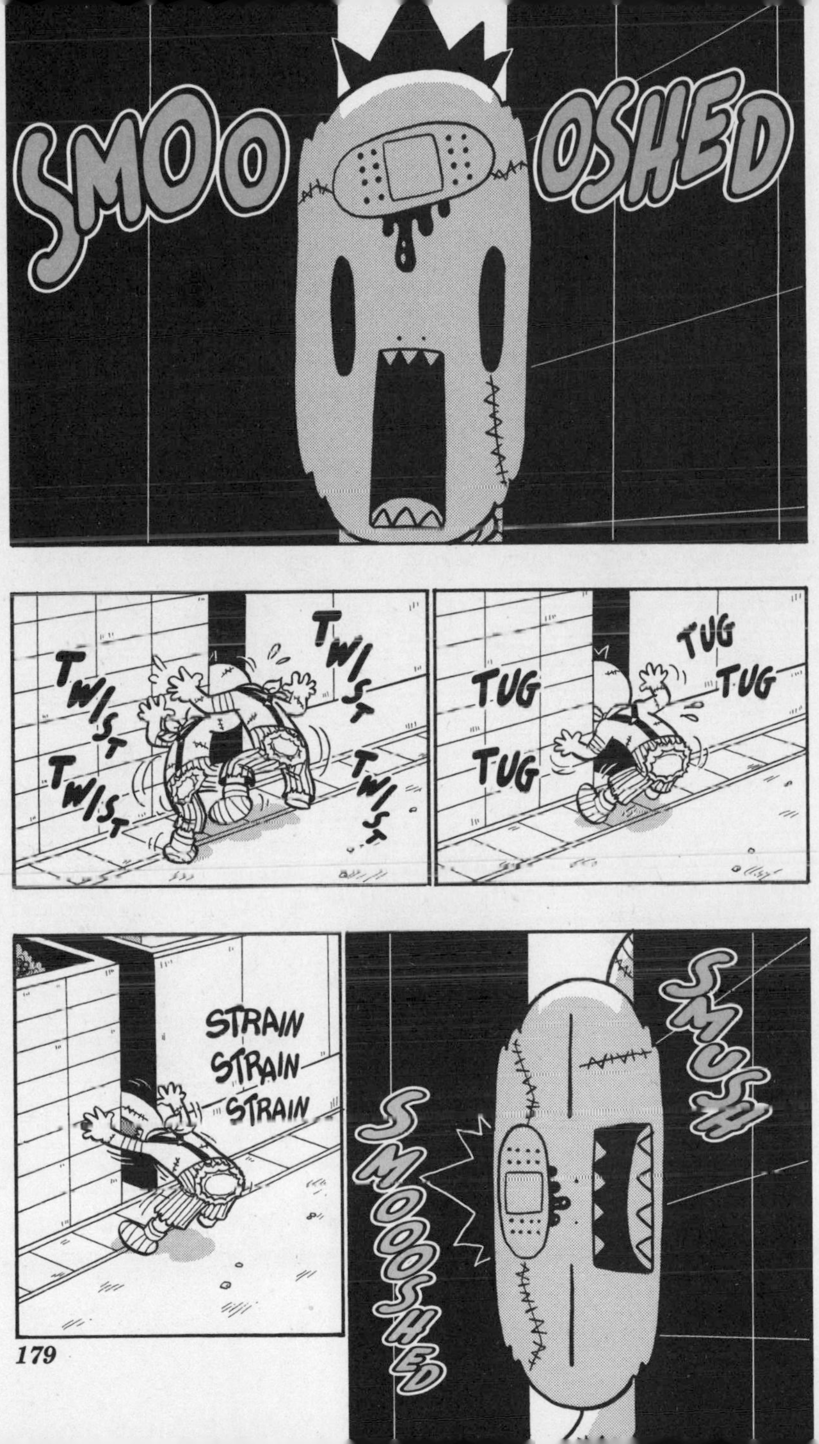
SMOO OSHED
TUG TUG
TUG TUG
TWIST TWIST
TWIST TWIST
SMUSH
SMOOOSHED
STRAIN STRAIN STRAIN

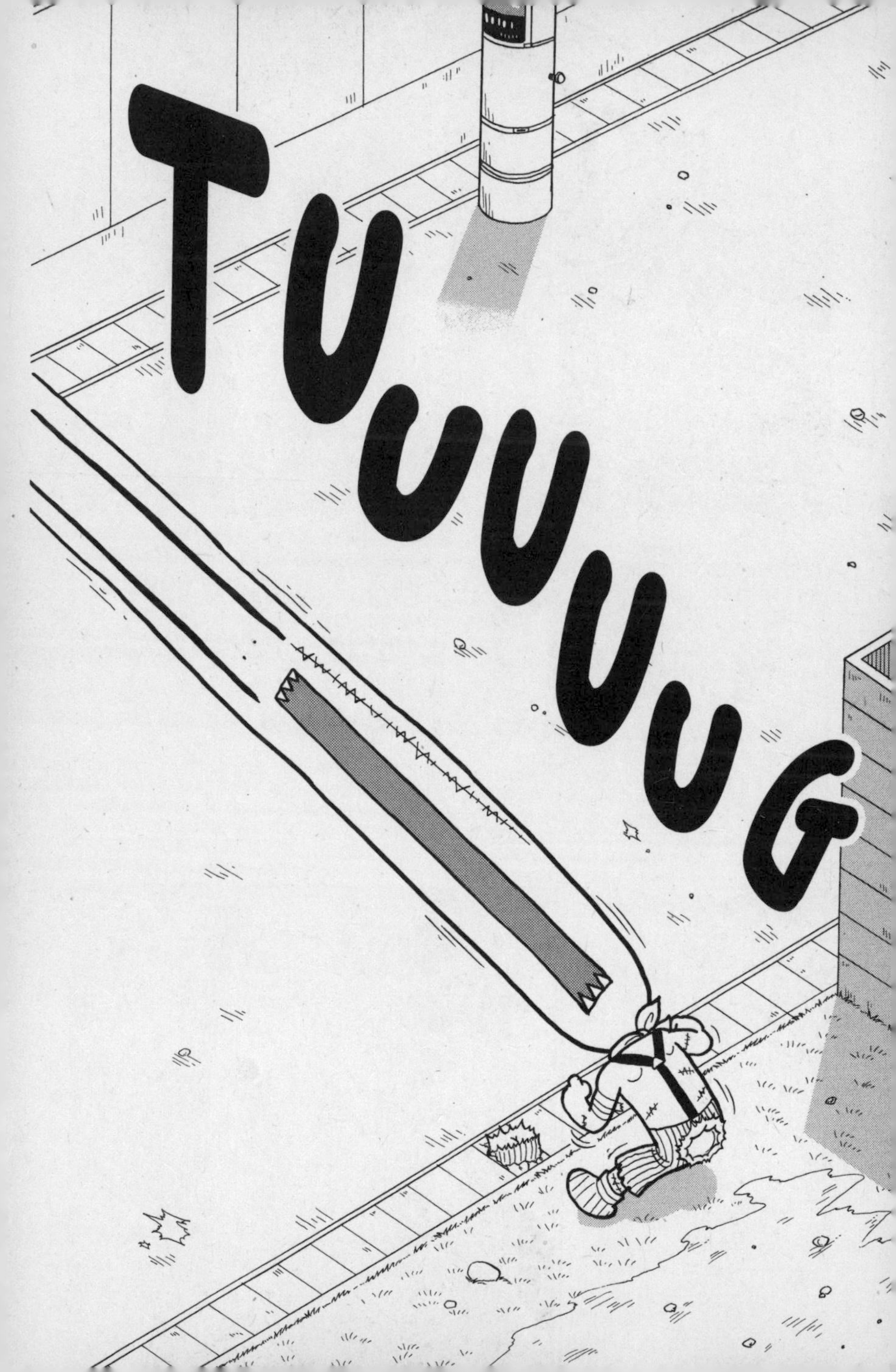
TUUUUUG

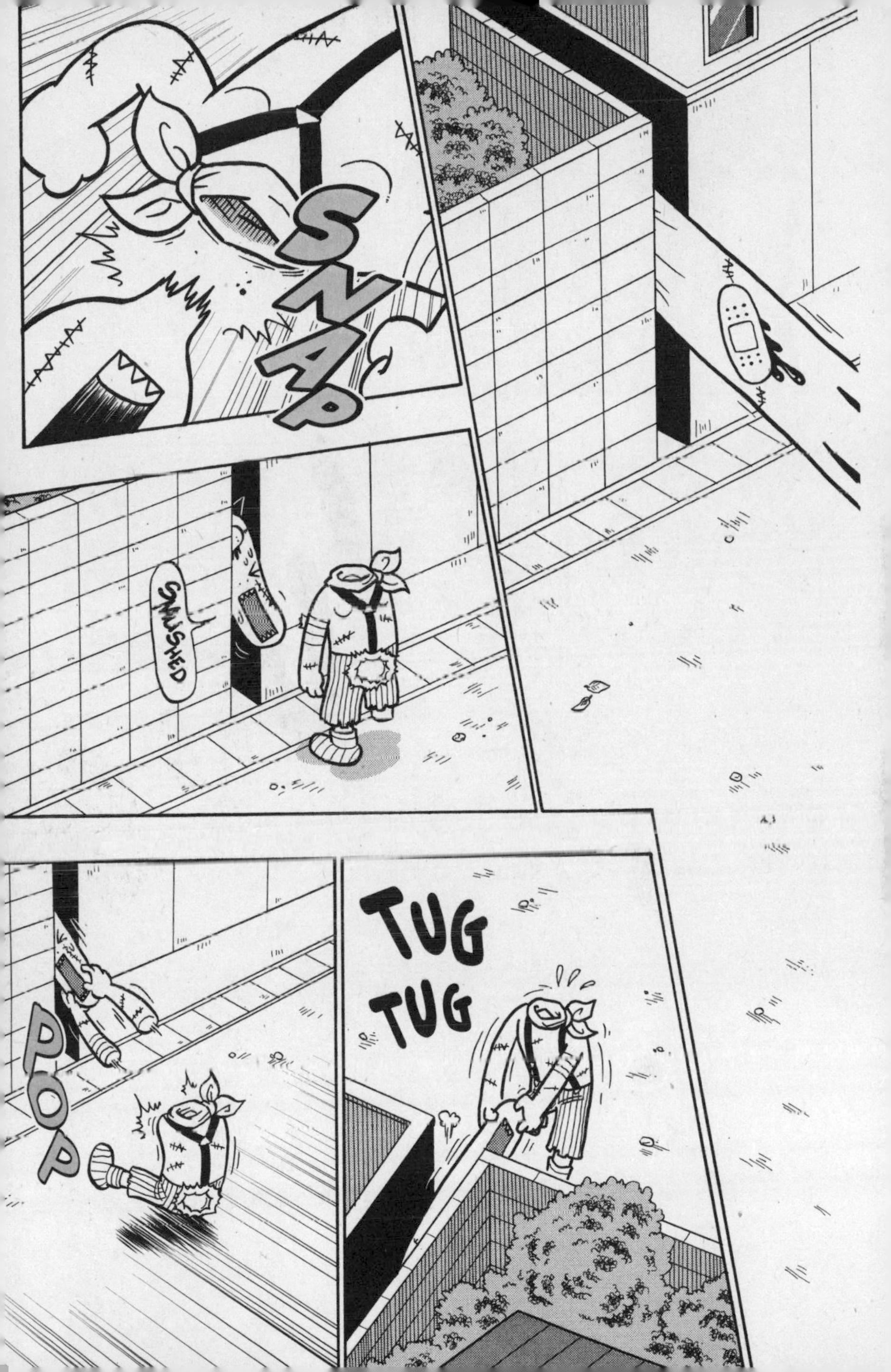
SNAP
SMUSHED
TUG TUG
POP

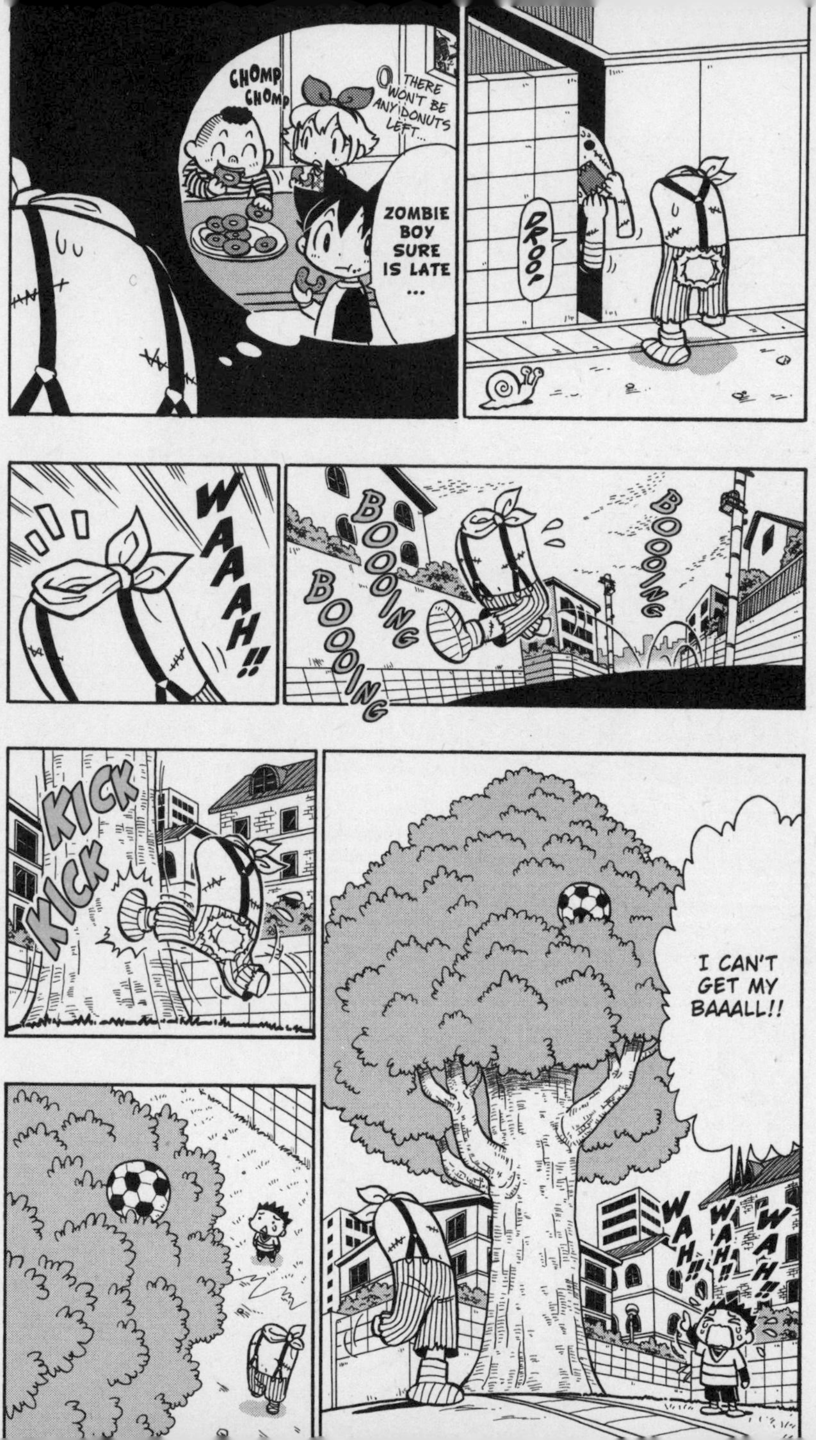
DROOL
THERE WON'T BE ANY DONUTS LEFT...
CHOMP CHOMP
ZOMBIE BOY SURE IS LATE...
BOOOING
BOOOING
BOOOING
WAAAAH!!
I CAN'T GET MY BAAALL!!
WAH!! WAH!! WAH!!
KICK KICK

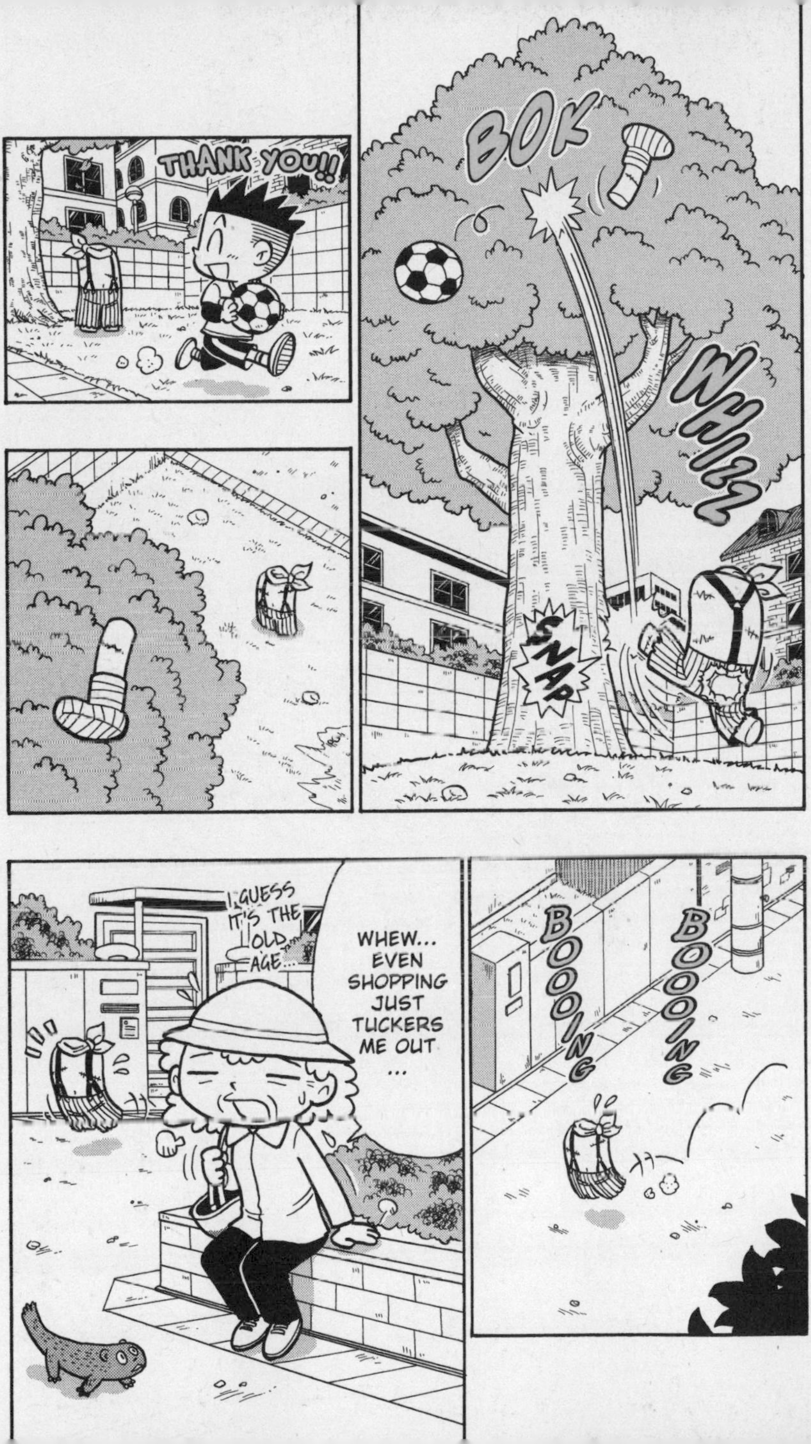
BOK
WHIZZ
SNAP
THANK YOU!!
BOOOING
BOOOING
WHEW... EVEN SHOPPING JUST TUCKERS ME OUT ...
I GUESS IT'S THE OLD AGE...

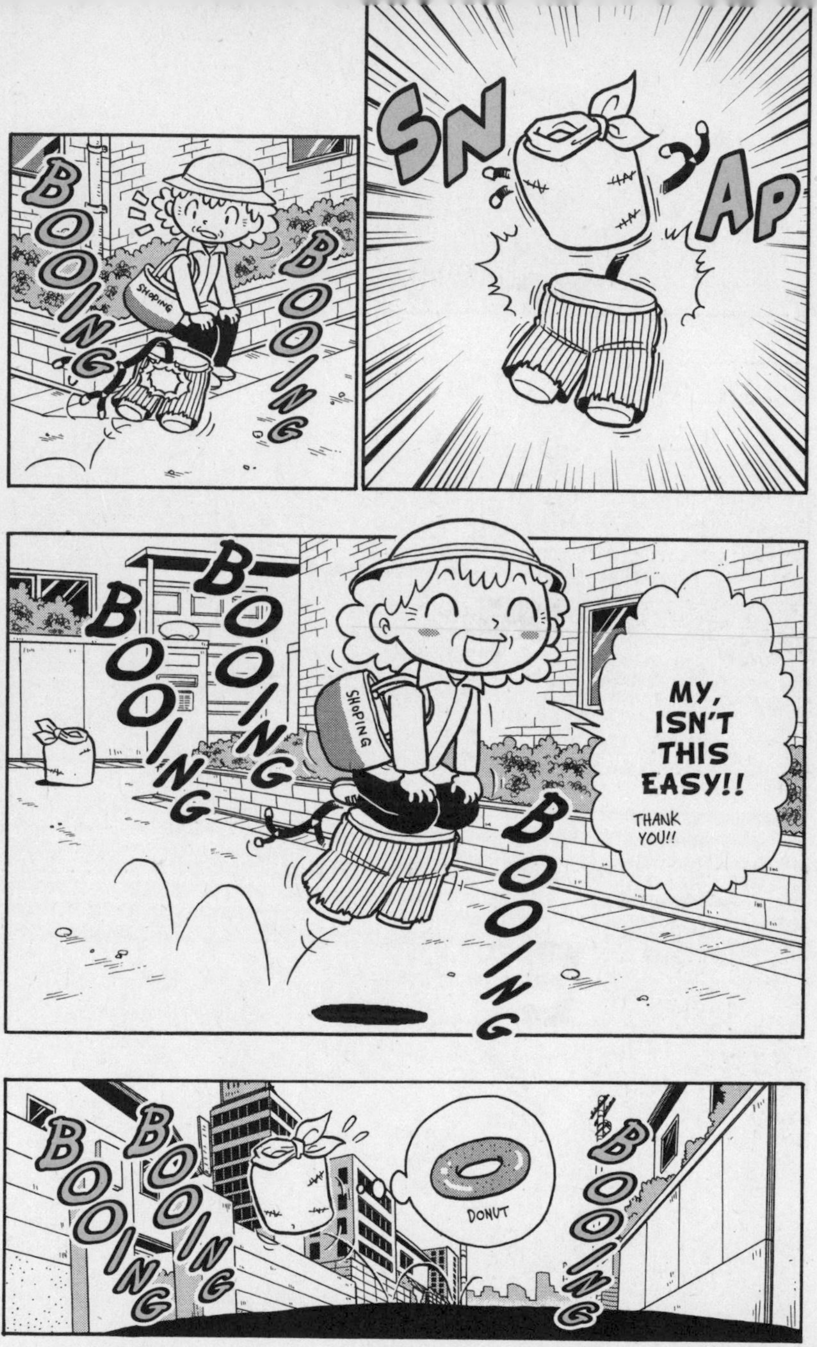
SNAP
BOOING
BOOING
SHOPING
BOOING
BOOING
SHOPING
MY, ISN'T THIS EASY!!
THANK YOU!!
BOOING
BOOING
DONUT
BOOING
BOOING

BEAT UP

MAIL

POST

THE RED PAINT ON THIS POSTBOX IS ALL CHIPPED. IT LOOKS SO RUN-DOWN!!

I KINDA FEEL BAD FOR IT...

OH NO...

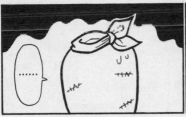

BOOING

THE DONUTS...

BOOING

......

GLANCE

SPEEEW

BLOOD
↓

POST

FWP

BOOOING

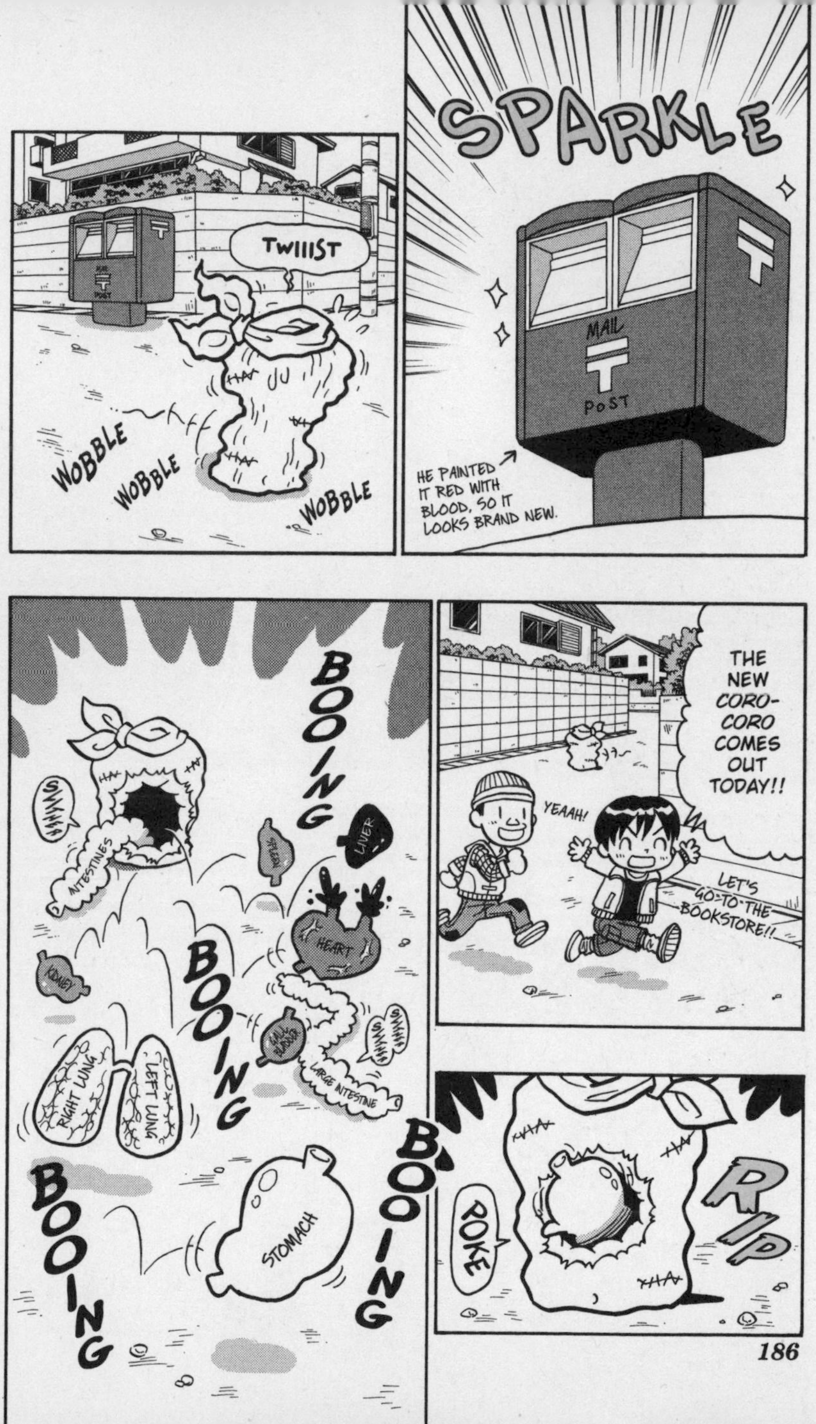
SPARKLE
MAIL
POST
HE PAINTED IT RED WITH BLOOD, SO IT LOOKS BRAND NEW.
TWIIIST
WOBBLE
WOBBLE
WOBBLE
THE NEW CORO-CORO COMES OUT TODAY!!
YEAAH!
LET'S GO TO THE BOOKSTORE!!
RIP
POKE
BOOING
BOOING
BOOING
BOOING
SWISH
LIVER
SPLEEN
INTESTINES
HEART
KIDNEY
SWISH
LARGE INTESTINE
RIGHT LUNG
LEFT LUNG
STOMACH

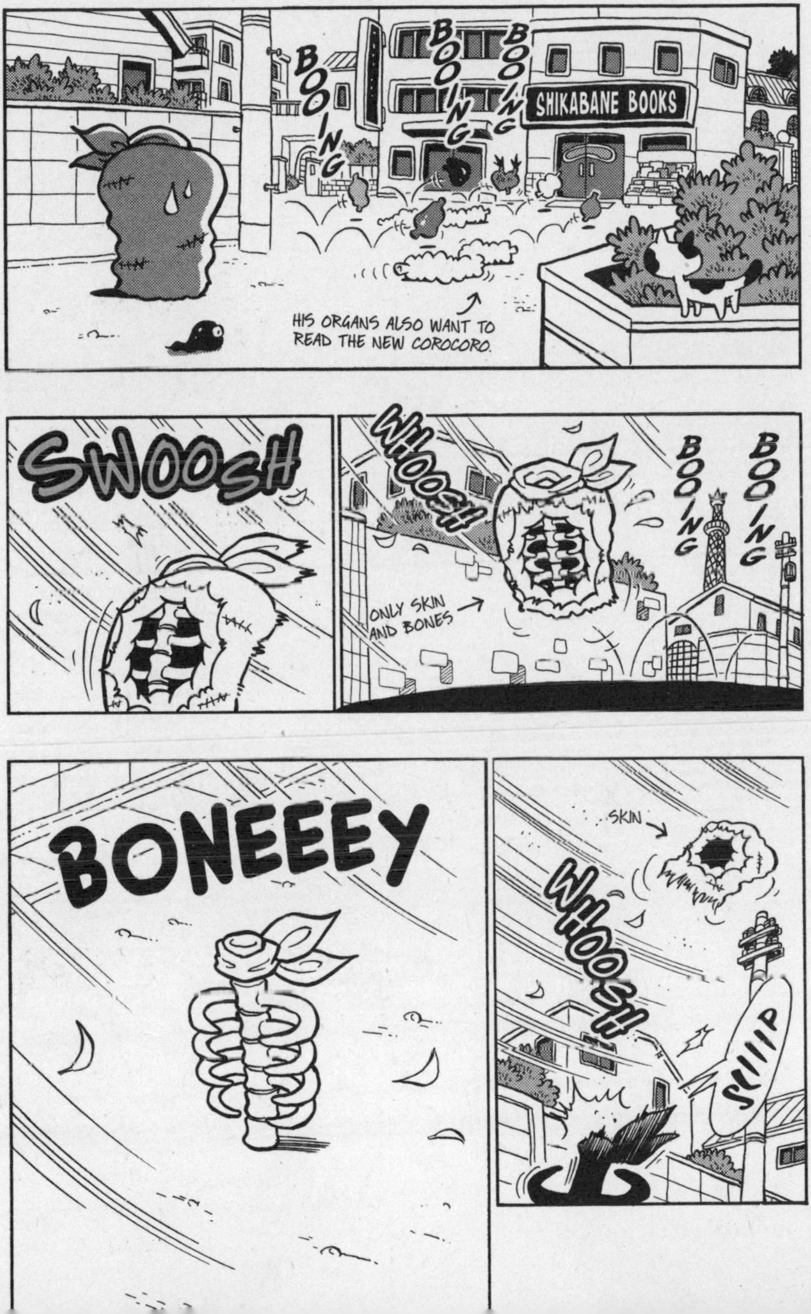
BOOING
BOOING
BOOING
SHIKABANE BOOKS
HIS ORGANS ALSO WANT TO READ THE NEW COROCORO.
BOOING
BOOING
WHOOSH
ONLY SKIN AND BONES
SWOOSH
SKIN
WHOOSH
SLIIP
BONEEEY

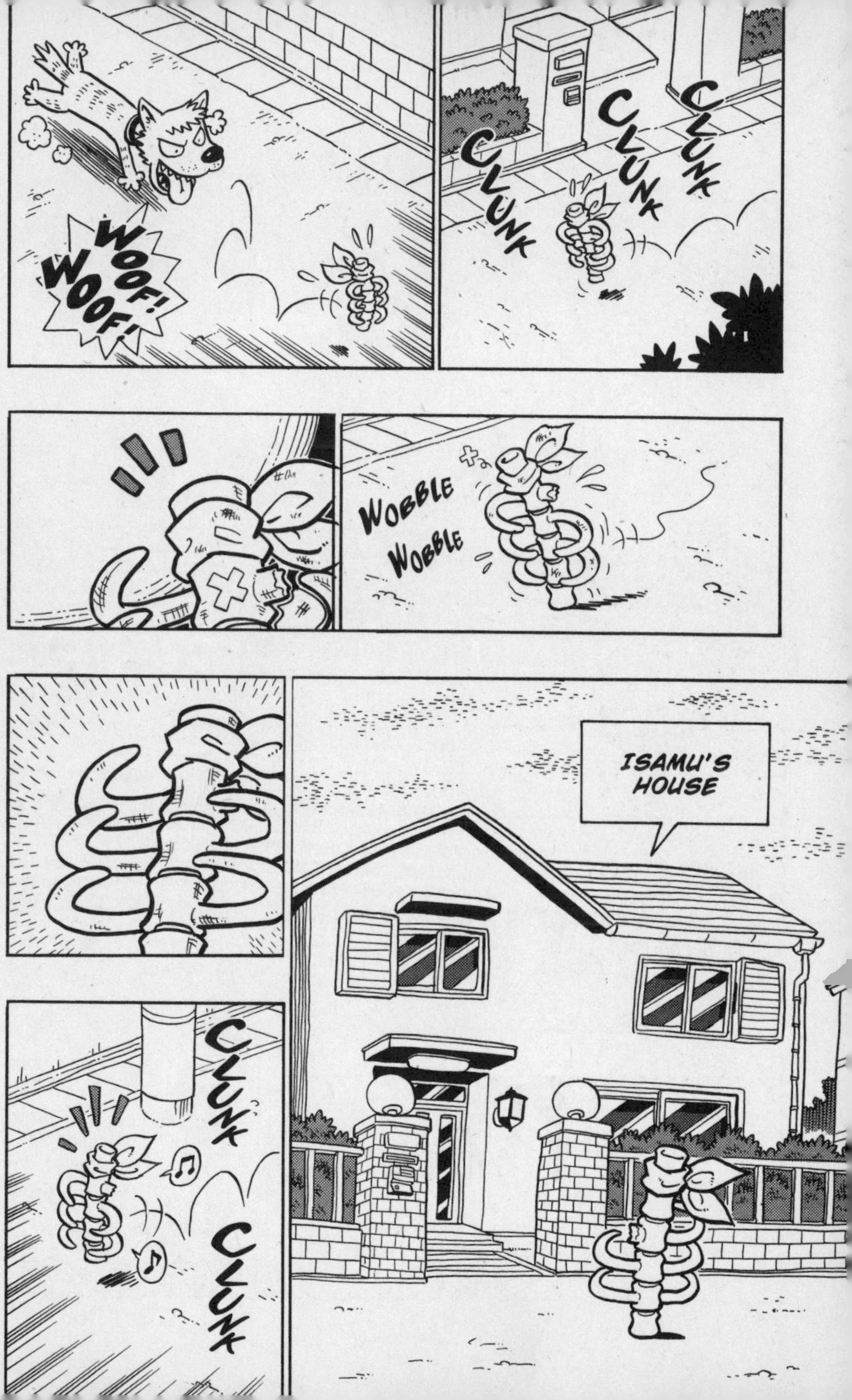
CLUNK
CLUNK
CLUNK
WOOF! WOOF!
WOBBLE WOBBLE
ISAMU'S HOUSE
CLUNK
CLUNK

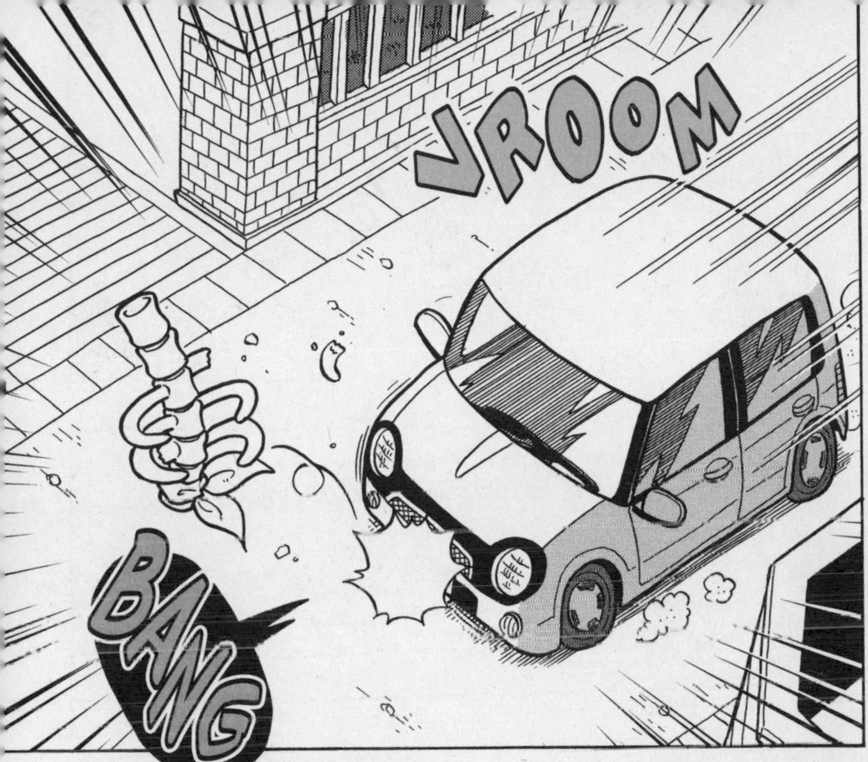
VROOM
BANG

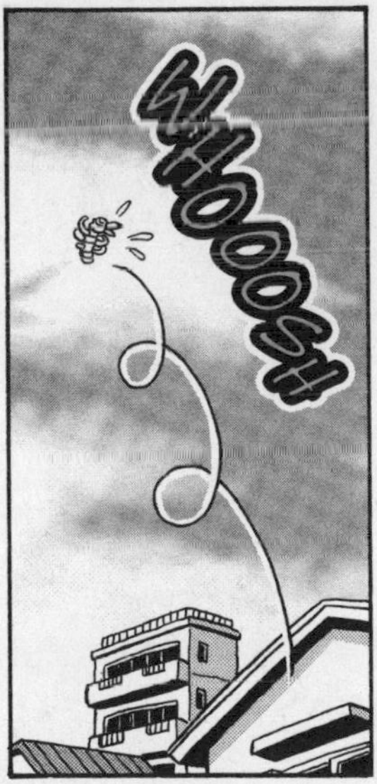
WHOOOSH

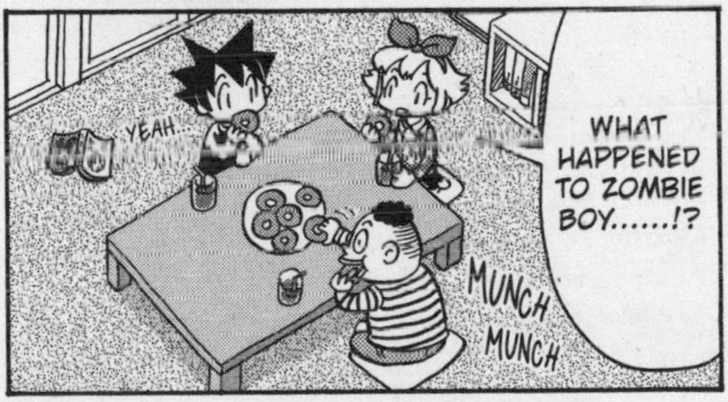
WHAT HAPPENED TO ZOMBIE BOY......!?
YEAH...
MUNCH MUNCH

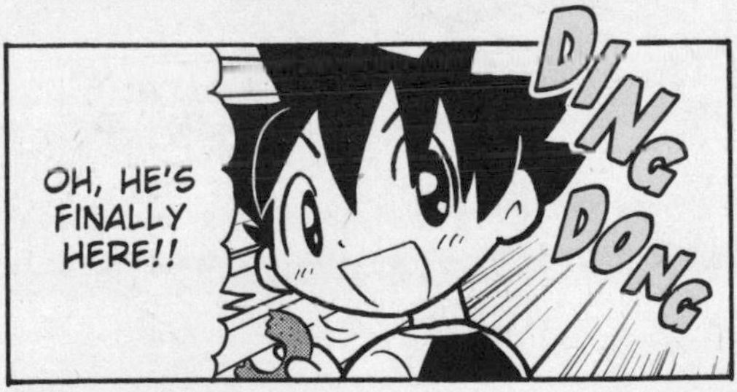
DING DONG
OH, HE'S FINALLY HERE!!

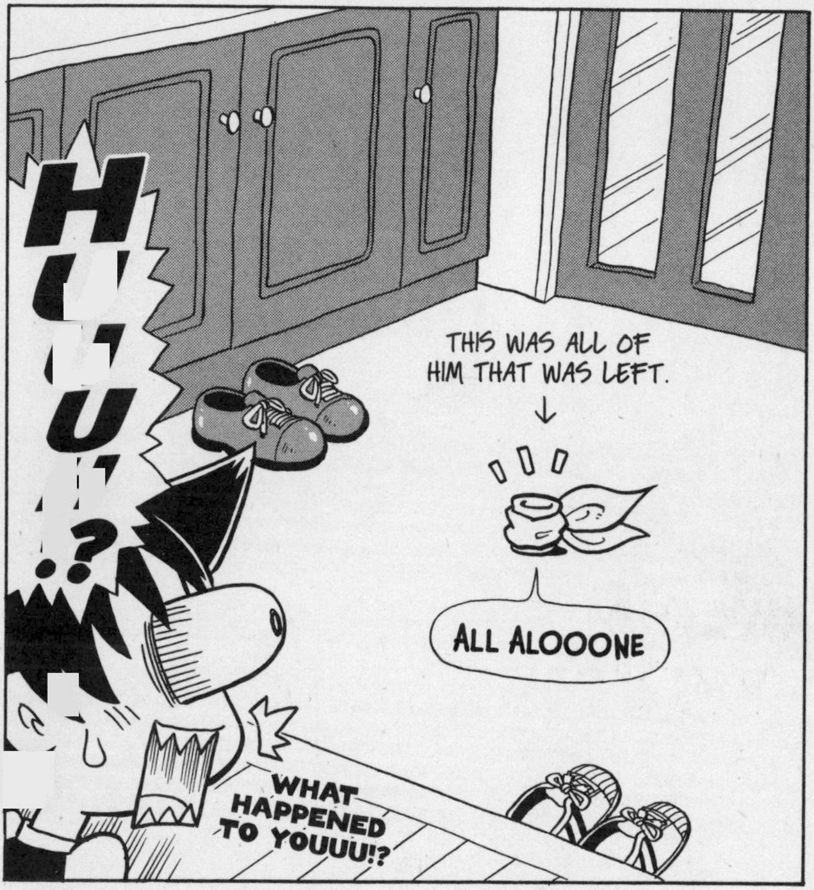
THIS WAS ALL OF HIM THAT WAS LEFT.
ALL ALOOONE
HUUUH!?
WHAT HAPPENED TO YOUUU!?

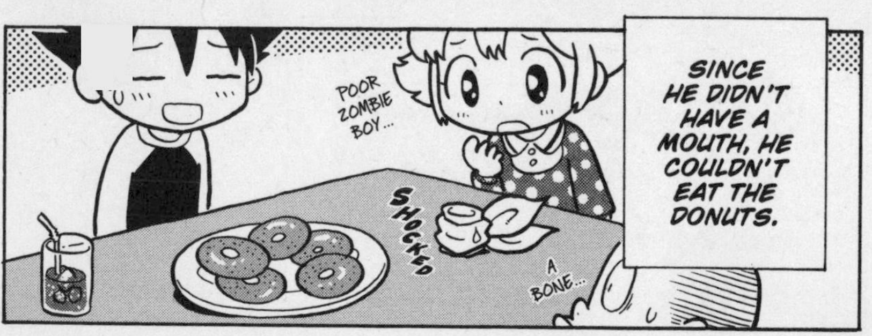
SINCE HE DIDN'T HAVE A MOUTH, HE COULDN'T EAT THE DONUTS.
A BONE...
SHOCKED
POOR ZOMBIE BOY...

SEE YOU AGAIN IN VOLUME 4!!

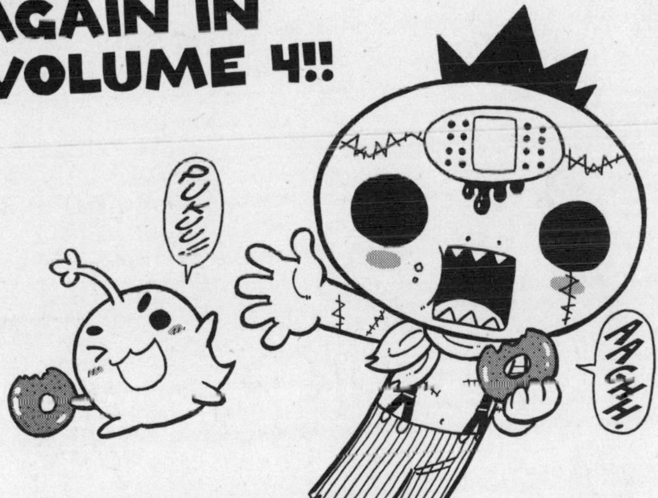
AAGHH.
PUKUU!!

ZO ZO ZOMBIE 3 THE END

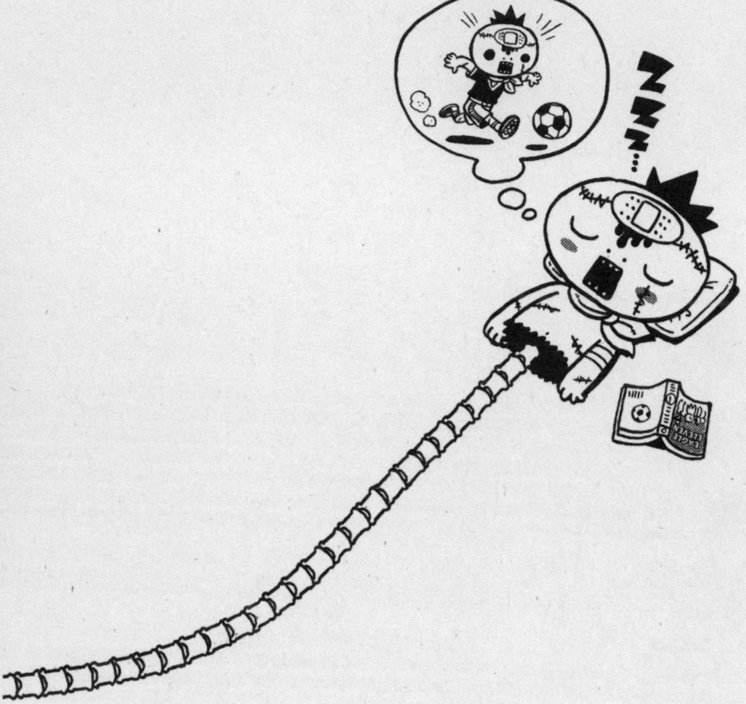
ZZZ...
EAGLE ELEVEN

ZOMBIE

YASUNARI NAGATOSHI

Translation: ALEXANDRA MCCULLOUGH-GARCIA ♣ Lettering: BIANCA PISTILLO

This book is a work of fiction. Names, characters, places, and incidents are the product of the author's imagination or are used fictitiously. Any resemblance to actual events, locales, or persons, living or dead, is coincidental.

ZOZOZO ZOMBIE-KUN Vol. 3
by Yasunari NAGATOSHI
© 2014 Yasunari NAGATOSHI
All rights reserved.
Original Japanese edition published by SHOGAKUKAN.
English translation rights in the United States of America, Canada, the United Kingdom, Ireland, Australia and New Zealand arranged with SHOGAKUKAN through Tuttle-Mori Agency, Inc.

English translation © 2019 by Yen Press, LLC

Yen Press, LLC supports the right to free expression and the value of copyright. The purpose of copyright is to encourage writers and artists to produce the creative works that enrich our culture.

The scanning, uploading, and distribution of this book without permission is a theft of the author's intellectual property. If you would like permission to use material from the book (other than for review purposes), please contact the publisher. Thank you for your support of the author's rights.

JY
1290 Avenue of the Americas
New York, NY 10104

Visit us at jyforkids.com ♣ facebook.com/jyforkids
twitter.com/jyforkids ♣ jyforkids.tumblr.com ♣ instagram.com/jyforkids

First JY Edition: April 2019

JY is an imprint of Yen Press, LLC.
The JY name and logo are trademarks of Yen Press, LLC.

The publisher is not responsible for websites (or their content) that are not owned by the publisher.

Library of Congress Control Number: 2018948323

ISBN: 978-1-9753-5343-8

10 9 8 7 6 5 4 3 2 1

WOR

Printed in the United States of America